PENGUIN BOOKS

ALL THE LITTLE LIVE THINGS

Wallace Stegner (1909–1993) was the author of, among other novels, *Remembering Laughter*, 1937; *The Big Rock Candy Mountain*, 1943; *Joe Hill*, 1950; *All the Little Live Things*, 1967 (Commonwealth Club Gold Medal); *A Shooting Star*, 1961; *Angle of Repose*, 1971 (Pulitzer Prize); *The Spectator Bird*, 1976 (National Book Award, 1977); *Recapitulation*, 1979; and *Crossing to Safety*, 1987. His nonfiction includes *Beyond the Hundredth Meridian*, 1954; *Wolf Willow*, 1963; *The Sound of Mountain Water* (essays), 1969; *The Uneasy Chair: A Biography of Bernard DeVoto*, 1974; and *Where the Bluebird Sings to the Lemonade Springs: Living and Writing in the West*, 1992. Three of his short stories have won O. Henry prizes, and in 1980 he received the Robert Kirsch Award from the *Los Angeles Times* for his lifetime literary achievements. His *Collected Stories* was published in 1990.

Wallace Stegner

All the Little Live Things

PENGUIN BOOKS

PENGUIN BOOKS
Published by the Penguin Group
Penguin Group (USA) Inc., 375 Hudson Street, New York, New York 10014, U.S.A.
Penguin Group (Canada), 90 Eglinton Avenue East, Suite 700, Toronto,
Ontario, Canada M4P 2Y3 (a division of Pearson Penguin Canada Inc.)
Penguin Books Ltd, 80 Strand, London WC2R 0RL, England
Penguin Ireland, 25 St Stephen's Green, Dublin 2, Ireland (a division of Penguin Books Ltd)
Penguin Group (Australia), 250 Camberwell Road, Camberwell,
Victoria 3124, Australia (a division of Pearson Australia Group Pty Ltd)
Penguin Books India Pvt Ltd, 11 Community Centre, Panchsheel Park, New Delhi – 110 017, India
Penguin Group (NZ), 67 Apollo Drive, Rosedale, North Shore 0632, New Zealand
(a division of Pearson New Zealand Ltd)
Penguin Books (South Africa) (Pty) Ltd, 24 Sturdee Avenue,
Rosebank, Johannesburg 2196, South Africa

Penguin Books Ltd, Registered Offices: 80 Strand, London WC2R 0RL, England

First published in the United States of America by
The Viking Press, Inc., 1967
Published in Penguin Books 1991

30 29 28 27

Grateful acknowledgement is made to Holt, Rinehart and Winston, Inc., for permission to quote, on page 209, from "To Earthward" from *Complete Poems of Robert Frost*. Copyright 1923 by Holt, Rinehart and Winston, Inc. Copyright 1951 by Robert Frost.

LIBRARY OF CONGRESS CATALOGING IN PUBLICATION DATA
Stegner, Wallace Earle, 1909–
All the little live things/Wallace Stegner.
p. cm.
"First published . . . by the Viking Press, Inc., 1967"—T.p. verso.
ISBN 978-0-14-015441-2
I. Title. II. Series.
PS3537.T316A78 1991
813'.52—dc20 91-18312

Printed in the United States of America

Oh, Sir! the good die first,
And they whose hearts are dry as summer dust
Burn to the socket.

—William Wordsworth

All the Little Live Things

How Do I Know What I Think Till I See What I Say?

A HALF HOUR AFTER I came down here, the rains began. They came without fuss, the thin edge of a circular Pacific storm that is probably dumping buckets on Oregon. One minute I was looking out my study window into the greeny-gold twilight under the live oak, watching a towhee kick up the leaves, and the next I saw that the air beyond the tree was scratched with fine rain. Now the flagstones are shining, the tops of the horizontal oak limbs are dark-wet, there is a growing drip from the dome of the tree above, the towhee's olive back has melted into umber dusk and gone. I sit here watching evening and the winter rains come on together, and I feel as slack and dull as the day or the season. Or not slack so much as bruised. I am like a man so stiff from a beating that every move reminds him and fills him with outrage.

In the face of what has happened, Ruth is more resilient than I, she has taken up little life-saving jobs. It would not surprise me to see a FOR SALE sign on the cottage that for me still trembles a little, like settling dust in evening sunlight, with the ghost of Marian's presence. But Ruth, making the cookies and casseroles and whole-wheat bread that she used to take there as offerings, puts the future under the pressure of sympathetic magic. She wills continuity, she chooses to believe that before too long we will hear the slam of the old station wagon's door down below, or have brought to us on the wind the voices of father and daughter talking to the piebald horse.

I? I came down here vaguely mumbling about finally starting on the memoirs. But the last thing I want to think about is what a retired literary agent used to do before he retired, and the people he used to do it among. I am concerned with gloomier matters: the condition of being flesh, susceptible to pain, infected with consciousness and the consciousness of consciousness, doomed to death and the awareness of death. My life stains the air around me. I am a tea bag left too long in the cup, and my steepings grow darker and bitterer.

Coming home this noon, Ruth and I said hardly ten words to each other. Our minds were back there on the lawn among the blunt stones. But when we eased over the stained and sagging bridge and saw the brush broken and trampled at its side, and a minute later when we rolled past the cottage with its weed-grown yard that I suppose expresses Marian without in the least resembling her, and a minute after that when the turning lane brought into view the gable of Peck's tree-house, something jumped the gap between us each time, a succession of those moments that you come to depend on during a long life together. But neither of us dared look fully at the reminding things we drove by. Ruth sat studying her hands, rubbing one white-gloved thumb over the other. In silence we drove through the open gates, between the big eucalyptus trees, and on up the steep shelf of road under the oaks.

October is the worst month for us. Nothing I saw

pleased me. The oaks were dusty, with many brown terminal twigs killed by borers. The buckeyes were bare. Only a few dull-red leaves dangled from the poison-oak bushes. Brittle weeds grew into the edges of the road, and as we swung around the buttonhook and onto the hilltop I saw in the adobe ground cracks wide enough to break an ankle in.

And there on the right as we coasted toward the carport was the cherry tree, its leaves drooping and its foolish touching untimely blossoms wilted. Ruth drew an audible breath. Cherry blossoms in October were exactly the sort of thing from which Marian would have derived one of her passionate lessons about life.

Ruth got out of the car. "I'm going to lie down for a while. Shouldn't you?"

"Maybe I'll work around the yard."

The white hand was laid like a policeman's on my arm. "Joe," she said, "don't take it out in highballs, now."

"What do you think I am?" I said, but her clairvoyance had put a barrier between me and a place I had half-consciously planned to visit. When I get sad or upset I can be a pantry drinker, and she knows it.

She pecked me with a kiss. "Poor lamb"—and then as our eyes met, "Poor Marian. Poor all of us."

I followed her inside and changed the dark suit for old garden clothes and poked morosely out into the yard again. I found that I had maligned the day. Until the rain moved in just now it was one of those Indian-summer days, warm and windless, brown-colored, even the air faintly and purely brown like the water of some Vermont streams. It smelled leathery and cured—the oak leaves, maybe. On the bank the pyracantha was ripening heavy clusters, and the toyon along the hill was top-heavy with berries. I stood by the carport looking down across the gone-by vegetable garden and the baby orchard, and of course what stood up in my view as if it were a hundred feet high was that cherry tree.

My hands began to shake and my eyes got moist—outrage, outrage. To take all that trouble of digging, fertilizing, planting, spraying, pruning, coddling, only to have a blind vermin come burrowing brainlessly underground to destroy everything! My head was full of some poet's bitter question: Was it for this the clay grew tall?

I walked down to look. The basin was disturbed by no more humps of loose dirt, but something drastic had happened underground. The leaves that a few days before had been green now drooped like heat-withered cellophane. Along the branches, here and there, were the browning wisps of blossoms that the tree had frantically put out when the gopher began working on its roots. Before I even saw that it had begun, it was finished. Trying to produce flower and fruit and complete its cycle within a few days and way out of season, the tree was dead without knowing it. The sore sense of guilt that I felt told me I should have done something. But what?

I took hold of the sapling trunk and wiggled it, and with a slight threadlike tearing the whole tree came up in my hand. Except for the tiny root I had just broken away, there was nothing. The thing was as bare as a fishpole, gnawed off and practically polished about six inches below the surface.

Off in the brownish air a great flock of Brewer's blackbirds flashed into sudden dense visibility, roughened the sky a moment the way a school of fish can roughen the sea, and flashed off again, disappearing, as they all sheared edgewise at once. It was like something seen through a polarizer. The big red-tailed hawk that lives in Shields's pasture was perched, I saw, high in a eucalyptus. Probably he was watching me with his X-ray eyes and wondering what I was doing, standing in my October orchard and brandishing the gnawed stub of what was once a promising Lambert cherry tree.

It was a fair question, and I could have answered it. I was pondering the vanity of human wishes and the desperation of human hope, the tooth of time, the vulnerability of good and the unseen omnipresence of evil, and the frailty and passion of life. That is all I was pondering, and I was overwhelmingly aware as I poked around that it was Marian who had exposed me to feeling as I had hoped not to be exposed again. I almost blamed her. Until she appeared, I had succeeded in being a retired putterer remarkable for nothing much except a capacity to fiddle while Rome burned and crack jokes while Troy fell. Now I feel the cold. I felt it up there in the orchard and I feel it now, I feel it as icily as I felt it after Curtis died. But where the death of my son drove me to find a hole and crawl in it, the death of this girl I knew for barely half a year keeps driving me into the open, and I hate it.

I threw the cherry tree onto the pile of cuttings that I would burn as soon as the fire hazard was over. The withered blossoms of that sapling, with their suggestion of unfulfilled April, put an ache and an anger in me where resignation might have been. Marian's philosophy of acceptance was never mine—I remain a Manichee in spite of her. The forces of blind life that work across this hilltop are as irresistible as she said they were, they work by a principle more potent than fission. But I can't look upon them as just life, impartial and eternal and in flux, an unceasing interchange of protein. And I can't find proofs of the crawl toward perfection that she believed in. Maybe what we call evil is only, as she told me the first day we met, what conflicts with our interests; but maybe there are such realities as ignorance, selfishness, jealousy, malice, criminal carelessness, and maybe these things are evil no matter whose interests they serve or conflict with. Maybe there *is* good life and bad life, good choice and bad choice, and unending war between them as in the Sunday-school hymns I sang as a boy. And maybe the triumph of the good is less sure than my Sunday-school teachers believed.

Nevertheless, Marian has invaded me, and though my mind may not have changed I will not be the same. There is a sense in which we are all each other's consequences, but I am more her consequence than she knew. She turned over my rock.

Looking at my ruined cherry tree, I could do nothing to repair what had happened. I could only act out a pantomime of impotence. Like a dwarf in a tantrum, some Grumpy out of a witch-haunted comedy, I dug in the basin of the tree until I found the run by which evil had entered and by which it had gone away. I set a trap facing each direction, knowing that even if I caught this gopher I would gain nothing but an empty revenge. If I ringed the hill with traps, others would still get through. If I put poisoned carrots in every burrow in Shields's pasture, some fertile pair would still survive.

I can see Marian smiling.

Riddled with ambiguous evil, that is how I think of it. All of us tainted and responsible—Weld, Peck, the LoPrestis and their sullen daughter, myself, John, even Marian. And yet until a few months ago this place was Prospero's island. It never occurred to us to doubt its goodness; we wouldn't have dreamed of trading it for our old groove in Manhattan's overburdened bedrock, or for one of those Sunshine Cities where tranquilized senior citizens (people our age) move to Muzak up and down an eternal shuffleboard court. Coming here, we kept at least the illusion of making our own choices, and we found that this sanctuary kept us physically alive, more alive than I at least have felt since those springs a millennium ago in Maquoketa, Iowa, when I used to go skinny-dipping in the creek with other boys and crawl out into an icy wind, shaking and blue, to pull on the bliss of a cotton union suit over my goose pimples.

For more than two years, physical well-being has been enough to make a life of. The expanding economy has had no boost from us. We have gone on no credit-card vacations to Oahu or Palm Springs, we never set off for the mountains towing a trailer or a boat, we belong to no country club, seldom dine out, possess no blue blue pool with lily-pad cocktail tables and expensive guests afloat in it. It will hardly do to confess aloud, in this century, how little it took to content us. We walked, gardened, read; Ruth cooked, I built things. We simplified feeling, as we had already anesthetized memory. The days dripped away like honey off a spoon. Once in a while we went for drinks or dinner to the house of someone like the LoPrestis, with whom our relationship was easy and friendly because it was shallow. Once in a while we were tempted out to San Francisco for a concert or show. That was all. Enough.

Yet if I had really been so fierce for withdrawal, wouldn't I have fenced Tom Weld away when I had the chance? Wouldn't we have kept Fran LoPresti at wary arm's length? Wouldn't I have sprayed for Jim Peck and his crowd before they got like weevils into everything?

I am as responsible as anyone. When we first met Peck in the bottoms I should have come away cackling and clutching my brows, crying, "A fool! A fool! I met a fool i' the forest, a motley fool!" Instead I came away implicated, entangled, and oppressed, and I knew exactly why. He was like a visitation—beard, motorcycle, and all, and his head rattled with all the familiar loose marbles. He angered me in a remembered way, he made me doubt myself all afresh. And there was a threat in him, a demand that he and his bughouse faiths be somehow dealt with or they would undermine peace forever.

But the Welds and the LoPrestis, who merely involved us in neighborhood complications, and even Jim Peck, who challenged every faith I hold, threatened our serenity far less than did Marian Catlin, who only offered us love.

These ironies are circular, without resolution. I drift from grief to anger, and from anger to a sense of personal failure that blackens whole days and nights; and from that all too familiar agenbit of inwyt I circle back to the bitter aftertaste of loss. All anew, I am assailed by ultimate questions.

The other night, standing in the patio watching the stars and the lights lost among the hills, I had a flash as if my veins had been shot full of menthol, a cold convulsion of panicked awareness that I was I, that for sixty-four years I have inhabited this skull which from the inside seems comfortably habitual, but which I might not even recognize if I could stand six feet away and see its hairless shine in the starlight. That old baldpate I? Good God. Is that what Ruth sees? What Marian regarded with affection and amusement? What Curtis rejected and was rejected by? And if I am so strange from the outside, am I so sure I know myself any better from within?

How do I know what I think till I see what I say, somebody asks, kidding the Philistines. But I can't think the question so stupid. How *do* I know what I think unless I have seen what I say? For two years I cultivated the condition that Marian called twilight sleep. Now my eyelids flutter open, and I am still on the table, the gown is pulled away to reveal the incision, the clamps, the sponges, and the blood, the masks are still bent over me with an attention at once impersonal and profound.

Escape was a dream I dreamed, and waking I am confused and a little sick. Sitting here sorting out the feelings and beliefs of Joseph Allston, while the rain sweeps in on gusts of soft Pacific air, I am sure of hardly anything, least of all of the code I thought I lived by. Some of it, yes; maybe more of it than I now think, for certainly I don't believe in conversions and character changes any more than I believe you can transform a radio into a radar by rewiring one or two of its circuits. But I do believe you can replace a blown tube or solder a broken wire. I have always said that the way to deal with the pain of others is by sympathy, which in first-year Greek they taught me meant "suffering with," and that the way to deal with one's own pain is to put one foot after the other. Yet I was never willing to suffer with others, and when my own pain hit me I crawled into a hole.

Sympathy I have failed in, stoicism I have barely passed. But I have made straight A in irony—that curse, that evasion, that armor, that way of staying safe while seeming wise. One thing I have learned hard, if indeed I have learned it now: it is a reduction of our humanity to hide from pain, our own or others'. To hide from anything. That was Marian's text. Be open, be available, be exposed, be skinless. Skinless? Dance around in your bones.

So I will have to see what I say about this sanctuary, these entanglements, these unsought amputations and wounds, this loss. In the saying, I suppose there will be danger of both self-pity and masochism. That Roman who drove a dagger into his thigh and broke it off at the hilt for a reminder, who would dare say he didn't enjoy the stoical spectacle he made? But I will have Marian at my elbow to mend me with laughter.

The rain has come on harder. I should go up to the house and bring in wood and light a grate fire and prepare such comforts as the first night of winter prescribes. Ruth has been by herself long enough. But I know I must come back down here to my study shack, regularly and often, until I have either turned light into these corners or satisfied myself that there is no light to be switched on. If every particle in the universe has both consciousness and choice, as Marian believed, then it also has responsibility, including the responsibility to try to understand. I am not exempt, no matter how I may yearn for the old undemanding darkness under the stone.

I

OUR SIAMESE CAT, called Catarrh for the congested rumble of his purr, has a habit of bringing us little gifts, which he composes on the door mat with an imagination that transcends his homely materials. One morning there will be the long grooved yellow upper teeth of a gopher, a sort of disembodied Bugs Bunny smile, gleaming up at me when I open the door. Once there was the simple plume of a gray squirrel, quite effective; once the front half of a cottontail rabbit, a failure; once a pair of little paws with their naked palms upturned as if attached to an invisible cosmic shrug. Many times there have been compositions of feathers, especially in March when the cedar waxwings sweep in on their way north and have a blast on fermented pyracantha berries. They overwhelm the mockingbird who thinks he owns those bushes. No sooner does he chase off one batch than another whirls in behind him and starts gobbling. He turns on these, and here come the first ones, reinforced. In a single day they can pick him bare. They sit in clouds in the plane tree and spit seeds on the bricks, and when they get really illuminated they try to fly through the plate-glass windows. Then Catarrh carries the casualties to the mat and makes jackstraw patterns of their yellow-tipped tail feathers.

This morning when I looked out into rain-washed sunshine, Catarrh had prepared a beauty: a gray nose, bristling on both sides with long whiskers, gleaming with four long teeth. Below and to the left, an intact paunch like a purple plum, enclosed within a coil of iridescent intestines. And along the top and down the right side, tying grin and guts together with a sweeping S curve that was pure dynamic symmetry, the nine-inch tail of a wood rat. Undoubtedly it was Catarrh's best to date—*Neotoma fuscipes* was his masterpiece. He sat in the entry in the sun, washing himself and waiting for compliments, and he made no objection when I lifted the mat at arm's length and hurried around the house with it. He understands that his art, like a Navaho sand painting, should not survive the hour of its creation.

I was so intent on getting the mat around without spilling its contents that I forgot we have been avoiding that side of the house as accursed. Now as I threw the wood rat's remains down the hill into the brush and straightened up with the mat dangling from my hand, I got the whole view of what Tom Weld had done to the opposite hill in little more than a week.

The eyesore dog pen and pigeon house were gone, but so was the great oak that once crowned the hill. Below the summit Weld had gouged a harsh bench terrace thirty feet deep, and from that led off a deep road shelf with a bulldozer asleep in it like a hog in a wallow. Beyond the bulldozer a bench of gray dirt ended in a long cone that spilled down the hill. The rain had cut gullies in it; I knew that our road at the bottom would be a foot deep in mud.

I looked Weld's work over with bitterness. The hill that once swelled into view across the ravine like an opulent woman lazily turning was mutilated and ruined, and Weld was obviously not through yet. Only an amateur planning commission unable to read a contour map could ever have approved that site plan; only a land butcher could have proposed it and carried it out. And though I had every hope that the people backing Weld would swallow him before the operation was completed, there would be no restoring what he had ruined. It reminded me too painfully; it made me sick to look.

I turned my back on it and went around the house. Too many miserable events in our recent life seemed to me in some way consequences of some ignorant act of Weld's. Perhaps he is where I should begin. *Am Anfang*, God created Weld, and Weld was without form, and void. And yet I know that Weld, however irritating, began nothing. From before the beginning he was, after all ends he will be. He is only the raw material of mankind, the aboriginal owner of the undeveloped tract called Paradise.

Neither was Lucio LoPresti a beginning. He too existed here, a prefabricated example, a dry run, a model and a warning, though I did not read him that way at once, and have never lost my sympathy with him.

Begin where, then? With Curtis's life and death, that uprooted us from habitual life and set us wandering? Not that either. My son is not what I want to examine now; I have examined him before, endlessly and without spiritual gain, and I can't undertake all that again. Nothing that I really want to examine begins until after we settled in this place. Once we found it and made it our refuge, we were as if in hibernation; exasperations, troubles with the neighbors, demands from outside, were no more than the fly-buzzings that persuaded us our sleep was sweet. It took something more to wake us—first a long, loud ringing of the alarm, and then something softer: a touch.

The alarm went off a year ago. The touch on the lips that brought us fully awake did not happen until last March.

2

Ordinarily this is not good walking country. In wet weather the adobe is like tar, and through the summer and early fall the open country is unpleasant with barbed and prickly seeds. In those seasons our walking is confined to roads and lanes. But when a rain or two has flattened the weeds and started the new grass without soaking the ground, then cross-country walking can be marvelous.

Last year, as this, the rains came early, and in October you would have seen us any afternoon, bald head following white head, country corduroy behind country tweed, me brandishing a blackthorn stick that an Irish poet once left at the apartment, starting through the Shieldses' pasture fence. We followed the path made by Julie LoPresti's black gelding, a path so uniformly double-grooved that it might have been made with skis. This ran into a trampled space under an oak where he used to sleep on his feet and switch flies, and then out again along the fence separating the pasture from Weld's apricot orchard.

Somewhere along there we always stopped to admire

the view, with our backs to the orchard and our faces toward the pasture and woodland rolling steeply down and then more steeply up, ravine and ridge, to the dark forested mountainside and the crest. Across the mountain the pale air swept in from remote places—Hawaii, Midway, illimitable Japans. I have never anywhere else had so strong a feeling of the vast continuity of air in which we live. On a walk, we flew up into that gusty envelope like climbing kites.

The Shieldses, who own the pasture, have been abroad for a year. We pass their lane, turn left, turn right again past the LoPresti entrance. Almost any afternoon we could look down and see Julie working her horse in the ring or currying the dust out of his hide, and at the house, Lucio laying up adobes for another wing. (Ruth suggested that he unraveled each night what he had laid up during the day.) Fran would be chiseling or sanding languidly at one of her driftwood sculptures, sometimes crowding under the shade of the patio umbrella, sometimes quenched under a straw hat a yard across. She has had a couple of moles removed by needle, and fears actinic cancer.

From Lucio and Fran, a wave, perhaps a minute of shouted conversation. From their daughter, nothing. She was not nearsighted, she was just a girl who didn't know how to smile, and was not inclined to acknowledge the flappings and hoo-hooings of neighbors who meant no more to her than her horse's droppings. She had a certain cold ferocity of antagonism to her mother, a contemptuous toleration of her father, and a passion of attachment to her gelding. Those, I believe, constituted her total emotional life last October. By now, a year later, her capacity for feeling should be enlarged.

Ruth believes that boys are not found around stables because what they like is taking things apart and putting them together again, and for this purpose horses are not so satisfactory as cars, motorcycles, and even bicycles, while girls adore horses because they are biological and have functions—just pat them and feel how warm! I wonder, on the contrary, if Julie didn't spend all her time with her horse because she had no other friends and because riding let her indulge her fantasies of having a bit in her father's mouth and a Mexican spur in her mother's side. She was a dark-browed girl, fifteen or sixteen, somewhat flat-chested, big in the behind. Off the horse she was rawboned and awkward; mounted, she was almost beautiful. She always rode bareback.

So there we went one day last fall. A wave from Lucio, a flutter of Fran's uplifted glove across some sort of mosaic panel laid out on sawhorses. No Julie—apparently not yet home from school—but the horse was hanging his chin on the corral rail waiting. We turned into Ladera Lane under big gum trees whose bark was starting to peel to reveal the delicate pastels underneath and whose fallen buttons, crushed by passing cars, filled the air with the smell I could never dissociate from the 1918 flu epidemic, during which we went around in gauze masks soaked in that pungent oil. Past the riding stable—more girls, no boys—and down a sudden gully smelling of bay and sage, around the corner of a walnut orchard to Roble Road and along it up a long hogback, the first crest visible from our house, until we came out on a windy plateau with puckers of woods below us and hills between us and the mountain.

It is a view that has the quality of bigness without actual size, and it used to comfort me to know that these little mountains, like everything else around, are very lively, very Californian. The range grows, they say, a half inch or so a year, and in the same time moves about that distance northward. It is a parable for the retired. Sit still and let the world do the moving.

The ridge was as far as we let our string out. Reeling in, we turned to the right across the clods of a plowed orchard, climbed through a fence beside a locked trail gate, and found ourselves in the pasture bought from Tom Weld's father a long time ago by a school district looking to the future. A wall-eyed white horse with a hanging lip and the black nose and black feet he had got from wading around in tarweed watched us; he had a decrepit Hooverville look like an old man dirty from picking through the dump. Angus steers, three-dimensionally black against the dun hill, chewed the cud under a dying grotesque of an oak.

Ahead and to the right the hills flowed into the valley. Roofs and trees and streets receded toward the bay, and in the unsmogged breezy clarity we could see the bridges—Dumbarton, San Mateo, even the Bay bridge—and far off on misty contracostal hillsides the white of continuous city.

Below or above the snuffling of the steers and the lazy rushes of wind through the oak I could hear the sough of traffic in the thousand streets of the valley, and I felt at once elated and besieged. A little more population pressure, that bigger water main that Tom Weld wanted, and our desert island would be quarter-acre lots and beatitude a memory.

A long slope led us down into the wood that thickened along the dry creek bed. There were dusty asters under the brush, an occasional scarlet gilia. Some trodden weed sent up a sudden minty smell. In the path I saw the scat of an animal, fox probably, all knotted up with fur and feathers, and I turned it over with the tip of the blackthorn. "Boy," I said, "that looks *painful.* How come a nice wild natural fox suffers from strangulated hemorrhoids?"

Holding her mouth as if she had been interrupted when just about to whistle, Ruth said in her mildest whisper, "I've got a Kleenex, if you want to take it home for your collection."

I made some suitably scatological remark and golfed the thing into the bushes. But there it was. I admire the natural, and I hate the miscalled improvements that spread like impetigo into the hills. But who can pretend that the natural and the idyllic are the same? The natural is often imperfect, and *Homo fabricans,* of whom I am one, is eager to perfect it. So I clean it up and grub out its poison oak and spray for its insect pests and plant things that bear blossoms instead of burrs, and make it all Arcadian and delightful, and all I do is help jar loose a tax increase, bring on roads and power lines, stir up the real-estate sharpies with their unearned increment, and get the hills cut up with roads and building lots. All our woe, with loss of Eden.

If I had three wishes—one would do—I would stop all development in its tracks and put the real-estate people to growing apricots again. Better a country fox with a hemorrhoid than a city fox with a pile. Aesop must have said it.

Through the brushy bottoms trail-riders had cut a ten-foot swath, but the summer's growth had half closed it in. Fronds of poison oak hung into the trail, dry cucumber vines and bindweed wove the walls of brush together. The ground, trodden by horses when wet, had dried again rough and hard as concrete. Passing under an oak, we got our faces full of late oak-moth caterpillars hanging on their threads, and Ruth was still pawing her face and shuddering when we came to the broken-down place in the bank where the riding trail crossed the creek between the Thomas cottage, then vacant and up for sale, and our south line. We slid down and clambered up, pulling ourselves by exposed roots.

And had a cold, visceral shock, a stoppage of the heart followed by a pounding pulse. For there, down in that quiet creek bottom where nobody but an occasional horseman ever passed, and where the only wheeled tracks were those of the man who periodically serviced our well pump, was this motorcycle sitting quietly, and on its seat this person in orange helicopter coveralls bulging all over with zippered pockets. The suit was unzipped clear to his navel, and his hairy chest rose out of it and merged with a dark, dense beard.

Caliban.

He was not surprised by us as we were by him; I had the feeling he had deliberately sat there soundless and let us startle ourselves. Teetering, tiptoeing his padded boots to balance the cycle (surely the feet inside those boots were cloven), he sat and looked at us. He was young, no more than twenty-two or -three. His hair was long and tousled, even matted where the helmet, now hung on a handlebar, had crushed it down. It crawled over his collar, and was pushed forward on his forehead, hiding his horns. His brown eyes, extraordinarily large and bright, gleamed out of that excess of hair, and his teeth, badly spaced, the eyeteeth long and pointed, were bared in a hanging, watchful, half-crazy grin. His coveralls and his shaggy head were splashed with green and gold as the leaves of the bay tree above him moved in the wind. He creaked like a saddle when he shifted, and he gave off an odor like a neglected gym locker.

The breeze was going in the top of the tree, but down in our hot pocket it was still. The wild mixture of things I smelled—this boy's rank body odor, bay leaves, crushed weeds, hot oil, gasoline—seemed to me the things I would smell in a camp of bacchants if bacchants rode motorcycles; and I was irresistibly reminded that the maenads were supposed to have intoxicated themselves by chewing bay leaves. In spite of the stillness of his face and body, in spite of his watchful grin, I was not in doubt about this fellow for a second. If I ever saw the incarnated essence of disorder, this was it. He emanated a spirit as erratic, reckless, and Dionysian as his smell, and I had not seen eyes like his since one day in the *suq* in Beirut, when a Bedu boy whom I knew for a pickpocket watched me buy Ruth a gold chain.

"Lost?" I said.

"Oh no." He had a soft, pliant voice. His hand went inside the open zipper and scratched comfortably at his ribs.

"I didn't hear your motor."

"I've been here a while."

Since he had to know he was trespassing, and since he might have guessed that I was the trespassee, I waited for him to explain. When he didn't, I said, a little sharply, "Doing what?"

The gappy smile widened, I became aware of very red lips among the red-brown beard. His eyes rolled upward eloquently, he seemed ready to laugh. "Meditating," he said. "Under your bo tree."

That was as fantastic as the helicopter suit. What is more, he spoke in a tolerantly amused way that said of course I wouldn't know what he was talking about, and who gave a damn? I said, "Bay tree, bo tree, that shouldn't make any difference. But I never heard of anybody meditating on a motorcycle."

I suppose there was some coloration of contempt in my voice. More than once, since that afternoon, I have wondered if, supposing I had responded to him heartily or good-naturedly, we might have begun and ended in good feeling rather than in suspicion and dislike. Marian suggested as much, so did Ruth. But I was jumpy from encountering him down there where I thought everything peaceful and safe; everything about him, from his repudiation of personal cleanliness to his mode of transportation, was a threat aimed straight at me, and I was bound to show it. He flicked his brilliant eyes at me—oh, he was alert, he was as sharp as a pin, he missed nothing in fact or by implication—and said in the tone I remembered too well, the tone of the son not quite keeping his temper before a censorious father, "Look close, and you'll see this is a Honda, not a Harley. Not everybody that rides a motor is a Hell's Angel."

No, I felt like saying, and trespass doesn't give you any right to get snotty. But I said nothing, for Ruth spoke up beside me, and I heard her warm, interested whisper as he must hear it: weakness, placation, a chink in the old bastard's armor. "How did you know it was *our* bo tree?" she said.

"Are you Mrs. Allston?"

"Yes."

"Well, I had a fifty-fifty chance, with only two mailboxes."

Somehow even the idea of his reading the name on our mailbox offended me. What the hell did he think he was doing, prowling around other people's property? But Ruth was still talking, saying, "Were you interested in the Thomas house? Because I think you need an appointment to see it."

"No, no, not the house." Perhaps it was only a slight narrowing of the eyes, as inadvertent as the gas-pain smile of an infant, that made me think he weighed a strategic move. He said mildly, "I was down here once before. It's a good place to sit in the quiet and let the air blow through you."

With his motives I couldn't quarrel. That bottom was lovely, and he did need an airing. But I didn't want him getting so attached to the spot that he would make it his standard meditating place, for I felt almost with panic—panic? yes, exactly—the threat of unpeace that lurked there from the moment he set his hoof in the dry duff under that bay tree. Turn away, have nothing to do with him. Danger, danger, danger.

"Are you a student?" Ruth said.

"Yes." He managed to make it sound as if he had confessed to having chancres under the helicopter suit.

"What year?" Ruth said—oh, interested, interested.

"I'm a graduate student."

"Studying what?"

"Philosophy."

"Philosophy! That should be interesting."

"Yes," Caliban said. "It should be."

His smile, I had determined, was semidetached. Whatever it had been at first, before he caught the edge of hostility in my tone, it now hung there, gap-toothed, unvarying, almost imbecilic, quite unrelated to the eyes, which were brilliant and speculative; and nothing to do with his last remark, which came with a sudden spasm of disgust like spitting sideways. His disgust, oddly, made him seem less dangerous, more juvenile: a delayed adolescent projecting his uneasy virility into whiskers and motorcycle, both absolutely standard, and his dramatized alienation into dirtiness and long hair, likewise standard, and his lust for visibility into that orange suit. I granted that it was more individual than the greasy jeans and black leather of the motorcycle corps, or the combat jackets, baggy khakis, and Jesus-sandals of the tribal Outsiders, but even so I felt that I could have made him up out of ingredients available without prescription at any off-campus coffeeshop, and for a small fee I would have offered him a motto for all his kind.

DISGUSTED? FIGHT BACK. BE DISGUSTING

And yes, when he flexed his right hand on the handgrip, sure enough he wore long horny nails on the middle and index fingers. A guitar-picker, naturally, a lover of the Folk, whom he would conceive as mystically as a 1931 Communist conceived the Masses. Who could persuade him that the Folk who lived simple lives and sang simple songs were also the people who discriminated, segregated, lynched, fought with switchblades, vulgarized everything they touched, saved for a rainy day, bought on credit, were suckers for slogans, loved gadgets, waved the flag, were sentimental about Mother, knew no folksongs, hated beards, and demanded the dismissal of school superintendents who permitted *The Catcher in the Rye* to appear on high-school reading lists? I knew all about the Folk—they were where I came from. I didn't know where Caliban came from, but I had an idea he came from books. If I opened his saddlebags I thought I might find Alan Watts on Zen snuggled up against Kierkegaard, Eugene Goodheart, Norman Brown, and Paul Goodman, and maybe the hallelujah autobiography of Woody Guthrie. And a copy of *Playboy*.

He was a very American product, authentic Twentieth-Century Mixed Style, mass-produced with interchangeable parts from five or six different machines. But seeing him plainly didn't make him any more attractive. So it was distaste rather than panic—distaste and a great weariness with everything he represented and recalled—that made me lay my hand on Ruth's arm to start her up the trail toward the gate near the Thomas house. To Caliban I said, "I'd just as soon you didn't make a habit of coming down here. One cigarette dropped in the weeds, and this place would explode."

"I don't smoke," he said. His mouth went on steadily smiling out of the beard, but his eyes were more than ever the eyes of someone about to pull something off. I held them; we dueled, in a way, without a word said. His eyes told me that he was not afraid of me, that he did not care a fig for old bald-headed bastards of my type, and that he dared me to deny him anything.

I broke off the ocular lunge-and-riposte. "Nevertheless," I said, and steered Ruth past him.

We had gone perhaps twenty feet when I heard the starter go down and the motor burst on. Here he came up beside us, rolling so slowly that he wobbled, balancing the cycle with his walking feet. He was saying something, ceaselessly smiling.

I stopped. He said something else, but I didn't catch

it because of the motor. So he said it again, and just as he said it, idly twisted the throttle so that the motor noise surged up. I said to myself, Don't let this punk get your goat, that's what he wants. So I waited, and he waited, a hairy grotesque, gleaming with teeth and eyes. In a minute I started us walking again, and then he goosed the motor to pull even, and shut it off.

"What is it?" I said.

". . . ask you a favor."

A favor. But as insolently as possible, to remove any taint of servility or inferiority. He said it as he might have said—and I was sure would have said if he had spoken his full mind—Fuck you, you old fart. And where did that antagonism come from? Did I incite it, or was it there between us like the suspicion between cat and dog? I am not likely ever to be sure.

"If it's O.K. for me to camp down here," he said.

At least he had the faculty of being unexpected. "*Camp*?" I said. "In a tent?"

"Maybe a tent. I'd have to have some kind of shelter for when it rains."

"Don't they have student housing at your college?"

He only rolled up his moist brilliant eyes and tilted his head and puckered his lips into the semblance of a turkey's behind.

"There must be apartments in town, surely."

"I'm not making myself clear," he said. "I want to *camp*."

We stood in the country stillness, eying each other. His pickpocket eyes were shrewd, but his voice had been soft, with a little burble in it. He didn't wheedle, he simply blinked once and stood there guileless.

"No," I said, "it's out of the question."

"Joe . . ." Ruth said. After a pause to see if she would go on—he was reading us as a sailor reads weather signs—Caliban said in his temperate, controlled voice, "Why out of the question?" He seemed genuinely and conversationally interested.

I should perhaps have told him straight out that I didn't want him on the place, as he already knew perfectly well. Instead, I weakly gave reasons, and not the real ones. "Fire hazard," I said. "Sanitation. Our well's right over there."

"I saw it," he said. "But I was thinking of across the creek. If you'll come back a minute I'll show you."

"There's absolutely no point." But Ruth's hand was on my arm, her eyebrows were up, she shrugged. Her signals were as plain to Caliban as to me. He put his Honda up on its kickstand and led us back under the bay tree. Following his back, brilliant as a tanager's, down the path, I said out of the corner of my mouth, "For Christ's sake, it's like being captured by Martians." Ruth said nothing.

Across from the bay tree the bottoms forked into two valleys, each with its dry stream bed, vertical moats ten feet or so wide and a dozen deep. These combined, between us and the Thomas house, to form a main moat, wider but no deeper. The horse trail crossed the trunk of the Y below the junction. Inside the Y was a little flat covered with poison oak, out of which rose two big live oaks with ropy poison-oak vines wrapped around their trunks. Back of the flat the hill rose nearly as steep as a cliff, choked with brush and trees.

"Over there," Caliban said.

I had to laugh, it was so inevitably the sort of place

twelve-year-olds would have picked for a woods hide-out. "You'd need wings."

"I can take care of that."

"So?" I said. "Why there? Why not right here under this tree, for instance?"

"Because over there you'd have your back against the hill and the creek in front and nobody could get at you at all."

"Why, is somebody after you?"

It was no effort for either of us. One look, one word, and we were circling like wrestlers looking for a hold. After a second he said, smiling and smiling, "I don't like being available to just anybody that comes along."

I felt like reminding him that if *we* hadn't been available to anybody that came along, we wouldn't be holding this preposterous conversation now. Instead, I only remarked that nobody ever came through here but us. And from the look in his eye understood that we were precisely the ones he had in mind. He made it incomparably plain by saying, "I'd respect your privacy, I'd expect you to respect mine."

After an incredulous second I permitted myself to laugh aloud. My amusement put a little extra fixity in his grin. There we stood, predestined antagonists, beaming at each other. He said, "I assume you *value* your privacy. You've got a PRIVATE ROAD sign out."

"Yes," I said, "I didn't suppose you'd noticed that."

Beam of that smile from ambush, unaltered watchfulness of the bandit eyes. To make my denial both final and reasonable, I said, "That's all poison oak over there anyway."

"I'd grub it out. Improve your property for you."

He said it like a dare, and I would have taken it, too, but at my side Ruth said treacherously, "What would you do for water?"

"There's a tap on the pressure tank at your well. I'd only need a pail or so a day."

"And sanitary facilities?" I said, knowing I shouldn't, I shouldn't yield even to the point of asking unanswerable questions, I should wipe out the whole proposal with a word.

"Chemical john," Caliban said. "It's no problem."

"You've got it all figured out."

"That's what I was sitting here meditating about."

As plainly as if she spoke aloud, I could hear Ruth asking me what difference it would make to us if we let a student live in that useless tangle. I was standing both of them now. I said again that I was afraid of fire. Even if he didn't smoke, he would have to cook. He said he knew where he could borrow a Coleman stove, and anyway he wouldn't be cooking much, he ate mainly nuts and fruit.

"Boy oh boy," I said. "What is it, a sanyasi withdrawal? You want to sit over there in a loincloth eating dates and raisins and say *Om Tat Sat* to the birds and squirrels?"

He looked at me, I thought, in surprise. Whatever his costume and the condition of his toilet, there was an elegance in the way one eyebrow went up. "You've been doing your homework."

"Plain living and high thinking and a low protein diet."

"Exactly."

"And to hell with the air-conditioned junk yard."

"Right."

"God Almighty," I said. "Do you mind if I summarize your case?"

"Go ahead."

"Let's see," I said, and began counting him out on my fingers. "You'd go into your spiritual retirement in a factory-made, chemically waterproofed tent. You'd have a chemical john utilizing industrial quicklime. Your water would be made available, thanks to myself, by a two-horse electric pump, a product of industry. You'd boil your tea on a gasoline stove—borrowed, but still factory-made. You'd go to and fro on a motorcycle built in Japan and brought to you by a complicated system of international trade supported by a complicated system of political agreements and treaties. The raisins you would live on would be mass-produced. Likewise the salted peanuts. In the evenings you'd relax—I see you play the guitar—with an instrument made in the Martin or Gibson factory. That's *withdrawal*?"

Caliban's smile modified itself as I spoke, until I couldn't help being reminded again how much lips surrounded by beard look like another sort of bodily opening. "Why does it bother you?"

"It doesn't bother me. I just wonder what you expect to teach the air-conditioned junk yard by a phony retirement."

"I don't expect to teach it anything. I get only one life. I'm not spending it teaching lessons to a shitty civilization."

"Let it go to hell."

"I've already said so."

"So long as it furnishes your personal thirteen hundred pounds of steel, five hundred pounds of cement, two hundred pounds of salt, one hundred pounds of phosphate, and the rest of the twenty tons of stuff it takes to support one individual in this society for one year, even if he pretends to withdraw. You want your Walden with modern conveniences, is that it?"

"If they're available, fine. If not, fine."

Obviously he thought he meant it. I might have told him that in California in the 1960s even the land to squat on came high—the taxes on that acre of poison oak were probably seventy-five dollars a year. But he wearied me, standing there stubborn, provocative, and smiling, turning nonsense into reality by the simple refusal to listen to anything but the ticking of his own Ingersoll mind. Yet he spoke some of my opinions, in his incomparably crackbrained way, and I was uneasily aware that in putting him down I was pinning myself. I had retired from our overengineered society as surely as he wanted to, and I lived behind a PRIVATE ROAD sign on a dead-end lane. And our argument, including the half-exposed contempt and hostility in it, reminded me of too many hopeless arguments in the past.

"Well," I said, "it's an academic debate anyway."

As she so often does, Ruth inserted a subject-changer just as I was closing the hall. She was still playing sweet old lady curious about youth, but it wasn't all acting. She *was* curious about this one. Where was he from? Where was he living now, that made him want to move to the woods?

He told us, in his soft, modulated voice, watching us all the time, his elegant eyebrow lifting occasionally to prompt our astonishment or amusement. He was from Chicago. Living? Nowhere. Who needed the *in-loco-parentis* university? A university was properly only students and teachers. So you put a toothbrush and an extra pair of socks and a sleeping bag in your knapsack, and you carried your housing with you, even to class. Want a shower, go over to the gym. (Alas, I thought, how many wasted opportunities.) Nights, you found a spot in the trees or down in the stadium. All last week he had spent the nights in the Auditorium, which was O.K. in that the seats were upholstered, but bad because you had to waste a lot of time hanging around to hide yourself before drama rehearsals stopped and the place closed up. And the janitors were early birds, up and working by seven. Caliban had heard that there were ways of getting through manholes into the heat tunnels, and so entering buildings where there might be hall benches and so on, but he hadn't bothered to investigate. He was more interested in the camping idea.

His recital got him animated. His flowing voice warmed, he shaped the scholar-gypsy life with his long thin hands. And he watched me all the time to see whether or not he was making it.

"All that to get an education!" Ruth said. He turned his head, big with hair, and pointed his bright eyes and anal lips at her, perhaps wondering if she was making fun of him. She was, but it would have taken somebody brighter than he to find it out for sure. After an inquiring pause he went on.

"One night the cops ran us off campus; I slept out here. Right under this tree. Birds in the morning, dew on the leaves, the whole pastoral bit." Quick as little crabs among seaweed and moss, his eyes went over me. "I could have slept down here every night since without anybody knowing it," he said.

And what was that? Pretense at candor? Threat? "I suppose you could have," I said. "But you couldn't now."

He stood five feet from me, scratching his hairy wishbone. Once again I had the impression that he was being deliberately outrageous, or alternately engaging and outrageous, as if he wanted my permission but only my unwilling or even hostile permission, as if it was worth more to him if it came out of my dislike. He would ingratiate himself only so far, and make no promises, and if I refused he would live in my woods in spite of me.

Ruth's mental telepathy was penetrating me like lasers. I felt unreasonably, in defiance of all sense, that I was being stingy, standing there saying a stubborn no to a proposition that, if I had liked this kid's type, I would have agreed to readily. My treacherous mind told me that the flat across there was pure wasteland, cut off from any usefulness, cut off from the horse trail, cut off even from prowling boys.

A jay bird charged into the bay tree and yakked at us and charged off. The smell of bacchic disorder emanated from Caliban's unzipped suit as rank as a goat yard. I wondered how anyone could sit next to him in a class. I wondered if he had any friends.

"Joe," Ruth said.

I said to myself, This is as stupid as you ever were, and you will undoubtedly regret it. Aloud I said, "All right. You can camp there, on certain conditions. The conditions are that you build no fires, shoot no guns, cut no trees, make a sanitary latrine, and bury your cans and garbage *deep*. And don't leave that tap open on my pressure tank."

I don't know what I expected—a change of expression, at least. He only watched me with his eyebrow up. "All right," he said. No thanks, no expressed pleasure or obligation. To force him, I put out my hand, and after a minute he shook it. His hand was thin, dry, hard, and gripped like bird claws.

"What's your name, in case the town comes around complaining?"

"Peck. Jim Peck." Still no change of expression, no unbending to a jocular or friendly tone. Softly, Jim Peck. Softly, but as if there were a jeer under the voice. There is something about all beards that is like the gesture of thumbing the nose. Thank you very much. Up yours. I regretted giving in to him before we had even turned away.

When we were halfway up the hill, walking slowly against the steepness and the shortness of our wind, I burst out, "In God's name why did you let me do that? You *wanted* me to do it."

"Yes."

"I wish I knew why."

She stopped, leaning uphill with one hand on her knee. Without turning her head she said, "Oh, Joe, you know! You couldn't miss it. There are so many of them it makes you think it's something they can't help. What if Curtis had gone to someone and asked for something like this, would you rather they said yes or rather they refused?"

"And after they said yes, would they be glad they had, or sorry?"

"Well," she said, "I can't help thinking it's healthier camping in the woods than sleeping in auditoriums and classrooms."

It was the same note she had struck when Curtis took up surfing: Anyway it's a *healthier* life than that zoo down in the Village. And look, I almost said to her, how *that* came out.

Her face, usually perky and sharp and amused, looked tired, and she went on putting one foot after the other up the hill with her eyes on the toes of her shoes. I knew she thought I had bristled at this Peck boy precisely because he was like Curtis. A chance, she was probably thinking. No matter how crazy they act, they have to be given every chance.

I wondered if she remembered how many chances Curt had, and how many he muffed. For all I knew—for we hardly talked about him any more—she might have persuaded herself that just one more chance would have saved him, that he was on the way out of his moral paralysis when he drowned. The bitterness, for her, might be that he never had the opportunity to demonstrate that he was saved. Or did she think an indefinite indulgence of one phase after another might have let him outgrow and survive them one by one? And for that lack of indulgence had she always blamed me?

3

I had thought I could make Jim Peck up out of the odds and ends of intellectual faddism and emotional anarchy and blind foolishness that have been improving our world for the last ten years, but in one way he surprised me. If all the idiocies of the later twentieth century had collected in his skull like DDT in the livers of birds and fishes, I shortly had to grant that something else had collected in him too.

For one thing, he was physically tough. He had none of that affectation of ill-health and that contempt for strength and well-being that I was used to among the literary intellectuals. For another, he liked to work with his hands. He was no good at it, he was a fumbling amateur, but he liked it, he was *Homo fabricans* at heart.

Driving out the lane a couple of days after our encounter, I saw brown movement through the trees, and stopped where I could see down to the creek. Peck, skinny and hairy in a pair of cut-off Levis, was testing a knot-ended swing rope he had hung in the bay tree on this side. A run, a takeoff, a swish, and he landed in the waist-high poison oak across the creek; a reverse run and takeoff, and he came swishing back. I saw him look my way, I saw him see me there in the stopped car, but he did not wave or nod. Presumably he was afraid I was going to invade his privacy. If he had acknowledged me, I might have gone on down and offered to help him get squared away. He didn't, and I didn't. Rather irritably, I drove on.

We did not see him again for ten days, though I observed that he had done some clearing in the little flat. Then one Saturday we heard the sound of hammering, and when I walked down for the mail I saw two motorcycles parked under the bay tree and Peck and a fellow beard building a platform of some kind across in the cleared space. Next morning a brown tent was pitched on it. A few days later, when we took advantage of the continuing Indian summer to make our loop up through the school land and back along the horse trail, we found that Peck had begun a bridge. Since he was not there to object, we violated his privacy and took a look.

He had sunk four strong six-by-six posts, two on each side of the creek, and strung two pairs of cables between them, top to top and bottom to bottom. Across the lower two cables he had begun to wire lengths of two-by-four for treads—a tedious job, obviously, not very neatly done and not more than a tenth completed. I set foot on the thing, but it was like trying to walk a horizontal rope ladder.

From across the creek we inspected Peck's domestic arrangements. He had built the platform considerably larger than the tent required, leaving himself a front porch seven or eight feet deep and a dozen wide. A green canvas patio chair, one of those bat-shaped things, sat on it beside a length of redwood log that acted as a coffee table. A beer can stood on the log. The tent was ill pitched, its ropes straining the canvas into wrinkles and its sidewalls drooping, but even so the place looked snug. Why the hell didn't *we* think of putting a camp down here? I asked Ruth. After Peck moved out we ought to build ourselves a teahouse, with a high arching Japanese bridge, so that in the rainy season we could go down there and brew a pot of tea and listen to the un-Californian sound of running water.

Saint Simeon Stylites with conveniences, Thoreau with amenities, Peck gave us glimpses of his Coleman lantern shining through the trees, and once or twice he himself moved in our vision, easing a yellow plastic pail of water across his bridge or working around the tent. But then the rains came on heavily so that it was too muddy to walk the horse trail or the bottoms, and we saw him only from a distance, and checked his presence or absence by whether or not the tarp-covered Honda was parked under the bay tree. Once, coming home in a downpour and seeing his tent blooming with light through threshing limbs and sheets of water, I half envied him his mixture of exposure and snugness. I can think of nothing pleasanter than to be close to danger or discomfort, but still to be protected, preferably by one's own foresight and effort. Civilization began somewhere around that feeling, and I didn't disagree with Ruth when she suggested that there was hope for any Caliban who displayed, however ineptly, the impulse to build his own shelter.

Since the day we encountered him in the bottoms, we had not exchanged words, but we were steadily and sometimes intensely aware of him. In a way that sometimes exasperated me, he imposed himself on us as a neighbor. We looked his way, driving in and out; we noted the sound of his motorcycle going and coming; we were aware when he was at home and when away. And sometimes in the evenings when we walked twenty times around the house because that was the only way of getting any exercise without wading in mud, we heard his guitar, so disarming a sound that it seemed no denizen of the hills was more natural and appropriate than Jim Peck. One morning after a big storm I caught myself looking across almost anxiously to see if he had weathered it.

"It seems so lonely for him," Ruth said. "He doesn't seem to have any friends, does he?"

I looked at her long and hard. "Are you maybe hinting we ought to have him up for a meal?"

It is not often I can fluster her, but she was flustered. She said defensively, "I wouldn't think it was completely out of the question."

"Thanksgiving, maybe?"

She flared up. "Well, why not? What would be wrong with that?"

"It isn't like you to be sentimental, for God's sake," I said. "Are you kidding yourself that he sits down there missing the comforts of home? Were you getting your mouth fixed to taste his touching gratitude for a home-made piece of pie?"

"He's young," she said resentfully. "He's human."

"Young yes, human hardly," I said. "Are you prepared to serve us up a Zen-diet Thanksgiving?"

"If I knew how, I wouldn't mind."

"No," I said. "I wouldn't sit next to him at table. What's more, he wouldn't come."

Probably he wouldn't have come, and almost certainly we would have had a hell of a time enjoying his company. But I wish now I had let him refuse us, rather than jumping to refuse him in advance.

Sometime before Christmas Peck's isolation began to break down. The beardie pal who had helped him build his platform came back, and his motorcycle was parked beside the Honda for several days. Immediately after that there came a Volkswagen bus with Illinois plates that stood for more than a week by the trail gate above the empty Thomas cottage. Every evening we heard the sounds of partying, singing, banjos and guitars. There was one girl with a voice so good I thought sure they must have Joan Baez down there. Then I concluded it must be a folksong troupe, one of those itinerant outfits that bangs around from hootenanny to festival playing troubadour. But about the fourth night of party the thing began to lose its charm for me. "What does he think he's doing?" I said to Ruth. "We didn't authorize a hostel."

"Oh, what's the harm? Nobody that age knows when to go to bed. You have to make allowances, Joe. We aren't really bothered, and there's nobody to bother at Thomas's."

"What's to keep a gang like that from breaking into the Thomas place and using it for a pad?"

"You want to find them guilty before they even give the slightest indication of doing anything wrong."

We were walking out our prebed constitutional, around and around the house in the cold night. Every time we rounded the bedroom corner the singing blew up at us out of the dark. I zipped the parka hood over my chilled skull and shut out some of the entertainment, but I couldn't shut out Ruth, and didn't really want to. Fifty steps of silence. Then I said, "Wouldn't you say we'd had experience? Wouldn't you say we know the type?"

"I wonder if we know very much about it at all."

"Remember the time the Wilsons let Curtis caretake their place in Roxbury?"

"Yes, but that was . . ."

"To hole up and write through the winter?" I said, walking on her heels. "Splendid isolation, high purposes?"

In silence she circled the carport and angled across the kitchen patio, me at her heels, gritting my teeth in the cold, hating myself, yapping after her like some feisty terrier. At the next corner the singing rose once more to meet us, and the very sound and style of it, familiar as the beginning clench of a migraine, made me savage.

"Remember? Remember what the Wilsons found when they went out there in January? Sink full of unwashed dishes, garbage pails overflowing with bottles, beds full of uninvited unwashed guests? You think I like to remember things like that? But you think I can forget them?"

"You don't know about Peck," Ruth said. I had to pull the hood off and turn my head to hear her through the throb and bang of their music. "He's been living next to the Thomas place for weeks, and no sign he's touched it. You just assume things."

"I assume them from experience," I said. "These people are so hell-bent to be individuals that they don't even exist except as gangs. Alone, they're nothing. Put all of them in one bag and they blow up the place. If Peck was going to open a hostel and have his goony pals sleeping three-deep all around, he should have asked, shouldn't he?"

"And had you refuse."

"Why not? Is it our obligation to shelter every underage kook that comes by?"

"Oh, wait and see," she flung back. "They're just visiting. They'll go away." On the next round she turned in at the bedroom door, and we went to bed in silence. Privately, I granted that my suspicions had no foundation; but I also felt, and I insisted to myself before I fell asleep, that if Peck would turn his camp into a hostel without asking, he would do a lot more. He was a kind of gas that would expand to fill any amount of space.

The Volkswagen bus disappeared the day after Christmas, perhaps bound for some place where the comforts were less spartan. For a while we saw only Peck. He was an incorrigible fixer. Because in the wet he couldn't ride his Honda across the bottoms, he cobbled together a wretched little shed beside the trail gate into our lane, an eyesore that offended me every time I passed it. (No permission requested, I pointed out to Ruth.) Observing from the lane, we noted other improvements. One day we saw him running his yellow pail across the creek on an overhead cable. Later we saw that he had rigged some way of pulling the whole far end of his bridge up into one of the oaks.

"What's he afraid of?" I said to Ruth. "I'll bet you he's got a half acre of marijuana planted over there."

"Grump, grump," Ruth said. "He's probably afraid of kids breaking in. He can't lock his tent, after all."

"In a hermit's cell there shouldn't be anything worth stealing."

"If he did live like a sanyasi, you'd be the first to call him crazy."

"He irritates me," I said. "He asks to put up a simple camp, being too poor to afford a room . . ."

"He never said that."

"All right. Being unable to stand the restraints of a room or apartment. Then he spends more on lumber and gadgets and rope than he'd pay for normal room and board in a year."

"Maybe he's having more fun."

"I wonder if he *knows* how to have fun."

"He has parties," she said. "He tinkers. Whichever he does, you complain. Why? You work on your think-house every afternoon of your life."

"I'm retired."

"So is he, in a way. Why can't you let him alone? He's not hurting anything."

He was the least contemplative sanyasi I ever heard

of. Every week there was a renewed outbreak of sawing and hammering. The one that began in mid-January went on for a whole morning, stopped, began again the next morning and went on through the day. Just after noon I went down for the mail. I could see the bridge, lowered into place, drooping crookedly across the creek. Beyond it was the front of the tent. I could hear the hammering but see no sign of Peck. What in hell was he putting up now? Steam-heated privy? Pergola? Studio? I told myself that I had better find out before he developed a subdivision over there, and went down through the mud to the bay tree.

When I was halfway across the bottom, I saw movement in one of the oaks, fifteen feet off the ground. In his orange suit, his John-the-Baptist hair crawling over his collar, Peck was squatting up there with his back to me, nailing away. He had laid joists across two nearly horizontal limbs and was spiking two-by-fours to them for a floor. The lumber was secondhand, and dark, and the live-oak leaves were dense enough so that from certain angles you could hardly see anything up there at all.

I coughed, and he twisted around. With his tangled mane and beard, he looked like some ridiculous lion out of a bestiary. And he was good and startled, as startled as I had been when we came upon him sitting his stealthy motorcycle under the bay tree. He grabbed a limb and glared, breathing steam.

"What goes on?" I said.

Peck rose until he stood crouching, one hand braced against the limb over his head, the other holding the hammer. I half expected him to heave it at me like a tomahawk, but all he did, finally, was make a little deprecatory gesture with it. He smiled. His voice was soft. "Little . . . treehouse," he said.

Looking up at this Tarzan, this fabricator, this retarded adolescent living a Swiss-Family-Robinson fantasy, I was full of conflicting emotions. Was I irritated simply because he had gone ahead and started something else without asking permission? Was it only an authoritarian insistence on being begged, an unpleasant property-owner desire to stoop grandly and confer favors, that made me angry at him? I was pretty sure he would have thought so, and I was ready to admit that there was some of that in my feelings. And yet wasn't I more exasperated at his refusal to acknowledge his *obligation* to ask? Manners, if not ordinary openness of motive, might have dictated at least a telephone call. Is it O.K. if? Do I mind if? I accused his type, as much as him personally. They took, they challenged, they acknowledged nothing.

It struck me, during our half minute of silent staring at one another, that I hadn't the slightest notion of what he might be thinking. What went on behind the beard and the dangling grin? What expression was that in his vigilant, feral eyes? Did I imagine our intractable antagonism, or was I only responding, stiffly and wrongly, to my finished but unresolved quarrel with Curtis? Certainly I could make no real case against the treehouse. The oak would carry it as easily as it would carry a jay-bird's nest. It would be out of reach, almost out of sight. Why should I care? Why should I feel that stiff censorious knotting in my bowels?

"What do you need a treehouse for, meditation?"

The upward eyebrow. He had regained his watchful cool. "Sleep."

"Too noisy in the tent?"

He was not one to respond to the jocular tone—not from me. He didn't even bother to reply, but stood smiling his fixed smile down at me, the interrupted hammer hanging in his hand, waiting for me to go away. He didn't say, as almost anyone in his position would have said, "Come on over and take a look." Why not? Something in him, or something in me? Or something that hardened like cooling glass between us whenever we met? Well, since I was the unwilling landlord, I would go over without an invitation. But when I set my foot on the treads of the bridge and took hold of the cable handrail, the whole think slewed sideways and threw me off balance, and I lay along the cable for a second before I could straighten up and step off. I looked up into Peck's happy grin. Uh-huh, it said. Walk on over, why not.

Ruth would have said I asked for it, going down there to spy on what he was doing. But I did not think I was going to abdicate control of my own property just because Peck made himself difficult to reach. Furthermore, he had not grubbed out the poison oak from any part of the bottoms except the flat where he had chosen to build. Scraping my shoes clean against his bridge post, using the diversion to take hold of my temper, I said I had come down to ask when he was going to get at the poison oak. It should be grubbed out in the winter, so that the new sproutings could be sprayed in the spring.

Well, that, he said from his tree. It didn't appear that he was going to be able to do that, after all.

Why not? That was part of the bargain.

Yes, well, at that time he had thought he was immune. But when he cleared out the flat he had got such a dose he had spent a week in the infirmary taking cortisone shots.

I could have laughed out loud. He gladdened my soul, that arrogant young poop. Trying to treat poison oak the way he treated people, he had found that poison oak insisted on its integrity.

"You'll have it again," I said. "That stuff will be up all around you again in a couple of months."

He said that when it came up he intended to spray it.

Fine, I said. When he sprayed his he could spray mine too.

The noise of the rain-born creek flushed away between us. It was cold and damp down there in the bottoms. Vapor was congealed on the hairs of Peck's beard. His eyebrow went up, his smile widened, his nod was almost a bow. I lifted my hand and turned away. As I walked the muddy path back to the gate, the sound of hammering resumed behind me, and I doubt that either Peck or I could have said whether its beat was triumphant because he had put me down, or irritable because he had had to give in.

The hammering went on for several days. From the lane we saw a birdhouse taking shape in the leafage of the oak, a tiny irregular building perhaps seven by nine feet, with a steep roof that shortly became more visible in a coat of red asphalt shingles. The whole thing was crooked and misproportioned. Ruth thought it charming. "It's like Hänsel and Gretel," she said. "It ought to have a crooked stovepipe with a cap. And look, he's got it oriented so the porch and doorway face east. Is that to face Mecca, or something, do you suppose, or just to get the morning sun? And look at that ladder, like an elf ladder leaned against a mushroom!"

"Curb your fairy-story imagination," I said. "That's no elf, that's an oaf."

4

Elf or oaf, nudge from the past, discomfort from an unhealed wound—and yes, prick of conscience, reminder of failure—Peck could not spoil the pleasure we took in mere weather, simple spring. Wet January passed into a warm and sunny February over which blew brief fresh showers. Spider webs at sunrise glittered, the birds were wild. We spent most of our time outdoors, just looking and learning.

It felt like renewal, and yet it was not the beginning of renewal, as in colder climates, but an advanced stage. Renewal had begun way back in November, with the first rain. In February we were already knee-deep in grass and flowers, and growers around us were cutting the mimosa branches that in New York and Boston would bring an irresistible foretaste of spring, at two dollars a branch, to people still trapped in slush and soot and black ice.

After a couple of cautious weeks, when I was convinced winter had gone for good, I planted carrot and lettuce seed.

Promptly on February first the almond trees had broken into blossom. Promptly on the fifteenth the first daffodils popped their buds. By Washington's Birthday the wild mustard was head-high in Sam Shields's pasture, and our daphne odora and clematis drugged us with sweetness when we went in or out the front door. In the woods along our hill the ferns were a lush chemical green. Above them the buckeyes spread tentative fingers of leaf more delicate than anything we had seen since the spring beechwoods of Denmark.

I set out tomato plants.

We walked a great deal, mostly on the roads and on our own lane, where the smell of mold was rich and woodsy. At the foot of our hill there was one stretch from which we had a nearly unobstructed view of the bay tree, Peck's bridge, and the tent, and above them in the oak the triangular gable of the treehouse. Peck had moved in, or upstairs; and obviously he had bought or borrowed another gasoline lantern, for at night a bright light swayed and stretched among the black shadows of the limbs, while down below the tent glowed amber.

One morning when we came along below the gate the sun was pouring in through the branches against the treehouse gable, lighting the little porch like a spotlight. As we walked along, turning our heads to look, a girl in a black leotard stooped out the doorway into the sun. She was laughing back over her shoulder, and she was bare to the waist. Outside she expanded opulent breasts in the sunshine, throwing back her head to let long dark hair shake down her back. Then her eyes left the morning and found us, and in one motion she closed her arms across herself and ducked back inside.

We had not even stopped walking: the whole vision lasted only while we took a half-dozen steps. "Oh my goodness!" Ruth said, half laughing.

I had perhaps enjoyed the vision more than she had,

but I probably resented it more, too. I said, "Well, what is our official position on hamadryads?"

"Oh, dear, I don't know!" But then she rallied a little, and said, "Well, we let him camp there, and we didn't say he couldn't have his friends in."

"Friends," I said.

"I certainly hope so," Ruth said. Then she burst out, jarred out of her habitual whisper, "Good Lord, can you imagine how that rockaby-baby bower would seem to a romantic-minded girl? He can probably have them lining up, if he wants to."

"O.K.," I said. "It's romantic. Just the same we have to make up our minds how much we're willing to sponsor."

"Do we have to sponsor it?" Ruth said. "I agree, I don't like to see young people as promiscuous as they seem to be these days, but is that our business, any more than if we had rented Peck a place? Don't we have to assume it's his own business how he runs his life?"

"So we ignore it," I said. "And he'll know we're ignoring it. She'll tell him—she's already told him—she saw us, and we saw her. So he'll know. And he'll think we're either approving his high jinks, or afraid to squawk."

Troubled, she looked at me in silence, and we walked on, and that's the way it was left between us, exactly as it was left between us and Peck: nullified by silence. I suspect that Ruth had some hope it was a real love affair, and I think she watched as we walked past, to see if the girl would appear again. She never did, not that one. Either we scared her off for good, appearing just when she was embracing the pagan wilderness, or it wasn't as romantic as Ruth imagined it. If you believe their novels, romance is not a thing that Peck's generation specializes in. In their books, and perhaps in their lives too, love is about as romantic as a five-minute car wash.

I put him out of my mind, for to tell the truth his amours were less interesting to me than those of the lizards, which began on these warm days to emerge onto the bricks and do their attention-getting pushups and chase their lady friends wildly across the patio and under the junipers. And there were other aspects of spring as notable as the amatory play of Peck, the lizards, and the birds—the sorts of reminders that I seem never able to ignore or forget, and that I catch myself reading as somber parables.

Often, putting our noses outside to sniff the fresh beginnings of day, we poked them into the affairs of the nocturnals, and sometimes these were corroborative of life, as when we looked out and saw deer standing on their hind legs to browse the high toyon berries below the terrace, or caught sight of a raccoon's tail just sliding out of sight into the brush, and sometimes they were not. I remember, for instance, out of the pictures of that spring, the morning I saw Catarrh doing a murderer's dance with a mouse.

It was a long-tailed white-footed mouse, one of the pretty kind. Catarrh dribbled it the length of the patio, fifty feet or more, feinting and changing paws. When he lost interest and turned away, the mouse tried painfully to fumble itself out of bounds. Just in time the cat woke up, scooped it inbounds from the fringe of junipers, tried a hook shot over his shoulder, got the rebound, dribbled around in a circle, grew bored, walked away, returned, prodded the mouse into movement, dribbled it some more. After quite a while the mouse had lost all its bounce and simply lay there. When Catarrh saw that it was going to provide him no more exercise, he lay down in the misty morning light that was like the dawn of creation, and ate it, head first.

He was not long about his meal, and there was nothing left over for door-mat art. From the bathroom window where I stood watching, I saw him give one last gulping swallow, and the tip of the mouse's tail disappeared like the tail of our resident raccoon, sliding home at sunrise.

II

IN JACKSON HOLE there is a Catholic church, named Our Lady of the Grand Tetons by somebody who didn't know what tetons are. If we had a Catholic church here (we don't, it would be zoned out of this bedroom town) it would also have to be called Our Lady of the Grand Tetons. A real dumpling of a girl, a Boule de suif, our local Earth Mother, and her clefts are dark with oak and bay and buckeye, gooseberry and wild rose, and—appropriately—maidenhair, and—perhaps not inappropriately—poison oak.

No outsider comes to our town for anything, unless to bring children to one of our three riding stables, or to make love and toss beer cans on our dark lanes, or to dump garbage by our roadsides. Progress waits on water mains, because the strata under us are broken and disjointed and wells are uncertain. The reason the strata are all scrambled is that we are in the zone of the San Andreas fault. Right beside Mother Earth, in the same bed, lies Father Earthquake.

In a cross-eyed sort of way I have been comforted by the thought of that crack under the smiling hills: the devil's in his diocese, all's right with the world. The lady who, more than a half century ago, was my Sunday-school teacher tried to teach me that the world was created innocent, and that evil sneaked in, but even then, at eight or nine, I was a Manichee and thought her more innocent than the garden she had faith in. Evil lay underground in Paradise before life ever appeared. It was part of the mud life was made with. It awoke the moment life awoke, like a shadow that leaps up rods long when a man stands up at sunrise. Though we may not like it, we had better not forget it.

Where you find the greatest Good, there you will also find the greatest Evil, for Evil likes Paradise every bit as much as Good does. What makes the best environment for *Clematis armandi* makes a lovely home for leaf hoppers. A place where Joe Allston hopes to enjoy his retirement turns out to be Tom Weld's ancestral acres and a place attractive to Caliban.

And look: here in authentic Eden, where plants grow the way fire goes up a fuse, you can't turn your back for two days without having the place taken over by things that wither or curl or frazzle the leaf, things that feed on the hearts of roses, things like mildews and thrips and red spiders and white flies and mealy bugs and borers, the blights and the rusts and the smuts, the bindweed that in the hours of my innocence, east of Eden, I used to call morning-glory, the wild cucumber that strangles half an acre in its octopus tentacles, the poison oak that is already bursting out in flourishing patches where six months ago I grubbed it up to make a walk or a hedge—yea, and the things like the moles and the voles and the meadow mice, and most of all the gophers, that in spring work inward from Shields's pasture, marking their invasion route by tailings of loose dirt kicked out of lateral holes, and when all else is brown arrive to set tooth to the succulent roots of the plants we have thoughtfully kept green for them.

Though I acknowledge these challenges, I do not accept them meekly. If God could not create a perfect world—and good God, how badly You failed!—Allston would lend a hand. So from February, when first spring broke, through November, when the battlefields were drowned by the rains, I was self-employed in a holy war against the thousand pests that infest Eden. Exterminator, that was the role in which Marian first saw me. Exterminator and clown. And I persisted in both roles, especially the last, for she bothered me. It was something like love at first sight, but something was obscurely wrong with the omens, and uneasiness, as much as my natural gifts, made a fool of me. And yet I did not mind being a fool; I would have turned handsprings like a show-off boy if I had thought she would take notice.

There are many kinds of perfect days here. The day last spring that I am remembering was one of those that James Russell Lowell had in mind when he inquired what was so rare as a day in June. The fact that it was March should not confuse us. Every clod felt a stir of might, believe me. The ground had been soaked by a good late rain, and it steamed with growth. Weld's apricot orchard that for two weeks had been a froth of pale pink was misty green as leaves began to replace blossoms. In our little family orchard the two almond trees were fully leaved and the fruit well formed. The plums, which for a while had been wedding sprays, were also setting fruit, but the sapling cherries were something out of Housman, or like young girls dressed for a lawn party in Charleston, S.C.

Ruth was cutting some gone-by daffodils on the slope above the parking area. Beyond her was the line of dark-red thundercloud plums, and beyond the plums, in the pasture, thirty acres of wild mustard so bright it yellowed the air. A cowslip under the chin of the sky: you like butter. From a hundred feet away I smelled the daphne in the front entry. A meadow lark was going crazy across the fence, and every male house finch had a head and throat as red as a tomato, the effect of love.

So here I am contentedly sprinkling cutworm bait along my row of young tomato plants and amusing myself thinking what a quaint idea it is to perfect Eden with poisons, and wondering (let us suppose) what Adam and Eve did without rotenone, melathion, lindane, chlordane, sodium ammate, and the other deterrents. In the days when the lion lay down with the lamb, did the flea lie down with the dog, or the gnat with the itching mortal? Did the aphid make friends with the rose, or the San Jose scale with the peach tree? Did the picnicking dame consort with the poison ivy? And as I am ruminating in this fashion, I see the tomato plant at the end of the row shiver, stagger, and sink two inches into the ground.

Within ninety seconds I am into the house and out again with the shotgun. "What is it?" Ruth is calling, and "Joe, be careful!" but I pay her no attention, tiptoeing down the garden path. The tomato plant has not moved. Down underground there the trespasser is still chomping and smacking his lips. As I wait, holding my breath, I hear voices, and a strange young couple appears at the top of our drive where it turns onto the hilltop. The woman wears a look of startlement as if she might scream, and for fear she will I make a fierce gesture for silence. We see hardly any people up here. Who the hell are these? Trespassers, shakers of the earth, scarers of the enemy. My eyes are fixed on the half-submerged tomato, my nose tickles with the dense garden odors, I hear the meadow lark splitting his throat, singing beatitude, and the murmur of Ruth's voice as she greets the strangers.

The tuft twitches, the plant goes down like the bobber on a fishline, and I pull the trigger. My ears are shattered by the appalling blast, and the two-foot circle of earth on which I have been concentrating splashes like water. I lay the gun aside, and dig, and behold him with a twig of tomato vine in his grooved teeth, a fat old bull gopher with a big head and naked-palmed feet: *Thomomys bottae*, the Evil One.

With my toe I scoop him onto the surface, and as he lies there on his back grinning his four-toothed yellow grin I see the fleas scuttling for cover through the thin hairs of his belly. Then I hear, from above me on the drive, this high, rather strained, but musical voice that says, "For heaven's sake, what have you gone and done?"

Now for sure I look up, and it is a rather odd moment altogether, because my ears and my eyes don't agree. I am prepared to reply to the voice in words of some acidity, but the first look corks my eloquence. She looks as if she had bloomed into this spring day, she has a tremble on her like young poplar leaves. It is hard for a sentimental man to say unsentimentally, and besides my heart is sore, but here is this girl—woman, rather, maybe thirty—with her hair a little blown, her face pale and strained but shining, her eyes most alive, and her lips parted in a look that mixes pity for the gopher with pleasure at meeting me even if I *am* a brute, and delight simply in the way the sun pours down and the browned daffodils lie in a sheaf across Ruth's arm. She is one of old Willie Yeats's glimmering girls, with apple blossom in her hair, and I admit to a pang. God knows what it is—maybe envy that someone is lucky enough to have such a daughter. I am old-fashioned. I believe that the human face was made for expression, and I like the way every emotion shows on this girl's mouth and in her eyes. I wonder how this kind of innocent eagerness got born into the same world with the beatniks and the glumniks; and all the time I am being captivated I am annoyed at her sentimental cry over the death of a pest.

So I don't answer her at once. I merely kick the gopher back into the hole and scrape dirt over him. Catarrh would eat him happily enough, but we prefer Catarrh to eat canned cat food. Ruth is whispering in her imperturbable voice, "Joe, these are the Catlins, they've bought the Thomas place."

"Allston," I say. "White hunter."

"It's not hahd to believe it," Catlin says in a down-Maine voice. He is a healthy crewcut, the kind that every now and then reminds you how virile New England still is. He looks bright, and he knows the uses of a smile. But his charming wife is another matter. She is going to have an answer to why I go around murdering harmless little beasts. She says to me breathlessly, "Why did you have to go *shoot* it?"

"Because he was eating my tomato plants."

"That's like hanging someone for stealing a loaf of bread."

"Today my tomatoes," I say. "Tomorrow my wife's daffodils—no, that's one thing he won't eat. Tomorrow the tuberous begonias, next day the agapanthus, following that the flowering quince. Pretty soon desert, nothing but poison oak and coyote brush again."

"I should think you'd have a nice natural garden where things are in balance and you don't have to kill anything. Is it fair to plant a lot of plants that were never intended to grow here, and then blame the gophers for liking them?"

She is laying it down, she really believes in this. But at the same time she has a serene, promising, transparent look as if, just as soon as this little cloud passes, she will bloom out again in sun. I say to her, and I am being neither scornful nor contentious, "You like little live things."

"You have no idea how accurate you are," her husband says. "I've given up fishing because she can't bear to think of the worms."

"Well," she says, "how would *you* like an old hook clear through you lengthways?"

There seems no answer to that one. I suggest that we repair to the terrace and have a drink and I will introduce them to some birds who are also fond of worms. As we walk through the kitchen patio, young Catlin says, half joking, half fond, the way he might speak to a kid sister he adored, "All right, get it over. Tell'm about your foxes."

"Laugh!" she says. "But you didn't *see* them!" Almost as if dancing, she swings from Ruth to me, back to Ruth. "Did you know we had foxes?"

I am tempted to tell her about the fox with the strangulated hemorrhoids, but she is a little new for that. I say only, "We've seen a few on the road at night."

"I saw *two*," she says. "Last night. Honestly, I never

had such a nice thing happen to me. I'd just put Debby to bed and was sitting by the window resting and wondering what sort of drapes to get, and there was this little scratching noise, and a fox came right up on the slab outside. He wasn't five feet from me, on the other side of the glass, with the light shining on him. I guess he couldn't see me because of it, or maybe he thought I belonged. I hope he thought I belonged, because he was the cleanest, sleekest, loveliest thing. . . ."

I suspect that I have much the same feeling, watching her, that she had watching the fox. I feel that I should move quietly, if at all. I find myself preposterously holding my breath. Then she sees us all intent on her, and her cheeks get pink. She flops into a patio chair with one foot under her, and laughs, flashing her eyes upward in an amused, challenging way.

"I don't care, he was beautiful. He looked right at me through the window like somebody shopping, and then he whined, I could hear him, and right away here came another one just as beautiful as he was. And you know what? They were in love. They kept nuzzling one another, and whining, and peeking in the window as if they thought it might make a good den inside if they could only find a way in. They must have been there three or four minutes, so close I could have leaned over and patted them. I could see every whisker on their chins. Now wasn't that a lovely thing to happen on our first night out here?"

We agree that it was. In fact, the Catlins themselves seem a nice thing to have happened, a big improvement over Thomas. In a sneaky bid for favor, trying to solidify a friendship by tying a former neighbor to the whipping post, I tell them how old Thomas used to sit in his back patio on Sunday mornings, dressed in pink pajamas, and hold target practice on the towhees and quail with a .38 revolver.

Marian Catlin is suitably horrified. But then she slants her wide, strangely shaped eyes at me, and completely undiverted from her original disapproval, says, "But you shoot gophers."

"You bet," I have to say. "Yes, ma'am."

"Who are you to say they haven't got as much right to live as quail? They can't help it if they're not pretty, and can't sing. All they're doing is just innocently digging away and eating the roots they run into."

"Did you ever look into a gopher's beady eye?" I ask. "*He* knows he's evil. He's got guilt written all over him. Wait till one innocently eats up your begonias."

"I haven't got any begonias."

"You will have."

"Nope."

"Carrots, then. Loganberries. Pole beans. Whatever you grow."

"We're not going to grow a thing," she says happily. "We're just going to *let* grow. While the house was vacant nearly everything dried up and died, and we're going to leave it that way—let it go back to the things that grow here naturally. We aren't going to tinker with nature one bit, we like it exactly as it is."

"Poison oak and all?"

"It doesn't poison me," she says, as if she has pull with the management.

"The immune are bad witnesses," I tell her. "I hope you're immune to beggar's-lice and cocklebурs and needle grass and foxtails, too. I hope your nylons are immune to screw grass."

"If I'm foolish enough to wear nylons in the country, I deserve to ruin them."

"Barefoot, then. Have you got a dog?"

"We might get a pup for Debby—that's our daughter."

"Is *she* immune?"

"We don't know yet."

"So. Well anyway, if you get a pup, get one without ears or eyes or feet. Otherwise you'll be taking him to the vet once a week, the way Fran LoPresti does her cocker, with foxtails in his tear ducts or his eardrums or the webs of his toes."

Her eyes, I have finally determined, are shaped like some exotic sunglasses, turned upward at the outer corners, but they are wide, not narrow and heavy-lidded the way Oriental eyes are. And they are as blue as my mother's were. She is watching me; the easy blush floods into her face. "Yes, but . . ."

"Not even barefoot nature lovers can find anything nice to say of the foxtail," I say.

"It's only following its natural way to reproduce. If it sticks in your stocking or in a dog's ear, it's only distributing its seeds."

John Catlin, who has been following the argument with a suspended half-smile, says to me, but with his eyes on her, "And if it's distributing its seeds, don't try to tell Marian it isn't O.K."

But by now I am beginning to rev up, because so far as I can see this girl seriously means the ridiculous things she is saying. I ignore the storm warnings that my good wife is beginning to fly, and I refill Catlin's glass and my own, and I bring up my strategic bombing command and prepare to plaster her off the map.

"You like nature as she is," I say. "Let me ask you. A gopher is nature, right?"

"Right. Just as much as any . . ."

"So it's O.K. if he eats my tomatoes. He's following his natural instincts. Is the tick on a gopher nature?"

"Sure." She is smiling, blushing, amusedly at bay, prepared to fight to the last man.

"So it's all right if the tick eats the gopher's blood. Is the germ on a tick nature?"

"Well . . . Yes, of course."

"So if the germ on the tick on the gopher happens to get off the tick and onto you and gives you spotted fever, you should fold your hands like the suffering Arab and say, 'God is kind'?"

"I wouldn't like spotted fever, no."

"It's only nature," I say with my district-attorney smile. "It's only those little germs distributing their seeds. From their point of view, which you seem to suggest is as good as yours, you're only a swamp where they have squatter's rights."

The girl says stubbornly, "You can become immune to germs just the way you can to poison oak."

"Some can. How much do you envy the people you know who became immune to polio the hard way?"

Catlin looks at me pleasantly, sipping his drink. I have the distinct impression that he wishes, in a friendly way, that I would shut my mouth. But good Lord, what this charming idiotic woman is saying! She wants to restore natural balances that have been disturbed ever since some Cro-Magnon accidentally boiled his drinking water. The Jains who go at night to break down the pest-control ditches, and build little bridges so that the locusts can get across onto their fields, are her appropriate playmates. Though for the moment I seem to have silenced her, I have certainly not put her convictions out of action. They are down there in the cellars and bomb shelters and among the rubble, and as soon as I drone away they will come out and go about their business as before.

"Isn't it lovely how violet the deciduous oaks look when everything is green around them?" Ruth says.

If she wants to pretend that the conversation has now exhausted its present topic and will turn to others, she is whistling in a wind tunnel. I fix Marian Catlin with my wise old eye, and don my curmudgeon look, which says that though I speak brusquely my heart is as mushy as a papaya, and I say, "My dear child, it's one thing to be fond of little live things—who isn't?—but you can't simply ignore the struggle for existence. There are good kinds of life and bad kinds of life. . . ."

"Bad is what conflicts with your interest," she says. This is more acute than I expected from her, and I grant her the touch.

"Yes, why not? We've become a weed species, we exterminate or domesticate species that threaten us, but we didn't invent the process. Every kind of life you can think of is under attack by some other kind."

"Of course," she says. "Everything's part of some food chain. But that doesn't mean we have the right to . . ."

"Even porcupines," I say, riding over her. "Even porcupines seem to have been invented just to feed fishercats. Is it news that nature is red with tooth and claw? The gopher I shot back there was crawling with fleas and ticks, and he probably had tapeworm—at least our cat gets tapeworm from something he catches. If he knew how, don't you suppose that gopher would eliminate all his pests and parasites so he could live happily ever after in my tomato patch? Do you think we could live here ourselves without fighting pests every day of the week?"

"Not if you want to live in a botanical garden."

Ruth's eyebrows are pulled clear up into the white widow's peak of her hair. Young Catlin yawns and stretches, squints at the view of Weld's shitepoke pigeon house and Tobacco-Road dog run across the gully, sips his drink, looks at me with a pleasant opaque expression. But I have to strike one more blow for sanity before quitting this silly debate.

"Look," I say. "Do you really like the woods and pastures as kind old Mother Nature designed them? Once they start distributing their seeds, which they will about May, you can't walk through them. The woods are choked with poison oak and wild-cucumber vines till they aren't fit for a rabbit to run in. And did you ever dig underground in these parts? It's underground that you really meet the evils. Ever examine the roots of poison oak? They're dead black, with red underbark, and if you cut one with a shovel or an ax it squirts out juice that will put you in bed for a week. Or these wild cucumbers. I dug one up once, just to see where all that vile vitality comes from that can sprout these tentacles twenty feet long. You know what's down there? A big tumor sort of thing as big as a bucket, an underground cancer. I very much doubt that any of these things are the friends of man."

As usual when I get high on my own persuasive powers, I think I am making quite a case, but when I glance at Marian Catlin I don't see any sign of conviction. She wears a delicate flinching expression as if she were forcing herself to look steadily at something ugly, or as if I am being embarrassing and she wishes for my own sake I would stop. Her husband stretches his legs abruptly. In a moment he will propose going home. And my good wife, who has been doing everything but kick my shins for five minutes, serves up at the conversational bar one of her patented dry murmurs, five-to-one with a twist of lemon peel. "Joe, lamb, you're being carried away."

"On my shield," I say, and let it go.

So we must leave the foolish girl in her foolishness, with a smile but not without some residue of combativeness. I turn the conversation by asking Catlin what he does for a living. The answer may not explain the nature worship, but it's consistent with it. He tells me he is an ethologist, which I understand to be halfway between an experimental psychologist and a veterinary. He came out here from Woods Hole last fall. His specialty is sea mammals—whales and porpoises and seals and such—and he spends a lot of time in the field. In the course of the conversation he tells me that a baby California gray whale grows a ton a month, a fact which, I feel sure, will agitate my mind on many a sleepless night. What in *hell* is in whale's milk?

We discuss other interesting matters, such as the objection that geese have to incest, and the way birds are imprinted, almost immediately after hatching, on the first thing they see that moves or makes a noise. Apparently, you can make an unfortunate baby bird believe that almost anything is its mother—an alarm clock, a mechanical toy, anything. There is a duckling somewhere that yearns for Charles Collingwood, before whom he was hatched on television. Catlin is full of interesting lore, and the ladies are having their own intimate dialogue, and my argumentative bumptiousness is passed over and forgotten.

Then a mockingbird swoops past, perches in the top of an oak below us, and sprays the whole hillside with song. He is in total disagreement with Browning's wise thrush, who sings each song twice over. This one is mortally afraid of repeating himself, and he sings so loud and long, and leaps into the air every now and then with such wild somersaulting glee, that he forces us to stop talking, and with pleased acknowledging looks at one another, to listen.

For a moment I have an acute awareness of how we look, quiet on the terrace in the bird-riddled afternoon, with the breeze dropped to nothing, the leaves still, the haze beginning to spread amethyst and lavender and violet between the layers of the hills, the sun dappling the bricks like something especially sent down from above to soothe our mortal aches away. Marian Catlin's face tells me that she has the same perception. This is the way she feels everything in her life—hungrily. Sensibility that skinless is close to being a curse.

I notice that her neck and face are thin; except when the easy blush comes on, she is pale. Her head is twisted sideward to hear, and against the strained cord of her throat a pulse is beating, a little hidden life. Her smile looks as if it pained her, and I swear her eyes are shiny with tears. I am ashamed of the way I hammered her down; it was like teasing an oversensitive child.

The mockingbird pours on, unquenchable. "*Listen* to him!" Marian cries, and because I have been caught in a kind of emotional nakedness I generally take pains to avoid, I cannot forbear to say, shaping the words nearly silently, "He does it on a diet of worms."

Even so inert a witticism, reviving our argument but in a way to call it off, gets me what I hope for: a wrinkling of the nose, a widening of the flashing, white-toothed smile. Friends, then.

The mockingbird swoops away with a flirt of half-hidden white feathers. A hermit thrush, winter resident for some reason hanging around well after he should have gone north, hops onto the terrace and examines us with a large round eye. A signal passes from Catlin to his wife. To keep them a little longer, because by now I am being willingly dragged in chains from the chariot wheels of this girl, I ask him what ethological circles say about the mockingbird. Does he really mock other birds, or do his old folks teach him his repertory, or is it built into the egg?

Marian tips her head back with a gurgle, the hungry look dissolves in laughter. "Oh, tell him! Tell him about Hannes and then we have to go get Debby."

So Catlin tells me about an Austrian friend who got a clutch of mockingbird eggs and incubated them in the dark and raised the young birds in total purdah to determine how they learned to sing. The only sounds they heard came from a tape recording of a man's voice reading Lincoln's Gettysburg Address, stepped up in speed until it was nothing but a high twittering. Hannes found that his mockingbirds did indeed learn by imitating: pretty soon he couldn't tell which was tape recorder and which was bird. But then his old scientific devil began to whisper to him, he started to cast covetous glances at the Unknowable. Like an ethological Faust, he dared too high. He taped one of his mockingbirds and then stepped the speed *down* to see if their encoded sound could be brought back to words. I see him bending, tight with suspense, above his speaker in some midnight soundproofed lab. The helpers have all gone, the whir of the electric clock is cut off by his pulling of the plug. The unmarked seconds drip away, there is a silent countdown. Hannes reaches out, his bony fingers turn a switch.

And does he hear the Great Emancipator's solemn voice beginning, "Fourscore and seven years ago?" He does not. He hears something that sounds like seven Ukrainians plotting revolution behind a thick door. Failure. Enter Mephistopheles on a puff of sulphur smoke.

"See?" Marian says. "Original sin. He tried to tamper with nature."

Just then the beagles across the gully, who have been unnaturally silent for an hour, erupt into a clamor. Still laughing, I stand up to see over the toyons, afraid I will see the owners in their padded corduroy-and-canvas shooting coats coming across the hill for their weekend sport with their shotguns over their arms. That would mean whisking the Catlins inside or around the house, because I doubt that Marian would enjoy watching this pair let pigeons loose and then gun them down for the dogs to retrieve. But there is no hunting couple in sight. Apparently, one of the dogs smelled something in his sleep and woke up yelling. That is the way the beagle mind works.

"Is it a kennel?" Marian asks. "Do they have pups for sale?"

"No," I tell her. "Only Tom Weld's latest way of making a dollar out of his pasture. His boy set it afire with a firecracker last Fourth of July, and burned off all the feed so he couldn't rent it out to horses any more. Now he rents it to some dog-and-pigeon people. When the grass gets a little higher he'll rent it for pasture again, without closing out the shooters, and before long one of them will shoot a horse, and I will sit over here watching and rubbing my hands."

Both Catlins are smiling at me, waiting. When I don't go on, Catlin says, "Weld is the man in the white farmhouse down on the county road, isn't he?"

"That's the least of what he is. He's the house on the county road, he's the busted bridge we all knock our wheels out of line on. He's that pack of pestilential beagles, he's Fran LoPresti's mongrel pup, he's irritations by day and alarms by night, he's the Adversary, the Id, Adam Aborigine, Old Mister Consequence. He's our fire hazard, our eyesore, our past, our future, our history, and our drama. You really want to know about Tom Weld?"

"Joe," Ruth says. "Not again. Not now."

But I am already in full cry, and with Marian Catlin's amused and attentive face before me, I outdo myself. Early explorer, old settler, garrulous gaffer, I regale these green immigrants with the hyperbolical perils of the New World. I start far back, when our relations with Weld were friendly and even funny, when he was a skin-clad native and we were white strangers who had quenched their prow on his beach, and I give it all its philosophical applications and extensions. It would have gone something like this:

2

There are certain orthodoxies in the associations between natives and new settlers. The newcomers land, see that the country is fair, kneel and claim it in the king's name, plant a flag and a cross, and advance making signs of peace, with muskets at the ready. Usually the local chief is friendly; if he isn't, a volley teaches him instant manners. He swaps corn, fish, squash, daughters, and other native produce for beads, mirrors, and needles. He throws a feast of young dog, signs a treaty of friendship for as long as grass shall grow or water run, and accepts a plug hat, a coat with epaulets, and a lead medal. He is offered raw alcohol cut with branch water and spiced with cayenne and powdered tobacco, and when he comes to, groaning, next day, his new friends thank him kindly for the gift of Manhattan Island.

Manhattan Island seems a small price for such enhancements of his life as the white men bring. He is employed as guide and hunter, there are new markets and job opportunities, the economy gets a boost. It even turns out that the newcomers value French and Iroquois scalps, will pay a dollar apiece and furnish the scalping knives.

So far, fine. But little by little the Indian finds that the white men have burned off the woods where he hunted, and drained the bogs where he used to pick cranberries and trap muskrats. Places turn out to be out of bounds, things are forbidden. Helping themselves to the white man's corn, Indians get slapped in the stocks. Shooting one of his spotted deer, they get thirty lashes. No longer red brother—now thieving redskin. Young bucks mutter threats, old chiefs counsel patience, winter comes, redskin cold and hungry, meat scarce, blanket ragged, tobacco and firewater impossible dreams. Appears at white man's door begging a meal and a smoke: *On your way,* you gut-eating vagabond! And keep a hundred feet clear of the chicken house as you leave.

That's the usual pattern. Up to now my sympathies have been with the noble and ill-used redskin. I have applauded when he shoots burning arrows into the thatch and tomahawks the women and children who run out with their hair on fire, and I have sorrowed for him when he is cornered and done in by the Miles Standish types. But the clash of cultures between Tom Weld and me has taught me that the white newcomer sometimes has a case. When I think about this Mohican I signed a treaty with, I feel as if somebody has wrapped a blood-pressure band around my neck and is pumping it up.

Ruth keeps saying we came out here to buy some quiet; we should accept the local culture for what it is. Weld's family has ranched these hills for sixty years with no success whatever—Ruth says because they never had a decent water supply, I say because all of them must have been cretins. These unirrigated hill apricots are small, and don't bring top prices from packers. In dry years the trees hardly bear at all. What would *you* do in those circumstances? Locate a decent water supply, or move to some land that could be farmed? But you're not a cretin. Cretins go on trying to farm it. Every time they hit a bad streak they sign a new treaty with the palefaces and dispose of another chunk of land. For the last twenty years it's taken a really splendid incompetence to lose money in California real estate, but there are the Welds with about thirty acres left out of two or three hundred, and nearly as strapped as ever. When Weld sold twenty acres to a developer, who resold our five to us, he needed money to pay for his father's funeral and to buy a new caterpillar tractor so he could go on raising minicots for a reluctant packing industry.

You can't see the Weld place from here, but the day the carpenters finished boarding our roof we climbed up and waltzed over the whole place, all full of euphoria, and from up there, with the binoculars, we saw this white farmhouse with a warped ridge and faded blue doors and window frames, inside a sagging woven wire fence. Also inside the fence—you can see most of it now if you look—there was a galvanized butane tank, uncamouflaged, an old truck with mustard growing up through it, a horse trailer with two flat tires, a secondhand culvert, lots of tin cans, plenty of paper, and a pile of fence posts that looked as if somebody had scattered them to get at a rabbit.

You think we were troubled then by that rural slum? Not a bit. Ruth even thought it was comforting to find that Weld lived a half mile off. A neighbor, that was nice. Not for fraternization, you understand, but just for emergencies. After all, we were after peace and quiet. So we waltzed around up there while a carpenter ran a machine saw along the edge of the roof, and down fell the ends of the roof boards like the ragged ends of our old life.

Then over in the pasture south of us we saw this Labrador dog coming with something big in his mouth that when he got closer turned out to be a red chicken. He came through holding the chicken high against the drag of the weeds and grass, and disappeared into the poison oak at the head of our road, and came into sight again a long time later far down below, approaching Weld's lane. The woven wire fence was in his way. He just left the ground and floated over it—a magnificent demonstration of what the dance people call *ballon.* Then he lay down and ate, and feathers blew around among the tin cans and old bones.

We didn't know LoPresti then, but we concluded he kept hens. Apparently, he kept them just for Weld's dog, because without any particular watchfulness I saw two more of them come through the pasture in the dog's mouth in the next ten days, and whenever I climbed high enough to see into Weld's yard his spread of mustard and thistles was thicker with the feathers of Rhode Island Reds.

Then one morning comes a short dark man to lean on a fence post and observe the building of our house. He wore faded suntans, and his hand that I shook was as callused as an oarsman's. This was LoPresti, who sounds like Parma but is actually third-generation California. He said he was building his own house, making his own adobe bricks as he went along. He'd been building for three years and might make it last a lifetime. He had this pleasant way of mocking himself in his talk, as if what he did struck him as mildly insane. His wife wasn't well—emphysema. They moved out here because it was smogless and because their daughter was horse crazy. He said there were a lot of deer, and at night they could shine flashlights out their windows and surprise raccoons and possums in the oak trees.

"Hard on your chickens?" I said.

"I don't have any chickens," said he.

"Oh? I thought . . ."

"I *had* chickens," LoPresti said. "Yesterday I chopped the heads off the five survivors and put them in the freezer. Though I'm not sure they're safe even there."

"So you know about that dog," I said. Oh, laughing—it struck me as very funny.

He looked off across the pasture and plucked great gut-bucket sounds out of the barbed wire and gave me to understand he knew considerable about that dog.

"Couldn't fence him out?"

"I did."

"Or keep the chickens inside a shed?"

"Did."

"But he got in anyway."

"Under," LoPresti said. "Over. Through. That's no ordinary dog."

"How come you didn't speak to Weld?"

"I did."

"What'd he say?"

"Said it was his brother's dog, he was just keeping it for him."

"That's a help. Did you talk to the brother?"

"I sure did. He said it didn't surprise him at all. He never knew a dog to beat this dog for hunting. Great rabbit dog, gopher dog, quail dog, mouse dog. It didn't surprise Charlie Weld one bit that he got after chickens. Dog like that, brought up in the country where he learns to rustle his own grub, it's no expense at all to keep him. Charlie was willing to bet me Tom hadn't bought a can of dog food since Charlie brought the dog out."

In my innocence, my inexperience, I cackled. "Did he offer to pay for the chickens?"

"Oh, no," LoPresti said. "Why would he do that? *He* didn't take them. It was the dog."

"And it never occurred to either of them that a dog like that ought to be tied up."

"Well, I suggested it, and Charlie admitted he'd tried. But that kind of dog, how can you keep him in? He just naturally unties knots with his teeth, chews his rope, busts his chain. Can't keep him in a pen either. Go over a ten-foot deer fence the way any other dog would go over a chair."

LoPresti pulled slivers from the fence post and flipped them humming into the weeds. "No," he said, "Charlie convinced me there's no way of looking at that dog except with regretful admiration. Which I do, indeed I do. He's got style. Yesterday he came over for his daily pullet and found the henhouse empty. You'd think he'd be put out. Hell, he never let it get him down for a minute. I was filling the woodbox with fireplace chunks, and I had my wife's cocker bitch tied to the clothesline for some exercise. She's in season, been shut in. So I get around the house just in time to be assured this mutt of Weld's won't die without issue. We'll have him in the God-damned family, multiplied by six."

LoPresti went home across the pasture, and Ruth and I had a big laugh. We had neither chickens nor cocker bitches.

That night the first rain blew in. We hurried out from

the motel where we were living to see what harm had come to our half-finished house, and right away got stuck in the mud of our half-finished road. So in the best tradition of the white settler asking native help, I walked back to Weld's wickiup, and he climbed into his pickiup and came and pulled us out. When I watched him get down in the mud to hook on the tow cable, I felt my years, and I was grateful to him.

When we got up the hill and parked by the lumber pile, there were these three horses looking out our unglazed window like Rosa Bonheur horses in a storm. From the evidence, which it took us a half hour to clean up, they'd been in our parlor all night.

I couldn't blame the horses. Weld had no shelter for them, and when he sold part of his land he hadn't altered his fences. Who was to tell these nags, which weren't even his, but boarders, that the south five acres were now out of bounds?

Still, somebody had to tell them. I walked back a half mile down the valley to do it. When I knocked on the faded blue door, out popped Weld's good-natured face. "Stuck again?"

No, I said, I just wanted to see him a minute. My feet were so balled up with adobe mud that I took off my shoes and came in my socks across five or six colors of asphalt tile. Somebody had been loose in the old farmhouse, fixing it up. Mrs. Weld gave me a smile and a wet rubber-gloved hand. Either she had taken advice from conflicting authorities or she had a friend who gave her samples. The walls were variegated like the floors: one wall rosebud paper, one combed redwood plywood, one birch. The fourth I didn't notice—window, maybe—but there was a large television in the living room with Weld's teen-age son magnetized to it. Mrs. Weld swooped through picking up Sunday papers in her rubber hands, and swooped out again.

Weld and I talked of the weather, and agreed it was wet. We agreed the road could stand a few more loads of base rock, which I planned to order. We said even if it was wet, the rain was welcome; out here it could sure get dry by November. We were mutually confident that it wouldn't take but a week or so before the grass would begin to come green.

After the preliminaries, I said, "Just now, when we got up to the house, we found your horses in it."

He was really pleased. "You did? They got in there, uh? It sure don't take a horse long to learn. Let it start getting wet and cold, and they're just like a person, if there's anyplace they can get under cover, they will."

"I wouldn't have mentioned it," I said, "only they do sort of mess up the house."

We laughed together, agreeing that a horse did, sort of.

"It doesn't matter much now," I said, "but later on they could do some damage. I wonder if we could work out a way to keep them out."

"Why sure, I should think," Weld said. "You probably want to put up a little fence around your place. I could give you a hand."

"That's good of you," I said, "but a fence means gates, and they're a nuisance to be always opening and closing. Wouldn't it be better if you fenced in the land you still own?"

There was a definite moment when he began to take it in. You could call it a moment of cultural shock. He looked at me blinking. "That'd cut out a big chunk of pasture."

"Yes," I said, "but you must have figured on losing it when you sold it."

He stood frowning and pinching his throat, looking at my stocking feet. "Well, yeah, I guess. But that'd be a big expense, that much fence."

I hadn't thought it would come for nothing. In fact, I had come over prepared to share the cost, as a sort of neighborly gesture. But it struck me that he hadn't yet admitted his responsibility to keep the horses on his own land. So instead of making any offer I remarked that the law was different in different states. Some places you were expected to fence loose stock out, but in California the law said the owner must fence them in.

"Yeah, is that so?" he said. "I s'pose. I never looked into it."

His face had gone a little mulish. In the kitchen Mrs. Weld was drying a saucepan and listening. The television scored on a long pass and burst into a roar, but when I glanced over, the Weld boy was watching me, not it. They had a kind of solidarity that made me mad.

"I don't want to seem unreasonable," I said. "But you can see that once the house is finished and the planting in, we can't have horses clumping around."

Weld had a habit of swallowing air, and the habit had grown on him as we talked. He pulled his dewlap and rubbed his jaw and swallowed and bent to look out into the rain that was coming down hard on a stiff wind. He said, "I should think you'd want a nice little fence around your place—picket fence, grapestakes, something like that. Looks nice, and all your planting is inside and you don't have to worry."

"That'd be fine," I said, "except that the landscape plan doesn't call for a fence, and I don't *need* a fence. *I* haven't got any horses."

I went to the kitchen door past Mrs. Weld, who managed a grimace about as near a smile as mine probably was. Weld watched my muddy shoes as I put them on. I suppose he was thinking that an hour ago he had done me the favor of pulling me out of the mud. So was I, for that matter.

I left him looking mulish, saying he'd have to see. A little later we drove down the hill and got stuck in the same mudhole where we had bogged down coming out. I wouldn't humiliate myself by asking another favor of Weld. I walked three quarters of a mile, clear past his place and on to the old horse ranch, and called a tow truck.

For a while we kept the horses out with barricades, which are not so different from fences that it gave me any pleasure to put them up. By January we had doors, and the house was safe; but in February, when the painters came, there were buckets and jugs to kick over. One painter came to hate the horses so bad he brought an air pistol to the job and lurked (at five or six dollars an hour, on my time) behind corners and partitions, trying to sting one good. I never saw him succeed. Myself, I relied on stones. But neither stones nor air pistols nor barricades kept the horses from bursting into the kitchen patio the night after the concrete was poured. You can see their footprints out there now. That time, I went to the trouble of looking up the impounding laws, and if it hadn't been for Ruth I'd have caged his wandering brutes and made him pay through the nose to get them back.

In April, when we moved in, the horses were spectators. I had piles of rocks handy, and I really let them have it. In their dismay they ran right over my back fence, which was continuous with Weld's. That evening Tom came leading them home, and when he had turned them down the road he started toggling the fence back together.

"That's O.K.," I said. "Don't bother."

He was good-natured enough, but swallowing air. "Well, my horses bust it down."

"It's all right," I said. "I'm planning to take that fence out."

Now for sure he swallowed air. "Then there'd be nothing keeping them in."

"Tom," I said, and I assure you I smiled, "there's nothing keeping them in now."

Victory. Within twenty-four hours we heard his pickup drilling postholes down along the road. I called the landscapers and placed an order. But a victory over old Massasoit is always partial or Pyrrhic. Instead of going on around and keeping road and bridge outside the pasture, he stops the fence at the bridge, and then he rips out alternate planks of the bridge and turns it into that fearful backwoods cattle guard we've got down there now. His horses can still come around the end of the fence and right up our road. I didn't even bother to squawk. He owns the bridge.

So there are still nights like the one when Ruth hears noises and wakes me up grabbing the front of my pajamas. I throw the switch on the burglar lights, and there is a horse looking in the bedroom window. He nods to us. I swear he swallows air. We can hear the others pacing the terrace like pickets. The one looking in the window has to be standing in the newly planted rose garden. I leap from bed, I ease open the door, I tiptoe to my nearest pile of rocks. They're pitiful: I want stones the size of softballs. The horses hear me, and bolt over a pair of Japanese maples that had just cost me fifteen dollars apiece. They thunder on down the road out of reach while I spraddle and curse and hurl my pebbles in the dawn and bruise my feet on harsh adobe clods, a figure of impotence.

We *still* had horses. Well, peace. Peace and rocks and eternal vigilance.

But beatitude too. You don't know yet, probably, how it is when the wind finally quits in May and the late spring comes on. Lyrical is the word. Dawns with choirs of meadow larks, noons celebrated by our mockingbird friends, afternoons that go down in veils of blue to the sweet sad Tennysonian intonings of mourning doves. The fields turn gold, the trees throw purple shadows down the hills, deer begin to jump the fences and go down to water at Weld's pump house. We took all that in, and nearly forgot Weld. Even the horses were beautiful when the girls who owned them came out and rode them in the evenings. They used to canter around the knoll over there like the horses of heroes in the Welsh and Irish ancient books—you know, the steeds that in their prancing threw into the air from each separate hoof a proud divot of turf.

The only excitement we had in several weeks was one night when I rescued a young opossum from Weld's dog, which had treed him in the carport. The possum was a real gentleman. He played dead while I drove the dog off, and still played dead when I reached him out of the rafters with a glove, and never cracked an eye while I looked him over. A possum looks like something left over from the Ordovician, and I was curious to see his marsupial pouch, but this one, being a gentleman, didn't have one. There he lay, though, as if chloroformed, and let me look. Finally I carried him out and put him on the low branch of an oak.

It was a night of white moonlight. The mockingbirds were making an unbelievable racket, piping like bosuns, squawking like jays. The oat grass had turned into cloth of silver, the shadows were velvet. I stood watching and listening for a long time before the possum moved. Then he lifted his snout and crept away along the mottled moonlight of the limb, and I went back inside and reported to Ruth that this backward little creature had restored my faith in the Earthly Paradise. He proved to me it was possible to get along with anybody if you would only make yourself harmless.

So what does she say? She whispers from her disturbed midnight bed and asks me how well the possum's meekness was working with Weld's dog when I intervened. All winter she preaches me sweet reasonableness, which is not my natural move, and then the minute I show signs of conversion she reminds me of the unappeasable aggressor.

3

Somewhere about that point I stopped. I was getting tired of my own prose, and a little uneasy about the figure I cut in my own story. Piling it on, making old cretinous good-natured Weld into something more than the mere irritation he was, sounded uncomfortably like

Joe Allston justifying himself at the expense of the neighbors. So I stopped.

They were both still smiling at me, waiting. "Yes?" Marian said. "That isn't all, is it?"

"Don't miss tomorrow's exciting episode."

"But what happened? Is the dog still around? Have you still got horses in your flower beds? Haven't you ever worked it out and got to be friends again?"

"The dog is in the happy hunting grounds," I said. "He was scavenging a run-over rabbit in the road and a truck got him. The horses went last July when the kid set the pasture afire and burned up all the feed."

"So now there's nothing to fight about and you're all reconciled."

"I wouldn't say that. Look at that eyesore over there, for instance." Ruth caught my eye pleasantly. "And the bridge," I said. "Shall I strike the body just once more?"

"Why not let it go," Ruth said.

"Just once," I said, for I found that I did want to justify myself to these people. I wanted it to be clear I was much put-upon, not merely cantankerous. "Of course Weld isn't home when his boy sets the grass afire," I said. "I went over with a shovel and tried to fight it, but it chased me up the hill with my shirttails smoking, and while I was up in the plowed orchard getting my breath, I saw the fire truck come out the county road and in our lane and stop at the bridge. Wouldn't trust the bridge to hold them. Eventually another truck came through the fences over the hill and put things out. But consequences, see? If the fire had swept the neighborhood, he'd never have comprehended that his refusal to fence his pasture had anything to do with it. He'd have blamed the fire department. He never has the right answer. If they had him up on the charge of fatherhood he'd say, 'Me? I never done one thing but sleep with my wife.'"

"But if *you'd* followed your impulse and offered to pay half the fence, maybe the bridge would be solid and we'd all be as happy as clams," Marian said. "Don't you sort of wish you had?"

"No," I said. "I'd look terrible with my nose that far out of joint."

The beagles break out again, and this time when I stand up to look, I do see the shotgun couple coming. The Catlins are making moves to leave. Quick, speed the parting guest, even though giving her a glimpse of that systematized slaughter would probably persuade her that I have not done Weld an injustice. It will be ten minutes or so before the shooting starts. Smile, rise, adjourn.

At the corner John Catlin slides his arm around his wife, not playfully but with a grave sort of protectiveness pleasant to see. As we walk around the house between the rose garden and the border of iris, I pause by a rosebush and examine its tip leaves. Just as I thought, a fat cluster of aphids. I tip the branch to show Marian. "This is one I'll send to you when it blooms," I say. "You like your roses with holes in them."

"Absolutely natural," she says stoutly.

She would rather be a canker in a hedge than a rose in my grace.

I start on again, but Ruth, proud gardener, leads the way along the bank that slopes up to Shields's pasture, obviously bent upon giving us what in Jane Austen novels is called a stroll in the shrubbery. I have had a curving asphalt path put in up there to keep us out of the mud. Now as the Catlins follow her single file, with me bringing up the rear, I see Marian squirm loose from John's hand and drop to her knees. Instantly he is bending over her. But she has not slipped, she has only seen something in the path. Her upturned face is that of an overacting child. "Oh, get a pick or something! Here's something I have to show Mr. Allston. I saw one just like it the other day."

At her feet the asphalt has been humped into three round hillocks almost as big as grapefruit. The dome of the biggest has cracked partly open. Gophers? Moles? I hope their fingers are sore from trying to tunnel through those four or five inches of steam-rollered asphalt. And I would rather ignore them now, and get the Catlins started home before the shooting. But I have no choice. I go down to the garage and get the pick, and Catlin takes it from me and digs out the biggest hump. You know what is down there, just about ready to force itself through all that macadam? A mushroom. A dinky mushroom the size of my thumb and as soft as cheese.

Marian's eyes absolutely blaze. To meet them is to have a shock of contact as if they were electrically charged. Her voice escapes her and goes fluty and shrill. She cries, "Now, you see? You wondered what was in whale's milk. Don't you know now? The same thing that's in a mushroom spore so small you need a microscope to see it, or in gophers, or poison oak, or anything else we try to pave under, or grub out, or poison. There isn't good life and bad life, there's only life. Think of the *force* down there, just telling things to get born!"

I have a moment's fear that she may break into tears. My mind tells me, *softly, softly,* while Ruth throws me an unnecessary tuck of the eyebrows and Catlin watches his wife with a concentrated alertness before he hides his mouth behind the lighting of a cigarette. But since I have been addressed in my capacity of Exterminator, I have to say something. Being a phunny phellow, I blink and sing:

> Oh de farmer took de mushroom
> And paved him underground.
> De mushroom say, "I'll be back up,
> Stick around, boy, stick around,
> Gonna be my home,
> Gonna be my home."

"Aha," Marian says. "I think you're licked."

"I'm licked." Privately, I am also relieved that the hysterical edge has faded from her face and voice. She is obviously tuned up ready to snap. It is astonishing, considering that she is both thin and pale, how she manages to give all the time the impression of vivid life.

Vividness is the last impression I have of her, for as they reach the bend of the drive they are silhouetted for a second or two against the greening apricot orchard beyond the fence. The afternoon light is full on them. The healthy responsible attentive New England face lifts, smiling; the thin one flashes like a turned mirror; then they are out of sight below the turn. A sort of thunderous silence remains behind them, cracked at its far edge by the clamor of the dogs on Weld's hill.

I turn and find my sardonic wife regarding me with an odd peering expression which changes at once into her skeptical-ironical one. I suppose I am responsible for Ruth's attitudes. She complains that her mind is shaped like a *jai alai cesta* from catching me and hurling me back when I come bursting out at her. Now, because I have been moved by that skinless young woman, I say rather crossly, "What's the matter, have I got a hole in my pants, or something?"

"Your doglike devotion was showing."

"Let it show. I like them. I think he's interesting and I think she's charming."

"She's enchanting," Ruth said. "*And* a little foolish. And sad."

"Sad, why?"

"She obviously isn't well."

"Then what's the joke?"

"You are, ducky," Ruth says with her abstracted, bothered air. "You tickle me." But it is clear I don't. She hooks her arm in mine and walks me toward the house, and after a few steps she squeezes me around the waist and says, "You should have had six beautiful daughters."

Since this comes close to what I have been thinking myself, I let it pass. I only say, "I suppose you're going to eat me out for bending her ear about Weld and arguing with her about the sacredness of life."

Ruth looks up from examining the buds on the dwarf orange tree against the garage wall. "You couldn't have known."

"Known what?"

"I don't suppose you noticed she's pregnant."

"No," I say. "*If* she is. How do you know?"

"How does anybody know anything? She told me."

"Well," I say, "don't act as if you got it by female

intuition, then. It isn't something she'd likely confide to me. How far along?"

"Just barely. A couple of months, maybe."

"Well, fine," I say. "Distributing her seeds. It couldn't happen to anyone who'd appreciate it more. But I can't say it seems to agree with her. I thought pregnant girls were supposed to go around blinking and placid and dreaming warm dreams and smelling of milk."

For a second Ruth looks as if she were going to be annoyed. She stands holding her hair away from her temple with the back of her hand. The meadow lark over in the pasture sets himself for some late-afternoon song with a whistle or two, clearing his pipes. "Ah," Ruth says, "that's where it could be sad. She's had an operation. Didn't you notice how she moved her left arm as if it were stiff, or even a little crippled? They took the breast on that side and all up into her armpit, all the little lymph nodes."

The shadow of the house has reached across the lily pool and halfway up the garage wall. Ruth's face is in the shade. I think of that girl, who is like a patch of sun-and-shadow woods, and of the obscene tendrils that have crawled through her, and of the withering that has already gone on. "But good God," I say, "she's so young."

"Yes."

"Has it recurred? Is that why she looks peaked?"

"No, I don't think so. She'd have told me, I think. She's very open about it."

The meadow lark has a different pattern from either the mockingbird or Browning's thrush. He sings neither doublets nor improvisations, but like a child going through a series of set pieces he sings one tune eight or ten times, switches to another for a while, switches to a third. I am aware of his mechanical rhapsodies almost with irritation, and of the continued uproar of the beagles from the other side of the house. Then the air whistles with wings, and a pigeon flashes over us, silvery in the sun, and circles and comes back. I see the purplish breast feathers, I hear the wing tips beating together. A second afterward, I hear the boom of the shotgun and the redoubled cracking clamor of the dogs.

Ruth and I stand looking at one another. A silent understanding passes between us. After sixty you are aware how vulnerable everything is, including yourself, but even after sixty you may need an occasional reminder. And though I am glad the Catlins got out before she had to go through the distress of the pigeon shooting, I am remorseful at the discomfort my big mouth must have caused her.

"Christ, I've got a gift," I say. "Why didn't you shut me up?"

"Shut *you* up?" Ruth says. "How?"

But her tartness is only habit. Going inside—for I find that I want to go in, I don't want to stay out and hear the boom of those shotguns or the excitement of the dogs as they quarter through the grass hunting the fallen birds—Ruth takes my arm again. Recalling that gesture, I understand it with every nerve in my body. I know what she meant to say to me.

We were once more exposed, and we were even more dependent on each other than we were when all our acquaintance was new, casual, and undemanding. Paradise, so late our happy seat, was lost, and lost not through any of the people I felt like casting in the snake's role, but through one to whom our hearts instantly went out. It is hard doctrine, but I was beginning to comprehend it then, and I have not repudiated it now: that love, not sin, costs us Eden. Love is a carrier of death—the only thing, in fact, that makes death significant. Otherwise it is what Marian pretended to think it was, a simple interchange of protein.

III

I BEGAN THIS rumination in the mood of an old-fashioned Christian who opens the Bible at random, hungry for a text. Because I could not reconcile myself to the way life cheated one who so loved being alive, I wanted to talk to her and about her, quietly. I see that I have been talking at least as much about Joseph Allston and how life has cheated him, who only wanted to retire and tend his garden.

Mischance is a collaboration, I have told myself; evil is everywhere and in all of us. Yet I am steadily tempted to poke around the garden looking for the snake. Sooner or later I shall find myself going (coming?) down my hole after myself. I do not forget the ambiguous serpent I dug out of the ground last summer, though I cannot make him fit any easy pattern of moral meaning.

None of us, surely, is harmless, whatever our private fantasies urge us to believe. Whatever any of us may have wanted in retiring to these hills, we have not escaped one another. The single-minded rancher anxious to capitalize on his remaining land, the Italian native son with the invalid wife and the sullen daughter and the narcotic adobe bricks, the threatened young woman desperate for continuity, the kook who lived in the birdhouse and this kook who lives at the top of the hill—whatever we wanted, we stumbled into community, with its consequences. And at the heart of our community was the Catlin cottage.

It sat on a shelf between our lane and the creek, a little higher than the rest of the bottomland. Its board-and-batten sides and its shake roof were weathered silvery as an old rock. To me it had an underwater look—that barnacled silveriness, the way three big live oaks twisted like seaweed above the roof, the still, stained, sunken light. It wasn't air you looked at in that pocket. It was an infusion of green and brown plants, it seemed always to have a faint murkiness of sediment sinking through it. The small hollylike oak leaves lay thinly on the ground, as unstirred as settlings on a sea bottom, and all through the spring and summer oak moths flickered and wavered among the trees. You half expected mermaids to scatter in clouds of bubbles from the picnic grove that Thomas had cleared down along the creek.

The moment we met Marian Catlin, we knew that this was her sort of place. Until we met her, we had thought it shabby. For six months or so, while the Thomases lived there, we had driven past with no more than a nod or a wave, and had never been inside the house or sat in the grove. Once the Catlins moved in, we were in and out of the house almost daily, and the grove became a place as familiar as our own terrace.

I find it hard to reconstruct how that intimacy happened. One day we had never heard of them, days later we were close friends. All our lives Ruth and I have tended to protect ourselves from people and cherish our privacy, and we have been more likely to reject individuals peremptorily—the way I suppose I rejected Peck—than to like them on sight. But we caught

Marian's affectionateness as if it had been a communicable disease: she was the Typhoid Mary of love. We have never had the kissing habit, knowing how little it usually means, but the Catlins we kissed on greeting and parting as if they had been our children. Which, by a sort of spontaneous mutual adoption, they were. For Debby, at Marian's request and by the terms of her will, we are now legally responsible in case anything happens to John.

We are a frail enough last resort, but our willingness gave Marian comfort, for she was anxious about the child and afraid of her aloneness in the world. John had no relatives closer than a brother whose State Department assignments kept him always in some Arab state or other. Marian's parents had been killed in an automobile accident when she was five, and she had been brought up by a grandmother with a pin in her hip, who took as much care as she could give, but who did give her an intense and sentimental love. Marian wanted at least that much for Debby. More, actually, much more. That was why she passionately and mystically bent herself to produce flower and fruit and create her a brother or sister. If she had a religion, it was biological.

The day after the Catlins' first visit, we passed down by the mailboxes a girl who had to be Debby—six or so, her hair pulled back in a pony tail from her thin wedge of a face, her eyes lost behind owlish little-girl glasses. Our waves got only a turning stare. Looking back as we crossed the bridge, I saw her moping along the lane touching mustard flowers with her fingers. "Moving is hard on children," Ruth said.

Next day, when we had to do our Saturday marketing, Ruth cut a bunch of rosebuds and some sprigs of daphne and put them in the car. As we drew opposite the Catlins' parking area we saw Marian pushing her daughter in a swing hung from a high oak limb in the grove. Their voices came up in chirps and cries, a sort of stinging musical spray from that brown pool. Marian saw us, gave the child a last running push, and came up the bank. I had not been mistaken about the vividness of her face; she brought light with her out of the shadow of the oaks.

Panting, she took the hand I held out, gave it a quick hard squeeze, and still holding it, stooped to smile through the car at Ruth, who was leaning to pass the roses across me.

"The worms we promised you," I said.

"Do I dare sniff them, or will I be inhaling DDT?" But she buried her face in the buds, and lifted it only to bury it again, though that variety, Fred Edmonds, does not have much odor. "I love them," she said, to make sure we didn't misunderstand her joke. "They're beautiful."

She was laughing at me through the bouquet—and what a blue her eyes were: cornflower, delphinium. The tilted updrawn look in the outer corners that women try to get with make-up was in her somehow wistful and young and vulnerable, since she wore no make-up at all and was in spite of the exercise so pale.

If I am really remembering, and not inserting feelings I had later, every movement she made troubled me with its intimation of the mutilation she had suffered. I could not help wondering if it was her scarred side she held the roses to. The left, was it? I could see no difference, but she had to pad herself, obviously. And would that seem offensive to her, that falseness? How did she feel when she looked at her ruined body, or when her husband looked at it? Mystically addicted to the distribution of seeds, did she feel herself crippled for love? She couldn't have, for what had she done as soon as she recovered from the operation but get herself pregnant? For just an instant I wondered if a husband in John Catlin's position might feel *used,* and then I thought of his good-humored, firm, guarded face, his eyes that followed her around, and I knew he didn't.

She chattered in the fluty, hyperthyroid voice, a thin girl in a faded denim skirt that showed no slightest sign of podding under its wide pocket. The orange-red roses lay in her bent arm. Behind her the weathered cottage stared, still curtainless, into unspaded beds of weeds. Ruth was offering slips, geranium or ice plant or something that took practically no care, but no, Marian insisted, they really weren't going to plant anything. Maybe she was a nut, but she believed that plants whose genes were adapted to an environment ought to be let grow in it, instead of being uprooted in favor of exotics that would die as soon as the gardener turned off the hose. Besides, why should she break her back gardening when the neighbors brought her such lovely flowers? In exchange, we must come and sit in their nice dusty grove, and get oak moths in our hair.

From that grove her daughter was calling. "Mummy! Come push me, I'm dying."

"I'm talking now, hon. Pump. See how high you can go."

"I can't, I go all crooked."

"Sit square in the middle."
"I *am*!"
Marian frowned, made an explaining face, seemed about to excuse herself and leave us. Across me Ruth passed the sprigs of daphne that filled the car with their scent. "Ask her if she'd like something for her buttonhole."
Sniffing—ummm!—Marian called, "Debby, the Allstons have brought you something nice."
The white nylon ropes jerked, twisted, and hung shaking. The girl came up the bank, flinching and frowning when she brushed against a thistle. She took the handful of perfume as if she had expected something a good deal more gorgeous, maybe a pony. "Smell," her mother said. Debby held the daphne against her nose and stared at us owlishly. Her mother hugged her shoulders. "Debby, this is Mr. and Mrs. Allston, who live up on the hill in a beautiful house and have a Siamese cat named Catarrh."
"What's catarrh?"
"Sinus trouble," I said. "We only call him Catarrh inside the family. His registered name is Otorhinolaryngitis."
She was not amused. Exit clown, to scornful laughter.
"Say how do you do, and thanks for the lovely daphne," Marian said.
"How do you do. Thanks for the daphne."
"I hope you'll come and see us often," Ruth said. "How do you like your new house?"
"All right."
"She hasn't had a chance to find playmates yet," Marian said. "John's at the lab all day, and she gets tired of just me. And she's had to change schools. We've

got to get busy organizing some of her friends to come out and play, or find some new ones."

"But you've got a beautiful swing," Ruth said.

"Ya," Debby said, "but she'll never *push* me."

"Hon, I can't push you all the time. If you'd learn to pump you could swing all day." To us, with a deprecatory down-drawn mouth, she said, "She's been simply *berserk* about that swing since John put it up last night." Again she hugged Debby to her hip. "We're a little lost, that's our trouble. But we'll soon get acquainted and like the country better than anywhere. Won't we? We're already making friends with the animals. We saw one of our foxes again, and a raccoon got in our garbage can, and three deer came by. You don't see those in town."

Held against her mother's leg, Debby seemed to resist the pressure without wanting to break away. "You forgot the man that lives in the tree."

Marian broke into laughter. "*Yes*, why didn't you tell us about our arboreal neighbor?"

"He never crossed my mind," I said. "As a matter of fact, I don't want him crossing my mind."

"Why not? He seems like a real original."

"Original?" I said. "You can grind out originals like that on a mimeograph machine."

"Oh, come on, how many people do you know who live in trees?"

"How many beards do you see running around on motorcycles?"

"But that's unfair. Should I call you a stereotype because you drive a car like a hundred and fifty million other Americans? As far as that goes, it's a shaven face that's unnatural. I think beards on men are handsome, sometimes."

"You've persuaded me," I said. "Starting right now, I'm growing a beard."

"Not in my house," Ruth said. "I have trouble enough with Catarrh shedding all over everything."

"Don't talk to me, it's her responsibility. She likes these dustmops, and what she likes, that's what I try to be."

"You're so amenable," Marian said. "Isn't he amenable? But I like your face all bare. I just think you shouldn't judge a person by how much hair he's got."

"Have you met this kid? Do you find him charming?"

"Well, charming, that's a word. He's pretty far out. But maybe that's because he cares about things."

"Cares about what? If he cared about things, he'd be down in Mississippi or carrying a sign in some protest march, not perched in a tree with his drawbridge up."

"I take it back," Marian said. "You aren't amenable at all, you're full of gross prejudice. If you don't like him, why do you let him live down here?"

"Softheadedness. Amenability."

"I'll bet. No, he really isn't so bad. Coming home the other night he rode his motorcycle by the window pretty loud, and Debby woke up scared, so we went out and talked to him while he was putting it away."

"I hope you did. If he disturbs you with that hoodlum machine, he's through roosting in that tree right now."

"Oh tush," Marian said. "He was perfectly good about it, he just hadn't thought. This morning he pushed the motorcycle past and started it down by the bridge. But he *is* about as odd as Dick's hatband, with the whiskers and that flying suit. John says he's got a bad case of disestablishmentarianism."

"I noticed," I said. "He's all broken out with it."

"And he eats only nuts and fruits and vegetables."

"He seems to tell everybody that."

"Did he tell you why?"

"No."

"His father's some bigwig in the meat-packing business in Chicago, and that's why he won't eat any meat."

"That's a great reason," I said. "Doesn't his father wear pants, too? How come Tarzan doesn't wear a sarong, or a toga?"

"You can't say those coveralls are exactly orthodox."

"Nor very sanitary," I said.

"Ah," she said, smiling and screwing up her eyes, "you like to sound like old Scrooge, but I notice he's still living in your tree. And that's going to disrupt this household, you know that? This one here has been after me all day, when she hasn't been screaming to be pushed in the swing, to go see his treehouse. And he obviously doesn't *want* people looking at his treehouse."

"But I could ask him," Debby said. "Why can't I ask him?"

"Because he's fussy about his privacy," her mother said. "Everybody's got his peculiarities. He likes privacy, Mr. Allston is grossly prejudiced, you've got bug eyes, I'm a skinny hysteric. But we've all got a right to be what we are. Haven't we?"

"I don't know."

"I do. So that's why he keeps his bridge pulled up and doesn't want us snooping around his place."

"Well I'm *going* to!"

"I hope not, baby," Marian said. "You'd embarrass us awfully if you did."

Ruth, leaning, said, "I'm afraid we have to go or we'll get caught in the rush-hour traffic. But please stop by when you're out walking. And bring Debby up to meet Catarrh."

I started the engine, mother and daughter stepped back, we were a rotating lighthouse of smiles. "You too," Marian was saying, one arm full of roses, one around Debby. "Soon as we get settled we want to . . . John gets a week between quarters, right away soon. Debby, wait, please! Sometimes I wish Daddy hadn't put that thing up. Talk about peculiarities, you're a swinger, nothing but. Say goodbye to the Allstons, baby. Goodbye, and thanks for the flowers. And the worms! The worms *especially*. . . ."

In the rearview mirror I saw Debby dragging her mother down toward the swing. "The kid's a tyrant," I said. "What she needs is the sound of a good firm no."

"I suppose Marian's trying to compensate for the upset of moving."

"And the gorilla man," I said. "Wouldn't you know they'd be all buddy-buddy within twenty-four hours?"

"Oh, buddy-buddy! They talked a few minutes."

"Sure, but I thought he despised square company. He could have grunted and climbed farther out on his limb."

"Joe," she said, "you're fantastic. You're jealous."

"Look who's calling *me* fantastic," I said. But of course she was right. I resented Marian's slightest acquaintance with Caliban.

When we came back around three-thirty, John was in

the yard with a golf-club-shaped sickle cutting down thistles. I stopped. "What?" I said. "Improving nature?"

"Thistles only," he said. "They prickle Debby's legs. I guess if we went around barelegged we'd have had them down before this. How about a beer?"

I looked at Ruth, with the thought she probably had herself: we shouldn't fall all over people, we shouldn't get *too* thick. But obviously we both wanted to. "Have we got any frozen stuff that will melt?" I asked.

"There are some frozen vegetables, yes."

"You hop out," I said. "I'll run up and put them in the freezer and come back."

I hurried, too, like a boy bound for a party. When I got back, I swung in against the trail gate to park, and there was Jim Peck's motorcycle with the white helmet hanging from the handlebar. As soon as I crossed the parking area and could look down into the grove, I saw him there among them in his orange suit, a satyr come to the picnic.

2

I see that grove as an eighteenth-century landscape, leafy at the top, meadowy at the edges, bronzy at the center where the figures cluster. The sun is low along the hill, and afternoon stretches into the grove in bars and rays to pick out Marian's faded blue, Ruth's red, John's khaki, the hot gold of beer cans on the weathered picnic table. The nylon rope, Maxfield Parrish touch not quite congruous with the rest, becomes a silver cord when Debby's swinging brings it into the sun.

John is pushing with one hand, holding a beer can with the other, turning his head to say smiling things to Ruth and Marian, who are stretched out in canvas chairs. Transparent flames lick up in the barbecue pit, for it is still spring, and not overly warm. The wood smoke that except for the disturbance of Debby's swinging would go straight up into the leaves is scattered and blown, to wreathe around among gray limbs and drift up to me scented with the nostalgia of a hundred pleasant outings.

Most orderly and neoclassic that pastoral grove, those noble trees, those gracefully disposed figures; most romantic the touch of gaiety and aspiration as the child soars upward in the swing. But also, inescapably part of the picture, the shape of Disorder stands a little apart, in shadow, gleaming darkly, the orange suit like a gross flower against the brown spring-fallen leaves.

Jim Peck is not one of those apostles of modernity who go stony-faced as if wearing a sign: ALIENATED. KEEP OFF. His wild hair, wild beard, wild eyes, are the components of a true satiric leer. Through his unvarying grin he peers out at the world of civilization and sense like a wild man through a screen of vines. He ought to be ridiculous or pathetic; I am sure his own version of himself contains a good portion of the saintly; and yet the picture that hangs in my mind, remembered or composite or imaginary, places him and half hides him in a way to corroborate my first impression that he is dangerous. He *is* dangerous, too, and all the more so because, as I now recognize, he has no more malice than he has sense, and has besides a considerable dedication to beliefs that he unquestionably considers virtuous. Dangerousness is not necessarily a function of malicious intent. If I were painting a portrait of the father of evil, I wonder if I wouldn't give him the face of a high-minded fool.

Dangerous or not, he is one of us. He has responded to the friendly kindness of the Catlins precisely as the Joseph Allstons have. I wouldn't allow the unwashed fantast in my house, but, I have to remind myself, it isn't my house he is being admitted to. And he doesn't bother me so much that I am going to give up the Catlins' company because of him. If he can stand me, I can stand him. I walk on down and join them in the fragrant shade.

I thought Peck looked uneasy in that pleasant grove, among those pleasant older people, and my entrance so obviously added to his social watchfulness that I had to remind myself, lest I begin to feel sorry for him, that in his pretentious withdrawal he was arrogant, and as much a dog in the manger as I had sometimes thought myself for resenting him. Moreover, among his own crowd, when he broke training and came out for a frolic, he was a long way from diffident. He could pick the guitar, sing, drink beer, bang the bongos or the girls, and play the bacchant with the best. I thought I had better keep in mind the occasional girls who rode in and out with him, glued as tight as beetle wings to his back while he leaned too fast into the curves of the lane or bounced across the treads of Weld's booby-trap bridge; and the vision in the black leotard who had emerged into the morning to demonstrate that one, at least, took Peck seriously enough to sleep with him. There was no need for me to feel any idiotic protectiveness. I was not the hostess here. If he was old enough to be playing saint and screwing girls he was old enough to take his chance in civilized company.

Not that they shut him out. On the contrary. Having hailed him out of friendliness, they made him welcome. A potentially squeaky hinge, he got early grease from both Marian and Ruth; so that, though I might have preferred to be part of the conversation that included Marian, I found myself talking to John about the coming town elections and the threat of a gravel quarry in the hills, while we pushed Debby back and forth between us in the swing. My ear, however, was cocked aside, as Debby's eyes were: her eyeballs followed Peck the way a portrait's eyes pursue a tourist around a gallery. It irritated me that I could not ignore him. Why, simply by being there, grotesque in hair and coveralls, did he focus our attention? And to hear what? This:

. . . healthy on his vegetarian diet? (Oh yes.)

What did he eat, exactly? (Oh, rice, whole-wheat bread, peanut butter, vegetables, fruit, nuts, like that.)

Did he have to avoid getting too much carbohydrates? Did he gain weight, or lose? (Never paid any attention. Never gained weight, no. Seemed to stay about the same.)

What was he dieting *for*, health, religion, or what? (Some of both. Also to protest the hypocrisies of meat eating. Every meat eater who thought meat came wrapped in neat cellophane packages should take a tour of the stockyards, he'd never eat it again.)

He seemed sort of—wasn't he?—sort of *Hindu*. Was it all kinds of meat he was opposed to, or just the killing of cattle? (All kinds.)

Well, was it the eating of flesh he opposed, or was it

the cruelty of the slaughterhouses? Meat eating was *natural*—guess who is talking—everything belonged to some food chain. Wasn't it simply the horror of the way animals were killed? (It was meat eating itself he was against. All the largest and strongest animals were vegetarian. He himself wanted to be absolutely *harmless*. He believed in ahiṁsa, nonviolence, harmlessness. Besides, the eating of meat had a bad effect on the clarity of his mind. He wanted to keep his mind crystal-clear. He was trying to think his way below all the surfaces, past all the boundaries. The world was shut in. It was the duty of thinkers and intellectuals to help free it. He was writing a book, keeping very full notes on himself as he projected his consciousness farther and farther into unknown or half-known states. If people only knew how, they could get rid of their hangups and their hostilities and come out on the other side into states of pure mind they never even suspected. The longer he stayed on his strict diet, the longer he worked on his exercises and his sessions of contemplation, the clearer he got, the less he was hung up, the less the world meant, the farther out he pushed the horizons of perception. He had hundreds of pages already, he worked sometimes all night, it came freer and freer, like automatic writing. The things he was discovering were so exciting he didn't sleep more than an hour or two. And that was something else you could control. You . . .)

His voice was soft, musical, with a throb of conviction and passion in it. He squatted, breaking twigs in his long thin fingers in a way that was a little too nervous for the theosophical doctrine he expounded. His eyes, too, retained their wild satiric gleam; he held the two women with his eyes like a pair of wedding guests.

Really? they said, intrigued. Did he do yoga too, was that associated with the diet as part of the way of consciousness? (Oh yes.) And what about organically grown vegetables, use of natural manure, avoidance of chemical sprays, all that? (He smiled; he indulged their worldly questions; he hadn't had time for any of that—all his effort went into keeping his mind and body transparent so that light could come through.)

Well, there was a health store in town, did he know? where they sold soybean steaks and blackstrap molasses, all the things with natural vitamins, rose hips, all that, an astonishing variety. (He didn't know. He didn't have much patience with all that hypocrisy that tried to make honest soybeans taste like sirloin. Simplicity, that was . . .)

But he was off the line. They had given him his turn, and were off on their own food fads, which were neither simple nor harmless. Left to listen to recipes for tiger's milk and other such messes, he crushed his beer can carefully into a four-sided shape and dropped it at his side. John left the swing and opened him another. Debby, coursing up and back in long arcs, yelled to be stopped, dropped her soft-drink can to the ground, dragged her feet, and scrambled out and went to the table to punch holes in a second. "Oh, Debby," Marian said, "not right before dinner."

Debby ignored her, prying. Soda fizzed and splashed her. "Here," Marian said, "let me, then." She punched two holes and passed the can to Debby, who took it back to the swing. Backing her behind into the board, her eyes already back on Jim Peck, she hooked her wrist around the rope and took a sip from the can in that hand. John pushed her and she went up and back, staring at Peck all the time. He winked a half-crazy eye and irradiated her with his satyr's grin, and when she came forward again there he was, waiting to push.

So promptly he found his own level. It was almost touching to see him gravitate to the one person there who obviously found him fascinating. I opened another beer for myself and sat down on the ground between Marian and Ruth.

In the brown grove where the oak moths flickered and the air sifted down its pollen and smoke scarved flat among the oaks, Debby went up and back in long white arcs between her crewcut amiable father and the bearded kook. I watched him, wondering if communication could ever be really established with him, supposing one wanted to make the effort. Could one do with a not-very-likable stranger what one had been totally unable to do with one's son? I was almost tempted to try.

But I thought of all the gibberish I would have to listen to, all the dyspeptic mixture of unmixables that it would be my duty to try to digest. There would be all the self-realization business, which was itself a mongrel cross between Socrates on the examined life and the Buddha on contemplation. There would be all those far-out states that Peck thought he could reach by diet, by yoga, by fasting, by drugs, and that would begin in Huxley's *Doors of Perception* and end in Leary's LSD cult. There would be a lot of Zen passivism scrambled with a sanyasi withdrawal, and mixed with both a portion of existential disgust. Though there didn't seem to be much civil-rights militancy in Peck,

I was sure he would have a full share of inert sympathy with civil-rights principles and a full share of contempt for the people who, trying harder than he to solve something, were not succeeding. There would likewise be at least a noise of sympathy with all the other activists, the sitters-in, the teachers-in, and the singers-in against authority of whatever kind and whatever degree of repressiveness or responsibility.

Could I stand to see humane feelings and noble ideals come half-baked from that oven? I doubted it. Also this boy would want pot made legal, which wouldn't trouble me, and he would angrily—or softly, since that was his style—demand the lifting of the ban on LSD and the other psychedelics, and he would have incontrovertible evidence that they were harmless. He would have a smiling sneer for people who took aspirin and denounced drugs, and for incipient alcoholics who objected to other ways of getting high. In the middle of all this there would be considerable heat about sexual conventions and hypocrisy, and a mystic faith in the perfect orgasm as one more way of reaching the desirable state of mindlessness. There would be a belief in the honesty of four-letter words, and a conviction that it was the duty of any disciple of freedom to use them at all times.

And so on, and on. Just thinking about it made my joints ache and my stomach rumble. One at a time, in some coherent order and relationship, with discrimination and with some sense of the possible, I might take and approve most of the ingredients that went into the great underdone pizza of a Jim Peck's faith, but I didn't believe I could take them in combination, the mustard on the blueberry pie, the asparagus topped with chocolate ice cream. We were ultimately and temperamentally strangers to one another. For some reason, the considered conviction made me irritable, for I half suspected that the irresponsibility of his search for freedom forced me to be more conservative than I wanted to be.

With the sun down among the trees that fringed the hill, it was growing cool in the grove. I could feel the chill puddling around my ankles, and beer was a drink I no longer craved. I hunched closer to the barbecue pit's warm bricks. Forward leaned John, up went Debby; forward leaned Peck, back came Debby. Down into the leaves came Debby's second soft drink can. John stooped between shoves to retrieve it and toss it into the barrel by the barbecue, and in his turn Jim Peck—reminded? showing off?—picked up *his* two cans and barreled them. Marian, glancing from her canvas chair, smiled at him brilliantly. The taming of Caliban. See the rude jungle beast behave like a well-brought-up middle-class boy. See the motorcycle-riding sanyasi, the hot-rod Spirit of Contemplation in his helicopter suit, suffering the little children to come unto him.

From the swing, staring Debby said suddenly—and I don't think she had said one word before that—"Do you sleep in your treehouse?"

"Of course," Peck said, and gave her outstretched feet a shove. She arched down and then up, and got a shove on the back from John.

"Do *things* come in?" she said, soaring back.

"Things?"

Up again, back again. "Animals and things?"

A push on the shoe soles. "Birds."

Up, back. "Could I see?"

"See what? The birds?"

Already caving away, drawn backward like yearning Eurydice, she screamed it out. "The treehouse!"

"Debby!" Marian said.

Forward she came, clenched to the ropes, dress blown into lap, shanks bare, glasses focused on the hairy grin of Caliban, who said, "You want to see my treehouse?"

"Yee-e-e-ess!"—in retreat, centrifugally backward soaring to the point of arrest, then arrowing at him, sneakers first. "Yes!"

"O.K.," Peck said softly. "O.K., sure."

"Maybe we could all see it," Ruth said a little plaintively from her chair—romantic Ruthie, secretly Jane in a Tarzan movie, ready to line a tree nest with sweet grasses and ferns. She only pretends to be sixty-five. Actually she is fifteen.

For a second Peck hesitated. I thought it somehow significant of our relations that he glanced at me, and that his eyes had that Arab-pickpocket speculation in them, as if they weighed chances. Maybe he looked my way because I was Ownership and Authority, and he wanted neither in his pad. Or maybe I only wanted him to acknowledge those aspects of me. Accepting me, who obviously made him nervous and aroused his antagonism in spite of his philosophical pretensions, he might come to accept the universe and quit trying to pretend it was something it wasn't. Anyway, he wiped his beard with the palm of his hand and said softly, fixedly smiling, "I don't know if you could get across."

"I'm a pretty good scrambler," Ruth said.

"Are you sure it's all right?" Marian said. "I told Debby under no circumstances . . ."

"No, it's O.K. Only I don't think any of you except Mr. Catlin could swing over, and the bridge is pretty wobbly."

"Oh, let's try it," Marian said. "If it wasn't hard to get to it wouldn't be Shangri-La."

Debby was all over Peck's heels as far as the trail gate. There, when he pushed the Honda off its kick-stand, he looked sideward at her. "Want a ride down?"

"Yes!"

He swung her onto the back of the long seat and stepped astride. "Debby!" Marian cried from behind them. "Oh good Lord!" Peck waved a hand—Don't panic, Ma—stepped on the starter, blasted the air with a couple of bursts, and roared down the path to the bay tree. There went Debby, wallpapered to his garish back, her pony tail bouncing, her little heart undoubtedly going pittypat. Give her another ten years and she'd be sneaking up his tree in a leotard.

We followed through the grass and then stood in the bay-smelling damp shadow above the sound of the creek, still flowing secretly from the rains. Since the last time I had been down, Peck's half-assed ingenuity had run wild. The bay and the oak opposite were a spider web of ropes and cables. The far end of the bridge was hauled up in the oak on pulleys and anchored there. In front of the treehouse, like a carrot before a rabbit's nose, dangled the ladder, also hauled up on a pulley. A security check would have found every avenue of ingress hauled up in the air, and the cables padlocked to ringbolts in bridge posts and trees. Another sort of check around the tent platform would have turned up every bottle, can, pliofilm bag, bread wrapper, and raisin box that Peck had discarded in six months.

"Do you remember our saying anything about burying his garbage?" I said out of the corner of my mouth to Ruth.

"Oh, come on," she said. "Don't be an old crab."

All right, I would not act the critical owner, I would be part of the curious throng. We watched Jim Peck with a businesslike air (he was proud, I saw with surprise) unlock a padlock that released a length of clothesline that in turn let down his knot-ended swing rope from the bay tree. "You wait over here," he said. With a run and a spring, he whooshed across the creek and hooked the swing rope to one side in a cleft stake.

Cheers. "Now me!" Debby said, jumping up and down. "It's my turn! Now me!"

"Wait," her mother said. "He'll tell us when." She and John were both laughing, shaking their heads in admiration, looking at me to corroborate their delighted sense of how wackily ingenious the whole place was.

"It's like getting into hell," I said. "All he needs is a Cerberus."

"You ought to apply," Ruth said, and she was looking at me with real irritation. "*Nobody* would look better with three heads." I suppose my feelings about Peck had been showing. Well, *pazienza.*

Across the creek Peck was unlocking a padlock that fastened a loop-ended cable to a ringbolt in the oak. Down dropped the treehouse ladder. More cheers.

Another padlock, this time on the bridge post, and now the bridge itself shuddered and started down. If he had had the wit to run the cable through a block, he could have handled it easily; as it was, the weight through the single pulley almost lifted him into the air, and the sag of the bridge pulled out of line the looped cables that were supposed to slip over the posts.

"Need some help?" John said. "Send over the swing rope and I'll come and give you a hand."

"No," said sweating Caliban. "I can manage." Eventually, with the cable belayed around his hip, he held the tottering thing still enough so that he could dart out one hand and force the loop over a post. With that secure, he strained and reached and got the other one hooked enough to hold, and then let go his pulley cable and pried it into place. At last the upper cables, the handrails. Still more cheers. Debby set her foot on the treads, but they shrank away sideward and downward, and she hung on, afraid. "Here, kiddo," John said, and with his hands over hers on the upper cables, his feet shuffling behind hers, most cautiously he edged her across. The worst part was after they passed the middle, and had to go uphill. As he jumped down beside Peck, John said, "I can see why you use the rope."

"It's O.K. when you get used to it," Peck said. "Some girls in high heels came across it the other night."

"Well," I said to Marian and Ruth, "if other girls can make it, you can."

While Marian was creeping and squeaking across, Ruth gave me the benefit of her eyebrows. But when her turn came, she got on the thing gamely, and with John helping her from the other side, made it in triumph. "Coming?" she said.

"I guess not." I said. "I'm not well enough insured to be crawling around on a thing like that at my age."

"Oh, come on, it's easy."

"No," I said, "I'm not that curious."

Peck, from the bridgehead, looked at me straight; we had these moments, not too infrequently, when we understood one another perfectly. After a second he smiled. The hell with you, I told him silently, and watched the three Catlins and Ruth, one after the other, climb up the ladder and into the treehouse. The tree nodded a little, the leaves shook. From inside came squeals and exclamations. A light went on, went off.

"Electricity?" I said.

Peck turned the gleam of his eyes and teeth straight down the bridge at me. His head hunched down a little between his shoulders. In his soft voice, his smile widening, he said, "I fixed up a flashlight rig for reading at night."

Marian's vivid face appeared in the treehouse door. "Hey, it's *gorgeous*!" she cried. "It's a real bug's nest. And it seems so high. You can see way up the ravine. It's like a *poem* up here!" To Peck she said, "No wonder you pull up the bridge and padlock everything. If you didn't, you'd have the whole world moving in with you." Her smile fell like sunshine on the hairy oaf as he leaned on his bridge post looking up at her, and probably up her dress.

"If the world was the way it ought to be, I wouldn't mind," Peck said. "It's only because of the way people are that I put the locks on. I don't like them, that's for sure."

I guess he thought that was original, or profound, and showed his purity of motive in an impure world. It seemed to me the justification of every lock ever built, but I kept my peace. He was an original, fascinating. He had built this marvelous mousetrap and all the mice were beating a path to his door. And one mouse that none of us had counted on. For while the Catlins and Ruth were still clustered on the treehouse porch, surveying the appointments and the view and speaking of the advantages of living in trees, there was a splashing, clumping, scrambling noise, the harsh barking of a dog, and there was Julie LoPresti on her black gelding, the horse flattened, ready to bolt, on the bank above the trail crossing. Beside her the ridiculous product of miscegenation between her mother's cocker and Weld's Labrador contracted its body in hysterical barking. It was a dog with a fat body and long legs, spaniel ears and a Labrador muzzle, spaniel coat and a long tail. Every time it barked its ears bounced.

Julie's face was twisted toward us, staring; the gelding moved nervously and she pulled him up. She shouted at the dog, who stopped barking but moved around behind the horse, watching us, his out-of-proportion body close to the ground and his ears down.

I smiled, I saluted. For neighborly reasons I always tipped my hat to that wooden Indian of a girl. As usual, I got no response. She was staring past me to where the four looked down from their perch, and Jim Peck, old Nick of the Woods, grinned at her through his vines. It must have been an astonishing vision to a girl who had just been going along minding her own business and hating her parents, not bothering anyone.

In fact, it was so astonishing that she had to acknowledge my presence. She came riding up beside me on the bank. "What is it?"

"Hello, Julie," Ruth said from the treehouse. "It's where Mr. Peck there lives. Isn't it something?"

Julie took in Peck, the tent behind him, the ladder, the crooked little gable among the branches, the littered flat. "Gee!" she said. "How *neat*!"

So it was unanimous. Would you win the feminine heart? Climb a tree.

"Marian," Ruth said. "John. I don't think you know Julie LoPresti. Her family live off Ladera Lane, over east a half mile or so. Mr. and Mrs. Catlin, Julie. And Jim Peck."

She was caught too far off guard to remember to be sullen. For once she looked what she was: young. Still getting an eyeful, she nodded at them. "We're having a house tour," Marian said. "Is it all right if she comes over and looks too, Jim?"

Jim, already.

For a man who spent so much time insuring his privacy, Peck seemed to be enjoying the intrusion. "Sure," he said. "She'll have to leave the horse, though."

Oh, very funny, ha ha. Julie blushed dark red, but she slid off, looking for a place to tie the gelding. There was nothing smaller than the bay tree, two feet in diameter, and she ended by laying the reins in the hand I held out. I too had a function and fulfilled a need. Hitchy-boy Allston.

Lifting one leg in the skintight jeans and giving me a view of her heart-shaped behind stained from riding bareback, Julie tested the bridge, then put her weight on it, got set, and went across like a squirrel across a light cable. When she leaped off the other end they applauded her—There's the girl the bridge was *made* for!—and Marian said, "Come on up, this is where it's fun. Here, I'll come down and make some room."

All but Debby came down. With a look under her

dark brows Julie went up, broad-beamed but agile. "Hi," said Debby's face, stuck into hers as she topped the platform. "I'll tell you, let's play I live here and you've come visiting." Beaming, not in the slightest the petulant little girl we had seen that morning, she waited till Julie was over the edge and then minced up with her hand dangling before her like a hurt paw. "Oh, how do you do, Mrs. Johnson, isn't this nice, come right into the living room where it's cool."

Yes, do. Join our social group. Everybody else has.

There was something extraordinary about the way the Catlins melted down the most resistant materials. Before five minutes were up I heard Debby asking if she could ride the horse sometime. (No, Julie never let anyone ride it but herself, she had trained it and it spoiled a horse to be ridden by more than one person. But there was a stable on Ladera Lane, she'd take her over there if she wanted.) Was Julie ever available for baby-sitting, Marian was asking (Yes. Yeah, sure.), and Julie was saying to Peck, "When did you build this, anyway? I was riding through here all the time till the rain started, and I never saw it at all."

I stood across the creek holding the horse. It was getting definitely chilly; the bottom had a damp, rank smell. Up in the treehouse, where Debby still played hostess, the light went on again—and that, I promised myself, was something I was going to look into. I doubted exceedingly that she was getting all that illumination from a flashlight, and I did not believe that on those nights when I had seen both tent and treehouse blooming with light through the rain, Peck had simply put in another gasoline lantern. Yet I could see no sign of wires leading in.

I was getting impatient with the afternoon, and was glad when they came tottering and reeling, one after the other, across the bridge. I handed Julie back her horse, which had slobbered green spit on the sleeve of my jacket.

Marian had me by the other arm, shaking me and scolding. "You should have come over. It's just terribly cute, everything is so ingenious and Rube Goldbergy."

"Maybe a little too Goldbergy," I said.

"I'm coming back to see you every day," said Debby from up on John's shoulders.

"You do that," Peck said. "Only when I'm home, though, all right?" To Julie, sitting her horse and watching, he directed his gappy Dionysian grin. "You too, Mrs. Johnson. When you're out riding, stop in for a dish of tea."

The dull red swept up through her neck and face, she gave him an uncertain look, jerked her head around and saw us watching her, and angrily kicked the horse into an instant canter. At the open trail gate she slowed only to a trot, then leaned the horse to the right, sitting him solid and easy and loose like a bag of flour. We saw the dark streak through the trees and heard the clatter of galloping, and then the *pick pick pick* as he took the hill at a fast walk. Our group let loose a flurry of thanks at Jim Peck, standing by his castle gate, and he lifted an indulgent hand. As we turned away he was already hoisting the bridge.

"Well!" Marian said as we walked across the bottom. "Quite an afternoon." Her eyes touched me, gave me a look of amusement and understanding and commiseration, and went on to rest on Debby, riding John's shoulders. "We saw the treehouse, and we found somebody who might take you riding and stay with you when we have to go out, and we had a little party."

To us, when we stopped by the car, she turned with a smile that literally blazed, excessive, intense, and troubling. "I *love* this kind of day," she said. "I love getting to know the new place, and new people. I like to feel us living our way right into it."

"You're doing that, all right," I said, depressed, and opened the car door. She was a very unsteady young woman. The light she shed was like the magneto headlights of an old Model-T Ford—it dimmed and flared again as the motor was accelerated or retarded. Now she went on blazing as if her machinery was going full speed, just when all *my* machinery had died down to a three-cylinder limp—cold hands, cold feet, a sodden irritability of spirit. Then all at once she stood on tiptoe and kissed me on the cheek. "We love it most that you're our nearest neighbors," she said. "I was telling John, it's as if we'd known you all our lives."

"Our unanimous family feeling," John said, and bending top-heavy with Debby he kissed Ruth and gave her a hand into the car. They stood watching while I backed out. During the minute or two while I maneuvered to turn around in the lane, Marian's smile was brilliant and strained. I had the feeling that it was maintained with an effort, and that it was directed at me to assure me that *she* didn't think I had been acting badly, even if Ruth did. She seemed thin and frail; it seemed that her friends should look after her and make sure she didn't overdo. The cobweb of her kiss clung to my cheek, saving the whole afternoon.

3

The first time I found myself down below when neither the Catlins nor Jim Peck seemed to be at home, I went down to Peck's pad and made a little reconnaissance of his less visible improvements. As I had expected, I found an insulated electric cable crawling out of the cutbank and drooping into the brush of the creek bed. On the far side it went underground, undoubtedly to emerge through the floor of the tent and from there to climb up the back of the oak to the treehouse. On my side it also disappeared underground. Short of ripping it up, which I was tempted for a moment to do, I had no way of following it, but I knew perfectly well where it led, and after snooping around the pole that held my meter box, over by the pump, I found the cable coming up the grooved inside of an old innocent-looking weathered board nailed to the power pole. Somebody more scientific-minded than Peck, I assumed, had tapped into the power line for him above my meter. A plus for the twentieth century. Even saintly tree-sitters may have friends with engineering skill, and thus put the callous capitalist world under contribution.

Undoubtedly, Walden was pleasanter with electricity. Our thanks to the Pacific Gas and Electric. The music for which I had given Peck and his friends total credit might not have been picked out on their own guitars at all, but could have come from a hi-fi; for all I knew, he might have stereo, with his speakers distributed between treehouse and tent. The girl who sounded like Joan Baez might well have been Joan Baez, recorded. And how cozy to chase away the winter damps with an electric heater, and lie in the treehouse bunk under a good bed lamp. I fixed up a flashlight rig, yes.

And power was not all he had brought to Walden. Under the bridge, drooping almost invisibly into the leafing poison-oak and blackberry vines, I discovered a black plastic pipe. This too disappeared underground on both sides of the bridge, but one inescapable intuition and a three-minute search showed it to be attached just below the surface to the pipe line from my well.

Plumbing too, then, this courtesy the Joseph Allstons. If I had felt like risking my neck I could have crossed the bridge, I felt sure, and found a complete bathroom—washbowl, shower, water closet, tub, tiled walls, chrome fixtures, the works. And perhaps a bidet for his lady guests.

A week earlier, I would have told him to dig up his improvements and tear down his bird's-nest and tent and get the hell off the place. But now I was caught. What, destroy the treehouse that was Debby's delight, and thus destroy Marian's pleasure in seeing her child happy, and her satisfaction at living her way into the new place? Put myself in the position of autocrat and policeman, appear petty and mean not only to Peck—whose reaction would not distress me in the slightest, considering the way he had chiseled on my bounty—but to the Catlins? It would certainly not break me to provide his water, and I was not under any special obligation to protect the P.G.&E. I was only infuriated at being made into a mark, and being helpless to do anything about it.

I followed my usual course: I went home and blew off to Ruth, who asked me why I cared, what did it matter, really? If I had not taken a hostile attitude in the beginning, he probably wouldn't have tried to put things over on me. I did not accept her analysis, but I did nothing. I was pretty sure all the time that I would not, for it is part of the script that Peck's Bad Boy should deceive his Pa, and that Molière misers like me should be tricked by the ingenious and irreverent young.

IV

DECEMBER 12, the calendar tells me. Two months since the Catlin cottage went dark.

All through the past weeks the storms have come spinning in off the Pacific, and the microclimates of the foothills have been swept together and obliterated in rain, like petty differences of opinion in a crisis. Each new storm arrives with a pounce, and our house anchored on its hilltop shakes to the padded blows of the wind, and the trees heave and creak, and our terrace is littered with twigs and berries. We fear for our windows, pounded and streaming, and look out across the terrace to see horizontal bursts of rain combing the treetops below us, blurring the ugliness of Weld's interrupted excavations across the gully.

Even the lichened oak outside my study window, with limbs larger around than my body, is uneasy in the wind. There is a stiff arthritic movement in it as if the 6600 volts of turmoil tearing through its upper branches have been stepped down, here in the underleaf cave, to a housebroken 110. The soggy duff on the ground is constantly kicked around by juncos and Oregon towhees and golden-crowned sparrows, and the presence of these birds, which we watch with pleasure and for which I have built a feeding tray out of Catarrh's reach, communicates a certain uneasiness to our minds, for they ought to mean spring and actually mean winter, and the winter they mean is so confused with spring that one used to the standard seasons is bewildered.

Much of what the eye sees is Novemberish. The apricot orchards are bare, and blown downwind and plastered against walls and fences are those leaves of pistachio, liquidambar, and Japanese maple that gave us a brief New England color. Like other immigrants, we brought the familiar to an unfamiliar place, our planting impulse no different from that of pioneer women hoarding in their baggage seeds of lobelia and bittersweet, or Johnny Appleseed scattering civilization along a thousand miles of frontier tracks. Call it the Law of Dispersion and Uniformity. Marian, who valued the indigenous over the exotic, was almost the only person I ever knew who didn't submit to it, and even she would sometimes take pleasure in the results.

A false autumn, then, imported but half persuasive. Now in December the earth smells Labradorean. If we had not lived through two California winters we would expect snow. And indeed we do get something wintry enough, for on clear mornings we may look out our windows and see the redwood screeds of the patio wearing a pelt of frost. Sometimes the bricks are lacquered with ice, and when we drive out on early errands the lonely untracked bottoms are white, and so are the rails and post tops of Debby's corral, and so are the treads of Weld's miserable bridge, still unrepaired.

And yet under ice and frost the sand between our patio bricks has sprouted in intersecting lines of bright-green moss. Within ten days of the first rain the bedraggled stubble of the hills could be parted with a toe and show tiny cotyledons of filaree and burr clover and tiny spears of oat grass. All during the weeks when the year has been darkening toward its end, the green has forced itself upward through the brown, until now at close to Christmas the hills are voluptuous lawns, and the lavender branches of the deciduous oaks spread against a background like April. The coyote brush, hardy and forehanded, has been blooming white since November.

Unsystematic, contradictory, unlike anything that habit and literature have led us to expect, the rainy season *is* a season, profoundly different from the summer it succeeds. It is green, not golden; wet, not dry; chilly, not warm; clear, not milky. It has real clouds, not the high fog that obscures the summer sky. It produces real sunsets, not tame quenchings of daylight. It attracts whole populations of wintering birds. It smells different.

Watching the still unfamiliar changes come on, I can't help realizing that nearly our entire acquaintance with Marian was on the other cycle. She smells in the memory of sun, sage, dust, the faint dry tannic odor of sun-beaten redwood, above all of tarweed. Her light is hot and yellow or warm and brown, never the damp green of this season. She moves from high spring to summer, and stops. In the chilly, fishy smell of wet mold or the freshness of a rain-cleaned wind off the skyline there is no trace of her. She does not go on. One must go back for her, and that means re-creating not only herself but the season she inhabited.

It was a season so fresh that, even remembered, it has all the feel of a beginning. That was Marian's doing. We thought of ourselves as old settlers, but she made us newcomers again. Until the Catlins came we hardly had a social life, only a set of comfortable habits, a finicky separation from our own and all other history, and a disinclination to all acquaintance except the least demanding. In her passion to live her way into the new place, Marian pulled us after her; or rather, she set us to thinking what the Catlins must see, whom they must meet. Who would respond with the proper enthusiasm to this girl's vividness? What persons, houses, views, would excite her? Who ought to hear John, in his dry down-Maine voice, tell stories of expeditions he had been on, or expound the sonar system of porpoises, or prove that whales were once land animals by demonstrating their modified limbs and residual hair?

A Californian who is just long enough settled to be able to mispronounce Spanish names correctly is a spider, he lies in wait to initiate others into the land of his temperate exile. Not quite anything, he has to show off everything. Somewhat to our surprise, we turned out to be that kind of Californian. The Catlins, who had spent the winter in a furnished apartment downtown, with only one car and John away part of the time, had had little time to look around. They were predestined victims.

How about our favorite walk, an easy three miles, delightful in this season? Lovely views, hillsides of lupine and poppies and blue-eyed grass.

Fine. The first available Sunday morning they walked with us through the opulent hills. Every three minutes Marian discovered a new plant which John identified with the infallibility of a botany book. We made the whole loop onto the hogback and across the school land and through the woods home, and saw riders strung out through the pasture, and put up a doe and fawn in a thicket. But it was a little too long. Marian was looking drawn by the time we crossed the creek below Peck's roost, and Debby had been complaining and hanging back for half an hour, and finished on John's shoulders. Next day she was broken out with poison oak.

By mutual consent we did not repeat that walk, but several times we came past at the end of our therapeutic miles and lured them up the hill for a drink or a meal, bringing Debby so she could wade in our lily pond. One of those times, as we were sitting on the terrace with our feet on the rail discussing with indignation the couple who slaughtered pigeons for their dogs' education (and also trapped the foxes who raided the pigeon house, Marian had discovered), the red-tailed hawk from Shields's pasture labored over us heavy and slow, and squinting up into the blinding purity of sky, we saw he had a gopher snake in his talons. The snake was by no means whipped. He was wound all around the hawk's legs, pulling them down. We could see his body work, only sixty or seventy feet above us, and sense how the hawk gripped and shifted, hunting a killing hold or trying to let loose. They struggled around the terrace twice, looking about to crash, before they took their unfinished drama elsewhere. Marian accused me of staging the whole business, just to demonstrate my tooth-and-claw thesis, and I was as proud as if I had. Ah, California!

They indulged our guidebook fervor, and they forgave us that our time was always free, as theirs was not. We made expeditions to Monterey and Pacific Grove, where John showed us the marine laboratory in which he expected to spend a good deal of his time. We did Carmel and the Big Sur coast, we visited the flowering orchards, remnants of what had once stretched the length of the Santa Clara Valley. We took in San Juan Bautista and ate tamale pie with a bottle of Cabernet Sauvignon. We had a picnic on the skyline ranch that Lou LoPresti owned with six or seven other people, and, from a ridge cropped as smooth as a Vermont meadow by cattle, we looked down through big wind-broken Douglas firs to the surf lacing the blue bulge of the Pacific. When school was out we planned to go together to one of the Music in the Vineyards concerts, and hear Pergolesi operettas in the winery yard and sip champagne at intermission, looking down over the vineyards and woods that plunge toward the smogged valley and the strident city of San Jose.

Come see, let us show you. It was all the California we knew, and we liked it better for the chance to share it. This is how the New World looks, this is what is happening in the vital madhouse of Eden, the vanishing Lotus Land. See it quickly before it is paved under and smogged out.

And the neighbors? A few. The Casements, Bill and Sue, rich, openhanded, openhearted, givers of great *fêtes champêtres* and barbecues. When the weather gets hot Debby might want to swim over there, all the young ones do. And the LoPrestis—Julie's word on them isn't sound, they're pleasant intelligent people; and if he is a little humorously housebroke and she takes herself a little seriously, only those of us who are without sin should throw stones. Because of her illnesses, real or imagined, they do not go out much, but when they do throw one of their Fourth of July or Christmas parties, they make history. She is artistic, sort of—creates mosaics and driftwood sculptures and things I can't help thinking of as button-box art because it is like the things I used to make at six or seven by sticking things from my mother's button box onto modeling clay. Lucio is an omnicompetent, knows how to build or do anything. Try his ranch olives.

Others? We come up suddenly against the true poverty of our acquaintance. There are the Canadays, admirable people who annually turn their ranch into a camp for blind and crippled children. We would gladly know them, but have got no closer than a hello when we meet on a walk. Over the ridge west is an even bigger ranch owned by some real-estate people jealous of their seigneurship and lavish with NO TRESPASSING signs that have kept us from knowing them, or wanting to. For though Ruth will trespass at the drop of a wire, she depends on me to talk us out of situations we may get into, and I do not like standing guiltily before hard-eyed people with hard questions in their mouths.

Next to the real-estate folks lives a former All-American center who married the daughter of an Italian chocolate maker from San Francisco. They are horsy and hunt-clubby, friendly when encountered but definitely Society. In the guest cottage on their place, living in astonishing simplicity, is the ousted dictator of a banana republic. Once as we were walking across country on a hot fall afternoon, we saw him on the lawn in shorts, being squirted with the garden hose by his tall and striking wife. But they didn't invite us in and make intimates of us.

That was about it. East of us the pressing suburbs and tracts, with a few stubborn ranchers clinging to residual orchards and vineyards. Down the road, Tom Weld, busy figuring how he could subdivide and make a million: nobody we wanted to show off to the Catlins. Yet shortly we saw that the Welds and Catlins were on friendly terms. The women stood chatting at the mailboxes, Weld's daughter played sometimes with Debby, though she was a dull little girl, somewhat retarded. Weld's son worked around the Catlin place cleaning and burning trash and making firewood. He was a willowy, sinewy boy, burned black with sun above the waist. He liked to wear a .22 target pistol in a loaded cartridge belt when he worked. His hair was skinned off and the top flattened so close that a bald spot showed on the crown. On his wrists he wore leather-strap supports that I imagine were more ornamental than orthopedic, designed not to support weak joints but to call attention to muscles. He drove a molded, raked 1957 Mercury so hiked up behind that its front wheels looked smaller than the rear ones. It went down the road like a ground hog just about to disappear in a hole.

Even these natives, illuminated by Marian's friendly interest, came to have a look of rightness. Like harmless weeds, they served to complete the local flora. What if they did give me hay fever? Marian and John, accepting them, persuaded me that even these had some place in nature's beneficent plan.

Once he got his spring disking done in the orchard, Tom Weld seemed to have a lot of business downtown. If I had known what he was working on, I would have watched less complacently from the terrace when, in bathrobe and slippers, I came out to consult the spring mornings and see what Catarrh had created on the mat. I would not have assumed so casually that the people who on several occasions walked around Weld's hill with him, setting the beagles crazy, were merely friends or potential renters of pasture.

Nearly every afternoon Julie LoPresti rode past, uphill or down, with her frizzle-chinned mongrel padding so close to the horse's heels that it was a wonder he didn't get his nose split by a calk. I remarked to Ruth that this misbegotten mutt was a rather apt symbol of the ties that bind family to family, and men to other men, and the living to the unborn, whether they elect to be bound or not. I thought I sounded rather like Joseph Conrad in an elevated mood, but Ruth only looked at me with her sharp raccoon face and said that it was clear whom I had been talking to. All right, I accepted the soft imputation. I talked to Marian every chance I got, and so far as I could see, so did everybody else around here.

And actually Ruth and I had more reason to see her frequently than anybody else did. We had a commission to keep an eye on her. One evening in April, before going down to Guadalupe Island off Baja California to study sea elephants, John came up our hill and asked us seriously, as a great favor, if we would sort of look out for her while he was gone.

He did not have any trouble persuading us. It was like being a small boy asked to hold somebody's thoroughbred. But his request gave me a fresh respect for John. Until then, I suppose I had looked upon him as a genial and attractive boy, fond of his wife but not really in her class. That afternoon, while he stood talking to us in the drive, I saw lines in his face that I hadn't noticed before, and they seemed to me lines of sobriety, responsibility, masculine resolution. It struck me that his life had been adventurous and daring, and that if he was overshadowed by his vivacious wife, he was so because he wanted to be. If I had been a father with a daughter I was anxious about I couldn't have found a son-in-law to whom I would have been more willing to entrust her.

"You know how it is with her," he said. "There's been absolutely no recurrence, and she goes in to the clinic every few weeks for a check. She seems stronger to me —it's been good for her out here. But pregnancy sometimes speeds these things up, female hormones seem to act like carcinogens. So I'd feel a lot better if I knew you were here for her to come to."

It would be pure pleasure, we assured him. And shouldn't she be kept from doing too much, shouldn't she rest more than she did?

That made him smile. "If you can keep her from doing too much you're better than I am. She'll do all she can do, and a little more. As long as I know you're here, and ready to help if anything should go wrong, I won't worry about her. If anything does go wrong, I wish you'd call this number in San Diego, Bill Barger. If you can't get him, try the Oceanographic Institute in La Jolla. We'll be in touch with both of them every day by radio."

He handed me a three-by-five card with the two addresses and telephone numbers typed on it. He shook my hand, he kissed Ruth's cheek, he said he would see us in about a month, he backed up a step or two, turning to go.

"Wait a minute," I said. "Does Marian know we're her keepers?"

John laughed. "Do you think I want to break up a fine friendship? No, keep it dark. She'd come to you anyway. I just wanted to ask you for that little extra watchfulness. She needs to be looked after, but she hasn't found that out yet."

Off he went, hand in air. Before he got to the turn he was running. We heard him thudding down the steep road, vigorous as a young hart upon the mountains. It was reassuring to think that Marian had all that health supporting her, and exhilarating to think that now we temporarily replaced it.

You would have thought, and you would have been right, that the principal lack in our life up to then was a little responsibility. Ruth never went by without stopping to see if she could take anybody anywhere or pick up anything at the market. I developed the habit of stopping every day when I walked down for the mail. There was rarely anything we could do for Marian, but we tried to do things for Debby. I spent a day building her a playhouse in the grove, but I never observed that she used it. Marian admitted a little apologetically that it suffered by contrast with Peck's treehouse, to which Debby and Julie went whenever they found Peck home. Marian was less inclined to object because she was troubled by the lack of children Debby's age in the area. The Weld girl was three years older, and her bus got her home late from school. Marian yearned for more playmates for her child. She believed in something called "block play," and she sometimes wondered if they should have brought Debby out into the country. She and John loved it so much they hadn't thought of Debby. This miserable only-child business. She knew all about it from her own childhood. Later on, with a little brother or sister, she'd be better off. Or if she had a pony. Julie LoPresti seemed to require nothing else in life.

Well, why not? I said. They could put up a ring, and a tack shed if they wanted, down there in the bottoms between their cottage and Peck.

Oh, she said, delighted, *could* they? Would I rent them that land?

Rent nothing, I told her. If I could afford to let Peck live in my tree, I could let them make use of a piece of unused pasture.

I was all the more willing because it appeared to me that Marian needed a pony more than Debby did. She spent half her time taxiing the child to piano lessons, to friends' houses, to parties, to the park, to the Junior Museum. When she wasn't taking Debby somewhere to be intellectually stimulated and emotionally refreshed, she was working with her to build birdbaths, feeding trays, frog-and-turtle pools, fern and flower collections. The introduction of a horse into that family would probably add twenty hours of rest time to Marian's week.

So we drove them around looking at stables and ranches until we found a fifteen-year-old piebald gelding, marbled like a cake even to the eyes. He was, the man said, as gentle as a kitten. As if to demonstrate, a pair of achromatic white kittens that had been chasing one another around the corral flew with their tails up along the fence and one of them raced up a fence post and the other, seeing a little darkly with its miscolored eyes, ran up the piebald's leg and hung there above the knee with its claws sunk in. The piebald only quivered. Marian bought him on the spot, to be delivered as soon as we could prepare quarters for him.

That was the week in May when the wind blew hard and dry from the north, and the hills under it went green-bronze and then gold, the whole landscape changing within three days, emerging into another set of colors like a drying color print. Against the gold hills the oaks were round, dense, almost black. The fields overnight were impossible to walk through, horrible with barbed seeds. I did not fail to point out the change to Marian, but I took some pleasure in it: it was another thing to show her about California. That seasonal change is as remarkable, in its way, as the stealthy spring that begins with the coming of winter. You go to bed on a May night with flowery smells on the air and the peepers singing, and awake to dusty summer, cracking adobe, and the first of the season's gnats.

2

Some sort of prologue ended with the finding of the horse and the swift coming of summer. Another act began when we drove down the hill one Saturday morning and found a horse trailer backed up to the trail gate and John, Dave Weld, and the stable man unloading the piebald.

We stopped, we shook hands, asked about the sea elephants, that sort of thing. John was as black as a pirate, blacker even than young Weld. With his shirt off he showed himself to be muscled like a prize fighter. "Sea elephants!" he said. "I hadn't been home ten minutes till Debby had me turned into a horse wrangler. Dave and I are taking his dad's pickup in for some fencing right now, to put in a ring. You're the indulgent owner, you can supervise."

"Supervise hell, I'll drive a nail," I said.

I sent Ruth into town alone, and I was waiting with posthole auger and shovel and hammer when the pickup came back with posts and redwood two-by-fours. By spontaneous combustion we found ourselves in a neighborhood work party. Julie was there, leading Debby around on the piebald and giving all sorts of trouble to her mutt dog, who insisted on staying at the heels of Julie's horse and kept getting stepped on by Debby's. Dave Weld, peeled to his walnut hide, with his target pistol strapped down to his leg and his transistor radio blasting out a Pirates-Giants game, was augering out postholes in the cementlike adobe. Gunslinger, strong and silent, he strained and twisted, gleaming with sweat and ropy with young muscle, his wrists strapped in leather, his face still and stern. Marian, catching me looking at him, half closed her eyes and made swooning motions with her head. She and Ruth, having fed us sandwiches and salad, were sitting in the back patio in the shade of a little walnut tree watching us swarm like ants around the bottom land.

"I'm going to trot him," Julie said, looking back at Debby as she led the horse across the flat. "Just let your legs hang. Point your toes out." She hunched her horse into a trot, sitting him loose and heavy and smooth, and Debby came behind on the stretch-necked piebald, bouncing on his fat back and screaming to stop. Julie stopped.

"She's *good* with Debby," I heard Ruth say. "She's going to be just right. You're lucky."

"Except I'll never get Debby into a dress again," Marian said. "Now it's jeans and an old sweatshirt with the arms cut off, notice?"

Through the heat of the afternoon we worked together in the sun and dust, young Weld digging holes, John and I setting posts. Actually I didn't work much. I held the level on them while he shoveled in earth and tamped it down with a length of two-by-four. Down in the grass, the transistor reported strike-outs, hits, double plays; the thin crickety roar of the crowd came up out of the weeds as if there were a trap door down into some region of the strengthless but unappeased dead. We talked about seals, their varieties, their migration habits, their breeding grounds, and the recovery of some of the species from near-extinction. Later on, in June, John was going up to the Pribilof Islands to be there when the female fur seals pupped. He wanted to study their learning rate. Any animal that could learn to swim and look after itself in a week struck him as interesting.

I eased my back, straightening up, and he did the same. I said, "You'll be gone part of the summer, too, then."

He knew what was on my mind; his heavy shoulders went up, his mouth went down, his hands went out in a gesture so Gallic it seemed he was imitating someone. "She won't hear of anything else. The gestation of seals is supposed to be more important to me and my career than her own is." I found his eyes on me. "She says she's gotten along fine. Is that right?"

"I think so. Ruth does too. She's gained a little weight, she's brown, she's out in the sun a lot. Don't you think she looks better?"

"I do," John said. "I'm grateful to you both."

"It's total pleasure."

He looked at me with his sharp blue fisherman's eyes, and smiled as if his mind were somewhere else. Exercise had gathered pebbles of sweat on his brown forehead, his chest and shoulders looked oiled. "What the hell," he said, "why are we slaving here as if we had a contract? I'm only going to be home three days. How about some feminine companionship? After sea elephants it looks pretty good." He threw the shovel clanging on the hard adobe. "Dave? Let's take five. How about a Coke or a beer?"

Young Weld drew a core of shining black adobe from the hole and knocked it out of the auger. Julie was leading Debby through the trail gate. The mongrel stood aside, ducking to try to get between the horses. His draggled beard was matted with burrs. As we walked up to where Marian and Ruth sat with a bucketful of iced drinks on the table beside them, the sweat flies buzzed around me with a noisy, frantic insistence to entrap themselves in the hairs of my ears, and I had an epiphany, an instant bright awareness of how that ridiculous dog must feel all the time.

Dave Weld stood a moment by the pail, slanted a look at us, and picked out a can of beer. He went halfway back to the corral and sat down with his back against an oak and pulled the tab off the can and drank. His eyes were fixed on something across the creek. I looked, and there was Peck, on the porch of his tent.

It annoyed me to see him there, spying on our pleasant neighborhood labors. Young Weld and Julie, both ordinarily part of the diurnal irritation, had been won over and brought in. And there sat Peck, watching us for God knew how long without even giving us good day. Why hadn't he swung on his Tarzan rope across the creek and offered to help? The Catlins had been kind to him, he knew that John was just back, all the junior admirers of his treehouse were present, why not join in? Was he, I wondered, annoyed that his privacy was going to be invaded by the horsy activities of those girls? I was myself annoyed enough to hope so.

"What's he doing, watching the squares work?" I said to Ruth.

Marian leaned over and motioned me to her side. From there I got a clearer view between the trees. "Watch!" Marian said, and shrugged her shoulders up around her ears like a gleeful little girl.

Peck was sitting on the deck, his head as big as a keg with hair, his bare back straight, his eyes fixed straight ahead into the brush, oblivious. The transistor talked to itself down in the grass to our left, and I heard Julie say something to Debby in the lane, but I paid no more attention than Peck did. He stared straight ahead, I stared at him.

"What is he, in a trance or something?" I said.

"Yoga!" Ruth whispered in scorn. "He's exercising."

"Are you sure he's alive? How long has he been there?"

"Ten or fifteen minutes."

"He'll wear himself out," I said. "All that violence is bound to have an effect on his system."

"Oh, *you* know about yoga, for goodness' sake," Ruth said. "You *do* it sitting down, a lot of it. You're exercising muscles deep inside."

"Every system has its own rules," Marian said.

"You're right," I said. "But a rule that might apply to all systems is that when people have been friendly to you, and you see them doing something laborious, you offer to lend a hand. Or at least you say hello."

"What a moralist," Ruth said. "Watch this, you might learn something that would be good for your back."

From our shade we looked across the blazing, trampled bottoms to the tree-backed stage where Peck sat between his legs in his cut-off jeans. I could not see him move one single muscle, though perhaps he was taking one of those locks, chin or tongue, or contracting his anal sphincters, or doing something else inward. After a long time he rocked suddenly forward and kicked himself into a headstand. His hands were clasped around the back of his neck, his elbows made a tripod on which he balanced a moment, wobbling. Then his legs, which had been folded insectlike on his chest, straightened until his bare toes pointed upward. "Ahhhhh!" said the admiring women on my right and left.

I held the watch on him until he curved his spine and rolled into a sitting position a few feet ahead of where he had sat before. "Three minutes and twenty seconds," I said. "What's the record?"

They were much too interested to pay any attention to my carping. They sat breathlessly watching. Braced against the tree, the beer can forgotten in his hand, Dave Weld was watching while the ballgame shrilled unheeded from the grass. Julie, bringing her pack train in the gate, saw us all sitting there entranced, and now *she* was watching. What the hell, we were all watching. With that many eyeballs focused on him he might have felt as if he were being caressed by the suction cups of an octopus. But he didn't watch us. He was above us, beyond us, way out.

In a pig's-eye. He was aware of us as an actor is aware of his audience. Intent on his act, he lay back and bridged from head to heels, thrusting his skinny rib cage into the air. Then he lowered himself until his spine was flat along the deck. Then he pushed up again. His upthrust beard quivered. Strain or heat waves?

"You still think it's easy?" Ruth said.

Peck rocked, and once again was sitting between his legs. "Pelvic posture," Ruth said to Marian. "That's a basic one." For a time he sat immovable, unless somewhere inside him some secret muscle was clenching and relaxing. At last he stood up and stooped into the tent, to come out again with a glass which he tilted up for a long mouthful. Leaning out over the edge of the deck, he brought his head and shoulders into a streak of sun, and in an instant his whole hairy top was haloed in spray. With a little more careful staging he might have made a rainbow.

"Elephant mudra," Ruth said. "You blow water through your nose. It's one of the cleansings. This is as good as a twenty-dollar lesson."

Peck took a handkerchief, towel, rag of some sort, off the back of the batwing chair, and pulling his tongue far out of his mouth, he massaged around in his throat. He spat over the edge, he tossed the rag into the chair, he sat down again and pulled first one foot, then the other into his lap. "Can you see?" Ruth was whispering excitedly. "That's the lotus posture. That's *hard*! It's the best one for meditation because your lower limbs are all locked and you've got a firm base."

"You think he's meditating?" I said. But when their heads turned—Marian's inquiring, Ruth's cocked like the head of someone turning to shush a talker behind her at a play—I didn't go ahead and say what was in my mind: that Peck was a long way from true meditation, that he couldn't have been more conscious of being watched, that down below there, *wink!* was going his little old anal sphincter, the window of his soul. *Wink! Wink!* Rubber, you squares.

I drained my can of beer and set it down, not softly. "How about finishing that fence?" I said. "If I watch this any longer I'll begin to twitch."

Peck sat immovable upon his locked posterior. The

Catlins were both laughing. "Joseph Allston, you have a closed mind," Marian said.

"Closed to phonies and show-offs."

"I don't understand you," Ruth said. "When Murthi was writing his book you were more interested than I was."

John and Marian looked inquiring. Who's Murthi?

"Murthi was a friend of mine, a client," I said. "He wrote a couple of books interpreting Indian philosophy for Westerners. Sure I was interested. He had a good mind, he was neither a phony nor a show-off. He didn't convert me, but I listened. When this kid comes out into the view of the crass materialist world to exercise his spiritual rectum, I'm *not* interested. I want to barf."

Ruth's eyes definitely disapprove of me, Marian's are merry and speculative and squinting as she tries to figure out whether I mean this or am mainly kidding. John stands up laughing. "I hope you never get mad at me," he says. He looks sideward at Peck, immobile and immutable on his pedestal. "Well, the show seems to be over. Shall we go work off your rage?"

"I never get mad," I said. "I only hold grudges. Ask Ruth."

It was casual and funny. And yet I really did think Peck had put on his show out of a trivial juvenile desire to show off, and I really couldn't laugh, as I should have, and feel indulgent. I was definitely grumpy as we went down into the sun where Dave Weld had begun industriously to grind away at another posthole. And it didn't do my state of mind a great deal of good when I looked over—just once, I couldn't resist—and saw Jim Peck, cleansed and purified, still blissfully unaware of our presence fifty yards away. He had a book in his hand, up on the deck of his treehouse, but it seemed to me that he was not reading; he was slyly watching us sweat down there in the sun. His right forearm made short, regular jerking motions that meant he was throwing salted peanuts or raisins into the pulsating vacuole in his beard.

About five o'clock all the posts were in. We left Dave Weld nailing on two-by-four rails and went around into the grove, where it was cooler, for a drink. Julie had led Debby off up the horse trail across the creek, but just as we were putting the tools away they came back and tied the horses inside the incomplete corral and went to work on them with currycomb and brush. I had an impression, which considering they were both fifteen or sixteen was natural enough, that Julie was inordinately aware of Dave's walnut torso working its muscles a little way beyond her, and that he in turn was elaborately oblivious to the presence of anyone else in the world. He set and drove spikes with great blows. His muscles contracted so, under his sweaty skin, that he reminded me of Julie's mutt dog, now asleep under an oak. Yapping, he contracted his body in just that convulsive way. You could see his bark in his anus. And guess what that brought to mind. *Wink!*

Maybe I *was* beginning to twitch. There were too many people around there exercising their muscles before audiences which they did not deign to notice. I was glad to get around the house and get a cold glass in my hand and lie back in a canvas chair and listen to John, who paid the most scrupulous and smiling attention to every member of his audience, tell us about the social habits of sea elephants.

After a while I became aware that the hammering

down in the ring had stopped, and I momentarily expected to see Dave Weld come past the house on his way home in the old Mercury with the red primer on the molded fenders and noise blasting from the twin pipes. But no sign of him, and no sign of Julie and Debby either. Then in a pause we heard the sounds of a guitar being tuned. Marian stood up and called. "Debby? Deb . . . by!"

"I'll take a look," I said, and went around the back of the house to the patio. The stage of Peck's tent was more crowded this time. They were all there in a cluster. Movie hero with his six gun, horsy girl with bareback seat, six-year-old with solemn glasses, they sat entranced around their hairy guru, under the bo tree.

3

So Peck never did exactly join us; he ran a rival shop. Telling myself that he was only a temporary squatter who could be evicted when I chose, I saw him spread like a wild-cucumber vine. He had his split-level pad beyond the defended moat which I could cross neither physically nor spiritually, nor wanted to. His Honda was housed in the unauthorized shed by the trail gate. Sometime in May, shortly after John returned to Guadalupe, and again without asking permission, Peck nailed a secondhand mailbox next to mine and daubed his name on it with a finger dipped in black: J. PECK.

The longer he stayed, the less time he spent in meditation or in solitude. Either his intentions matured during the months while he was getting his tree in order, or he had discovered students whom he could influence.

He began, clearly, to think of himself as a guru, and his attractiveness was obviously enhanced by the improvements he had made in my poison-oak patch.

If the Catlins had been bothered, I might have run him out—or would I? *Would* I? I don't know. When I wasn't being excessively irritated by his willingness to stretch into an ell every inch I gave him, I was willing to admit that he was simply a kid, maybe a bright kid, with most of his generation's idealistic fantasies and a pretty good sense of theater. And yet I never lost my sense that we were adversaries, and that he knew it as well as I, but that Marian and John, who looked upon him and his crowd as anthropologists might have looked upon a village of picturesque head-hunters, had no comprehension of the emotional antagonisms that lay in us like surly dogs at the end of a chain, ready to leap up and growl at a step. If I had eradicated Peck's nest to simplify my life, I would have been guilty of subtracting from the pleasure the Catlins took in *their* new life, and I probably would have hated myself to boot. Nevertheless I could not keep my mouth shut.

"Do you think Julie should be taking Debby over there all the time?" I asked Marian one day. I had dropped in after picking up the mail, and found her in the patio hulling strawberries. The air was rich with the smell of boiling jam. I saw the black gelding in the corral with the piebald. From across the creek came the sound of the guitar. As her stained fingers pulled blossoms from the berries and dropped blossoms in one pan, berries in another, Marian looked at me in the scented shade in the amused-serious way she had, as if giving a ridiculous remark every chance to make sense before she laughed at it. She shook her head.

"He and his bunch are all right. In a way, they really *are* sort of saintly."

"Saintly! My God."

"They're kind," she said. "They don't push anybody around. They treat children like people. Debby adores them."

"Naturally. They're all about her age."

"What's wrong with that? Don't you believe all that about little children and the Kingdom of Heaven? Here." Reaching, she stuck a great strawberry between my lips, but as soon as my mouth was clear of the succulent pulp I said, "One of the dangers of grown-up little children is that they have a child's judgment and an adult's capacity to do harm."

"What harm could they do Debby?"

"Oh, I don't know. Give her beer?"

"John does that."

"Pot, then. They all swear it's so harmless, and they're so kind."

About to answer, she heard or smelled something in the kitchen, laid her pans aside, and rushed in. A minute later she came out, and reassembling her work in her lap she said seriously, "Maybe they do smoke pot, I suppose they do, everybody their age seems to. But I'm sure they don't give her any."

"How can you be sure?"

"I can't, I guess. I just trust them not to."

"What about Julie?"

Marian had continued to spend much of her time cultivating health. Her arms and hands and legs were deeply tanned, she had gained more weight, her eyes were a clear blue and white flash in her brown face. She frowned. "Yah," she said as if disgusted. "That *has* bothered me a little. They treat both her and Dave like mascots or apprentices or something. They might think it was a joke to initiate them. But if it's harmless, and John thinks it is, more or less, then it's no worse than if a couple of fifteen-year-olds had a few drinks, is it?"

"The police would think it was a little worse."

"Well, what would you do? I can hardly forbid her to go over."

"Her mother could."

"I wonder," Marian said. "That's such a *fierce* girl, sometimes. She's so full of rebellion, what her mother tells her not to do is exactly what she has to do."

"Does Fran know she goes over there all the time?"

"I don't know. I suppose she thinks she's here baby-sitting." She moved her hands irritably in the pan of berries and scowled at me uncertainly. "If I didn't have her as a sitter, she'd be over anyway. Maybe it's better if she has Debby to keep an eye on."

"Well," I said, "I guess she's her parents' problem, and she's probably insoluble."

"Ah," Marian said, smiling, "she'll get over it. Given a chance, we all grow up. Julie wants to be taken as an equal, not as a child. That's why she finds Peck's crowd so much more interesting than her mother. They aren't really hoodlums, Joe. All they do is sit around and talk about the good life, the ideal life. That shouldn't corrupt the young, should it?"

"It depends on how they define the good life."

"They define it as freedom. *Absolute* freedom."

"That's what I thought," I said. "Anything goes, is that it?"

"That doesn't seem to be it—well, *technically* it might be, but mainly they seem to believe in the natural virtue of primitive man. They're romantics, I suppose. Man is naturally good, but he's corrupted by society." She giggled suddenly, eying me as if she thought I might explode. "Did I tell you they've painted a motto on a board and nailed it to the tree? BE YOURSELF. GOOD IS THE SELF SPEAKING FREELY, EVIL IS WHAT PUTS THE SELF DOWN."

"Oh, that's pretty!" I said. "Did Peck write that?"

"I guess so. Maybe he borrowed it. Why, don't you believe in freedom?"

"Not to any great extent," I said. "What's Peck doing when he sits down to his yoga? Speaking freely?"

Looking at me doubtfully, she pulled the blossoms from three or four berries. She waved a wasp away from the pan. "But yoga is *self*-discipline," she said. "Is that what you mean? That he's contradicting himself? They aren't opposed to self-discipline, only to the traditional and conventional kinds that they think are antilife."

"He's improvising his exercises, is he?"

Studying me with a frown, she said, "What are you getting at, you debater?"

"No debater," I said. "I just want to keep this conversation on the track. Yoga is a system of very strict rules, none of them invented by Jim Peck. Absolute freedom, my foot. You can't open your mouth or move your hand without living by rules, generally somebody else's, and that goes for those birdbrains across the creek, too. It's the beginning of wisdom when you recognize that the best you can do is choose *which* rules you want to live by, and it's persistent and aggravated imbecility to pretend you can live without any. But if you say they're harmless, they're harmless. I only brought them up because I hoped they were a nuisance to you."

Smiling, torn between hearing me out and dealing with a renewed emergency in the kitchen, she was sidling toward the door, and at the last word she bolted in. After a time she came out with a pot of jam in one hand and a great spoon in the other, lifting red spoonfuls into the air and letting them drop back, testing.

"Oh, damn!" she said, and knocked the spoon clean and fished for the wasp that had dived in. Carefully, she lifted him out and carried him to the hose bib. The water flooded him out onto the ground, and she rinsed the spoon and scooped him up again, slimed with jam and stickily crawling, too encumbered even to buzz, and washed him a second time, gently, and set him on the window sill to dry off.

4

So I went on picking up my daily beer cans along the lane where the freedom force threw them, and every day or so I built a little bonfire on the asphalt road by the mailboxes to get rid of the throwaway newspapers, boxholder letters, free samples, and other junk mail that began finding its way to Peck, as to other mortals, the hour he announced himself in residence. He never opened any of this, or carried it away, but pawed it out contemptuously onto the ground, where it lay or blew until I gathered and burned it.

As if they were ordinary people, and not fantastic adolescent freaks, I gave good day to the unkempt young men and apache girls who came in and out, most of them in the Illinois Volkswagen bus that had now reappeared, apparently to stay. I used to see them filing around Debby's ring toward the bridge, bearing sacks of groceries and six-packs of beer. Invariably they wore a look of excitement as if headed for an audience with the Most High. The Most High Himself moved among them with a new, pantherine dignity, smiling his ambush smile and gleaming with his hypnotic eyes, benevolently dispensing sanction and welcoming all to the uses and premises of absolute liberty.

But newcomers, Julie told Marian, who told me, were not necessarily admitted to the Presence. Sometimes they spent a whole afternoon and evening there and never saw the holy one, who stayed up in the treehouse with favored disciples. This reservation of the sacred person was so fantastic that I slapped my naked head when I heard of it. I asked Marian what had happened to the absolute-freedom rule. Why didn't the neophyte, speaking freely and not letting anything put the self down, simply climb up the ladder and barge in?

Self-restraint, she said, baiting me.

Yes, I said, taking the hook. Taking it? Gulping it, plunging for it. Yes, self-restraint enforced by a rule, or by a taboo, which was worse. Holy holy holy. Was it death to eat out of his rice bowl or touch his coveralls?

She only laughed at me. She thought of them as kids playing Utopia.

Which, if I could forget the harm they were capable of, I might admit they were. By few and many I observed them sitting or lying around Peck's untidy flat beyond the web of ropes and cables and the crooked loop of the bridge—safe from intrusion, escaped from Babylon and the parental university, absolutely free to submit their minds to Peck's charisma. I saw the favored ones sitting with him on the treehouse porch, throwing their beer cans down into the brush. Put away your nets and follow me.

Once their college closed in June, the group settled down to six or eight regulars, including the Volkswagen crowd. They were as fully in residence as Peck himself. The Honda had been removed from its winter quarters in the shed, and stood under canvas by the bay tree. The shed was filled with mattresses, folding chairs, card tables, cartons of books, wastebaskets filled with junk, the sort of shabby indispensable paraphernalia that passes from student to student or from student to secondhand dealer and back to student, and into storage and out again, providing at intervals the sitting and sleeping needs of generations of the penniless young. Maybe this stuff was being kept for someone during the summer, maybe it was being stored against some planned enlargement of the establishment. I saw it, as I passed back and forth, with uneasiness and nostalgia. To have so little, and it of so little value, *was* to be quaintly free.

Many nights we saw them sitting around a fire and heard them singing. (No fires, remember? But that was a rule imposed from without.) The first time I saw the fire I was furious all over again at Peck's calculated challenging of every restriction I had laid down. But even in my anger I don't believe I ever contemplated going over and making him douse it. I told myself that by now his flat was trampled so bare there was little hazard; that the creek, after all, made a firebreak; that the horses had picked the bottom land down to the adobe so that nothing could spread; that anyway Peck had all the water in my well to fight fires with. The fact was, I wanted no confrontation with Jim Peck; and I avoided it not because it would bother him, but because it would bother me.

It was a permanent gypsy camp. Mornings, sleeping bags lay like khaki cocoons around the tent. Mealtimes, smoke arose and girls in jeans moved around the fire: either Peck had given up his vegetarianism or he did not insist on it for his followers, for I often smelled hamburgers broiling. Afternoons, a lot of bare feet and sandals might be propped against the lower corral rail and a lot of eyes might watch through altogether too much hair while Julie gave Debby lessons in seat and hands around the ring. Apache girls exposed a lot of leg, climbing on the old piebald for a turn. Unkempt boys leaped aboard the startled old thing and kicked him into a canter up the lane, showing off as if they had been normal adolescents, while Julie sat firmly aboard her gelding to prevent anyone from trying to ride *it,* and Peck looked down indulgently, lounging in the treehouse door. Play away, my children. Anything goes, even fun.

It was so incongruous to see those refugees from an intellectual coffeehouse disporting themselves in country pleasures that I half liked them, and this despite the probability that they were as promiscuous as a camp of howler monkeys. I began to recognize faces. There were two girls who were always around, and so far as I could see, they belonged to no one in particular or everybody at large. John told me, with some amusement, that the one called Margo was a founder of something called the Committee for Sexual Freedom that had chapters at all the colleges in the area and had staged spring demonstrations in some of them. We did not see their faces in the newspaper photographs of sit-ins and vigils that came up that summer all over the Bay Area like alkali salts in a drying lake bed. They did not go in for anti-Viet Nam parades, they did not picket the makers of napalm. They went to the heart of the matter: sexual freedom. The only time I saw Margo's face in the paper, she had been photographed while conducting a rally to legalize abortion.

"My God," I said to Ruth, "it's the Oneida Colony all over again. First thing you know they'll begin to manufacture silverware. Every time I remember that we're the sponsors of this outfit, I doubt my sanity."

"Not sponsors," Ruth said. "Neutral observers. So observe."

"O.K.," I said, "I'll observe. But if I were Marian I'd observe with less complacency, and if I were the LoPrestis I'd observe with no complacency whatever, and if I were Tom Weld my hair would be standing on end with horror and disbelief. Have you seen what that gun-toting rural Adonis is turning into? Did you see him up on the bulldozer the other day, grading the road?"

For there was no doubt that Peck, who never appeared in the papers and who had no cause but absolute freedom, had captured the neighborhood youth. More than once, after Debby had been called protesting in to supper, I saw Julie sitting cross-legged among the bohemians around the tent, tilting and rocking with laughter or laboriously learning the changes of some guitar tune. More than once, as we came home at night, we saw Dave Weld's molded Mercury parked by the trail gate. He brought down his father's chain saw and made the bacchants a woodpile, using his muscle and his country skills (and my trees) as an entree into the society he coveted. He quit carrying the pistol: old ahimsa got him. And by the end of June the flat-top haircut that had once been so short his skull was tanned had grown out to a prickly reddish brush. I offered to bet Ruth that it would go all the way to a John-the-Baptist bob, and I would have won, too. It used to fascinate and frustrate me to imagine the comments that hairdo got from Tom Weld, who whatever he was was no longhair. On the other hand, he probably never noticed; he was not much for noticing.

Peck's whole ménage, neighborhood and otherwise, piled in and out of the Catlin cottage as I had seen the summer crowd pile in and out of places on Vermont lakes. They were completely relaxed with Marian, and with John when he was at home. With us, or at least with me, they had a wary politeness about them—*non timeo sed caveo*. All except the Margo girl, one of those who are aware every waking minute of every square inch of their bodies. She, I thought, was provocative, but I withstood her charms.

As for Peck himself, assuming that I did not misread his attitude toward me, it must have tickled him to have me in a position where I would permit the whole camel to creep into the tent rather than seem petty. He robbed from the rich and gave to the poor, that one. His morality, which I was sure did not all come from the Upanishads, would have told him that he was making it, and that to make it was good. On the other hand, he seemed as willing to evade a direct confrontation as I was, for he never discussed any of his theosophy-and-water faiths and two-candle-power illuminations in my hearing. When I was around he was invariably quiet, polite, soft-voiced, and he smiled as if he knew something. I got his beliefs secondhand from Marian, who patiently attended his philosophical regurgitations. I say philosophical: occasionally a philosopher was his source. More often, his enthusiasms were straight out of old James Dean movies and Ginsberg poems. That was one of the things about him that was hardest to swallow. There was so much Dean in his Ginsberg.

5

One day I came up from the mailboxes just as Peck was mounting his Honda in the Catlins' little parking area. He came toward me along the foot of the hill, bare-chested, bare-legged in his cut-off Levis, insect-headed in the white helmet, and as he passed with a gust of hot air and dust-and-oil smell, he gave me his gleaming, knowing, wordless smile through his beard. Ten feet down the road (did I imagine this?) he goosed the motorcycle into a derisive snort. I turned to look after him. He was just crossing the bridge, attentive to the narrow tread his wheels followed, but as he reached the other side he looked back. We exchanged some sort of message before he whipped out of sight behind the trees.

Walking on, I saw Marian stretched in the old lounge in the grove. She waved me down, and I went, though I was not overjoyed to be succeeding Peck as her visitor. And I couldn't ignore him, as I probably should have. I had to spit him out of my mouth. "Been having a discussion with our friend?" I said.

Braced back in the lounge with a paperback book in her hand, Marian cried, "Why so glum? Isn't it a gorgeous day—again? Discussion is right. I think he's been trying to convert me." She lifted the book.

I put my bundle of mail and magazines on the ground and sat down in a wicker chair. Why so glum indeed. This was the best half hour of my day, this pause on the way back from the mailbox. On days when I found her gone, or Debby home from school, or somebody's car in the parking area, I could count on my heart wavering down through me like a flat stone dropped in a water barrel. And just to see her there, fizzing, an open and inexhaustible bottle of champagne, did make it a gorgeous day in spite of Peck.

"Converting you?" I said. "That must have been fun. Has he got a mind? Is anything going on under all that hair?"

"You wouldn't believe me if I said there was."

"No. I don't believe you're going to say so, either."

"It's funny, I really don't know," she said, with the quick switch to earnestness that often made me regret having chosen a joking tone. "A lot of the time he's absolutely predictable, a sort of conditioned response—young anarchy—*you* know. He's twenty-four, he says, but it's a young twenty-four. And sometimes he just seems to be drifting in this cloud of abstract ideas and sometimes he's literally reforming the world. He thinks you could make it over, he really does, and he has a lot of enthusiasm—" she glanced at me under her eyelashes—"when he trusts you not to laugh. If he thinks you're laughing at him, he gets stiff. Just now he was reading to me, sort of explaining where he starts from."

She held up the book again, and then dove into it, hunting through the pages with that bright, laughing, now-you-listen look of hers. When she found it and began to read, her voice was artificially high, like a child's reciting.

> "The community of masses of human beings has produced an order of life in regulated channels which connects individuals in a technically functioning organization, but not inwardly from the historicity of their souls. . . ."

"*Historicity* of their *souls*?" I said.

She frowned me down with her eyebrows while still smiling at me with her mouth.

> "The emptiness caused by dissatisfaction with mere achievement and the helplessness that results when the channels of relation break down have brought forth a loneliness of soul such as never existed before, a loneliness that hides itself, that seeks relief in vain in the erotic or the irrational until it leads eventually to a deep comprehension of the importance of establishing communication between man and man."

She stopped. It seemed I was supposed to comment. I said, "From the quality of the prose it's probably Kierkegaard, or maybe old Jaspers."

"Joe, you're incredible! It *is* Jaspers."

"So?" I said. "One of the four cloudy gospels. Once I read them all, trying to understand something, but I never succeeded. Do you understand what the historicity of the soul is? Or loneliness of soul, which is so much worse than ever before in man's history? Do you too take refuge in vain in the erotic and the irrational? Are you too dissatisfied with mere achievement?" The mere phrase made me start to roar. "*Mere* achievement! Jesus. Well, you've answered my question. There isn't a mind there, there's only a phonograph record cut on litmus paper."

From the way she laughed, I knew she had thrown

the passage at me just to *hear* me roar. (I have it in front of me now, and it is as ponderously banal as ever.) "The trouble with the people to whom that sounds profound," I said, "is that they're dissatisfied with mere achievement before they're in the slightest danger of accomplishing any. Is Peck having trouble with his great book, is that why he's getting sick of achievement?"

"Who told you?"

"Nobody told me. Is he?"

"You know," Marian said, studying me with her head on one side, "if you weren't so irascible you'd be very impressive. As a matter of fact, he's given the book up. He says it was only a preliminary exercise anyway, to help clarify his consciousness. It was part of his withdrawn phase. Writing is a dead art. The future belongs to interpersonal relations—communication between man and man, the way it says here."

I should have felt justified, I suppose, since Peck seemed to be fulfilling my prophesies for him. But all I felt was my old weary exasperation—years old, much older than my acquaintance with Jim Peck. I said, "His recent sociability is philosophic, not accidental, is that it? He's given up contemplation? Too much loneliness of soul there? How's he going to start the flow of communication between man and man?"

"He's going to organize a school," Marian said.

"*Organize*?"

"All right, improvise. He's already started improvising. The last time John was back, before he went up to Alaska, he and Margo and that blond one, Peter Whatever-his-name-is, were over here all one evening asking him how to approach the foundations."

"That figures," I said. "Let the Establishment fund the

Disestablishment. I hope John wasn't fool enough to help them."

"Oh, he gave them some names. He was sort of touched, they're so earnest and naïve. It hasn't got a chance anyway."

"I wonder," I said. "I've known some foundation people. They've all got projectitis. This could be just idiotic and far out enough to strike some board as interesting. What kind of school?"

She giggled. "Can't you imagine? No courses, no admissions requirements, no administration, no degrees, no faculty."

"No faculty," I said. "Now that's getting right at the root of the evil. They'll teach each other, is that it?"

"Of course."

"Under some bo tree."

"I suppose. In the country, anyway, outdoors as much as possible. There's a lot of frontier, pioneering enthusiasm in Jim, did you ever realize? He's sort of like a homesteader, over there."

"Squatter," I said.

"What?"

"Squatter. Nester. Intruder. Interloper. Trespasser."

"All right. Anyway they'll build their own meeting room and library, that's all they'd need."

I brooded for another while. Naturally I had read about this "free university" business. Naturally, since it was a contagion epidemic among his kind, Peck would think it a brilliantly original idea. He had no immunities, that boy. I said, "Except for the building and the bookshelves, I can't see but what they've got their school already, right there across the creek. Professor Peck's Outdoor Academy."

Sprawled in the lounge as if she had thrown herself there and alighted anyhow, with legs doubled under and brown arms hanging down, she watched me with the impish expression of a child waiting for the firecracker to go off under auntie's chair. "Did you look at his mailbox today?"

"I burned his daily trash. With my daily irritation. But I don't think I noticed his box. Why?"

"You didn't see the initials under his name? U.F.M.?"

"Unimaginably Foolish Man? Universal Federation of Morons?"

"University of the Free Mind," Marian said, and burst out in giggles again. "You've *got* it! It's in operation. It's being presented to Ford and Rockefeller and Carnegie as a going concern, with ten students. Including Julie and Debby."

Her laughter was so infectious that I laughed too. I was always willing to laugh with her, even at myself. One on me. A going concern, Oh ha ha ha.

We were sunk like minnows in the brown shade. John had been in the Pribilofs for ten days. Debby was away somewhere, perhaps riding with Julie. The Volkswagen bus had not been at the trail gate when I came down the hill. I could hear no sound from Peck's camp, screened by thick trees and brush. Maybe they were all out stealing books for the library. I said a little grimly, "A going concern that just might go out of business about tomorrow."

"Would you do that?" Marian said. "Are you that out of sympathy with young idealism?"

"Young idealism has been making a mark out of me for six months."

"They're just thoughtless. If you'd unbend and get to

know them better you'd probably like them. *I* like them."

"You like whate'er you look on."

She smiled, looking at *me*. "And you're old Scrooge and hate the young. Why are you so hard on these kids?"

"Look," I said. "Look!" Without warning my hands were shaking and my tongue stumbled over words. "Look, I've been *through* all this, I know it backward and forward, I could predict every insanity this fool will find his way to!"

As I said it, wishing that I wasn't saying it, or that I could say it without that agitation in my voice, I understood that I had been wanting to say it for a long time. To her, for her sympathy. Half ashamed, half hopeful, I looked into her vivid face, which in instant sympathy had lost its laughter and shaded itself to my tone. I found there the understanding I had been fishing for, and behind it—or was that something my own shame put there?—a sort of reserved judgment. I wondered if she sat there now listening to me with the same amused and scrupulous tolerance she showed Peck. But I didn't believe so; her eyes were full of wry love. "Your son," she said.

"My son, yes."

"Ruth told me."

"What else did she tell you? That I was a stiff-necked father and drove him to it?"

"No, because of course you weren't. Only that you were a lot alike, too much alike to get along, and that he never found anything he could *be*."

"And looked in all the wrong places," I said. "Just like this one-eyed king of the blind over here."

I was already sorry I had exposed myself, and irritated that in exposing myself I might have seemed to give too personal an explanation for my objections to Peck. I told myself that I would have found his beliefs and his activities dangerous nonsense if I had never had a son, or if my son had not wretchedly thrown away his life.

"I gather Peck has a father too," I said, "and blames every act of his own life on the old man. Papa was rigid, therefore all discipline must go. I wish he'd come around and spill his insides to me, I'd spray them with turpentine."

She had attractive, young, abrupt gestures, such as the one in which she now drew up her brown legs and pulled the denim skirt tight over her knees. "Don't you suppose he knows that? That's why he avoids you."

"He avoided me before he ever met me, practically. The first day he rode in here he had a chip on his shoulder that he kept daring me to knock off."

Marian sat smiling at me speculatively. Every thought that crossed her mind showed in her face like cloud shadows crossing a meadow. She said, "Maybe that was only his way of knocking off the chip he thought *you* were wearing."

"Maybe," I said, offended.

But she would not let me sulk. She leaned toward me and smiled me back to friendliness without losing her air of urgency and earnestness. "But that's too bad! Because you're somebody who could teach him all kinds of things if you could ever get close."

"If he'd let anybody teach him anything. You just admitted he avoids me."

"Yes," she said, and sank back thoughtfully. "I guess I did. They all quote that bromide about not being able to trust anybody over thirty. It might have to be someone closer to his own age."

"Somebody such as you, evidently."

"All right, I'm willing. I feel sorry for young people. They seem to find it harder and harder to believe the world values them or has a place for them."

"That's what comes of sneering at mere achievement. The world has a place for anybody who can *do* anything."

"Joe," she said, "I think you *want* to keep your prejudice against that groping boy."

"Groping!" I said. "Good God, he's the Mahatma, he's got the confidence of a road agent."

"You think so? If he really felt that way would he have to keep on acting so sure of himself? I think he's as uncertain as he can be—look how he hunts and hunts through all those yeasty philosophies for something to believe in. I do feel sorry for him. People his age have every right to be appalled at the world they find themselves in, the bomb and all the rest of it."

"Could Peck make a better world?" I said. "As for the bomb, I'm sick of the thing, hanging up there on its thread. It's no different from what's always hung there. And if anybody ever pushes the button, it'll be some nut like Peck, some wild-eyed enthusiast with no sense of history. It's his *temperament* I don't like—that True-Believer stance, and his faith in the emancipated individual. The whole history of mankind is social, not individual. We've learned little by little to turn human energy into social order. Outside the Establishment these kids despise so much, an individual doesn't exist, he hasn't got any language, character, art, ideas, anything, that didn't come to him from society. The free individual is an untutored animal. Society even teaches him the patterns of his revolt."

It was the kind of tirade I sometimes threw at her head just for the pleasure of arguing with her. This time I thought I meant it, but I said it like a vehement joke because I was still upset. Marian, a chameleon of moods, looked at me seriously with her great tilted eyes and said, "All right, maybe so. But if we're still talking about Jim, at least give him credit for good will. *He* isn't going to push any button. He hates violence. And don't you agree with him it's terrible what the human race has sometimes organized itself *for*?"

"Yes," I said. "Yes. We've learned how to do it for technology and war, not for much else. What does he want to do, resign? It's just about the way it's always been. I can't see anything different about the modern race *except* its technology. Whether that creates a record-breaking loneliness of soul I wouldn't know."

"And you don't think it can be improved."

"The technology? It's improving all the time."

"Come on, Joe Allston. The race."

The brown light was warm on her skin. It seemed to me that when the joking tone and the verbal sparring didn't tempt us into being merely provocative with one another, she was the one person in the world to whom I could say something I deeply felt. So I said, "You want to know what I think about the race?"

"Yes."

"It'll be a mouthful."

"I'm braced."

"All right," I said. "I think the race will multiply, for it is unfortunately very fertile. Since marriage is one of the conventions the Pecks are busy breaking down, more and more children will be illegitimate or deprived of the dubious advantages of what we used to call a home. Because of that and other strains, more and more adults will be hoodlums, criminals, and the effectively dispossessed, and from these both our demagogues and our novelists will increasingly take their morals and their attitudes and their lingo. First we help create these underworlds, and then out of guilt and sympathy we imitate them."

"Oh, but wait a minute!"

"No," I said. "You said you were braced. We imitate it out of pity, and we create it out of pity. Any civilization that achieves anything has losers—one of the reasons it achieves is that it has clear ways of telling its losers from its heroes. We have given up heroes—they go in for achievement. So we have more and more surviving losers, whom we imitate because we can't be ruthless enough to put them down. Are you still listening?"

"Not very quietly."

"I know. You're pitiful. So am I. But I try to be pitiful and still keep my head clear. The law, including the moral law, is never either just or merciful. It's just necessary. So the residual believers in order and stability and law and achievement will go on rigidifying the imperfect discipline of their society against the subversion of the criminal artists and the criminal saints. Are you attending?"

She nodded, an attentive, serious, half-smiling pupil. "Which are you?"

"Neither. I've resigned. I've really done what Peck used to think he was doing. But let me wind this up. We'll go on synthesizing new proteins and carbohydrates for the feeding of our growing billions. We will get very ingenious, but never fully successful, in disposing of the wastes we multiply. We'll invent new weapons and new defenses against them, and new forms of political threat and blackmail—or no, those are already well enough developed, in that area there's nothing new under the sun. Then one day we will succeed in doing what we've been headed for ever since the first halfman in Leakey's Gulch picked up a stick or a rock. Somebody *will* push the button, or one of our improvements will backfire, and our technical tinkering will finally destroy all life, and ourselves with it."

She was shaking her head, her smile widening. "I don't believe it."

"Wait," I said. "Hear me out. Everything's blasted, not so much as a virus left. There is a gap of geological time—geological? Astronomical, cosmic—and then patient old Mother Nature will start over, assuming we've left any nitrogen and other elements around, rolling her Sisyphus stone upward from the atom to the molecule to the polymer to the cell, and from the single cell to colonies of cells, and from colonies to forms with specialized organs, and through millions of experimental forms until she stumbles on something that will work for the Higher Tinkering—in our case it was a brain and an opposable thumb, but something else might work as well. Then consciousness comes into the world again, and tools, inventions, languages, arts, symbolic systems, and history begins, and nations form, and science begins to add one law to another, and the conscious creature handles his environment always more roughly, and overcrowds it too drastically, and things get competitive and hostile, and somebody pushes the button, and boom goes the stone to the bottom of the hill again. That's what I think about the human race."

She was looking at me steadily, unsmiling. Stretched on the lounge, still thin, five months pregnant (this would have been at the end of June), she looked as if she had swallowed a grapefruit. If she had not had that small perfect head, and those facial bones, and the great tilted eyes of such a sudden blue, she might have seemed almost grotesque, like one of those medieval Eves with a beautiful simpering face and a pot belly. Her hand lay on her abdomen now, as if protectively.

"You surprise me," she said.

"You never heard me deliver a sermon before."

"No, seriously. Because we're not so far apart as you seem to think, only you're gloomy about what you think, and I'm not, and you think consciousness comes into the picture a lot later than I do. I think it may be there even in the atom, because the atom is the first sign we can detect of *order*. Isn't it funny, I agree with you even about that. Order is the basis of everything. John and I sort of believe Teilhard de Chardin that all evolution is only a perfecting of consciousness. Do you?"

"I haven't read him."

"And if consciousness *is* being gradually perfected, then the area of choice is being gradually enlarged, isn't it? That's why, if I believe in order, I have to believe in *search* too, even if it seems as silly as Jim Peck's. The alternative's petrifaction, isn't it? Everything would just stop. So we have to risk disorder to keep the order of the universe expanding and consciousness growing. Doesn't it thrill you to think that, an inch at a time, we may be creeping toward wider and wider consciousness, until eventually man may just sort of emerge out of the tunnel and be in the full open?"

"That's what some of these modern kids think they're doing with drugs."

"No," Marian said. "I mean, I know they do, but I don't believe that. It couldn't be that easy. It has to be *earned*, to mean anything. It goes very *very* slowly, but we can't destroy the process any more than we can stay embedded in the sort of consciousness we have now, which we seem to have inherited from neolithic hunters. I think we'll perfect ourselves, finally, not destroy ourselves."

"If it depended on people like you," I said, "we would for sure."

"No, be serious."

"I was never more so."

"All right, if I could drop you a curtsy without getting up, I would. I'm the kind that will save the world and justify mankind. But I gather you think there are too few of me."

"There's only one of you."

Her head tipped back against the cushion, and she filled the grove with her laughter. "You're such a *courtly* old Gloomy Gus. How can you be so courtly and so gloomy about the world at the same time? Or how can you blame Peck for feeling alienated and hunting for panaceas?"

I was glad enough to be back on Peck. Whenever we verged on biology and reproduction I got uncomfortably aware of Marian's pregnancy, and of the mutilations under her checked boy's shirt. She struck me as at once too devotedly bent upon that baby and too systematically cheerful.

"I guess it's his stupid confidence that puts me off him most," I said. "I hate people with confidence—it's the surest sign of defective brains. Peck doesn't know any better than to believe he can improve things."

"If he's foolish you ought to feel sorry for him," Marian said. "Don't you feel sorry for me? Because I'm at least as hopeful of something better as he is."

"His kind of optimism I've seen before," I said. "Yours is something new, I'll have to think about it. At least it isn't just a rationalization for enjoying your kicks. The trouble with Peck, he doesn't realize that the world he lives in is holding itself together in desperation, with sticking plaster and patching cement and Band-Aids, and needs the support of every member. He thinks he lives in a society of bigots, hostiles, fuddy-duddies, and squares who conspire to limit his freedom and his fun. I wish there was such a conspiracy, I'd be its Brutus."

"That's just what I was saying. You declare war on him, you won't give him time to work things out."

"I didn't declare any war. He declared a revolution, he and all the others like him. That ruthless and healthy society I was just talking about would tell them to shape up or take the consequences. Our society is afraid of them. But I see no reason to open the palace doors so they can loot the wine cellars and turn the art gallery into a latrine. Youth is barbarian, you can't let it run you or it will run you down."

"Ah," she said, "but sometimes out of all its anarchy and groping it comes up with the idea that saves us."

"Maybe," I said. "You're speaking of a kind of youth I've never seen."

She watched me with her head tilted, as if trying to

make up her mind whether or not I was as conservative as I sounded. She began to smile. "But you still let Jim Peck live in your tree."

"Yes, curse it."

"Why?"

"Why? Because you keep suggesting that I'd be a flint-hearted monster not to—you and Ruth both. But also because I'm the sort of half-wit who won't take his own side in an argument for fear of sounding illiberal."

We sat laughing at each other, the brief minute or two of seriousness dissolved and gone. I was always totally happy in her company, even when we argued and even when our subject was something as frivolous as Peck. Even when her directness forced me close to things I had no intention of talking about, though I might hint them to get her sympathy.

"I have one further question," I said. "How can you stand to talk to him, now that summer's come on?"

She squinted her eyes and wrinkled her nose in the mischievous-child smile. "Ah—outside he's all right. He does a lot of exercise, after all, and he doesn't have all the facilities for bathing."

"On the contrary, he's got a plastic pipe hooked to my water line."

"Maybe he isn't aware."

"Come on," I said. "You can't believe that. He's just deliberately and calculatedly dirty. I was reading a book the other day that said something about the lairs of all carnivorous and omnivorous beasts being unseemly. One step in the progress you believe in has been to make human lairs a little less unseemly. But here's old Peck, vegetarian as he is, doing his best to unravel that little knot of progress, and his lair is as unseemly as he can make it. I think he's dedicated to the purpose of smelling worse than his daddy's stockyards. It's a mystery to me how those girls of his hang on, and why."

"He's quite good-looking," Marian said, "and he's got a marvelous voice."

"I suppose. Nevertheless, I have trouble believing my eyes about his love life. The mind boggles."

"I wonder if he really has a love life? Somehow he doesn't seem quite the type."

"Take my word for it. He seeks relief—I hope in vain—in the erotic and the irrational, on his way to shedding his loneliness of soul and promoting communication between man and man, or man and woman. And the hard way, the hard way, against all probability. Next time you see him tell him I've got a new motto for his ashram."

"What?"

"Be Yourself. Evil Is a Bath and a Haircut. Good Is B.O. Plenty and Pussy Galore."

It set her giggling again. "Maybe I should have John suggest a man's deodorant."

"Deodorant?" I said. "Hell, he probably uses Accent. Let's change the subject. When's John coming home?"

"Pretty soon, a couple of weeks probably."

"Then he won't make the LoPrestis' Fourth of July party."

"I doubt it. He should stay till he gets everything he went for. Then he'll be home the rest of the summer."

"Good," I said. "We'll pick you up for the party. But we'll be glad when he gets back. You shouldn't be left alone so much, especially with old Comus and his crew next door."

That really did make her laugh. "Oh Lord," she said, "what a *limitless* imagination! I may be scared of a hundred things, but not of James McParten Peck."

"I'm glad to hear it. I'm also glad to see you lying down here, for a change. You do too much. How's the baby coming?"

She patted her abdomen. "Coming right along."

"When's B-day?"

"End of October."

"I'll mark it on the calendar."

We remained smiling at one another, run-down, a little awkward. When I stood up Marian put her legs carefully over the side of the lounge and hoisted herself upright. She batted her brilliant eyes and smoothed the podded front of her denim skirt. Plaintively she said, "Never have a baby, Joe. You can't imagine what a chore viviparous reproduction is."

"Don't kid me," I said. "You want this baby very much."

"Yes," she said happily, squinting at me in the sun-spattered shade. "Very *very* much!"

6

Friday night, July 3

Dear Marian,

Maybe I will send you this letter, maybe I won't. But the more I think about our talk the other day, the more I feel inclined to write it. You thought I was pretty rough on Peck, and I have the impression you think I am suffering from some unhealed trauma about my son, Curtis, and am taking it out on Peck. It isn't impossible,

I suppose—few things are. But as I told you, I have been through all this before. Since Curt died I have been over it ten thousand times. If I could convince myself I was to blame, do you think I wouldn't accept the guilt along with the grief? Do you think I would deliberately repeat history with this Peck boy, who reminds me so much of Curt? I can find plenty of things to blame in my temperament and my actions, but I can't find the specific things that caused Curt. I can't find adequate causes for somebody like Peck, I weigh his beliefs against mine and I can't conclude that I am wrong. I have to believe, in fact, that it is my moral duty—which I'm not exactly performing—to resist him.

It would embarrass me to say to your face some of the things I expect to write down here. I was never one for the couch, I don't unburden readily. If my conscience visits me in the night I assume it wants to be alone with me. To repeat our dialogues seems to me too often a sort of self-justification. But I will try to repeat them to you with as little of that as I can manage.

One of my difficulties in Curt's case was that every time I acted according to my principles I was instantly at war with him. Every time I swallowed my principles, or let Ruth persuade me to be indulgent, I felt ashamed. So far as I can tell, I have not changed since Curt died, which doesn't mean I don't still have bad times over his memory and am not full of regrets. But my trouble is not the prick of conscience. It's guilt, I suppose, but a guilt that I can't justify. If I had it to do over again, I can't see how I would have done it differently.

I am probably the last one to say what Curt really was, since I never understood what he thought he was trying to be, and was never sure he was trying to be anything. Maybe he was trying *not* to be anything.

He was crosswise in the channel of his life for thirty-seven years—he was born crosswise. I am not modern man at all, but he was modern youth to the seventh power. He never got over being modern youth. He was crypto-communist youth during the late thirties, pacifist-internationalist youth in the forties, and overage beat youth in the fifties, and nothing very seriously, and nothing for keeps. As I look back at him, I see that he *wasn't* much of anything, he was simply against. I have read his life, and arranged for its publication, two dozen times: rebel in uniform, nonconformist who runs in packs and sings in close harmony with his age group. He was willful child, sullen boy, prep-school delinquent, army reject, postwar lush. Whose fault? It is usual for distressed parents to accept the blame our psychologists are eager to hand them, and I think Ruth and I would accept it if our judgment told us we must. Sometimes we did accept it, against our better judgment, and tried to cope with him by dealing with ourselves. But appeasement never worked, and no matter how many ways I tried to persuade him of my concern and my affection, I never found his guard down, and my patience was never long enough to outbox him. Put that down as one thing I accept blame for: impatience. Maybe you can make an explanation from it. I can't. It explains a little, but by no means all.

Many of our friends probably explained him with that glib formula about sons with high-powered fathers, doing me the honor of thinking me more high-powered than I am. It could have been the other way around. He may have felt some secret shame that I was only a nursemaid of writers and not a writer myself. The apartment was always full of them, he grew up among celebrities, and he could have made comparisons. But that should have led him to treat me with contempt or condescension, perhaps with pity. Not with hatred.

Principles, I said a minute ago. Values—a very unfashionable word, since to hold any you have to deny the validity of their contraries, and thus seem censorious. I honestly believe that the counsel I gave Curt was mainly sound, and I don't think too much of it was holier-than-thou. After all, we lived in the world, not in a parsonage. I tried to give him a code to live by. He wanted not one scrap of it, he didn't agree with a single value I held. I had got my values from wherever we do get them, out of the air or out of books or out of contact with people I had to admire, and he got his in exactly the same way except that he was immune to mine. Mine, say, were old-fashioned bacterial values. His were viral, and from my point of view virulent. He went absolutely unerringly to attitudes that he knew I disapproved or despised, and the only way to live with him in peace would have been to submit to his beliefs. Ruth was more willing than I was—after all he was her only child, and she loved him—but she liked the way he was going no better than I did.

I would not submit to his beliefs. I believed, and I still believe, that some periods of human history and some phases of human culture are better than others, and that it isn't always the creeping toward perfection that I know you want to believe in. Some codes are better than the codes that displace them; and I believe this is a corrupt age because it accepts everything as equal to everything else, and because it values indulgence more than restraint. I guess I honor the Roman republic more than the empire. The one believed in austere virtue, and the other had bread and circuses, like ourselves.

There is a book of Ford Madox Ford's, one of that fat tetralogy, that he called with characteristic ungrace *Some Do Not*. He was adenoidal, and they say he smelled like Jim Peck, but he had something. Some do not, if only to show that they can refrain. You don't have to shoot yourself like a Dostoevski intellectual to assert the will. You don't have to commit whimsical existential crimes to prove your freedom. You can take hold of yourself, like training a horse, and that is both pleasure and morality.

I never persuaded Curtis. I was neither a good enough teacher nor a good enough example. Train yourself for what? he would ask. To sell bonds? To be a good corporation man? To demonstrate shaving between the halves of televised football games? To make a lot of money? To contribute to this vulgarian's nightmare they call a civilization? To acquire things? No, I would tell him, beginning, God help me, to roar. To be a man. Isn't that enough? To be a man whose word is trusted and whose generosity can be depended on and who doesn't demand something without giving something himself. Fair trade, he would answer me. Inviolability of contract. The morals of the stock exchange, which never cheats a customer but which goes up on every brush-fire war and skyrockets on every big one.

What should one do? If Ruth had had any better luck with him I would have thought that he simply had to attach himself to antifatherly gods until he proved himself a man in his own terms. Ruth was infallibly gentle with him, though tartness is more her natural style. She didn't push him, she followed him clear to the bottom of his burrow, trying to understand, she forgave him incessantly, she was the pacifying force when he and I clashed. And he went out of his way to treat her with even greater impatience and contempt than he treated me. His wretched treatment of his mother was one of the commonest sources of our quarrels. Sometimes I wondered if he didn't abuse her because she tended to take his side—he wanted no mediator between us.

It does me no good to reflect that filial rebellion is common. Mutual respect, though perhaps not common, is possible—I've seen it. It becomes impossible only when the value systems of the two antagonists are irreconcilable, as they seem to be between Fran LoPresti, who is conventional, and her daughter, who is hell-bent not to be.

Curtis could have disagreed with us incessantly if we had felt in him some integrity that gave his disagreement weight. We couldn't. I have to blame myself for not finding any way of reaching him, but I can't feel that either Ruth or I had anything much to do with his corruption. The twentieth century corrupted him, the America that he despised corrupted him, industrial civilization corrupted him with the very vices he thought he scorned in it. It encouraged him to hunt out the shoddy, the physical, the self-indulgent, the shrill, and the vulgar, and to call these things freedom, and put them above the Roman virtue that, so help me, is the only moral stance I can fully admire. And like Peck, he always had smoke screens, political or aesthetic, to hide his hypocrisy from others and perhaps from himself.

He was drunken, disorderly, and promiscuous from early adolescence. We might have thought those irregularities normal and exploratory if he had shown even temporary contrition about them; but he indulged them as if he must, to maintain his self-respect. *Non serviam.* All right, we could have taken that too, if we had found any fallen-angel grandeur of mind or spirit in him. But we had to observe that he was ungenerous, that he gave nothing and took all he could, that he felt responsibility for nothing, love for no one. He had such a gift for the wrong companions that it was fair to think of him, not them, as the bad influence. He had a good body that he abused, and a good mind that he used for nothing but searching out new forms of challenge and insubordination, new kicks, new ways to evade obligation. He sponged on people, especially women; he betrayed friends, especially women; and he fell for every crack-brained groupy arty-intellectual fad over a period of twenty years.

In his earlier teens he had a political phase, walked picket lines, attended meetings of the Young Communist League, collected money for the Spanish Loyalists. Fine. For a while, though he alarmed us, we were even rather proud: he showed signs at least of a compassionate social conscience. Actually, he had no more political interest than a snowshoe rabbit and no more economics than a grasshopper. He liked secrecy and rebellion and dusty basement meeting places, and emancipated girls in lisle stockings, and the sound of broken-down mimeograph machines cranking out insurrection and intransigence.

When the war came on, he was swept naturally into pacifism—his canoe was already on those waters, he didn't even have to paddle. Later, when he spoke of his troubles in prep school, he liked to imply that he was thrown out for his pacifist beliefs, and it is true that he was one of a group that in 1941 marched in tin hats and gas masks, bearing scornful placards, outside the classroom windows of a master who was hot for war against Hitler. But Curt wasn't thrown out for his conscientious beliefs, and he was thrown out more than once. One school sent him home because he had been scraped up drunk off the lawn three weekends in a row, and was insolent to the masters who reprimanded him. The second fired him because he and two other boys smuggled a girl into the dorm and kept her there for three days. A master coming to remonstrate mildly about the pacifist picket line found her there, locked in the bedroom with a lot of girly magazines, a bag of caramels, and a bottle of sloe gin.

For a few months in 1944 Curt was in the army, but he came out quickly with a PN discharge—homosexuality. From what I hear of the army, it does not throw you out on those grounds unless you go out of your way to be challenging in your aberrations. I don't think for a minute that Curt was a fairy. He wanted out of the army and he had no more self-respect than to get out that way.

It is a painful chronicle, and I gain nothing but renewed distress by writing it down. There were two cheap marriages and two cheap divorces. There was a banjo-picking phase and a barefoot-saint phase. He rode a motorcycle across the continent, he tried Zen and poetry, the Village and Sausalito. I found him jobs and he lost them or quit them within weeks or months. Once he worked quite happily for half a year as a mechanic in a garage (was it dirty enough to suit him, or did he find some queer heartbreaking security in the untaxing performance of a simple skill?). That ended in a traffic accident and a drunk-driving fine. Mainly he lived on us and on the little trust fund that Ruth's mother had been so ill-advised as to settle on him before she died. It gave him just enough to leave him free. You asked me if I didn't believe in freedom and I told you I didn't, not much. Freedom was the worst thing that could have happened to Curtis.

Once in a while, after he had passed his twenties and could no longer pretend that he was just postponing his life until he could "come to grips with reality" and "find himself"—my God the cant that apologists for these lost souls use!—he made half-meant, convulsive efforts to do or learn or be something. These fits came on him when, because he was ill or broke or at odds with some woman, he came back to the apartment for a spell of fatted calf. During those spasms he would be brisk and energetic; we heard him sing in the shower; he wore coat and tie when he went out on important errands. Heartbreaking, because we knew it was a false front, and yet it gave us glimpses of what it might be to have a son with whom we could get along.

False starts, he made a dozen. Once he signed up for a writing course in Washington Square—did you ever notice how pitifully these people are converted into believers by the word "creative"?—but he found the instructor tedious and retired to somebody's cottage up in the Housatonic valley to write on his own. He and his guests wrecked the place and cost us a friend. Once he was going to study architecture—this when he was past thirty—and talked his way into a job as a draftsman on the strength of his facility at free sketching. Two weeks that lasted; he said he couldn't stand drawing other people's lines. One year he spent a lot of time in the Village, painting he said, and taking some extension class or other. That too faded away. There was a long and relatively peaceful year when he was abroad, living in an unheated room on the Nyhavn in Copenhagen, a place he was drawn to because he had heard it was the toughest of Europe's waterfronts. Yet I wonder. I had a Danish phase myself, I went back there too, looking for something and not finding it. I wonder if Curt was trying to follow some raveling thread back through his labyrinth? It saddens me to think so, for I'm sure it broke, he ended up lost in the same old mazes.

Every time he failed to perform, or lost his job, or lost interest, he fell back into the Village or wherever he happened to alight. Right back into his old galvanic-twitch life. His personal motives were freedom and pleasure, and he misread them both.

Then a little less than three years ago, thirty-seven years old, with not quite a prep-school education but with a record of scorn for practically everything the human race ever thought worthy, he had another of those painful spasms of the refurbished will. Because his aptitude scores were high and friends of mine would still write letters for him, he got himself admitted to San Diego State College. He expected us to applaud, and we did. After all, we were penitent, we were clearly not good for him and never had been. Any college reckless enough to admit him had our gratitude, any move he made that looked serious stirred our hope.

In September he drove across with a friend. Contrary to custom, and promptly enough to encourage us, we had a letter. The school was O.K., better than he had expected. Freshman classes were infantile, but he had goofed off so long he had something coming. He thought he could take an overload and go to summer school and so crowd the degree into three years. He had an apartment over a garage, pleasant and quiet. The weather was as advertised, the beach marvelous. The big thing around there was surfing: decrepit as he was, he was giving it a try. Mother would probably raise a cheer on hearing he had shaved off his beard—it hadn't seemed quite appropriate on the beach.

He exaggerated our concern with trivial stigmata. I am no lover of facial hair, but I would have applauded a beard as long as Rip Van Winkle's if I could have been sure that Curt was finally, after so much disastrous self-waste, going to pull himself together into a package, even if the package turned out to be a Southern California Natural Man.

There were no more letters. In November a friend, asked to look him up, reported that Curtis had dropped school and given up his apartment. After some detective work, he had found him living in a trailer colony near the beach, with a girl and a surfboard. Our informant said it was not a very attractive colony, more a motorcycle bohemia than a surfer's camp: plenty of black leather, greasy jeans, long hair, late parties, and raids by the narcotics squad hunting backyard and window-sill weeds.

Well, so the more he changed the more he was the same thing. We swallowed the news without real surprise. If he was indeed a custard pie, he was not going to stay nailed to any wall. I suppose we finally gave up on him then, though we had given up on him several times before, and though one night Ruth, reading a magazine article about surfing, looked up at me and said, "You know, surfing sounds like fun. And it isn't only kicks, it's a cult. You have to have real skill and nerve." Yes, I said, so I had heard. "It ought to be a healthy life, hadn't it?" she said. "Healthier than that zoo down in the Village, anyway?"

"Ah, Ruthie," I said. "Ruthie, Ruthie, Ruthie!" But I had had the same sneaking thought myself. At least there was nothing false or contemptible about surfing, even if it didn't seem quite the highest end to which a man might devote himself.

That would have been about Christmas time. In February we had a call from the La Jolla police. Curtis was dead, drowned in a surfing accident, his body recovered.

Ruth was getting over an operation. I persuaded her to stay with her sister in Bucks County and flew out to bring Curt back. I saw his girl—a trifle, a tanned gewgaw, string-haired, ready to be defiant if I gave her a bad time. But why should I give her a bad time? She cried, saying he was the greatest guy she ever knew, he wasn't satisfied with anything but the very best out of life; and looking at me out of her wet slightly crossed eyes she whispered, "Sometimes I wonder if he really slipped and got hit. Sometimes I wonder if he didn't let go. He was capable of it."

I had wondered the same myself, but I didn't feel like joining in her speculations. When I left her she probably went off with one of the other great guys who lived in the clutter of trailers, campers, and converted delivery trucks scattered along that scabby little ravine. Or maybe she stayed on in Curt's, which I sold on the spot to a couple of motorcyclists with sideburns clear to their jawbones.

They didn't show me Curtis there. I saw him only

back in Bucks County, at the funeral. It seemed I looked through a scald of tears at the total failure of his life and mine. I thought he had a manly face. Without the beard he had worn ever since beards emerged as part of the uniform of alienation, he reminded me of the bronze charioteer in Delphi. The beach life had been good for him. He looked fit and young, and his brown hair was streaked. Sun or peroxide? Inescapable as it was, the question shamed me. After all, he was thirty-seven years old.

I still can't think of his face composed on the final satin without a clutch in my chest. The hair might have been as false an emblem as the beard had been, but the face had given up all its poses and looked merely young, incredibly young, far younger than it had any right to look, the very face of kicks-crazy America, unlined by thinking, unmarked by pain, unshadowed even by years of scrupulous dissoluteness, untouched by life—or by death either—except for a slight discontented droop at the corners of the lips. I could not answer the suggestion of resentment and dissatisfaction in it. Maybe, if the girl's suspicion had any basis, he had sidled into death as he had taken up every job and project of his life, and then found that he couldn't quit it as he had quit everything else.

Somehow Ruth and I had always had some groundless faith that he would come around. The boy having trouble becoming a man would eventually, perhaps late but eventually, overcome his trouble. These oats would be sown, he would get over having to sniff at every post where some existential junky or disengaged beat or criminal saint had lifted his leg. There would come a time when he wouldn't have to snarl at his gentle humorous mother, and when he and I might talk, go to a ballgame, have a drink, discuss a book, without that miserable stiff-legged father-son suspicion and that unsleeping awareness of our differences. Without admitting it to each other, we had counted on time, and now time was run out. Never never never never never. If Lear was an old fool, and he was, he was by the end a contrite and suffering fool. So was I, for I could not put aside the thought that perhaps, out in those glassy rollers inside the violet band of the kelp beds, Curt had looked it all in the face, himself in the face, and let go the board. There had been no wounds or signs of injury on his body. Most suicides, I believe, are spiteful. If Curt was really a suicide, did he go hating, or did he go hopeless? Either way, it meant he couldn't bear any more. Neither, thinking about it, could I.

Sometime after the funeral, the girl—there was something human and touching about her little act of responsibility—sent on a box of Curt's personal effects, including his books. I could have listed them without opening the box: Miller, Albee, Kerouac, Sartre, Genet, the Marquis de Sade, Ginsberg, Burroughs—a poison garland from the Grove. I could not have told you then, and I can't tell you now, whether those books really corrupted him. I think they only corroborated him, without quite giving him the confidence of his convictions.

That ends Curt's story. I think I must go on a little with my own. I felt that I had to be steady for Ruth's sake, and for a while I seemed to be. But in the end she bore it better than I, for no amount of thinking could reconcile me to the way our only son had died, irresponsibly and frivolously, incongruously uniting in himself a sun-worshiper and a nauseast; and if unhappy, as he surely was, unhappy by his own asserted will. I judged him, yes I did, even in death and even while I was stricken with the sense of his unhappiness, and I judged myself for judging him, and could find no way of avoiding judging him.

February and March were a dull sad endless time for us both. I wasn't sleeping, but when Ruth tried giving me sleeping pills I made a virtue of an old prejudice against tranquilizers. Probably I was punishing myself. I have already admitted that I believe in guilt, not as an indulgence but as an essential cautery of the soul. One of my troubles was that I felt guilty without being able to persuade myself intellectually that I could have acted any other way.

So I ground the coals to my breast in my private dark. I had exiled myself to Curt's old room on the excuse that I didn't want to keep Ruth awake, but what I really wanted was Curt's ghost to myself. It was the worst time of my life. Night after night I went on composing dialogues, revising his life and mine, explaining away estrangement with reasons that I did not fully believe, being wiser in these fictions than I had ever been in fact, putting into clear prose this clash of values and the need for self-discipline, self-respect, clear purpose, all that. I said persuasively everything that at one time or other I had said angrily or hopelessly. And every time, I disgusted myself with my own mouthings, I never persuaded myself that I would have persuaded him. I felt that I couldn't leave even his ghost alone to be itself as it wanted to be. Why? Because I couldn't accept him, living or dead, as he had wanted to be. I wanted reconciliation, oh yes, but on my terms, because I couldn't convince myself that my terms were wrong. I defined myself as bigot without shaking my convictions at all.

Within weeks his living face had begun to fade into a few waxwork expressions: an impish boy (what ever happened to him, where did he go?) caught in motion while he played with a terrier on a wide New Hampshire lawn; a sandaled beat who leaned his head against a wall and raised his unclean reddish beard in contemplation; the athlete whose composed handsome discontented face burned upward from white satin under the carefully brushed streaked hair.

To the fading or frozen expressions that hid my son's unreachable privacy I tried to speak my heart, and I had the advantage of endless revisions; but the dead listened no more than the living had. He would have none of my love unless it came unqualified and uncritical and in spite of every provocation—and it is simply uncanny how much of that spirit I detect in Jim Peck, who isn't of course after my love, but who is certainly trying to corner me without losing any of his own men. It is not a kind of love I am ever likely to be able to give. I don't think any human being is entitled to it, and anyway I can't separate love and respect. Curt demanded what I couldn't give, I insisted on what he wouldn't accept. Never never never never never.

Trying to explain myself, I told him about my own life, including some shameful episodes, but all that did was revive a lot of unhappinesses that I had lived down and put aside years before, and remind me of old guilts that were not unlike Curt's. Thinking filled my days with boredom and my nights with self-loathing. Out of my son's death I plucked the conviction of my own imperfection and failure, and yet I could not name the ways I might have taken so as not to fail.

There were times in the office when, faced by some contractual quibble or other, I was drowned in disgust; times when dictating a letter I heard my voice like a twittering of sparrows. By the end of March, Ruth was saying to me, "Joe, you've got to take a vacation. You've got to get away for a while."

I could easily enough have justified a trip to Rome or London or Paris. But I would have run into clients in any of those glamorous capitals on any afternoon. I found too that I didn't want any two-week interim followed by a return to the office. I wanted to wipe the board off clean, not with a dusty eraser but with a kerosened rag, the way we did it every Friday afternoon in Northfield, Minnesota, when my mother was keeping house for a professor at Saint Olaf College and I was briefly a Danish kid, possessed of an unexpected identity between the Swedes who snooted the Norwegians and the Norwegians who scorned the Swedes. A blackboard as clean as Miss Tidemann's fifth-grade room on a Friday afternoon, a mind emptied of all that could not now be helped, a full retreat of the soul.

Nel mezzo del cammin di nostra vita
Mi ritrovai per una selva oscura . . .

Nel mezzo? Quasi alla fine. I was more than sixty, past the age when I should have had to settle ultimate questions. But ultimate questions were the only kind I wanted to ask, such questions as might divert my attention from Curtis, who was past hurt or help, and onto myself, who felt ambiguously but bitterly responsible.

It may have been only Ruth's insistence on a trip that got me to believing the cure for my unease might lie in a place. I had never had a place of my own, I had spent my life in motion even while I persuaded myself I was domesticated. A housebroke vagrant. Call me Ishmael, but add, Jenny kissed me. I had an alley cat's appreciation of stability without having a place either of origin or of domicile. We had camped in Manhattan for thirty-seven years, with at least one trip abroad during each of the thirty-seven. When I began to wonder if it might be possible to go back and find where the road forked (*Che la diritta via era smarrita!*), I couldn't think where I might go.

If I had had a home town, I would have gone straight back to it on one of those middle-aged pilgrimages to search out the boy I was, the man I started out to be, and I might have half expected to find myself barefooted and with a fishpole, like a *Post* cover by Norman Rockwell. Young America, freckled and healthy, the finest crop grown in the soil of democratic institutions. But I had been raised on the run by an unfortunate woman whose first husband, my father, shot himself in the barn, and whose second, a drunken railroad man with D.T.'s and periodic paralysis, was finally backed over by a switch engine in the Saint Paul yards. After he died, when I was six, we moved from place to place. My mother, with a thick Danish accent and no education beyond her twelfth year, had no skill to sell, and no beauty, only her hard hands. She kept other people's house and tended other people's children.

We lived in shallow, laborious, temporary ruts, and over their rims she was always seeing some dawn or rainbow, the kind of rainbow that had brought her to the States, only now it was one that always promised something better for me. Generally she waited until the school term was over, and then we were gone to where a letter or a rumor or a chance conversation over coffee had persuaded her she must go—another town, another house, another job, strange faces, strange rooms, strange smells, strange streets to be learned. Sometimes I have felt that I could smell my way backward down my life from stranger's house to stranger's house, like a homing dog, by little tokens left on maple or elm or light pole. I would know one place by the smell of crushed mulberries, another by the reek of trying lard, still another by the dampness of laundry hung on a clotheshorse under which I lay hidden and heard the surf of adult voices overhead. There is no plan or continuity or permanence. My first sixteen years of going to and fro in the earth were a passage from vacuum to vacuum.

My teachers thought me gifted; eventually I found my way to a scholarship and a part-time job at the University of Illinois—it really *is* a land of opportunity and there really *is* such a thing as disinterested human kindness. Or the intention of kindness, for like many good intentions, the help of my high-school principal had mixed results. I was exploded into books and ideas and the company of people so different from those I had known in my maid's-room, boardinghouse life that they might have been another species. I was in a constant tremble like an overfilled glass. I discovered that I *was* bright, and it made me drunk to realize it. And it never occurred to me, though I had worked summers since I was twelve, that instead of blotting up teachers' attention and devouring books I might be out earning some money to make my mother's life easier. When we're young, we take so casually every sacrifice offered by the old. At least I did. Also I know that if it *had* occurred to me she would never have permitted it for one hour.

She would have thought even a year, even a semester, a catastrophic wasting of my talents, though I was only sixteen and could have spared it easily.

I had been a child unnaturally self-contained, I had had to learn early to be seen and not heard. I had hidden myself in corners and window seats and backyards and sheds with books or projects of my own, knowing even at seven or eight that the maid's child would be suffered, and sometimes sentimentally made over, but not indulged. When college blew up all those inhibitions, I must have been insufferable, the sort of cub who would now set my teeth on edge. Anyone who did not accept the opinions that I had developed within the hour, or read in a book ten minutes ago, or advanced in argument because the argument obviously called for them, was an idiot, and apart from thee and me there were a lot of idiots in the world. You know me—I have not substantially changed. Among other things, I remember resolving that I would live without emotion. I had some hot debates in which I disparaged poetry because it was irrational and therefore unreliable. An emotion, I said, was an imperfect thought. I would live in the thin pure air of reason. (Ashes on my head—I was preposterous. Yet I was recognizably the ancestor of the intemperate old fool you know.)

My mother could find no job in Champaign-Urbana, or pretended she couldn't. After coming down with me from Elgin, where we had been living, she warmed herself for a day among buildings, stadium, lawns full of students and squirrels, and then she went away again, probably out of pure delicacy because she could see she embarrassed me, and got a job in a boardinghouse in Chicago.

I saw her go with relief. Later I hid her letters from my roommate, because I was ashamed of their lined tablet paper and their penciled, misspelled, mixed Danish and English. Though I thought I loved her, and told myself that I would rescue her and bring her to my mansion as soon as I finished college and had set my life on the track to some star, I would not for all the praise I hoped to win and all the money I expected to make have had it known that my mother was a maid of all work in a rooming house, a servant to clerks and shop-girls.

Not too many of her letters had to be read in haste and hidden in a drawer. In December of my first college year, going down cellar to stoke the furnace, she caught her heel in a rotten step and fell. My only visit back to Chicago was to her funeral.

Luckless and deprived, she lies in a South Side cemetery in an unvisited grave, a clumsy Danish servant girl without one relative besides myself on the American continent. She had married, supported, and buried two weak husbands, and thereafter given herself up to making a life for her son. It all reads like one great cliché. But maybe love and sorrow are always clichés, ambition and selfishness and regret are clichés, death is a cliché. It's only the literary, hot for novelty, who fear cliché, and I am no longer of that tribe.

I hadn't thought of my mother ten times in twenty years, but in the bad time after Curt's death she came every night to join the spirit of my dead son. Between them they drowned my heart and mind, for I had to set her devotion to me, which was the best thing in my life until I met Ruth, against my own unwillingness to accept or forgive Curt. Would she have judged me, no matter how selfish and demoralized I might have become? Would she, in my place, have been able to reconcile herself to a scapegrace and give him the uncritical love that I was half convinced he had been demanding of me? And if she had, would I have approved? Down in my heart, wouldn't I have thought her sentimental, and abused her for the love I knew I had not earned?

My two ghosts kept Ruth from getting close to me, and they made me sick for what I had done to people I loved, and what they had done to me. If I forgave Curt, I had to forgive myself. And there were the talents I had got from the great Grab Bag—I had failed to make anything of them, but I couldn't determine whom or what I had failed, for I couldn't refer myself to any source, tribe, family, region, nation, tradition, gene pool, or anything else to which the wastage of my life could be called a loss. I grew to hate the thin dispersal of my relatives, my mother in Chicago earth and my son in Bucks County, each alone among strangers. And here was I, random and now childless, making meaningless orbits in the Madison Avenue void.

Lose a dog in the woods, no matter how *oscura*, and he will follow the back track to the place where he went in. At past sixty, rather deep in the woods, I was lifting my nose from among the mold and mushrooms to sniff at any cold scent that promised to lead me somewhere. But I could find no place that was mine. The crisscrossing trails of my mother's life had confused all the scents.

In the end, we made, one after the other, the two moves that are possible to Americans and lost dogs. We smelled our way back to the old country and sniffed for a while around Copenhagen and around the little island of Taasinge in the southwestern Baltic where my mother was born. We learned something, perhaps, but that is another story. What matters is that I didn't smell one thing that was familiar or that meant anything personal; not a person, not an echo, not a whiff from the past. Europe was cut off, no longer anything to me.

So we did the other thing that Americans and lost dogs can do, we quit trying to backtrack and went forward. We turned our backs on everything remembered and came out to make a new beginning in California. It wasn't a radical act, in a way. It was a habitual one, it conformed to twenty generations of American experience. We would have pooh-poohed the idea that we were living by the Garden myth, but we were, we are. We expected to become less culpable by becoming more withdrawn. We shook dust from our garments and combed bewilderment like twigs from our hair and we abandoned the woods. I am determined not to fight shadows any more, or sit like a nitwitted old woman sorting guilt and blame. I wouldn't be surprised if Peck and I were unanimous on the subject of harmlessness, at least in theory. I don't want to harm anybody, I don't want anybody harming me.

So you see why this Peck exasperates me? He reminds me of things I don't want to remember. He threatens me, he endangers my peace. If he and Curtis are the future, then I am an irreconcilable past. They leave me nothing, not even the comfort of blindness, because I think I see them very clearly—as clearly as I see my own incapacity to accept them or deal with them.

And, of course, can't dismiss them either, any more than I can make up my mind to shoo Peck out of my oak tree.

Well, I have been writing you for two hours, trying

to say a little more intelligibly some things I said too uncompromisingly the other day. I have come at you like an old weepy barfly, and cornered you, and taken your hand in my damp hand and told you the story of my sad life. I am a continual surprise to myself: I had not thought I was one to spill my guts in this fashion. Usually I am nimbler at ironies and evasive tactics than at the confessional business. Except to me, none of this that I've written you is in any way important. But it is personal and it is serious, two things I have always found it troubling to be.

This letter I found recently under a stack of old papers in the study. I had never finished it, signed it, or sent it. But it reminds me that even back in midsummer Marian had begun to force or coax me out of the burrow where I lived with the gophers and the moles and the other creatures of darkness.

If Peck was a threat to peace, what was she?

V

ONE KIND OF midsummer day here starts gray, with a cool sweat of dew on the leaves, a smell of wetted oat grass, dark wetness in the angles of fences and on the patio screeds. The sky is obscured by the unmoving unmottled ceiling of high fog that will burn away about ten. Once it does, the rest of the day will be warm and even until the evening chill comes on.

But two or three times in a summer we will get up to find the morning cloudless but milky, with a red sun and a vinegarish taint of smog even up here in the hills. The valley is murked out, the near ridges are dim, the far ones gone. If there is any wind, it is a light drift from the inland valleys. The newspapers will speak of inversions, and record a climbing smog count, until, after three or four days of increasing heat and smarting eyes, the built-in air conditioner that lies off the Pacific shore will move inland and hang over the skyline in rolls of cottony fog, blowing us instantly cool again.

The Fourth of July was one of the red-dawn days. When I got up at seven and went out on the terrace the sun was like an orange through Weld's orchard. The air was sour and still. Between the cinderish bricks of the patio the screeds were warping upward at the ends. Thinking how that brick lawn would radiate heat later, I had a disloyal moment of yearning for the cool grass and broad-leafed shade of rainier climates.

Catarrh had left nothing on the mat. He was not a summer hunter. The first year he had eaten a lot of lizards, but they obviously disagreed with him and he had given them up. He was too lazy to hunt widely, and once he had cleaned out the vermin from the immediate yard in the spring, he relapsed into apathetic snoozing in the flower beds and scavenging the occasional bird that broke its neck against the windows.

I was congratulating myself that at least, now the adobe had dried like cement, Catarrh's spring extermination would last. Then I walked around the house and discovered that within the past twenty-four hours a gopher had come boring straight under the walk, leaving collapsing bricks in his wake, and was already throwing up mounds of dirt in the rose garden.

These things make me swear out loud. They're infallible, they find your weakness like heat-seeking missiles. The walk was my only remaining weakness, for within half a year of completing the patio itself, all laid on sand and with sand swept between the bricks as the landscape plan specified, I had discovered that the system was not made for gopher country, in which it got undermined, or for adobe soil, which in the dry season cracked so wide that all the sand went down to China and the bricks caved after it. I had already taken out the entire patio—nine thousand bricks, a brick at a time—and relaid it section by section on a concrete pad. But I hadn't yet got around to the walk. Presto, this pest finds it.

It is not easy to trap gophers in the loose earth of a

flower bed. The usual result is that they kick your trap full of dirt and pack the hole so tight you can't pull it out. But I couldn't leave this vermin loose among the roses; I would have to deal with him after breakfast. So I went inside and plugged in the percolator and made toast and orange juice and grilled a couple of little breakfast steaks and carried the tray into the bedroom, where Ruth was just stretching herself awake. For a woman who rather scorns physical indulgence she takes a suspicious pleasure in the last luxurious half hour of morning sleep. We breakfasted in the bedroom as usual, with Catarrh curled up on the electric blanket, and after breakfast we read aloud in *Il Gattopardo* for nearly an hour. Ruth insists on these exercises, lest we deteriorate. Only after the Italian lesson did I get out and start for the rose garden with a spading fork and a couple of traps. By then it was already hot.

You can tell a gopher's general direction by the way the lateral mounds lie. Dig across the line of these and you cut his main tunnel. This is the only effective place to set traps, one facing each way. His instinct is to plug up the place where you have broken into his passage, and backing over the trap dragging dirt under him with his forepaws, he backs his behind into the pan and is speared just behind the forelegs by the sharp wire jaws.

The mounds here ran irregularly toward the corner of the house. As I dropped the tines of the fork to the ground, estimating the angle, I was indulging in a fantasy, thinking how it would be for some ambitious gopher, digging along by that radar or sonar they seemed to possess no less than porpoises, if he ran into the solid gunnited wall of a swimming pool. Aha, he would say to himself, they're protecting something really precious here. Look how solid, observe how immovable, see how deep. They value this, whatever it is, but they can't keep it from me. Claws that dig in adobe will never be blunted by cement. Away he digs into the concrete, his full length, twice his length, and pauses for a breather and goes at it again. By his sonar he can hear the wall getting thinner. The cement under his claws becomes damp, then wet, and he thinks, Yea, by God, I'm almost there. I'll bet it's a freshly watered flower bed full of roots, or maybe a cold frame of tomatoes, my favorite. And *whulp* comes the whole swimming pool into his face.

Oh happy culmination. Oh well-deserved denouement. But this one I would have to get the hard way. I stepped down on the fork and sank it full length and pried upward.

It came up heavy and struggling. The dirt broke away and left a knot of black and white coils that clenched around the tines. Right out of the earth in one motion, when I had expected only clods and hopefully the dark opening of the tunnel, came this king snake that had lain secretly under my feet.

His writhings sent shudders up the fork handle into my hands. Standing there holding the struggling thing, I was cold goose flesh all over. Horrible. But beautiful too, dusty black crossed with diagonals of white, a creamy belly, a clean whiplike body. And wounded, speared through, blood on the bold coils. Above all, ambiguous, a creature marked with extreme visibility that had been struck because he was underground where his visibility didn't help him. No hawk would ever have stooped on this one as the redtail last spring had stooped on the gopher snake. The black-and-white whip would have warned him off: too hot to handle. So *I* stoop on him, myself as blind as a mole, and he never sees his death blow.

I slammed him to the ground and scraped him off the fork, and he gathered his broken body, thickened at the middle with the unmistakable bulge of the swallowed gopher, and faced me with diamond eyes and flickering tongue. But I gave him no moment for defiance. I beat him to bloody twitching with the fork, and at once enlarged the hole out of which I had speared him, and buried him. I reacted as if to an enemy, or to evil itself. Yet he was the natural bane of gophers, mice, moles, rattlesnakes, all the pests hurtful to me and my garden. Though he worked in darkness and shook my pulse with his suddenness, he had been doing me a favor when I killed him.

Queasy and upset, sweating with heat and shock, I stepped out of the trampled flower bed with the spooked feeling that the snake was an omen or symbol whose meaning I ought to catch but couldn't. Now, I would read him as a riddling revelation of the inadvertent harm we all do, as if our very clothes were deadly, as if harm rose not only from malice, hatred, love, and the other focused passions, but from the most casual contact and the most commonplace act. Step out to watch a sunset and crush a bug—that sort of thing. But that is now. Then, I was sickened and bothered. A day that had not started well anyway was already spoiled.

Well, *absit omen*. I went into the kitchen and poured myself a gin and tonic to quiet my stomach, and got caught at it by Ruth, who lost her temper with me for drinking at midmorning on a day when I would probably blot up ten highballs at the LoPresti party. Think of my liver.

So I sat on the terrace the rest of the morning thinking of my liver and listening to the noise of firecrackers from the eastward, over in subdivision country. Every municipality in California forbids private fireworks, but still I was hearing the shotgun boom of big ones and the musketry rattle of strings of little ones every few minutes. Every time one went off, the beagles in their pen right under my eye rushed back and forth with their saber tails in the air, and put their paws against the wire and stretched their muzzles upward. *Owooooo. Owooooo.*

"Wouldn't you think one of those half-witted Welds would get it through his head those damned hounds are a nuisance?" I said.

Ruth lifted her face out of a magazine. Our fuss about the morning drink had been sharper than usual, and we had been a little stiff with each other since. And she was wearing shorts, though I have suggested plenty of times that shorts are for women under fifty. I took these not as a concession to the heat, but as a deliberate challenge to me.

"I don't know," she said. "Why don't you call them up and tell them?"

"Tell them!" I said. "You know the answer I'd get."

She shrugged, ever so indifferent. "Why don't you just sit quiet and console yourself by thinking how if his place catches fire this Fourth of July you'll let it burn?"

"You should read minds," I said. "How are you at tea leaves?"

For a half minute she looked at me, pursing her lips. Then she said, "Tea. That's not a bad idea," and smiled —having dug me good, she could smile again quite naturally—and went inside. After a time she came out with a glass of iced tea and fruit juice. Maybe it was a peace offering, but I chose to read it as her way of telling me what I was permitted to drink before five o'clock. I took it from her and set it on the bricks beside my chair, and it sat there till lunch time, with its ice melting to scum and wasps drowning in it.

Around noon the pick of hoofs went down our road: Julie going to work for Marian or to visit her kooky friends in the treetops. In my shade it was still and sticky hot. The ugly clutter of pigeon house and dog run on the opposite hill offended my eyes. Every few minutes *boom* went the sullen air, and *owoooo* said the hounds. Standing on the railing with the binoculars, and looking down to the county road, I saw that Tom Weld had run up a flag before his house. Oh, say can you see.

Lou LoPresti could not have picked a worse day for his potlatch if he had consulted an astrologer.

2

At three o'clock I awoke from my nap to find the air of the bedroom as motionless and water-saturated as the bottom of a pond. My skin was greasy, my head stuffed. I could taste smog at the back of my tongue. The windows, closed and curtained to keep out the heat, also kept out any possibility of a breeze. But outside there was no more breeze than in the bedroom, and the smog taint was worse. The sun had moved around to curl the oak and toyon leaves motionless below the terrace rail. The wooded ravines lay simmering in air as gray as dishwater. The beagles sprawled in their doghouse, and the patriots had run out of ammunition, but our flag was still there.

Warte nur, said the ghost of Goethe to my discontented mind, *balde ruhest du auch.*

On the patio side I found Ruth, barefooted and in shorts, walking the narrow shade picking dead blossoms off the geraniums. Between her and the bank of pyracantha the bricks blazed, colorless with heat. Straightening to look at me, she accidentally put her foot down outside the line of shade, and her expression as she hopped back was eloquent. A fakir used to hot coals would have found that patio up to specifications.

"A great little day for the barbecue," I said.

Without answering, she bent again and went on picking withered blossoms into the garden cart. It seemed that reconciliation was up to me; evidently that untouched tea offering had made her mad. Well, I had not calculated to alienate her permanently—the only way to live with a woman is in amity. So I unrolled the hose from the reel and turned on the water, which at first came out hot enough to shave in, and then ran cool. Under it the bricks steamed: when I turned the hose away I could see the wet disappearing in them like the fog of breath evaporating off a windowpane.

I took off my shoes and sprayed my feet and ankles. Delicious. I was absorbed. Then, watching my chance, I caught Ruth when she was bent over the geranium bed, and turned the hose full on her stretched backside.

She came up yowling. "*My hair!*" she said. "Oh, damn you!"

I said, "It would be in strings anyway, in this steam bath. Want some more?"

"No, that's enough! Now quit it!"

I made her dance, popping water at her feet, and when she turned I gave her another good one on the bottom to suggest that shorts deserved no quarter—ladies over sixty would be safe only if properly dressed. Then to forestall reprisals, I turned the hose up in the air and let it rain on me until my shirt and pants were soaked. The humidity was so high that even soaking wet I was warm.

"Turn on the fountain," Ruth said. "At least we can *sound* cool."

I went into the garage and turned the switch; the motor hummed in its box. By the time I was back in the patio the jet was toppling into the steel basin above the pool, and shortly the basin began to overflow from its shaped lip. Our scorching hilltop filled with the sound of grottoes. A couple of times we walked from the shade, across the warm wet bricks, and with the sun beating on us stood mid-calf-deep in the pool to let our blood cool at the ankles. We were standing there, wet and reasonably comfortable, when Marian came up around the buttonhook turn at the top of the hill.

Across the fence I watched her stop briefly to rest. Her hair was tied back in a pony tail like Debby's, her dress was one of those maternity wrap-around things, indefinitely expandable and guaranteed not to look well at any size. Its shade of green didn't particularly suit her. I thought she looked tired, a stick woman with a bead for a head and a larger bead for a belly, and not even her smile, flashing like a heliograph when she saw me watching her, could remove the impression of fatigue and drabness.

Walking slowly, she came up the drive and around the end of the pool, and in comic collapse fell into the chair I turned for her. Her sandaled feet sprawled before her, she puffed out a great breath. "I ought to have auxiliary oxygen for that hill."

"You ought to have your head examined," I said. "Why did you walk up? I was going to come by for you."

The unbecoming green dress made her brown hair look dull; there were shadows under her eyes darker than the summer tan. As if to see whether or not I was really annoyed at her, she looked at me out of the corners of her eyes. "I'll get my breath in a minute. I know, you said you'd come by, but I got . . . I don't know, Debby went off with Julie to swim at the Casements', and I felt sort of smothered down there alone, as if I'd been popped into a double boiler. So I came on up."

Ruth was staring at her with the absolutely expressionless expression she wears when she is concentrating on something that bothers her. "Are you all right, Marian?"

"Why, of course!" Marian said. Her eyes jumped to Ruth's, then to mine. Something trembled on her mouth, a begging flicker of the lips gone so fast it might never have been there, and she was saying serenely, making a show of relaxing deeply into the chair, "Just as soon as I get my breath."

"You sure picked a lovely day for a walk."

She stirred, I saw her argumentativeness reviving like

a game, exhausted puppy at whom somebody has made a playful pass. "I don't know," she said. "I sort of *like* the heat."

"You're sun-struck," I said. "Here, take off your sandals."

"Why?" She looked suspiciously at us both, apparently seeing us clearly for the first time. "You're both soaking. What have you been doing, falling in the pool?"

"Making a sane response to the weather." I turned on the hose and squirted her feet, sandals and all. She jerked them back, then stretched them out again, pulling her dress above her brown knees. "Oooo, dreamy! It's like Keats eating red pepper and then drinking cool wine."

"The first of the bolts-and-jolts boys," I said. "Anybody in his right mind would skip the pepper."

The haggard look which Marian had worn when she arrived was smoothing out, almost as if it had been only the effect of the heat and the hill. I looked for the scared or distressed or begging expression I thought I had caught earlier, and all I saw was her usual amused combativeness. She said to me, "Pain is a form of pleasure, don't you know that?"

"You mean when it quits."

"No, pain itself."

"Only for sadists and masochists," I said. "For thee and me, pleasure extends only to the near edge of the uncomfortable."

Considering, she had already begun to shake her head. "But when it's summer, don't you like it to be real *hot* old summer, and when it's winter don't you like to *freeze*? Pain makes things valuable. How would women feel if having babies was as easy as picking apples? Don't you get pleasure—satisfaction—no, *pleasure* it really is—out of all the rough, hot, cold, scratchy, hard, uncomfortable things?"

"No."

"Oh you do too!"

"No I don't either. And I don't think John would want you taking all that pleasure running up hills in a heat wave. You looked ready to collapse when you came in here just now."

"Really, Marian, he's right," Ruth said.

She had a way of seeming to consult some core of seriousness inside her even while she was engaged in one of these joking arguments, the way a girl laughing at something might in the merest flash out of the corner of her eye check her hair in a mirror she was passing. Her hands smoothed the dress over her knees so that the outline of her thighs showed through. She seemed momentarily astonished to find her lap so foreshortened. Then she lifted her clear blue insistent glance and said, "I was as comfortable as could be down below, and that didn't keep me from being low and lonesome and wishing John was home. So I came up to see you, and now I feel better. That's what John would want me to do. He wants me to do the things that are good for my *spirit*. Do you know that poem of Frost's?"

"Of course. Which one?"

She made a completely happy face. "All right. I don't remember its title. I only remember the last lines. It's about hard pleasures."

Primly, ready to laugh, but serious too, meaning it, laughing not at the poem but at the spectacle of herself sitting there *spouting* it, and meaning too that we ought

stretched, with a sheen on it. The physical details say nothing, and they do not recall the essential magic of her smile to me now. It was her spirit that smiled, it bubbled out of her like the bright water bubbling from the fountain. Remembering, I could knock my forehead on the ground.)

Her fine small head, shaped by the back-drawn hair, tilted to listen. Her eyes went around the patio in a flickering circuit. "And look what sort of shade you arrange to bicker in!"

Forced by her attention, we attended. She had the faculty of making you look and listen and smell and taste. The motor hummed, almost imperceptible, from its box. The stem of water rising five or six inches above the nozzle wavered and toppled with clunking, gurgling sounds. I saw that the jet was trying, against the interference of its own toppling weight, to rotate clockwise, like all volatile Northern Hemisphere things pulled by the spinning earth. Now and again the basin hummed out a deep reverberating note, like a gong. From its lip a smooth thin stream curved to shatter in the pool, and from the splash circles spread, overtaking each other, rocking the single yellow water lily afloat on its green raft, and from the spreading circles the sun knocked reflections that fluttered on the fence and crept among tongue-shaped clematis leaves. A hummingbird buzzed the orange tree by the pool's corner and shot away.

"You wouldn't have made this so beautiful if it didn't please you," Marian said, "and it wouldn't please you so much if it wasn't so hot and dry all around. Remember the argument we had this spring, the very first day we ever came up here? How I got after you for not leaving everything natural? Well, that's the way I'd still do it myself, but yours is so good it almost persuades me. What's an oasis without a desert around it? What's a garden if you don't come into it from a dirty street or a closed-in house? You *need* it hot in this patio. You wouldn't turn on that fountain in the rain."

Her vividness troubled the air as the blur of the returning hummingbird troubled the corner by the orange tree. I sat smiling, dabbling a stream of water on her sandals, and as she threw out her hands in a triumphant Q.E.D. sort of gesture I saw the slight, awkward stiffness of her left arm.

A cold finger was laid on my insides. I could not help appraising the false breast swelling above the real swelling of her pregnancy. I saw her brown throat, too vulnerable. Would I have so doted on this girl if she had not been maimed and threatened? Was it to herself or her danger that I responded with so much anxious solicitude? Talk about the need for contrast in a garden! She was herself, if one believed her thesis, the indispensable reminder of danger and pain to make this sanctuary blessed. She saw stars by daylight because she lived down a well, and she watched them with passion because any day the cover might go on and she might be bottled forever in the dark.

For that single intense instant the image of the king snake glared in my mind, the bloody coils bulging in the middle as Marian bulged. I saw him smashed and twitching, stuffed into a hole with the dirt falling on him. It was no more than an association of shapes, but the cold spot in my guts contracted in a spasm, and on my arms every little hair bristled from its crater of goose flesh.

I was dismayed at the violence of my feelings, and

said angrily—but angry at what? At it, at her danger, at her brightness and bravery, I suppose—"Pain is fine when you can turn it off. It may even be good for the soul in small quantities, the way strychnine in small quantities is good for sick hearts. But they don't arrange pain in this world so you can turn it off when you want. Feel the earth rough to all your length, sure, fine, but for God's sake don't cultivate pain. Pain is poison, you poor demented enthusiast with whom I am madly in love. Pain is *poison*! Don't go hunting for it. Never praise it. Avoid it all you can and bear it if you must, but never never never mistake it for something desirable!"

It was an outburst, and it left them both staring. In my embarrassment at the way my feelings had snatched and shaken me, I squirted their feet with care and turned off the hose. Ruth's half-dried shirt was stuck against her, showing the wiry outline of her torso and the white shape of her brassiere—a healthy and durable woman. But the flesh of her thighs sagged a little, her hair was pure white, and looked all the whiter because her eyebrows were still black. I felt a gush of tenderness, not so much because she had been my wife and my intimate for forty years, as because she was mortal and threatened like the girl beside her. They read me the same lesson in helpless vulnerability. Neither could have had the slightest notion how hard it was for me not to reach out and touch them, one after the other—groping for contact like a hippo or a walrus, one of a species that cannot live without rubbing against its fellows.

I met Marian's eyes. She smiled tentatively, willing at a hint to forget this awkward moment and go back to the playful heckling that was our minds' habitual disguise. I thought she might understand what my anger had been trying to say; after the long letter I had written her the day before I somehow felt that the masks were permanently off. But clearly she didn't understand, and I had to remind myself that she had never seen the letter; I had poured myself out without an audience, I had fallen in the forest without an ear to hear my crash. Now, I saw, Marian would have tried to say something cheerful if she had been sure what I meant or what I needed.

But to cheer me just then she would have had to annul her mortality, Ruth's, my own, the mortality of every blob that twitched with sensation anywhere on the indifferent earth, and fled the too violent sensations it knew as pain.

What a job of work was done when we crossed the fatal boundary between the polymer and the cell, and began stumbling toward the perfected consciousness that Marian was so sure we would ultimately reach!

The telephone rang, and I went with relief to answer it. It was Fran LoPresti, apparently without a thing to do but chat, though she had a hundred-odd guests coming at any time. She is dreadful to talk to on the telephone. Her voice absorbs you like quicksand. Unctuous and caressing, full of soft emphasis and boneless stress, she went on about the heat, and who was coming and who couldn't come, and what ought to be done to keep Ansel Sutton sober. The telephone was wet in my hand, a fly kept lighting on my bald spot, the voice oozed on until mercifully some little plug of lead melted in my overheated skull and a connection shorted out and communication became only a soothing murmur.

I couldn't imagine what she had called for. Anybody in his right mind would be sitting in a cool tub. Maybe that was where she was. I saw her, pink and white, sitting in the bathtub stirring the water with a pink toe, her mouth smootching the white telephone. From that, for some reason, I progressed to a vision of pink new-born mice being lifted by their tails and dipped into honey and lifted out dripping and smoothly swallowed.

It struck me that the murmuring had stopped. "Mmmmm?" I said.

"All around the patio," she said. "We've been working like *fiends*. Every one of the mural things and all the driftwoods, and even the big one, the welded one. I finished it last night, out there with the perspiration simply *pouring* off my nose and bugs flying into the torch. You just don't have any idea how I suffer for my art."

"All art is suffering," I said.

"Well," she cried, "I hope not for *you*! I'm *very* anxious to hear what you think of them, especially the welded one."

I said I couldn't wait to see them. The receiver crooned and sighed and warbled at my ear.

"And, oh, Joe," it said. "I knew there was something else I wanted to ask you. Have you seen Marian? Julie said she had to baby-sit, but I've rung and rung, and nobody's home."

"Marian's here with us. She said Julie and Debby have gone over to the Casement pool."

"Oh." She sounded softly jolted, as if she had stepped down a step that wasn't there. "She *is* with Debby, then."

"That's what Marian said."

"Well, all right then," Fran said vaguely, and then her voice rose a little and lost its syrup, and I found myself speculating that in a crisis she could probably even scream. "I would have *bet* she was down with that gang of beatniks again. Do you know, I found out she goes there *all* the *time.* And she lies to me, my God how that child lies! It's the most awful age, I can't do anything right, I can't open my mouth without making her hate me. And that gang makes her ten times worse. Who owns that land across from you, Joe? Couldn't we find out, and see if we couldn't get them put out of there?"

"God help us, I own it," I said.

"*You* own it? But why ever did you . . . ?"

"I gave permission to one, and he became seven or eight by mitosis or something."

"But you don't *want* them down there."

"Not particularly."

"Oh, good," she said. "Oh, *wonderful*! Maybe we can do something. I'm sure they shouldn't be permitted in the neighborhood, they're as vicious as can be, and dirty, and all those long-haired bearded boys. Ugh! Oh, you make me feel *so* much better! Let's talk about it—not at the party, I want you to have a good time and I want you to look at my sculpture *very carefully.* Later, right away soon. Mmmm? Oopsie, there's a car, they're starting to arrive. Byeee. Come early. Bye-eee."

I want back out to the patio. "Who was so endless?" Ruth asked.

"Fran. Mainly worrying about whether Julie is down with Peck's crowd."

Immediately I wished I hadn't said it, for Marian was dismayed. "Oh dear! Is she upset?"

"Well, yes. She'd like me to run them all out."

"Are you going to?"

"I don't know," I said. "The fact that Fran is upset seems to me the least good of several good reasons why I might."

"Oh, I'm going to have to talk to her, and to Julie too. Maybe I shouldn't hire Julie any more."

"Then she'll go anyway, as you told me yourself," I said. "Well, the hell with the surly young. I read some counselor the other day who was convinced the only thing worse than being a parent is being a child. He had it backward. Are we going to this party?"

"I suppose any time now," Ruth said.

"Sun's far enough over the yardarm, you think?" It was a provocative remark, but she only looked at me pleasantly and impenetrably. I suppose she did think it was now a legitimate time for a drink. She has these little rules, and when they are satisfied, she is. And I suspect that she had comprehended my outburst when Marian began trying to persuade us, or herself, that there is virtue in pain.

"Are we going across country?" Ruth said. "Let's not, let's drive around."

Marian looked at us both and said, "Honestly, if you two can stand it, I'd *rather* walk."

"Of course we can stand it, but you can't," Ruth said.

"Just because I got winded on your hill!" Marian said. She seemed genuinely upset. "I ought to walk, the doctor says so. Anyway, don't I have to be consistent and choose the uncomfortable way?"

Softly, I said to myself. Don't argue with her. For some reason she's got her backbone straight, she's screwed up tight like the first day we met. So I said, as if it didn't matter, "O.K. Have you got some sort of wrap, for coming home after it's cooled off?"

"I'll take an extra stole," Ruth said.

A light trembling, not quite a smile, moved on Marian's lips. "Joe, are you mad? Because I don't really care. Just because I'm a pig and like punishment is no reason . . ."

"I agree with John," I said. "You have to do the things that are good for your spirit."

"I'm afraid you *are* mad."

"Not at you. At *it,* whatever it is. I've been mad at one thing or another all day. So just stick your feet in the water and stay cool and we'll get dressed."

A little later we were a tiny procession between brass earth and brass sky, little coolies in straw garden hats, me carrying a preposterous sweater and two stoles. It was so hot I shivered, and flares went off behind my eyes. My nostrils were coated with the dust-and-manure smell of the trail we followed, and I felt the tug of burrs at my cuffs, the prick of foxtails in my ankles. High over the hazed ridges the redtail was riding the thermals, looking not as if he were up there hunting, but as if he had gone up in search of a breeze.

Beyond the Shields pasture and the hot lane, a short-cut path hooked down into the willows around a pump house and tank. There was a head-clearing whiff of witch hazel, an illusory breath of coolness. Sidling through the turnstile, we passed the empty chicken house whose torn wire was a memorial to Weld's brother's dog, and climbed the gradual lane of oaks, almost defoliated by oak-moth caterpillars and clotted with dark mistletoe. Naturally, being a parasite, the mistletoe was unpalatable to any pest. The more ravaged the tree, the more healthy those kissing-clusters.

As we came up the lane we heard the sounds of the party as volubly unintelligible as an Italian traffic argument, and then we came to the top and it was spread out before us in the enormous patio.

A Renoir picnic on a construction site. Among random piles of lumber and sand and tile, between cement mixer and bench saw and sawhorses, women in bright dresses and men in bright shirts coasted and clustered. There were only three little fig trees for shade, but a red beach umbrella bloomed like a poppy in the blazing center. The shadow of the western wing of the house cut the patio about a third of the way, and against the shaded wall, by a white bar table, a man in a white coat dispensed respite and nepenthe. As he lifted a glass to pass it to a woman, the ice cubes caught the sun and threw me a brilliant blue wink.

Marian turned. Her smile for the moment was as bright as the wink of the ice cubes, but as we started in toward the crowd I saw her back, splashed with the mixed sun and shade under the desolated trees. Her shoulders drooped, her green dress was wrinkled in back where she had sat on it. However much I might want a cold drink with a touch of company, *she* looked as if someone should in kindness lead her off to a darkened room and put her to bed.

3

The other day, between rains, Ruth and I waded through the mud to the LoPresti place, carrying a little Christmas present with the notion of patching up our relations, sadly out of whack since the Fourth of July. We found no one at home but the sculptures, on whom I suppose I might have put some of the blame for Fran's sense of grievance. And the whole vast patio in which they sat or stood or hung had been tiled, bordered, grouted, polished, planted, cleaned up, finished. Cement mixer, bench saw, generator and tank and torch, piles of sand and tile, were all gone. And not a muddy footprint besides our own, no sign that since the wind left them there the leaves in the corners had been stirred by anything bigger than an earwig, nothing busy about the place except a stream of ants that poured up and down the grout lines between the tiles. I got, somehow, the feeling of a bleak and tidy desolation; the *aim* had gone out of that once-busy yard, it was like an unhappy woman with a tight mouth. And for that I was partly responsible.

They say that more people are alive today than have lived in all previous human history. I find that hard to believe. It is so long a history, and so laborious, and it sits so heavy on the mind. Alive for what? I wanted to ask, up to my ankles in ants that I could have melted to goo with one blast of an insect bomb. Busy for what? But I knew well enough. We move because we move, we build because we build, we reproduce because our loins thirst for the profound touch, and then we divert upon our children, who have their own sort and do not want ours, the hopes that for ourselves are no longer mentionable without a grimace. Standing in Lucio's courtyard before Fran's ill-omened sculpture, I had a quick, comical impulse to get out of there and go home and do something useful—lay some stones, say, in the retaining wall I was building along the drive.

This job was too aridly closed up, and there was no sign of a new beginning. Yet Lucio had walked a treadmill of incessant new beginnings. The cement mixer, his heraldic emblem, was always rampant somewhere above a cone of spilled sand. Lumber piles and litter got incorporated into the living routines as people use the stumps and outcrops of a picnic site. I have seen Fran in her abstracted way flatten down the top of a two-ton pile of sand and throw a cloth over it and use it as a coffee table, and it was standard practice for Lucio, on party days, to fill the cement mixer with ice for the cooling of beer. Even worn-out tools never disappeared. With her torch, a real antique, one of those that generates its own acetylene gas out of calcium carbide and water, Fran welded them into art.

We were looking her major creation right in the eye, or would have been if it had had an eye, and I found myself actively disliking the thing. Troublemaker, pretender, parody of something sad and unattractive—in its maker? in its viewer? both, probably—it brooded back at us, its exposed torso shiny with welds like scars. Most of Fran's art was either ragged messes of junk (she talked a good deal about learning to think in the medium) or mosaics of old teaspoons, safety pins, coins, and kinks of copper wire embedded in fused glass like the leavings of litterbugs in a Yellowstone hot spring. But this thing was frankly, even darkly, female. Back on the Fourth I had indulged my alcoholic humor at her expense, but now I thought she leered at me with a knowledge that was sinister, sad, and accusing.

A woman, of a sort, nearly life-size. She wore for skirt a cut-off galvanized boiler with rivets running like a row of buttons from belt to hem. Rising out of the rounding top of this skirt like a jutting pelvis was an old shovel whose handle made a spinal column linking pelvis and thorax, as in a wired skeleton. Midway in the spine, moved by some whimsy that I never did understand, but that I would investigate if I were her psychiatrist, Fran had drilled a hole in which she had set a lens from a pair of eyeglasses. For some reason, it was inescapably obscene to look right through that thing's bifocal navel. Filthy X-rays.

Bracketed to the spine in place of a rib cage was a portable typewriter rescued from the dump. Its movable parts were fused with rust, its keyboard made a panel of gangrenous guts, its necklace of rusty type hung down between ribbon spools like round rudimentary breasts. To enhance the resemblance, Fran, thinking in anything but the medium, had touched each spool with a bright nipple of solder.

The neck was a hammer handle wrapped with leather like the neck of one of those African women stretched with circle after circle of copper wire. The face was composed only of the hammer's down-hooking claws. Curving up over this tooth-face as halo or sunbonnet was a bamboo lawn rake with some broken rays. Both hammer and rake were tilted slightly on the stiffly upright body, so that the faceless teeth under the sunbonnet wore an indescribable look of coquetry. You expected her to sidle up and say in a voice like Mortimer Snerd's, "How'd you like to look through my navel, a-huh, a-huh, a-huh?"

"What in hell do you suppose Fran had in mind?" I said, when we had stood looking for three or four minutes. "She couldn't have arrived at that thing by accident. And she takes it seriously or I wouldn't have hurt her feelings so on the Fourth."

"She's a pretty vague woman. I imagine it's just an iron doodle that turned out gruesome."

"You know what I think? I think it's a portrait of Julie."

"Julie, or Fran's feelings about Julie?"

"Well, isn't every portrait a self-portrait?"

"Fran wouldn't like the idea," Ruth said. Then she said a strange, bitter thing. "If you did a portrait of Curtis, would it resemble you?"

We stared at one another almost with hatred. Her eyes ducked away, her lips moved in a deprecatory slight smile, as if she begged me to take her remark as a joke, and she went back to studying the caricature standing above us on its pedestal. "Isn't it just that hammer that makes you think it's hostile?" she said. "After all, she didn't make that, she just found it lying around."

I found it easiest to adopt her casual and speculative tone. "If she'd been making it out of affection she'd have found something else lying around to use, a saucepan with dimples, maybe. And why those white-hot titties? To emphasize femaleness in a dangerous, unpleasant way? Or those half-formed breasts that are like the scary outcrops on your adolescent child? And all those corrupt guts, and that window navel. Doesn't that say, in the voice of a furious and suspicious mother, 'I can see right through you?' "

"You're free-associating," Ruth said mildly. "After all, she started this a long time before."

"Then it was prophecy."

"Oh, I don't know," Ruth said almost impatiently.

"She wasn't afraid of Julie as a *girl*. She was afraid she'd grow up beat, or a lady vet like Annie Williamson. She wanted a nice sweet feminine domestic girl in nicely pressed dresses who would be on the honor roll and play the piano and make little art things."

"But virginal."

"Oh yes. Maybe a little Pre-Raphaelite in a nice way."

"And got this stormy creature she could neither understand nor approve."

"Yes."

"And that neither understood nor approved her, nor granted her authority."

"Yes."

"Like a lot of other parents," I said. It was the point we had been circling for minutes, as her oblique look acknowledged.

"Why don't you say all parents?"

"Because I don't believe it," I said. "There has to be an occasional parent-child relationship that works. When it doesn't work, one side or the other is to blame."

"And you think it's usually the child."

"I didn't say that. I didn't even imply it. If I implied anything, it's that people are too ready to assume that it's the parent."

A drift of wind moved in the empty, chilly patio. The air was soggy with unshed rain. The expanse of tiles gleamed like an abandoned Roman bath. It would have made a splendid place to open your veins.

I said, "Did you read about that fifteen-year-old who killed his parents the other night? The one that had taken the family car and wrecked it so they had his learner's license pulled? So that night he went into their room and brained them both with an ax. Who's to blame in that one?"

"A boy like that is obviously a psychopath."

"And therefore all the more in need of control, isn't he? They were doing the only possible thing when they grounded him. But there are millions of people who will sympathize with that murderous slob. He was frustrated in his normal desires. All his friends had cars. His society taught him to equate the driver's license with the passage into manhood. And anyway we must feel sorry for wrongdoers, they're unhappy people. Well the *hell* with it! I'm going to save my sympathy for that tormented pair trying to instill a sense of human responsibility into their brat, and getting their brains knocked out for their pains."

"Oh, *well*, Julie didn't murder Fran and Lucio, after all."

"No, but how the blood flowed in fantasy! Why? Because her mother wouldn't let her do everything her hormones and her teen-age rebellions suggested. Fran is a kind of fool, sure, but the kid is a monster. And don't tell me consequences caught up with her. They caught up with a lot of other people too."

"She isn't that bad," Ruth said, "and she may be one of the kind that never learns except by making mistakes."

"So youth must be served," I said. "They must be left free to work out their lives. You know what youth is? Youth is a pack of barbarians. That's why I've resigned from the God-damned world, because it's abdicated its authority, it's *abject* before these underaged goons that think they know everything and know nothing at all, not one damned thing!"

Ruth's lips were pursed, her eyebrows arched, rueful and dubious. I was aware of the sound of my voice dying out between the blank wings of the house. I had been shouting. Her hand came out and patted my forearm quickly, twice. "Yes," she said on an indrawn breath like a sigh, and then, "It's going to rain, we'd better get back. I wish they'd been home, it might have smoothed things out some if Lou could have shown off his finished patio."

She stooped and laid our little offering between the screen and the massive homemade plank door. I have seen that thoughtful, relinquishing, regretful expression on people as they lay flowers on a grave. We had honestly liked the LoPrestis. It seemed to me, as I know it seemed to Ruth, that we would be better employed consoling one another than avoiding one another.

"I'll bet you something," I said. "I'll bet you he liked it a hundred times better when it was a corporation yard as rough as a lava field, full of tools and people and noise."

4

Which is the way it was when we looked into it on the Fourth from the lane of ragged oaks. We stood a minute under the last tree, two hundred feet from the bar. It was like looking in toward home plate from center field, with the crowd overflowing out of the stands into the infield. People saw us, heads turned, teeth glinted, hands waved. A police car with its radio turned on squawked out something from where it was parked off the corner of the eastern wing, and I thought perhaps we already had trouble until I saw the city manager of a town up the line, standing under the red umbrella with a big-time subdivider and builder, keeping his ear to the air, evidently combining pleasure with a proper Independence Day alertness. I saw Bill and Sue Casement, both brown with summer golf, and our resident All-American and his porcelain wife, who were by the bar with our resident dictator, the man in the white coat I had mistaken for a bartender. I should have known better. Lucio's parties ran on a do-it-yourself basis.

Beyond the white coat I noted two incongruous dark ones, the only coats there besides the dictator's. Strangers, and sticking together like nuns. Also I saw Annie Williamson, our lady vet, hunt-clubber, raiser of beagles and borzois and Tennessee walkers, judge at all the region horse shows and dog shows and gymkhanas, a woman with the wrists of a laborer, the shoulders of a bantamweight fighter, and a voice like the Hewgag of E Clampus Vitus.

Likewise college professors, gentleman-farmers, honest-to-god farmers (not Tom Weld, never Tom Weld in that patio, though he was represented by his Labrador's by-blow), retired generals, airline pilots, advertising men, the widow of an internationally famous oil geologist, the wife (in the midst of divorce proceedings) of an internationally famous architect, a Nobel Prize winner in medicine, and others unknown, a great swarm to the number I should say of three thousand six hundred and thirty-two, not counting the little children, who were all still up at the Casement pool.

Now here came Fran across the blazing patio to greet us. We waved her back, starting out of our own shade to prevent her exposing her susceptible skin, but she came on anyway, and we met by the cement mixer, which stood about where the shortstop would be playing with a man on first and a right-hander up. She was looking most Gretchen in a dirndl, and she had her fair hair in one thick braid that hung over her shoulder nearly to her waist. Her arms and neck were soft, white, palely freckled; her eyes were brown and moist like her cocker's; her voice reached out like her hands to lay a caressing touch on us. For company she always put on what Ruth called her *haut blancmange* manner: you had the feeling that if a fly alighted on her it would sink and disappear without trace. And yet a warm sort of woman, almost tediously female, as affectionate as she was affected. She came lamenting the heat and hoping we were not simply *dying* of it, and she gave me a soft look of gratitude when I draped one of my stoles over her arms and shoulders. I meant it as a joke; she took it as a thoughtful acknowledgment of her actinic peril.

"Oh, I'm just *sick* about this weather!" she cried. "I wanted to have a really *nice* show, and now nobody can stand out in the sun long enough to look at things."

I began badly. Turning to the cement mixer, fuming from its maw of ice, I said, "Ah, but this is one I've been admiring. No—don't tell me what it means. Or isn't it intended to mean anything? Do I have to think in the medium?"

"You come here with me, you scoundrel," Fran said, and hooked her arm in mine. "There's one over here I *do* want your opinion of."

"I ought to get these ladies into the shade."

"Just on your way past, it won't take a minute. I want them to see it too."

As we picked our way over rough concrete and across projecting headers, people in the shade cried *Hi* and *Welcome,* and *My God, did you walk? You poor souls. What's all the cold-weather gear, Joe? Man, you out of your mind? Hello, Ruth. Hello, Marian. Where's your handsome husband? Still off with those lady seals?*

We stopped before the figure in the skirt of tubular iron and I looked her in the teeth. I looked her through the navel. I inspected her rusted viscera. I observed the little flames of the nipples. Though we were under the red umbrella, it was almost as hot as in the open sun. I could see Marian wilting, I myself was oozing sweat, and it made me impatient to be trapped into a lot of dishonest art criticism the minute we arrived. I wanted my hand around a sweating glass, what is more. But with my forked tongue I said, "This is a real departure. This is something *new.*"

"What do you think?" Fran said, her braid in her hand. "Tell me honestly, now."

"It's different from anything of yours I've seen."

"Yes, I think I . . ."

"You didn't just throw it together, either," I said. "This was *created.* It will stand a lot of looking."

"You just look all you want to!"

"It's ominous, though," I said. "Is it meant to be a little frightening? Because that's the way it strikes me."

"Well, yes, I guess it *is* meant to be a little frightening. It sort of took hold of me as I worked on it. . . ."

I saw Lucio coming, his dark face shining with heat, his shirt mooned. Fran was saying happily, "And if you don't think that was a perfect *stinker* to weld, with that old torch! I ought to get a new one, Lou keeps telling me. But I sort of like doing it the hard way."

"Every woman I know is a masochist, apparently," I said. "But I know a couple who have suffered all they should, for now. Excuse me, Fran, will you? Marian ought to sit down. I'll study this some more and talk to you later. You should feel very good about it, I think."

I escaped, carrying with me her soft, radiant smile and her expression—arch would be the name for it—that said *Don't you forget, now! We've got a date, remember!*

"I damn near called you this morning to come over and earn your supper by helping me dig the hole to roast the beef in," Lucio said, "but then I remembered you're an old retired bird and probably couldn't take it. What were you doing about nine or ten? Lying in the shade?"

"Digging," I said, remembering the king snake.

"Brother, I wish I'd known that."

"So do I," I said.

I got the ladies gin and tonic, I poured a good one for myself, and I led them into the shaded angle looking for chairs. The dictator did credit to his upbringing by rising promptly for Marian, and a man I did not know got up rather less willingly for Ruth. Sue Casement came over just as I was tucking the sweater and stoles under a chair and telling Marian, "Now that the pain is over, try cultivating comfort for contrast."

"Pain?" Sue said, with concern in her rosy face. "Is something . . . ?"

"Joe is being a mother hen," Marian said.

"Run along and play," Ruth said. "Sue and I will look after her." So I talked with Sue a minute and then wandered off, dangerously unattended, into the party.

It was quite a party. In the heat everybody gulped and everybody got quickly tight, and not the least swift of foot among those who ran with the god was Joseph Allston, who had started the day crooked and had been itching to set it straight. The old Dutchman was right, we get too soon oldt and too late schmardt.

I talked with acquaintances, I heard a few stories. Then I discovered that the two dark suits were Russian "students," men of forty or so, with hard Party faces, whom Fran had met on some committee and captured for the day. She wanted them to see an American neighborhood gathering, and what better time than Independence Day?

I am as willing to wag my tail at foreigners as any other old dog, but these people were hard to wag at. Mostly our talk was about vodka. It turned out that American vodka was less potent than Russian vodka. But also we spoke of languages. I discovered that all Russians spoke English, German, and French at least, but that few Americans knew anything but English and none knew Russian. After a few minutes of this I excused myself and drifted back to the bar for a second inferior American gin and tonic. Looking toward Ruth and Marian, I saw them in a conversational ring with several other women. Marian's brown legs were stretched out, her head back. She listened peacefully, as if half-asleep.

Four two, said the police car in right field. *Four two. Accident at Squawk and Squawk-Squawk.* The city manager, who had suspended his conversation to listen, once again turned his ironical attention to the Russians. The developer, leaning his weight on two women who screamed with laughter, was demonstrating how he could drink from the glass held between his teeth.

Hilarity recollected in tranquillity can be depressing.

With respect to this particular hilarity I am like Don Marquis's party guest recalling his last-evening's conviction that Mrs. Simpkins's face was a slot machine, and that the macaroons were pennies. It seems to me that on the Fourth I took several Mrs. Simpkinses by the ears and tried to shake chewing gum or stamps out of their double chins. Get old Joe Allston high and he kills you. What a comical old rooster. A prince—and spell it the way we used to spell it in my youth when we applied the term to someone we especially admired. P-r-i-c-k, prince.

Let me get it over. Father, I have sinned. I have put an enemy in my mouth to steal away my brains. I have shamed my gray hairs. I have mocked a friend in such a way that she will never like or trust me again. I have waggled my ass's ears among the foolish and the drunken.

For instance. The developer, who for quite a while had been feeling no pain, had been feeling other things, including several bottoms. The city manager and I, squatting to examine Fran's old relic of a blowtorch, observed his wandering hand. The manager looked at me and pulled his deadpan joker's face down. I was equal to the occasion. Showing him how the torch worked, I dropped some carbide into the tank and added the ice cubes from my glass. When I closed the tank and opened the valve and struck a match, I just happened to be holding the thing close to the developer's rear end, and the pop of blue flame from the nozzle set his shirttails afire. His friend the manager put him out with a flat-handed slap that moved him six feet.

Later, Lucio and I made an acetylene cannon out of a length of soil pipe, and shortly Lucio, the city manager, the Nobel Prize winner, the All-American, Bill Casement, and a half dozen more of us were happily blowing tin cans and plugs of wood fifty feet down into the gully. I heard Fran explaining to the two Russians that fireworks were traditional on Independence Day, though for safety reasons—and Americans were *much* more careful in that way than world opinion credited them with being, look at the comparative statistics on traffic accidents in Europe and America—they could be fired off only under permit. The city manager's presence made us sort of legal, though he wasn't *our* manager.

I didn't hear the Russians' reply, but I thought I could paraphrase their response: *Warlike, barbarous, technically advanced, the Americans demonstrate even in their toys and playthings a martial and destructive spirit, though their improvised ordnance seems definitely inferior to the Russian. . . .*

Coming up past them after we had exhausted Fran's supply of carbide, I gave them a cheery greeting in Italian, but they only stared.

The intolerable day was cooling toward evening; the daylight-saving sunshine lay like custard on the oaks and mistletoe, the patio was three-quarters in shade. Carrying my empty glass, or somebody's empty glass, I made my way back to my women, to whom I had paid no attention for an hour. But someone had kept their glasses full, or else they had nursed their first ones, and their circle was still deep in the sort of talk that women get into—about clothes, children, P.T.A., local politics, conservation, world affairs, art, music, books, that sort of thing—and they looked at me with some amusement and waved me away. So I refilled my glass and turned to see what further entertainment the party offered.

The first thing I saw was Annie Williamson burrowing into the cement mixer, evidently in search of a beer. Even on tiptoe, with her arm in to the shoulder, she could not reach the bottom, and in exasperation she hopped up and put head and shoulders inside. Right then, behind her, I became aware of the city manager with the mixer's power cord in his hand. Following his wildly pointing finger, I saw an outlet in the wall. He flung me the cord across twenty feet of patio and I plugged it promptly in.

The mixer grated and started to turn, Annie's tiptoeing feet left the ground, her rump reared up. There were muffled sounds of bears attacking bulls and dinosaurs being gelded, and then Annie's feet found pavement and her head popped out, red, wet, and roaring.

The city manager liked the deadpan pose, but he was definitely breaking up.

"Laugh!" Annie roared at him. "Honest to John!"

I handed Annie my handkerchief, saying, "That was a kid trick if I ever saw one. It's a pity people drink when they don't know how to hold it. Public officials at that. What will our Russian friends think?"

They were standing together with their impassive lumpy faces and their stony Party eyes, and I read their minds. *Among the overprivileged Americans drunkenness may be called the standard. Weak as their liquor is, they do not carry it well. Far from creating the happiness that they say they are in pursuit of, their capitalist system encourages self-indulgence and alcoholic deviation. . . .*

The police car squawked. Wet-eyed, shaken with seismic rumblings and convulsions, the city manager lifted his head to listen. He hopped across the headers and leaned in and took a microphone from the dash and talked into it. The squawk box replied unintelligibly. The manager slid inside and slammed the door. The motor caught, the turret light began to revolve. He shouted something, still laughing; gave us a sassy twirl of the siren, skidded his wheels on the slippery oak leaves, and bolted out the drive between the parked cars. There he went, a boy on a man's errand, accident or fire or gang fight or something. Shoulder to shoulder the Russians watched. Pravda *reports law in America enforced by alcoholics.*

Several times during that sweaty afternoon I had caught Fran's eyes on me, or caught her working in my direction. Evidently the shell game I had played on her hadn't satisfied. She had peeked under my remarks and found no pea, and she was going to make the old thimblerigger go through his act again. No, that was unfair. She didn't suspect me of rigging anything, she only felt she had missed the full discussion. Pontifex Maximus, that was who I was, and she hadn't been able to read my bull.

But I didn't feel like Pontifex Maximus. I felt like Josephus Arbiter, the Master of the Revels, and so I slipped Fran's unaggressive but persistent pursuit. I kept clots of people between us, I failed to catch glances, I made strategic retreats to the toilet.

When I finally did find myself confronting the statue, I could feel the alcohol in my balance and my tongue, and I was again in the company of Annie Williamson. The patio had half cleared to watch Lucio and others dig out the pit where a hundred pounds of beef had been roasting in foil packages since noon. Some of the ladies, Ruth and Marian among them, were clearing the bar table and setting out plates and silver. I registered Marian's activity long enough to be exasperated: Sit down and be *enceinte,* let somebody else do that. But my eye was promptly recaptured by the shadow that the statue's coy leer threw on the east wall, a thing to scare you to death, and my ear was tuned to Annie's confidential whisper, which would have rustled palm fronds at forty rods.

"Now you tell me," she said. "You *tell* me. What is it?"

"Annie, you've been a judge in too many dog shows to be baffled by art. Look her over. Check out her points."

Annie's face was as brown and shiny as a buckeye, her arms were brown, her legs were brown, her badger-brush of hair bristled, her eyes were beginning to frost over. She gave me a look through blue cataracts, put her can of beer behind her and balanced it on her tailbone, and began to rotate around the figure. She examined its rear end for a good while, hands behind her, head sunk, lower lip jutting. If she had had a cigar she would have looked like a transvestite Winston Churchill in a fright wig. She bent, and her bifocally magnified eye glared at me through the navel. She straightened, shaking her head.

"It beats me. It's got points, like you say. It's got class. It could be Best of Show. But what the hell's the *breed*?"

"I thig it's a gollie," I said.

Annie opened her eyes wide in contempt. Her bristly scalp snapped down and snapped back. Circling, she peered up under the hammer claws. "Good bite," she said, and then, excitedly, "Say, the roof of her mouth is purple. That means chow blood."

"But if she's chow shouldn't she have red hair?" I said. "You notice she hasn't got *any* hair. And look at that brisket. Could she be a Mexican Topless?"

"Haw!" Annie said—one blat from an old rubber-bulb Model-T horn. She touched the carriage bar, which dangled like a withered right arm from the typewriter's shoulder. "A pointer?" She leaned, trying to read the label on the rusted machine, and shook her head again. "Who ever heard of a Royal pointer?"

With her knuckles she knocked once, experimentally, on the galvanized skirt, which hummed out a resonant A. Old Joe Allston, that bald-headed cutup, threw a finger in the air, slopping his drink. "Annie, that did it! We've got it!"

She waited, glowering.

"My dear Watson," I said, "it's an Ashcan Hound."

Babble, clatter, blurt, crash, Annie came down in laughter like somebody falling through a skylight. She fell upon me and embraced me, roaring. And as she did so the camera changed its angle and looked with Joe Allston over the damp gray head, straight into the face of Fran LoPresti, a dozen feet away. For the instant of contact her eyes flared as hot as the spit of her torch. The soft face wore every expression I never expected to see there—disappointment, rage, a distended ugly vanity, and hatred, hatred. Then the hostess look melted over her mouth and eyes, her face moistened and softened into the rubbery indulgent smile. Of course. Only Joe making one of his jokes. That vixenish expression? Illusion. How could you make a harpy out of blancmange?

But there for a split second had been the spirit that

created Snaggletooth. And who had fetched it into the open? I, Pontifex Maximus, with my papal infallibility.

Damn people who puttered together junk art in their backyards and thought themselves Leonardo. Why couldn't this foolish Fran LoPresti be a culture-club woman like anyone else? Why not concentrate on Russian visitors? Why not grow camellias? But my anger was more than half contrition, for I liked the silly woman. Sober, I would have taken pains to protect her from scoffers like myself.

For somewhere under the soft smile, soft voice, soft movements, away down below the cultivated emphysema and the skin that wouldn't take sun and the hands that wore gloves for the slightest task, there was a dream. There was this woman, the dream went, who worked quietly, satisfying her own demanding standards without thought of fame, and in her country patio she accumulated statues, busts, herms, figures, mosaics, groups, shapes, forms, until one day a visitor, some Pontifex Maximus in a Homburg, found his way to that garden of art. How did he stand? He stood amazed. What could he not believe? He could not believe his eyes. He got out his checkbook, he claimed this, and this, and this. Tell no one, he said. Trust me. And hurried away to inform collectors and gallery owners and directors of museums. Within weeks the garden was a place of pilgrimage like Milles' place outside Stockholm, and it was peopled with copies and castings of her works, plus some originals that she would not part with no matter how the world clamored for them. In later years she would receive there, gracious and brilliant, and her charming quiet daughter would rise from listening, and go out softly and come back bringing tea, being careful not to clack the cups and saucers while the visitors' tape recorders were still on.

Oh, Jesus. Too soon oldt and too late schmardt.

Annie backed out of my arms wiping her eyes, saying, "Joe, you slay me. What did you say you were before you retired? One of the Marx brothers?"

"Shhhh," I said. "Our Russian friends are easily offended." And escaped, leaving her haw-hawing.

5

Backed against a tree in left field, I had time and sobriety enough to reflect that I had done to Fran precisely what I most loathe when it is done to me. I remembered an assistant coach at Illinois nearly fifty years back, who came into the locker room one day when I was alone in there, stripped, yanking at a stuck locker door. He stared at me with a dawning smile, put out a hand that closed clear around my biceps, and passed on, saying with a burble, "Take it easy, there, Muscles, you'll pull the joint down." Nothing he could ever have said to me, no subsequent friendliness, could have altered my perception that he had expressed his absolutely honest mind, and that therefore I hated him and always would. And *did*, standing there outside the party for the purpose of hating myself.

Or that box supper in Maquoketa, the shadow social where girls brought boxed meals and walked in turn between a light and a hung sheet so that men recognizing a shadow shape would bid five, ten, fifteen dollars for the cooking and the company and the Ladies' Aid would raise a round sum. When a half dozen had crossed, and posed, and been bid up and knocked down, and come giggling and blushing off to join their purchasers, then what was that balloony shadow that appeared, a thing that even as shadow had three left feet? Laughter erupted all over the hall, most hearty and spontaneous. Hoots, wolf whistles, a bid of two bits, a raise to thirty cents, more laughter. The shadow hung a moment, lurched, spread, and was gone to the sound of heavy running feet. A door slammed. Suddenly silent, we sat there in front of the dusty American flag with the laughter dying off our faces, and would not look at one another.

I saw that girl every day in the bakery where she worked after school: a girl hastily helpful, easily embarrassed, hotly flushing. Time and silence will not have healed her. If she is still alive I am sure she has nights when the memory of those thirty seconds thunders in her ears and turns her body cold and brings sweat to the palms of her hands. Why not? It does that to me, one of those who laughed loudest. Inasmuch as He has done it unto the least of these, and even when He has made me the instrument, He has done it unto me.

I would have to hunt Fran up and try to laugh or explain or apologize away my crude humor (it was the dhrink talkin') and lead her back to the welded woman and fill her full of perceptive appreciation. I would have to lie my head off, because here the only kindness was to lie. I might even have to offer to buy the damned thing, and what if I should succeed? That scarecrow in our patio would drive away even the buzzards.

The locust swarm of young, wet-haired from swimming, came streaming in the drive. The olive and potato-chip crops were gone in seconds, the nut bowls emptied. While the younger ones prospected for Cokes in the cement mixer, the older ones poured themselves drinks under their indulgent parents' eyes. I saw Debby, slippery and fast as a minnow, dart through the crowd to jam against her mother's knees, talking excitedly around the neck of a Coke bottle. She made a brief, attractive picture, framed in Marian's arm: Happy Childhood, authentically adjusted to country living. Marian had no need to worry about her any longer.

But then came another figure in a faded blue jersey and cut-off jeans, slouching with her face closed. Her dark hair was lankly wet, her legs heavy, her hips wide. On her seat the slick stain of bareback riding was a part of her natural coloration, like the scut of a deer. Not Happy Childhood she: Junior Alienation, rather. I saw Fran LoPresti, from the table, note her daughter's presence. For a breath or two she stood with knives and forks in her hands, watching, before she turned and again began laying out the silver in handy piles. Julie skirted the edge of the patio as if to avoid people, and she looked out of the corners of her eyes to note and hate those who observed or greeted her. Expressionless, she noted and hated *me.*

She made her way to Marian's chair and stood talking. Her hands were jammed unladylike in her hip pockets, her haunch swelled like the haunch of a Percheron mare. Opulent, in her way, a forming reservoir of fecundity. Give her a year to discover she was female, and Fran would look back upon her present difficulties as the golden age. Marian's face was turned upward inquiringly. She looked concerned. She shook her head, saying something, and Debby took the Coke bottle out of her mouth and said something else. Julie shrugged, looking over her shoulder.

Now came a crowd of men and boys bearing smoking bundles of foil on a sheet of plywood. They set it on the end of the table, Lucio whetted his knife and with its point flicked the foil from a great roast. Women pressed paper plates into the hands of children and stood them in line. The developer came from inside with a gallon jug of wine in each hand. The alcohol-heightened shouting talk roared outward from the paved triangle like the barking of a thousand sea lions. When I could see again through the press, Marian had stood up and was getting Debby into line. Julie had gone.

From over near the west wing Ruth was flagging me to come and eat, but I, out in left field where I felt I belonged, indicated with my raised glass that I wanted to finish my drink first. I watched Fran, in her best *haut blancmange*, maneuver plates into the hands of the Russians, who fell back against the wall and sat down on a pile of planks, looking behind them first as if for tacks. By the time I had got them settled and looked for Fran again, she was hurrying around the house, heading toward the car-jammed driveway and the front yard.

It is a moment I would just as soon not recall. I am like a Monday-morning football fan watching the movies of a lost game, and arriving at the point where the home quarterback cocks his arm to throw the pass that will be intercepted and run back for the winning touchdown. Don't throw it! groans the fan. Don't go after her, I urge myself in recollection. But I was full of the half-drunken conviction that I must make my difficult peace.

Like so many things, it comes back by way of the

nose. My memory hunts by scent, like a beagle, among a banquet of smells: the rich aroma of Lucio's carving, odors of green concrete and adobe dust, a whiff of acetylene gas, the faint chlorine scent that the young had brought in their wet hair, the tang of gin and lime from my glass. In those odors is the whole jammed patio, the sticky, fading afternoon. And there goes Joseph Allston, a jaunty sport-shirted figure with a tanned head, around the corner after Fran LoPresti, whom he has just seriously offended. Brilliantly inadvertent, he bumbles right into mother and daughter, nose to nose in a bitter quarrel.

Julie was backed against the bumper and grill of a parked car, but she looked as if she might come out clawing at any minute. Fran was crowded close to her, her head sunk to bring her face close to that of her shorter daughter. Her throat and cheeks were mottled, she poured words into the girl's face in a harsh, cutting whisper as different from her ordinary soft voice as the crackling of a down high-tension line is from the bubbling of a percolator. . . . *spectacle of yourself . . . dressed like that . . . too good to say hello, is that it? . . . not lift a hand to help . . . all by myself, a hundred people . . . other people's daughters . . . out with those beatniks, were you? . . . now you listen to me, don't get that look on your face . . . never again, you hear? You HEAR? Answer me. . . .*

They heard or saw me, their heads jerked around from their mortal duel, their eyes stabbed me, Medusa and basilisk. Her lips still pointed like a beak, Fran grabbed her Gretchen braid in one hand with an exclamation. I saw her eyes flick off me to something behind, I saw the girl's slow dark smolder of eyes on me for an instant, and then Fran had swung around and was walking toward the front door, and Julie, pushing herself away from the car's radiator with a hunch of her behind, slouched off the other way, toward the stable. Turning myself, ready to flee or tiptoe, I saw the Russians getting into an old Plymouth. They were what Fran's eyes had flicked to in the very moment of my interruption: one more grain of sand to her burden—obviously the Independence Day revels had not fascinated them.

I tried to tell myself that it was just as well I had interrupted. Whatever Fran was demanding of Julie, it did not look as if Julie was in any mood to submit, and their argument might have got even shriller, and drawn a crowd. But I didn't persuade myself. I knew that the essential thing was that on top of my snickers at her art, I should demonstrate my infallibility by stumbling into them when the masks were off. Exposure of that kind she would hate as much as she hated ridicule. So I sneaked back and got my plate filled and found a seat beside Ruth and Marian and sat chewing Lucio's delectable beef as if it had been unboiled rawhide. With food, the party noise had diminished, but it was still loud.

"Did you talk to Fran?" Marian said.

"About what?"

"About Julie?"

"No. Why?"

"I wondered. Julie was asking me if I didn't want her to take Debby home after a while, and put her to bed, so I could stay at the party."

"What did you say?"

"I said we weren't staying longer than just to the beginning of the fireworks. I thought maybe she was wanting an excuse to slip off to Peck's."

"You think very clearly."

"Is Fran upset?"

"Yes, I'd say she's definitely upset."

Her clear glance was clouded by a frown. Her mouth looked tired. "Damn! What should I do?"

"Nothing," I said. "Anything you could do would be wrong. Leave it to Fran to do something."

It was growing dusky, but not so dark that I couldn't see the droop of her mouth, the sag of her shoulders. She looked sad, her plate was hardly touched. It irritated me that she should fret herself over that goonish girl—in fact, it irritated me that the LoPresti family existed, at that moment—but I had no spirits left for cheering her. The only illumination in the patio came through the rectangle of the door, through which I could see two couples dancing, trying in their drink to be as young as their children, doing the frug or the watusi or the jerk, one of those rope-climbing, joint-dislocating dances. The bang-bang music pounded out through the door and I felt it get the beat and start synchronizing with the dull beginnings of a headache.

Somebody flipped a switch. Cones of light burst out above the shapes of driftwood and iron. Directly in front of us the welded woman stepped tall into the bug-streaked beam of a spot. *Ahhhh!* said the crowd, pleased at this ingenuity. I squinted, trying to see Fran, hoping she would come out and accept some dishonest praise and start feeling better. No sign of her.

"Do you really want to stay for the fireworks?" I said.

"I couldn't drag Debby away before."

"We could take you home and I could come back for her in the car."

"Joe," Ruth said, standing behind Marian with her hands on the slim shoulders and her eyebrows up into inverted V's, "why don't you go get the car now, and then we'll all be ready to go as soon as Debby's seen a few rockets."

"Of course," I said. "Good idea. I should have thought of that myself." When I stood up, my legs told me that I was still not fully sober, and my head added that I would soon be hung over.

"But Joe's been the life of the party!" Marian said. "Oh dear, I really botched everything, talking you into walking. I'm sorry. Please don't leave because of me, you're having so much fun."

"An orgy of high spirits," I said.

The smile, sympathetic, friendly, amused, lightened her face in the diffused glow of the spot. "What's the matter?" she said. "One too many? Maybe Fran's got some vitamin B. John swears by those."

"No," I said, starting away. "I welcome the hangover. It's what I drink for. You take it easy. I'll be about a half hour."

Under the oaks it was as black as a coal hole. As I groped down toward the pump house I heard a rustling on the right, and discerned a pair of glimmering presences sitting on the bank—no faces, only the faintest pale outlines. "Boy," I said, stumbling a little more than I needed to, "this is like being lost in an elephant's bowel. There *must* be a way out." They did not laugh or speak. Who? The All-American and the architect's wife? I had no evidence and no interest.

By the time I got out of the willows into the lane my eyes had adjusted. By the time I reached the pasture I could see the golden grass. The sky spread out, full of dim stars. From back of me radiated the full renewed volume of the party's noise.

Then I heard sounds from ahead and below. I stopped and listened: a loud banging and pounding, and when it ended, a clamor of shouts and laughter that faded so that I could hear under it the tom-tom thumping of amplified guitars, Beatles or such. Natchez-under-the-hill was celebrating the glorious Fourth too.

Through brittle weeds I went over to the fence, and from there saw a glow of light on trees below me, and heard voices male and female, and the random picking of a banjo in a lull. Then began another three or four minutes of that tremendous banging, as if someone was pounding out a dented fender. What in hell *were* they doing? I could see nothing but the flicker of firelight.

From the covering dark I spied on them by ear, thinking with derision of Marian's belief that they spent all their time debating the good life. If that wasn't an orgy down below, I never heard the noise of one. With little effort I could imagine gleaming eyes and teeth, joints passing from hand to hand, and off in the edges of darkness the sounds of rut and riot, apache girls running naked and laughing through the brush until their hair caught in the poison oak and hairy hands grabbed them, and at the end, maybe, the tearing of the goat god, some victim whose blood the orgiasts could dabble in and whose flesh they could devour. Maybe that was what Peck wanted mascots like Julie and Dave Weld for.

What did go on at their parties? Mass hysteria? Mass

fornication? Or only drunkenness, noise, and disorderly conduct such as that coming across the hill from the party I had just left? I stood between the revelry I despised without knowing what went on and the more elderly revelry I despised because I had just been part of it. And away off in the hills, audible in faint, excited bursts, I heard the yap and bugle of hunting hounds. The beagles must have got out. So every God-damned element of disorder in the universe was running loose with hair streaming and foam on its teeth, and there I stood by a fence post, tightening my eye muscles around a growing headache and thinking bleak thoughts.

Was this all there was to do? Was I all there was to be? Did we come west for no better reason than to set shirttails afire and make brainless sport of touchy friends, and periodically overturn habit, custom, order, and quiet in binges indistinguishable from those that went on down in the University of the Free Mind? Had we gravitated, despite ourselves, from suburbia to its cure, which is orgy? I had a considerable distaste for the good life as prescribed by Jim Peck, I disparaged his affection for the disorderly and irrational and his faith in chaos. But what better could I suggest? My withdrawal was even more finicky than his, and I preferred alcohol to pot. There was the real difference. Pot, I understood, did not leave hangovers. Maybe that was my total reason for repudiating Peck's brave new world. It is bad enough to live with yourself *with* hangovers.

The dark fled away, I emerged into visibility, I saw my hand on the post, my hairy forearm, the ragged grass; and turned to meet the air coming at me with a soft heavy concussion and see the sky streaming fire. Apocalypse, and never better timed. With my socks full of foxtails I groped along the fence to the turnstile and through it into our drive. Rockets and cheering broke out of the dark behind me. An awakened mockingbird began to pipe in the screen of *Eucalyptus globulus* around the water tank.

6

When I curved into the level stretch below the hill I could see the bacchant camp: red fire, glare-and-darkness angles of tent and treehouse, moving silhouettes. A green rocket hung its doomsday light above the trees, and their cheers broke out raucous as the cries of savages. My lights picked out the corral, and in it Julie's black gelding with his chin hung over the withers of Debby's piebald. So she had made it, and mother be damned. For a slow-motion second the two pivoted at the base of their lengthening shadows, while a web of elongating legs and enlarging bodies and sharpening angles of corral posts raced counter-clockwise along the creekside brush beyond, and with a leap of overstretched darkness joined the shadows around the fire. My turning lights touched the Volkswagen bus and Dave Weld's molded Mercury at the trail gate, and reached past them to reveal the gray, abandoned-looking wall of Marian's house.

In my remembering mind that wall has a waiting look. It sits dark, quiet, and patient while bedlam howls through the woods around it, and while across the hill overprivileged middle-class revelers run cackling from the star shells they fire at the dim sky. Something is waiting in that cottage—maybe serenity, maybe sanctuary.

Nearly fifteen minutes later I got back around the five miles of crooked hill roads and found Lucio's place boiling like a plowed-up anthill. The celebrants had set the oat grass afire. A bunch of them were beating and stamping along the edge of the parking area, and Lucio and others were squirting silver streams of water across my headlights. There was no wind, the thing was already over, but someone had seen the glow and turned in the alarm, and now before I could find a place to pull out, here came a fire truck in behind me, and after it eight or ten carloads of passers-by hunting excitement. Within minutes, one of them backed into the ditch trying to turn around, and the lane was clogged with happy pushers and angled cars and the not-very-amused members of the fire department. Obviously it might be an hour before we could get out.

But Lucio had a Portygee gate in the fence above his pump house, and rummaging in his garage, I found a pair of wire cutters. For the third or fourth time I caught Debby and got the door shut on her. I collected Ruth and Marian, standing off to one side with their stoles around them, and we nosed down the pump-house lane and out into the road. A stop for another Portygee gate, and we bumped through crackling weeds across the pasture. On our side I cut the fence to let us down into our drive. I was working in sullen, headachy silence, trying to get the day over. Ruth broke into lamentations when I cut the wire, saying what about Julie's horse. I said, irritable with headache and depression, that there were more important things than that horse. I would fix the fence tomorrow, and hunt the horse if I had to. Marian said nothing at all; Debby, leaning against her, was already asleep.

We turned down the hill, and Ruth, seeing the fire across the creek, said, "Oh look, Peck's having a party too."

"A nice loud one," I said. "We'll be hearing it till rosy-fingered Dawn creeps out of Tithonus's bed." Then we pulled up into Marian's parking area, and there were two cars that had been parked there beside her station wagon. "Damnation," I said. "They think they own the world."

"It's all right, they won't bother me," Marian said.

"They'll carouse all night and start grinding their starters under your window at five a.m."

"No, really," she said. "I'm not sleepy anyway, I'll probably read in bed." Carefully she propped Debby upright and reached for the door. I hopped out and opened it, and she got out, awkward with her pregnancy, holding onto my arm. "Won't you come in?"

"You don't want company at this hour," Ruth said. "It's pretty late."

"Late? It's only ten-thirty or so."

"But it feels like two to this aging playboy," I said. I lifted Debby out and heaved her sacklike onto my shoulder. Her hands hung down loose as strings. In the diffused glow of the headlights Marian was looking at me oddly. "If you didn't . . . mind waiting for a minute while I roll Debby into bed, I wish you *would* stop."

I looked at Ruth. The last thing I wanted was to talk, even with Marian. I had the feeling I wasn't fit company for her; I was skewered from temple to temple, Debby was heavy on my shoulder, her breath warm against my neck. "Why of course," Ruth said. "We'd love to."

Well, maybe she was afraid of entering her dark house alone. I should have thought of it. Dutiful but dull, I hoisted the warm slipping girl higher and carried her in. Marian switched on a floor lamp, then a wall switch that showed me the hall leading to Debby's room. Marian was waiting with the covers turned back, and her smile flashed, but tiredly, as I eased the child down. "I'll only be a second," she said.

I went back into the living room where Ruth sat. The redwood paneling was so old it was almost black. It drank the light and was darkened by it as blotting paper is darkened by wet. "I never realized before," I said. "This is a *gloomy* room."

Eying me thoughtfully, she nodded. She rubbed one thumb over the other. We heard light sounds from the interior, then steps, and Marian came in and eased the door carefully shut. "Would you like something? A beer?"

Thanks, we wouldn't. I wouldn't, at least. I glanced at Ruth. She frowned, with a quick, impatient shake of the head. Her eyes were on Marian, and her air of watchfulness was so marked that I roused up, blinking. Almost diffidently, Marian sat down in a corduroy-covered chair. With her hands in her lap and her eyes downcast, she looked like a little girl going over in her mind a piece she would have to recite any minute. Then her eyes came up. A hot, painful flush burned briefly in her face, and faded almost as quickly, as if she had forced the blood out of her skin by an act of will. We stared back at her in the slack light. "Marian," I said, "in God's name, what is it?"

"I wanted to tell you," she said carefully and steadily. "I saw the doctor yesterday. It's back. I've probably got two or three months."

Sickly staring, we took dumbly what we had wholly feared and half expected. I saw the fine tanned skin tightly drawn across the temples, the violet shadows under the eyes. All day, all through that hectic party, she had had that locked up in her. She had carried it up our hill, it had sat beside her in our patio while she quoted us verses celebrating the hard pleasures.

The air in the room was as thick as syrup, tumid with unspent heat. Marian's hands were in her lap, thin, long-boned, long-tendoned, sheathed in skin as fine as silk. She turned them over. The palms were unnaturally pink. She blushed for that deadly stigma as if it had been shameful.

I find that I can't remember that night except as a numbness, like a dream suppressed that persists only as discomfort. When I try to recall what we said, I slide off into things we said at other times. When I try to remember how I felt, I am like a man who wakes sweating and clutching the blankets, but what he wakes to, what he clutches, is not what he clutched in the reality of the nightmare. In the blunt minute when she announced her death, I suppose we felt it necessary to deny, doubt, comfort. If we didn't shed tears, we held them back only to spare her. She herself did not cry. She wore one unchanging expression: fortitude had been turned on and left burning.

I suppose we must have suggested the last-ditch treatments we had seen other friends suffer through, trying to reverse the inevitable—cobalt, male hormones, radiation.

She said she was not going to take any radiation treatments. The baby.

Patiently she waited while I burst out at her, calling her a sentimentalist, crazy. I said she was making the choice that the heroine of a sticky novel would make. When I was through she said, "It isn't a choice, Joe. It's a race."

I turn from it now as I turned from it then. I said I simply didn't believe John would let her risk her life for a life that didn't yet exist. I couldn't understand why she would want to.

So in her quiet, controlled voice, looking at one or another of us for corroboration or approval, she told us: They gave her no hope that they could save her, radiation would only slow things down. Radiation was hard on the patient, which was all right, but the worst was that none could say what it might do to the fetus. They might keep her alive until she could have the baby, but the baby might be a monster, or damaged somehow. If she didn't take treatments, she might not live long enough to bear the child, but it would at least be normal, and they could take it, if necessary, at the end.

She used the word "end" without a flutter, but for me it was as shattering as the crash of breaking glass. It destroyed all my will to argue with her, for though I could not believe she meant what she said, or would stick to the decision she had leaped to when they posed her her intolerable alternatives, I knew she *thought* she meant it, and it seemed cruel to make her defend it. We put our faith in John. We tried to get her to let Ruth stay the night. She would not. She didn't want to evade it, she wanted to come to terms with it, and she would do that better alone.

We kissed her, we found smiles to answer the one she flashed for us, we made her promise all over again to try to reach John the first thing in the morning and bring him home no matter if he missed everything he had gone up there for. We told her to call us, no matter what the hour, if she got lonely or afraid. We said we would be down in the morning right after breakfast. Then we were out in the parking area, and the door that had framed her as we said good night was closed.

"Oh, God damn, God damn, God damn," I said.

We did not get into the car, but stood as if waiting for something. Ruth came close and put her hand under my arm, and I squeezed it against me with my elbow. It was an unnaturally warm night, the air soft and damp. The living-room light went out, then some remoter light, and the cottage squatted blackly before us. I visualized Marian walking softly into the back bedroom, where she would undress her mutilated, misshapen body and lie down. Would she stare at herself in the mirror, searching for signs of what was happening within?

Then I became aware of the undiminished forces of disorder in the night. The intrusive automobiles were still parked without permission beside her old station wagon, the hounds were still baying off in the dark hills, the raffish crowd at Peck's burst out bawling to a guitar, singing with gusto.

"Give me that old-time religion,
Give me that old-time religion,
Give me that old-time religion,
It's good enough for me."

On the sluggish air moving down the gully I smelled the wild fragrance of their fire. All the restless blood in that well-tempered exurb was out and roaming, turning night into day and yelling the delights of chaos, the mystical and curative pleasures of uncontrol. And in the gray cottage, in the still bedroom, in the organs and blood stream of the girl who liked the hard and painful things because they could so persuade her she was fully alive, and who believed the universe began in order and proceeded toward the perfection of consciousness, the stealthy cells, rebellious against the order that had created them, went on splitting to form their fatal isotopes.

7

The song bawled on through another verse and into the next chorus. Bleakly we stood and listened, and when it stopped we looked at one another doubtfully in the dark and I opened the door of the car for her to get in. Just as I did so the terrific banging that I had heard from the hill began again, this time in the beat of the singing. *Gimme that* BANG BANG BANG, *Gimme that* BANG BANG BANG, *Gimme that* BANG BANG BANG BANG BANG BANG BANG!

"Oh for Christ's sake!" I said. I dug the flashlight out of the glove compartment and shoved Ruth across under the wheel. "Drive up to the foot of the hill and wait for me. I'm going to put that hoodlum outfit down."

"Joe," Ruth said, "do you think . . . ? She said she didn't mind."

"Maybe she won't be sleeping," I said, "but she might want to think. She's got plenty to think *about*."

I was going through the trail gate by the time she got

turned and started. I didn't need the flashlight because of her brightening lights that showed up the cars, the ratty shed, the path, the corral beyond. And the fire, with its jumping shadows, made a target for me to walk toward.

The lights moved past me up the lane and left me in deep darkness. The intolerable din across the creek stopped abruptly, and was succeeded by hoots, yells, screeches, laughter. "Next! Next! Hey, Miles, come on, emancipate the old ego! Man, that puts *bees* in your head!"

Easing along the path by feel, I ran into the corral fence and stopped to let the red glow of the fire fade off my retina as a green afterimage. It smelled like a Navaho encampment there in the bottoms—horse, woodsmoke, dung, leather, dust. The horses snorted softly, their feet thudded in the powdered adobe. I saw the shadow of a head and neck against the sky, the shine of an eyeball, and putting out a hand I felt a velvet nose and the moist hot blast of breath. The head pulled away, a shoe clinked on a rock. From my zone of darkness and soft sounds I saw the red light and black shadows across the creek, and heard the cacophony of their voices talking loudly and all at once.

I did not even then flick on the flashlight, because I was curious to know what that banging had been, and I didn't want to scare them off whatever they were doing. While I stood there one of those amplified guitar records came on—loud, loud. Was there something the matter with their ears, that they needed that level of noise? Was it a protective result of growing up in an overcrowded, rackety world that they couldn't have a good time without a boiler-factory uproar? And did they have no awareness that people who lived within range of that raucous uproar might take less delight in it than they?

I guided myself along the corral rail until I was as close as the corral came to the bay tree. Between me and the fire, which now threw up a shower of sparks as someone poked it, the looping bridge and all Peck's rigging of lines and cables hung like lianas across the face of some fantastic jungle. Any minute bands of apes could have come swarming out on them hand over hand. But the apes, and I supposed their Tarzan too, seemed to be busy doing something else. A cluster of them was gathered over to the right of the tent; others were watching from the tent deck and from the porch of the treehouse. I moved a little to get a better look at those off to the right.

A tight group of figures, hard to tell in that light whether male or female—for that matter, in broad daylight it would have taken a medical examination to determine the sex of some of the kids I had seen coming in and out of there. They seemed to be gathered around something, some shed or low tent. Then their mass divided and I saw the dull corrugated gleam of a section of highway culvert four feet or so in diameter and five or six feet long. Someone had evidently done a little nightwork at a road-construction site, and it must have been a job to roll that thing home and get it across the creek. Great energy in dubious causes, that was Peck. But what were they doing with it, or in it? I saw one, then another, crawl in. Some erotic mystery, some rude Eleusis cave? Some refinement on the Marquis de Sade? Several of the group, I saw, had clubs or sticks of wood in their hands.

"O.K.," somebody said. "Pull in your brains."

The music blasted out again from the tent, and lined up on both sides of the culvert, the orgiasts began to beat it with their clubs. *Blam! Blam! Blam!* BLAM! BLAM! BLAM! The culvert hummed like a steeple, the blows exploded and reverberated, the yelling settled into a rhythmic chant. No wonder I had heard it up on top of the hill. They must have heard it in San Jose. And inside, where the kicks-hunters crouched with their skulls in their hands, how would it be in there? It was unbearable where I stood, a hundred feet away, and I knew it must be pounding against the windows of Marian's room.

BLAM! BLAM! BLAM! The clubs came down, one side, then the other. The club wielders capered, yells streaked off into the dark, the firelight shone on eyeballs and teeth and off the tanned hides of some who were stripped to the waist. You couldn't have found anything to match it short of New Guinea.

One of those inside the culvert came scuttling out crabwise, then the other. The pounding tapered off into ragged thumps, then stopped. The rhythmic chant broke into the jar and clash of separate voices raised above the tom-tom booming of the music that was itself loud enough to vibrate the leaves on the trees. The victims reeled around wowing and hooting and holding their heads. One sat on the edge of the tent porch and pounded his head with the butt of his palm like a swimmer with water in his ear. The music blurted off.

"How'd that go, man? Way out?"

"Holy shit, I was in orbit. I still am. *Jesus,* that drives you right out of your skull!"

Right where they all wanted to be, out of their skulls.

Well, that would be enough disturbance for one evening. I took a step toward the bridge and flicked on the flashlight.

Its cone lifted and widened across twenty feet of trampled ground and came hard against the gray trunk of the bay. I saw a hasty tangle of limbs, bare skin, the white eyes of startled turning faces, a swatch of long dark hair. Then they rolled and scrambled and were gone behind the tree and into the brush. But not before I had recognized, in the face framed by the lank dark hair, Mr. and Mrs. Lucio LoPresti's difficult daughter.

I had stopped instantly, as startled as they were; my thumb had pushed the flashlight switch to let them escape the light that had nailed them for a panicked instant against the tree. There I hung, on the brink of turning away myself. I guess it actually shocked me to catch Julie in that state of coitus alarmus. For one thing, I had been inadvertent enough for one day, I hated my capacity for blundering. For another, sexual revolution or no sexual revolution, pill or no pill, I believe that society should restrain kids that young from playing with something of whose explosive consequences they can't possibly know. And for still another, I was dismayed that my remarks about Peck's crowd, made more than half facetiously, turned out to be approximately true. They *were* as promiscuous as howler monkeys, evidently, and they were not careful about confining their activities to the reasonably mature.

I was sorry for Fran, grieved for Lucio, exasperated at Julie, angry at Peck, and it never left my mind that while this orgy went on, Marian lay over there in her dark bedroom, alone with her death. It all came out as rage. In a bound, it seemed, I was at the bridgehead, flicking the flashlight across the faces around the fire, up into the treehouse, over to the crowd by the culvert. I meant to bark at them, curt and peremptory and commanding, but my tongue was so stiff in my mouth I managed only a harsh roar, right into the blast of sound from the record player.

My roar or the light—more probably the light—brought them around like an order to throw up their hands. Their heads jerked around, their faces stared, one half rose as if to run. There were maybe a dozen of them, beards and smooth faces, longhairs and shorthairs, he's and she's. I recognized two boys I had seen earlier pouring themselves drinks at the LoPresti party; they sat over there in Pecksville, incongruous in pipestem white jeans and sport shirts, evidence that more of the neighborhood than Julie and Dave Weld had been sucked into the crowd. Peck built quite a mousetrap. I saw Miles, the rather amiable boy who was one of the most devoted disciples, and the sex goddess Margo, but I did not see Dave Weld. Had it been his unkempt head beside Julie's under the bay tree? And where was Peck? Off in the bushes or up in the treehouse, conducting one of the less public Mysteries?

The boy who had started half to his feet slipped off quietly toward the corner of the tent, and I put the light on him to let him know he was seen. He bolted: off to warn somebody? bury the can of pot? In my anger I took satisfaction in their obvious fear. Like a cop or a night watchman, I moved the light across their faces, and like cornered safe-crackers they stared back into the eye of my accusing lamp. Some now put hands to their eyes, shading them, trying to see. The music banged away unheeded behind them. "What's the matter?" one of them yelled. "Who is it?"

I held the light on him, one of the Volkswagen boys, with a skimpy reddish beard. "Turn off the music."

"What?"

"Turn off the damned noise!"

One of them darkened the triangle of the tent opening; the music squawked out. Questions, bending and peering faces, whispers. *Who the hell is it? Can you see? Is it the fuzz, or who?* A face looked out the treehouse door, and I switched the beam of light upward: female, unknown. I switched it back onto the wispy beard. "You're making too much racket," I said. "Turn it down."

They were beginning to unfreeze. The group by the culvert began to drift to the fire, trying to see. And now someone turned a flashlight on *me*. The white coal bored into my eyes, dazzling me. There I stood in my bald head and my sport shirt, obviously not the police. Though I could not see against the flashlight, I could hear the buzz and stir of their relief. The insolent light moved down to my feet, then up again, taking me in. "Who says?" said a high voice, incredulous. A girl laughed.

Bang! went my adrenals, and there I was again, shouting at them. It was a time for quiet moral authority and the dignity of an elder. Instead, I roared. "*I* say! Now turn it off and keep it off!"

The light bored steadily into my eyes. "Who's I?" someone said. The high voice said, " 'Ell, I'm 'igh meself. If 'e's any 'igher than I am 'e's *really* 'igh." A gust of laughter. Whispers. *What's buggin' him, anyway? Christ, it isn't even eleven.*

I counted ten before I said, "Is Peck over there?"

It seemed to me that heads turned. Through my slitted eyes I thought I saw the red firelight gleam in the turning eyeballs of a girl near the front. Then I swung the light up toward the treehouse and there Peck was, the god himself, bushy-headed, hairy-chested, skinny-legged, lounging on the rail. "Hello there, Mr. Allston," his soft voice said—oh, soft, imperturbable, cool, friendly, a rebuke to my shouting. I felt all the ridiculousness of the police function, but I had no intention of backing off.

"Your party's too loud," I said.

He was surprised. "Loud? Well, maybe it is, we couldn't conduct this experiment *without* some noise. But who's close enough to be bothered?"

"Anybody within a mile and a half," I said.

He laughed. "Oh come on, this is the *country*."

"Where people expect quiet," I said. "Anyway, Mrs. Catlin isn't a mile and a half away, she's a hundred yards."

"Did she send you?"

"It makes no difference whether she did or didn't," I said. "I won't have her disturbed, and I'm telling you to keep your party quiet." My hands were trembling, and I snapped off the flashlight. The boy by the fire left his on me. Up in the tree Jim Peck's figure darkened and dimmed almost out, then emerged again, touched with red firelight. He put his hands on the limb in front of him and leaned there as if pondering. In the door behind him the girl's face hovered.

"Well now look, Mr. Allston," Peck said finally. "You've got some kind of wrong idea. This isn't really a party, we're not just putting on a blast. We've got an experiment going, we're getting close to something very important psychologically."

"And making much too much noise in the process."

"I told you," he said patiently, "it can't be done *without* some noise."

"Then cancel it."

A pause. "I don't believe you mean that, Mr. Allston," said the soft voice from the tree. "After all, you gave me your *permission* to live here."

I quote him accurately. That is exactly what he said. Permission, he said, forgetting the stolen electricity, the stolen water, the unburied litter and garbage, the fires, the unauthorized sheds and mailboxes, the paper and the beer cans. And now this unendurable music and this deafening banging on a stolen culvert in the spirit of scientific research.

I keep wondering now, as I think back on it, what might have happened if I had explained. If I had said, "Look, Mrs. Catlin is ill, the last thing she needs is to be kept awake all night." If I had crossed the creek and sat by their fire and had a beer with them. If I had turned their experiment and their brawl into a bull session and let them try to tell me what they thought they were about. I wonder if they would have let me in or shut me out. I wonder if I might have gone home that night understanding them any better or liking them any better. I think not, but I almost wish I had tried.

For instead, I got mad, and getting that mad leaves me fluttery and nauseated. And I bawled out a grown man, or what passed for one, which is nothing to be enjoyed.

"Permission?" I said. "I now take it back. I gave you

permission to camp, not to start a fleabag ashram. And I take it back. You've got a week to get your place torn down and get out of here. And you'll close up this party right now."

I stood there, and Peck leaned in his tree with his hands on the limb. The others were silent, letting the Mahatma cope. For a while he said nothing—he had that knack of keeping his cool, so that my fury reverberated in the succeeding quiet. Finally he said mildly, "You seem all upset, Mr. Allston. O.K., of course we'll keep the noise down, if it bothers you that much."

"You'll turn it *off*," I said. "If you don't, you'll be entertaining some guests in uniform, and I doubt that you'd welcome that. Also there are two cars parked in Mrs. Catlin's drive. I want those out of there right now."

"We're staying all night," a voice said.

"I don't care if you're staying the whole last week, get those cars moved. You had no business parking there in the first place."

"Right *now*, you want them moved?"

"Right now."

They looked up at Peck. He was still leaning casually, but I felt the lines of antagonism between us as intricate as the web of lines and cables in the tree. At last he shrugged. "All right, we'll move them. Whose are they?"

Two boys, one of those in pipestem pants and one of the beards, stood up and started to shuffle across the swinging bridge. Behind them rose a murmur of complaint and anger, not loud. The Mahatma had failed them, the Establishment had the power to put him down. It was not exactly triumph, it was more like disgust, that moved me when I thought how impotent he was against the ownership, authority, and law that I could bring to bear on him. I would much rather have been representative of something he had to respect for its manifest solidity and goodness, not for its power. And for that, who was to blame? Peck, with his compulsion to break all laws and deny all authority, or I with my emotional inability to accept anything he stood for? Had I oppressed him in a way that he obscurely wanted to be oppressed in? They hate us Youth, was that it? Something he had to prove, and so kept pushing and pushing until he brought it about?

The boys came off the bridge and passed me in single file, eying me sourly. One had a row of buttons pinned across his shirt like service ribbons. JESUS WAS A DROPOUT, one said. Another said, WANT COLOR TV? TRY LSD.

I said no more to Peck, but followed the two across the bottom and stood by the gate while they started their cars and drove them down to park them by the mailboxes. In silence, they came up past me and went on across toward the fire. "Thank you," I said as they passed. They did not reply. No noise from the camp except the low sound of voices. The light through the drapes on Marian's window lay dimly against the oak in the patio. No sound from there, either. I wondered if she had heard me shouting at the revelers. Without using the flashlight I walked up the lane and climbed heavily into the car beside Ruth.

Altogether, the Fourth had lived up to its omens. The air, as we crossed the patio to the front door, was sour with smog. The mockingbird that had been disturbed by the fireworks was greeting a last-quarter moon with querulous chirpings.

VI

ON JULY 6 I was at the San Francisco airport three-quarters of an hour ahead of John's plane, and I was in the front line at the gate when he came up the ramp with the unloading passengers. He must have left Saint-Paul Island on an hour's notice, for he was wearing khaki pants and field boots and carrying a stained quilted jacket. In his other hand, along with a flight bag, he had an aluminum rod case, and I had a moment of irrational dislike of him, as if he had been irresponsibly off fishing while Marian made her bleak choices at home.

He saw me waiting, tilted back his head and smiled. His face was sun-blackened even after three weeks of Aleutian fogs; his clothes, when he made the top of the ramp and shifted his luggage to shake my hand, had a wild, gamy smell. His eyes searched my face.

"Joe," he said. "It's good of you to meet me. How is she?"

"How is she?" I said. "Brave. Undaunted. Which means nothing at all, because she's given up."

I felt him watching me as we edged around a knot of people and into the open corridor on the way to the baggage claim. His eyes were streaked, his face the square, strong, rather coarse-skinned face that makes athletes look older than they are. "How do you mean, given up?" he said.

"She won't take any treatments. She says they might harm the baby." Though I looked for signs of surprise or dismay in his face, he did not seem surprised. He only knitted his brows slightly and walked on in silence. Still in silence, he stepped on the escalator and rode it down with one hand on the rubber rail. At the bottom I said, "Doesn't that seem to you . . . mad? Totally wrong?"

"It's something she's talked of, as a possibility," John said.

"With *you*?"

"Yes."

"And you *let* her? You could have stopped that before it ever got fixed in her head! Do you want this baby more than you want her?"

Standing by a pillar while the baggage chute began to spill suitcases onto the slow ring, he gave me a quick, sharp, streaked glance of dislike. "No," he said briefly.

His canvas B-4 bag was one of the first pieces of luggage that tumbled from the chute. He grabbed it before I could get hold, but let me take the rod case. The irritation that had showed in his face creased into an expression sober but friendly. He hit my shoulder lightly with his free hand as we went out into the parking garage.

"When did she find this out?"

"The third."

"Why didn't she try to reach me sooner?"

"Why ask me?" I said bitterly. "I don't understand anything she does. I guess she didn't want to interrupt your work. When she told us, the night of the Fourth, we made her promise to call."

"Hmm," John said.

"Didn't you talk with her? How did she reach you?"

"Radio out from Anchorage," John said. He threw the B-4 bag into the back end of the car when I opened it, and stood rubbing his hands down the thighs of his wrinkled khakis. "All it said was that the doctors had given up on her. Is that right?"

"That's what she says." I followed the yellow arrows around, rolled down into the street, slid into the fast traffic headed for the Bayshore Freeway. "But good God, John," I said, not willing to look at him but not able to keep still either, "good *God*, she doesn't have to accept what they say! How can they make a statement like that, that she hasn't a chance? Not one chance? How do they know? They can be wrong like anybody else."

"She must have thought they had the evidence."

"All right!" I said. "Suppose they did? Miracles happen all the time. Somebody could make a break-through tomorrow. Keep her alive an extra sixty days and she might live another fifty years."

His cheek was as weathered as an old board. Only the bloodshot whites of his eyes showed that there might be a limit to his taciturn impassivity. When he rubbed his hand back and forward over his bristly scalp his shoulder bumped massively against mine. I wanted to shout and pound at him; it seemed to me he could not possibly realize what had brought him home; I thought him a block, incapable of feeling, dense even.

"Maybe they're wrong," he said. "Maybe she's wrong.

We'll have to see. She was never one to kid herself." Accidentally almost, when he fished for a cigarette, his tired eyes touched mine, and I realized that he could not have slept at all the night before, unless for catnaps in the Anchorage and Seattle airports. His voice was slightly hoarse, the Maine accent strong. "It takes some getting used to, even when you're braced," he said, and said hardly another word all the way back. Only when we had entered the hills and were going up through the little canyon on the county road he stirred himself, the way a dog riding into familiar ground will stir sometimes, and begin to whine out the window. He was sitting forward when we bounced over the rattletrap bridge, and before I had quite stopped in the drive he had the door open.

No one was in sight. Then the house door banged back against the wall and Debby came flying to hurl herself around his legs. "Daddy! Daddy! Daddy!" He lifted her and hugged. "Ah, baby! How's my girl?"

I got out and lifted the B-4 from the trunk and set it by John's feet. "John," I said into the chattering and the kissing, "you've got to persuade her. You *must*!"

With his lips still at Debby's cheek and ear, he turned, sober-faced, to say something. Then I saw his eyes switch their direction, and his body grow still. He was looking past his daughter's fair head to the doorway where Marian stood smiling.

I waved blindly, I got in and stepped on the throttle and drove out of there and left them alone with it.

Up on the hill I couldn't get the tableau of their meeting out of my mind. It was no use trying to talk to Ruth, who had been with Marian almost constantly for a day and a half, and who was now lying in the darkened bedroom with a migraine. In default of anything else I patched up the cut fence, and then I started taking turns around the house. Catarrh followed me for the first couple of rounds, and then sat down on the bricks and let me keep coming back to him. The weather had made its dramatic change-over from the heat of the Fourth: the fogfall lay in a cottony roll along the skyline, fingers of mist reached down across saddles and into ravines, and though the sun was bright the wind was chilly. I went on around and around.

Then I heard the noise of a motorcycle on our hill, and as I came into the patio I saw Peck in orange suit and helmet coasting toward me. It was the first time I had ever seen him on the hilltop. Hastily, to prevent his ringing the doorbell and disturbing Ruth, I went out into the drive to meet him.

He had cut the motor as he topped the hill, and now he sat balancing with his padded boots a-tiptoe. He wore a sly smile among his whiskers, and his voice was the soft, warm voice, almost as caressing as Fran LoPresti's, that he had cultivated since giving up meditation in favor of interpersonal relations. He used it the way women use their eyes; I did not doubt that on occasion it was accompanied by the palms-together gesture of Hindu greeting. Love, love, that's the word. "Ah, Mr. Allston," he said.

"Mr. Peck," I said.

His smile widened. If he had not been astride the motorcycle he might have embraced me and kissed me on both cheeks. He oozed good will and warmth. His helmeted head was tilted a little to one side, his alert eyes studied my face. "I don't like to bother you," he said. "I know you value your privacy as much as I do. But I thought I'd better come up and apologize if we disturbed you the other night, and make sure you didn't mean that about moving out."

How was it that I somehow always found myself dealing with him when I had something else, generally something distressing, on my mind? He had a faculty for the inopportune as great as what I sometimes disliked in myself. And yet I didn't want to think about Marian and John down there talking; for an hour I had been trying to walk off my feelings and forget them. I should probably have welcomed this diversion, but instead it only irritated me. I said, "Suppose I *did* mean it."

Peck laughed. It seemed I had said something amusing. "I don't blame you for being upset," he said. "I thought I'd better—*you* know—explain."

Though his voice was tuned to suggest a relaxed afternoon conversation between friends who understood one another, everything about him was in motion. He rolled his shoulders, squinted his eyes, tilted his head, drew down his mouth, bounced on the Honda's seat, took his hands off the handlebars to make gestures as if he were releasing birds into the air. Trying to equate this jittery, confidential smooth-talker with the Peck I knew as lordly, superior, and amusedly alert, I concluded that he was uneasy, he really was afraid I would throw him out. All the time I felt his watchful eyes.

I waited.

"I told you," Peck said. "We were conducting a little experiment."

"I remember, yes."

Hunch of shoulders, humorous downturn of lips, spread of hands. "Nothing very far out. People have done it with drums for centuries. But the increase in sound level, that was the idea. See if it helped people shake their hangups, get them over being jealous and hostile and all that, you know? Just compare it with other methods, like."

With the afternoon sun straight in his face, he was lighted as if for a camera close-up. He smiled and smiled, squinted, rolled his shoulders. I thought him the most preposterous fool I had ever looked at, all the more intolerable for his apparent conviction that he was snowing me, giving the old square a glimpse of the true faith.

"You know—people get hung up, especially kids," he said. "Parents ride them, they can't make it in school, love problems, all that. They're shut in, all tangled up in rules, all screwed up, *you* know. I mean, there have to be ways out, they have to tear out of the net. There are all kinds of ways, we've been doing some interesting work on some of them down below. Diet, *you* know, exercise, fasting, music with a beat—folk rock, like that." He jiggled, squinting, fixedly smiling. "Drugs, some people use. Take a trip, planetary, leave the whole screwed-up world behind you, you know?" His squint opened into his half-crazy grin, like a nudge, as if he reminded me of things he knew I knew. "*You* know. Orgasm's a way. Love is basic. Swim with the world's big vibrations instead of across them. Read love poetry, it gets the love words out in the open instead of leaving them in there with the dirty words. There're all kinds of ways. We've experimented some, there's a lot more to do. What you heard the other night was just one step."

"I thought what I heard was a very loud party."

He was pained that I would not understand. He took his hands off the handgrips and shook them, palms up and fingers spread, as if he expected the words that would enlighten me to come drifting down and settle in them. "Mr. Allston," he said, "I don't know if you'll believe this. But I took notes, I interviewed each one. The informants had different reports—*you* know, personalities are different, things hit them differently—but every person that went into the culvert the other night testified that he came out, *you* know, really cleansed. Purified."

I held his eye; it didn't waver. Fantastic con man, or true believer, or nut, or a voice crying in the wilderness, Prepare ye the way of the Lord? He smiled with his head on one side.

"Then what?" I said. "After coming out purified, what did you all do? Did everybody there go home, kiss his parents, forgive his enemies, make up with his girl? Did Julie LoPresti go home and get reconciled with her mother? Are you going back to Chicago and shake your father's hand and ask his blessing?"

Not nut, not con man; and if true believer and prophet, then also Adversary. Our incomparable and incorrigible mutual gift for dislike was between us like sudden kicked-up dust. Peck's lips moved secretly, as if tasting, in the brown beard. "Not quite," he said. "There's too much that has to be changed in the Establishment before anybody could be reconciled to *it*."

"So hostility survives your therapy."

"I didn't ask you to subscribe to the theory," Peck said. "I only came up to explain that there was, *you* know, a serious purpose to the noise."

"You're seriously telling me that?"

"You don't believe it?"

"No."

A short silence. His brilliant eyes glittered like wet stones in the sun. He looked away, pressing his red lips together, then looked back. His shoulders lifted and dropped carelessly. "All right, that's your privilege. But we did turn it off when you asked us."

"Yes," I said. "Yes, you did. But it's hardly anything you can take a lot of credit for. Because I didn't ask you, I told you. You'd have been in trouble if you hadn't."

"Yes," Peck said, studying me. "I wonder if I can explain this so you'll understand. We're in trouble now if you make us move. It would crack everything just—wide open. I've invested a lot of time and thought and money down there. We're just beginning to make headway with the school. A lawyer friend of mine has applied for tax-deductible status for us, and we've got three people ready to put up money to get us off the ground. We're just . . ."

"School?" I said. "What school?"

The question obviously made him impatient. He didn't reply.

"Mr. Peck," I said, "I don't know what you take me for. One minute you tell me you're developing noise therapy, and the next it turns out that without asking me or even telling me you're founding a school. If I objected to that noise once, doesn't it strike you I might object to it as a regular classroom exercise?"

"The noise therapy isn't basic," Peck said. "Anyway, we've done the fundamental experiment. We can let it go."

"Fine," I said. "But what is this school? I've never been asked if you could start a school down there. If I had, I'd have said no. I don't want the traffic, I don't want the fire hazard, I don't want the garbage, I don't want the liability, I don't want the nuisance to the Catlins."

"I spoke to Mrs. Catlin," Peck said. "She wasn't bothered."

"You spoke to her? When?"

"Just now."

"Just *now*? Wasn't John there?"

"Yes, they were all there."

"Oh, good Christ!" I said. "You rang their doorbell just now, a few minutes ago?"

"Sure. Why not?"

"Never mind," I said. "It just makes it all the more necessary that you move out. I gave you a week. You've still got five days."

He straddled, head sunk, his arms braced down on the handlebars. His hands squeezed the brakes and let them out again. His feral eyes came up to meet mine. "Why do you hate us?" he said softly.

"I don't hate you."

"Oh yes you do!"

"I disapprove of you, I disagree with you, I think you're dangerous. You want to know why I disapprove of you?"

"Not particularly," he said with a curled mouth. "But if it will relieve your hangup."

I had trouble keeping my hands at my sides. "Maybe

it will," I said. "So I'll tell you. From the minute you showed up here, you dared me to. For some reason I equal the Establishment. Do I remind you of your father, or what? You felt for some reason you had to challenge me. You asked me if you could camp, and you wanted to bait me into giving you permission without wanting to. You agreed to several conditions and you deliberately broke them all. You expanded your pad and you put in a shed and a mailbox and you moved in your gang and you threw garbage around and you built fires and you stole power from my pole and water from my well line and now you start a school. Doesn't it occur to you I might have a right to disapprove?"

"That's it, that permission bit, isn't it?" Peck said. "You've got to be asked. You want your authority recognized."

"I'd like my rights recognized, and the rights of some other people."

He was studying the gravel of the drive, and he wore no trace of the smile that I had thought a permanent fixture of his face. "As long as we're speaking of rights," he said, "what about the improvements I've made in that property for you? Shouldn't those be taken into consideration?"

About that point I found myself as weary as I have ever been of any human being—weary, weary, sick to death of him, and reminded too, as I always was. He was Curtis all over again, but worse, madder, more insistent. I understood him no more than I would have understood a Martian, but I understood the evil things he did to me, the way he had of making me be less than myself. I turned away from him. "That's fantastic,"

I said. "I'll have to burn the place out to sterilize it."

I started toward the house. To my back he said quickly, "Wait. Wait a minute. What's the answer, then?"

"The answer to what?"

"Do we stay, or don't we? Make your conditions."

"There are no conditions, because there never was any question. Of course you don't stay."

He jerked so furiously on the teetering Honda that I thought he was going to leap off and attack me. Then for a second he glared downward between the handlebars, thinking. His hands tightened on the grips, he dropped head and shoulders in a spasmodic, furious gesture. His foot kicked down, the motor caught. There he went, spattering gravel back toward me in a pebbly rain. There he went—wronged innocence, repudiated idealism, frustrated science, thwarted aspiration. And left me feeling how? Relieved? Justified? Oh no. Sick, half nauseated from anger, baffled and unsettled and vaguely guilty.

2

Peck didn't even stick out his legitimate week. I was walking in the lane—accidentally, though he wouldn't have believed that—when the Volkswagen bus pulled out the gate with a load of miscellaneous junk and Peck came straddling after it on the Honda. I stopped, giving him a chance to get by without an encounter, but he paused at the gate to settle the helmet over his tangle of hair. The morning was overcast and gray. He sat there screwing his neck around, getting the chin strap under his beard, while the Honda chuckled under him. The Catlins had gone to Carmel for a few days, a move that I thoroughly approved, even though it left Ruth and me adrift and wretched. There we were, Peck and I, just the two of us; and there was tension between us like a stretched wire.

He turned his hairy face—he had been aware all the time that I was there. His eyes glittered under the helmet's round brow, the smile that had been his trademark for months was missing. Spaceman, kook, barefoot saint, seeker, searcher, rebel, lush, pothead, idealist, bughouse intellectual, Modern Youth, whatever he was, he looked me in the eyes for a second that contained our mutual recognition and abhorrence.

"We can't take it all yet," he said. "I'll have to leave the stuff in the shed till later. All right?"

It was not a request, it was still a challenge, but I shrugged. "All right."

"Thanks a lot." So I granted him one last favor, with dislike, and he thanked me with sarcasm, and he gunned his motor and was gone out of my life as abruptly as he had come into it. He left me feeling as if I had just shaken off something slimy that had crawled on my skin, and yet I had too the unsatisfied sense that all through our association of many months I had failed to do something I might have done. What? Try to teach that baboon something? Try to *learn* something from his gibberings? Try to reach whatever sense of responsibility he had? Build up a moral nature in that wilderness? There had never been a meeting between us, only a handful of confrontations. What if, early in our acquaintance, I had crossed the creek?

Alone in the quiet bottoms, too early for the mail, I

crossed it that morning for the first time. I found the bridge, which they had left down, difficult but passable, and as I inched across, I wondered why Peck had not destroyed it. Better surrender it to the Philistines than wreck the product of his own creative labor? Or had he left the whole shebang for Debby? Or had he left it simply because it never occurred to him to clean up after himself? Or maybe because he wanted to emphasize his deliberate disregard of my demands?

Whatever his reasons, it was a grubby gift for Debby, an effective means of giving me the finger. I stepped from the swaying bridge into inch-deep dust. Before me the stained platform, wearing the cleaner rectangular mark of the tent, was littered with rags, papers, gutted books, beer cans, beer bottles, wine jugs, sink sponges, leaves, socks, a woman's moccasin, a broken peel chair. When I kicked over a fruit basket I exposed a dozen fierce earwigs. Ants were moving up and down the trunk of the oak and clotting around some spilled syrup or honey in a shelf nailed to the tree. Below the shelf their unretrieved, perhaps outgrown motto greeted me from its faded board, the end of it broken off. BE YOURSELF. GOOD IS THE SELF SPEA

The ladder to the treehouse, like the bridge, had been left down. Climbing it, I put my face in the door of what had been holy of holies, Ark of the Covenant, love nest, what else: a crooked little room with an old sweater hanging on a nail and the floor drifted with feathers, evidently from a torn sleeping bag.

Vaguely disappointed—yet what had I expected to find, snooping around where during Peck's tenancy I had scorned to go?—I stooped inside. As I did so I kicked an electric wire, and produced a sear of blue sparks, a tingling foot, and a smell of ozone. They had salvaged their electric equipment by simply yanking it off the wire. A true Peckism. If he had left the bridge and treehouse for Debby's use—and I did not entirely deny the possibility—he had managed to leave it so that she would electrocute herself the first time she came to play.

My anger was as hot as the sparks. I would have to clean up his leavings, and not for the first time. But then a few minutes later I stood out on the deck and looked across bare buckeyes, ragged oaks, and green bay trees that filled the gully southward. It occurred to me that Peck, insane as he was, had had a genuine affection for this place, and had availed himself of it with some imagination, and had left it with regret.

Against the hill that rose sharply behind the tent the poison oak was thin-leafed, already turning red; among the tangle gleamed dozens of beer cans. But even that testimony to Peck's slovenliness could not drive out of me the feeling that this place without its semihuman occupiers was forlorn. Standing among the Freedom Force's shabby leavings I had a haunted sense of *déjà vu,* and immediately I located the source of the feeling: Curtis's room, mornings when I stood in it and looked with distaste at the results of a week of his occupancy.

Perhaps it was for Debby's sake, perhaps for other reasons, that I scraped out the treehouse with a flap of cardboard, and kicked together the worst of the refuse on and around the tent platform, and tore the motto and the crooked shelf from the oak, and set the pile afire and waited nearly an hour while it burned out. The culvert at the edge of the brush hummed like Fran

LoPresti's welded woman when I knocked it with my fist. I thought of rolling it down into the creek, just to get it out of the way and prevent someone's thinking I had stolen it, since it was on my land; but in the end I left it there.

On the other side I disconnected the hidden wire from above my meter box. I was finding the chores rather pleasant, like tidying up after friends' children have been playing around the place. Though I contemplated unhooking the water line as well, I decided to leave it, thinking that Debby, more or less in the spirit of the former inhabitants, might want to make mudpies. For a moment, forgetting, I even revived a previous notion that Ruth and I might build a teahouse there on Peck's flat, with a high arching Japanese bridge, and I had a brief vision of the Allstons and the Catlins having tea there together on damp winter afternoons, while the creek went secretly past below us, entangled in its blackberry and poison oak. Brief, a moment only. Then I remembered why the Catlins were in Carmel, and the prospects we all had before us.

After a week, when Peck's outfit did not return for it, I removed their mailbox, completing the cleanup except for the shed with its miscellany of odd junk. But I could not feel good about closing up the University of the Free Mind. For one thing, I had done it in anger, not after reflection. For another, I knew that Marian would regret their going. She had a mystical confidence that by trying many things they might eventually learn something that we who tried little would never learn. I had agreed with her more than once, but insisted that they also forgot more, and wasted more, than we who weren't revolutionary would ever forget or waste. Still,

I regretted having to explain why the ashram had left so abruptly, and though the flat beyond the creek was now open territory, I found myself avoiding it. I didn't even like crossing the dry creek bed below it at the end of a walk. It seemed to me that the culvert up there, hollow and resonant, Peck's perfect monument, troubled the air at intervals with a faint, swarming hum when the wind blew through it.

3

My promptness in dealing with Peck had not reinstated me with Fran. In place of the old neighborly unction, she now treated me on our infrequent meetings with distant politeness. All kinds of connections seemed to be broken. Dave Weld I hardly ever saw any more: it turned out that he had located the ashram in its new place up on the skyline, and being mobile in his Mercury, he spent all his spare time up there. Once or twice I saw Julie with him in the car; more often I encountered her at the Catlin cottage or on the trail or lane, riding with Debby. If I met her in the house, she left the room. If she saw me coming on the road, she turned her gelding into the brush.

Lovable old Joe Allston, everybody's friend. Was it my fault? A lot of people thought so—even, I was afraid, Marian. She thought I took Peck too personally, as if he were my moral responsibility. And she was quite right, I did. But we did not spend much time discussing him, except when he got his name in the papers. Most of the time, Marian had her ear tuned inward, not outward. All the tumult among the careless and the rebellious must have seemed like the meaningless traffic noise outside a sickroom. For through late July and August she was learning how to get ready to die, and because she had that other preparation too, that baby to whom I thought she too readily gave up, she felt that she had to stay in good health for her dying.

Fascinated and miserable, we watched her coddle herself, not giving up her routine duties, but resting often, going to bed early, forcing down those health-food mixtures, tiger's milk and such, that she thought gave her the most calories per mouthful. When I saw her during one of her rest periods, stretched on the old redwood lounge in the grove, abstracted, lightly frowning, I imagined she was focusing her will on her body, willing the growth in her womb to speed up and the deadly growth in pancreas and liver to slow down.

Watching was about all we found to do. It was no use talking to John. More than once, in the beginning, I came at him with suggestions—male hormones, why not? They were said to be effective in some cases. What if they did produce masculine characteristics? Wouldn't he rather see Marian with a beard like Jim Peck's than . . . submit . . . . fade? But they had talked it all out on that trip to Carmel. They had a secret, impregnable solidarity that excluded us from their decisions while we were still welcomed to their company and their affection.

Having made her choice, she left none to us. Forced to attend helplessly, I watched her with the apprehensive alertness of a young man in love. If I missed seeing her for a day I grew anxious. Some days I walked the hill three or four times just on the chance that I would see her and have an excuse to stop. The more I saw them drawing together the more I hated my own intrusions and the less I was able to keep from intruding, especially after they sent Debby off for three weeks to the Canaday ranch camp and there were chances of catching Marian alone. Increasingly, I found myself searching for revelations in her face. It remained the face of Marian Catlin, it paid us its usual compliment of eager interest, total attention, warmth, love. It remained addicted to laughter.

Too addicted to laughter? Hysterical? Afraid? But I would no sooner begin to wonder than I would catch her eyes on me so tenderly, so reassuringly, that I put my anxiety down as obscene. She deserved better of us than this morbid watchfulness.

But we noted changes. As she began to expose herself less to the sun, her summer tan paled to a sort of translucent gold, the kind of skin you sometimes see on beautiful Eurasian girls. In repose she appeared utterly serene, purged of every impurity, and she went about her work quietly, without strain.

Once we watched her and John walking toward us where we stood by the boxes waiting for the delayed mailman. They came slowly, holding hands, watching the ground but absorbed in each other, confidential and intimate and intent. Ruth's eyes flew from them to me, to see if I had seen what she saw. Tears massed in them all at once. Biting her lip, she turned away, and was barely able to greet them when they looked up and saw us.

Marian let John limit himself to a half day at the lab, but she did not exempt herself from the duties that can make even dying seem a troublesome interruption of more important things. I suppose there was a degree of support in familiar routines, though it grieved us to see her occupied with shopping, laundry, meals, housework, and when Debby was at home, the incessant taxiing to swimming pool or park or piano lesson or the house of some friend. We hated the obligations she undertook to entertain visiting professors and faculty wives, and when we saw strange cars in the drive we avoided the cottage, feeling excluded and aggrieved.

Yet as I think about it, it seems that we did see her often alone, as if she often got John and Debby out of the house in order to be private with her two inward guests. Especially about noon, when I made my walk to the mailbox, and especially when Debby was away at camp, I used to see her resting in the grove, eyes closed, hands folded on her podded abdomen, her body otherwise thin and straight like an effigy on a tomb, and her face burning upward, a waiting lamp in the dry shade. The moment she heard my step her face would turn, her eyes open, her smile flash out, the rheostat of her spirit turn up ready for company. I never caught her with the lamp turned clear down. Perhaps that was why I never lost hope. I couldn't believe she was really waiting for what she was waiting for.

Once, when I had stopped like that, I asked her if she had any pain. "No, thank God," she said. "I worry about it. I don't know if I could stand the kind of pain there is sometimes."

"It seems to me you can stand anything."

"The bones are the worst, apparently," she said. "Nobody can stand it in the bones. But I don't have it there." Turning on me that unforced radiant smile, she knocked lightly on the wooden frame of the lounge.

"I wish you'd agree to some sort of treatments," I said hopelessly.

But she put me down with an admonitory lifted hand and a humorous breathy sigh. "Joe, please, it wouldn't be any use. I don't want to be fooled, or soothed, or kept expensively alive as a morphine vegetable. All I want—no, of course I want more, but I'll *settle* for time to have the baby. When the other gets close, I hope I have the nerve to let it come. I hope I'm conscious enough to help it along, not slow it down for no purpose. That's why I worry about the pain. I'm afraid it'll be bad and I'll miss it."

"*Miss* it?"

"Miss the experience. It must be one of the greatest, and it's certainly the last."

"Oh, Marian!"

"Oh, Joe!" she said, mocking me, and banged her reddened palm on the frame of the lounge. "We all wear such tough *hides*! We cover ourselves up so! You can't blame me for thinking about it a lot. I swear we never know half what life means, not even what it feels like. Birth and death are the greatest experiences we ever know, and we smother them in drugs and twilight sleep."

"The hard pleasures," I said. "You'll tell me next you had Debby behind a bush." If I had not made a joke I would have had to leave her.

She shook her head with a reminiscent half-smile. "I wasn't good enough. I wanted to do it without anesthetic, but the doctor wouldn't let me; he thought

I might have a bad time, I'm so narrow. So I got him to set up a mirror I could watch in, and when the pain got too bad I raised a little flag and the anesthetist put the cone over my face till I could feel myself going, and then I raised the flag again and he took it off. I experienced part of it, but I wasn't good enough to get it all."

I had to look away from her bright serious face, down into the tangle of blackberry and poison oak and maidenhair that hid the creek channel. It was a warm, still midday, everything stuck on dead center. The heat and smog of the valley were being pushed up into the folds of the hills, and the brown shade smothered me.

"Joe," she said, and put her cool hand on the back of mine. "Don't feel bad. I'm glad you love me, but I hope you and Ruth won't grieve. It's right there should be death in the world, it's as natural as being born. We're all part of a big life pool, and we owe the world the space we fill and the chemicals we're made of. Once we admit it's not an abstraction, but something we do personally owe, it shouldn't be hard."

"But you love everything about your life," I said. "You're more alive than anybody I . . ." It was more than I could do, I couldn't sit there calmly discussing her obliteration. I said, "If you were my age, maybe I could stand it."

For a good while she said nothing. When I could look at her again she smiled coaxingly, inviting me to join her on that plateau of impossible tranquillity she had somehow reached. "Isn't it complicated to be human, though?" she said. "Animals seem to give up their lives so naturally. Even when it's violent it seems natural. They mature, and reproduce themselves, and a lot of the young are taken but a few survive, and the phylum is safe so the old ones can die in the stream like salmon, or get pulled down by wolves like old caribou, and it's right, it's what they expect and what nature needs."

I made some inarticulate sign—assent, dissent, *nolo contendere,* something.

"And after all," Marian said, "I've done it. I grew up, I married John, I had Debby. So *knowing,* being able to understand and forecast and even predict an approximate date, shouldn't make any real difference. I guess consciousness makes individuals of us, and as individuals we lose the old acceptance."

From the grove I was looking up at the golden glare of Weld's hill on the other side of the lane. A buzzard was cruising around the top, tilting, fingering the air delicately. I could see his head crane as he looked down, and then he banked and was out of sight behind the trees.

"The one thing," Marian said in a voice that went suddenly small and tight, "the thing I can hardly bear sometimes is that I won't ever see *her* grow up. She'll have to do it without whatever I could have given her."

I saw her bite down on her lower lip, her eyes fled mine and turned up into the roof of leaves. In her throat the pulse fluttered, tethered and frantic. But only for a second. When she spoke again her voice was back to the controlled, modulated, musical, rather high tone of normal conversation.

"Time, too," she said, looking upward. "Time and everything that one could do in it, and the chance of wasting or losing or never even realizing it. It's so important to us because we see it so close. We're individuals, we're full of ourselves, and so we're bad historians. We get crazy and anxious because all of a sudden there's so little time left to be loving and generous as we wish we'd always been and always intended to be. John is always saying ontogeny repeats phylogeny. Do you suppose I feel the shortness of time because I want to experience everything and feel everything that the race has ever felt? Because there's so *much* to feel, and I'm greedy?"

I could not answer. Around us, as we sat, the silence revealed itself to be not silence at all, but a deep vibrant hum, the distant roar of the hot acquisitive society that we both half repudiated, and under it the small reassuring noises of the natural world. A jet came over from the south, already letting down for San Francisco, and blotted everything out. Then, as it faded northward, the little noises came back. Among the oak leaves, dry and horny as the cast shells of little crabs, a lizard made a sudden stir. The birds, I realized just then, were starting to sing again after the long preoccupation with nests and young. From the hill a meadow lark piped sweet and piercing, and apparently a long way off, deep in the ravine, I heard the three plaintive dropping notes of a wren. It seemed too much life for anyone soberly to consider leaving behind.

"Do you know how magnificent you are?" I said shakily. "Do you know how many people in your situation grab for every petty selfish indulgence? How many really *are* greedy? How many go into blind panic, or turn their backs and pretend they haven't got what they've got? And you sit thinking how little time there is to be loving and generous."

"To my daughter," she said. "To my husband. To my

friends, a few like you and Ruth. They're my pleasure, after all. If I managed to be what I'd like to be, I *would* be indulging myself."

I stood up, because I couldn't bear for another second to have her smile so at me, and bent blindly to kiss her, and went away. But afterward, those few minutes were between us, a secret, and I realized she had come out of herself and admitted me to her confidence because she wanted to comfort and reassure me. I am certain she made the same effort for each of the people she cared about, and that each of them kept it as something private and precious, and talked about it no more than I did. When we came to see her, we were the ones who were comforted. She made us all confederates in her preparations, and I know that Ruth and I, at least, picked up strength from her. She had so much she could give it away. Her biological confidence was so serene that she could accept even the blind coffin worm as an essential part of the biota.

4

Changes, symptoms, stigmata—we watched for them, unable to help ourselves, and slowly, a trace at a time, they appeared.

"Have you noticed how indifferent Marian is getting to Debby?" Ruth said one day, one of those blurred indistinguishable days while summer droned on and she burned toward her end. "It's as if she's so intent on having the new baby she's forgetting the one she has."

I said I hadn't noticed any such thing. If she seemed

indifferent, it was because she was tired all the time, and who could blame her?

"I wasn't blaming her. I've just been noticing. It started all of a sudden. It's more than tiredness."

"That doesn't sound like Marian. She adores that child."

"Adored," Ruth said. "She's changed. You watch. John's the one who's attached to Debby now."

"Naturally, he's saving Marian all he can."

"That wouldn't make her act so cold. It's like a repudiation."

"If I were in her place I'd probably think of nobody but myself," I said. "I can't think it's any more than that. What are they going to do when John has to go back to teaching?"

"I thought you knew. He's taking the quarter off."

I brooded about that, trying to imagine how it would feel to conduct your life as if you were driving soberly, carefully, well within the speed limit and in accordance with all the traffic laws, toward an intersection already in sight, where you knew a crazy drunk out of control was going to hit you head on. It is no good to say we all conduct our lives that way: most of us can't see the intersection, and so can pretend it isn't there.

Bitterly I said, "They figure three months will take care of it, is that it? It's almost obscene, they're like conspirators. Are they going to have signals, you suppose, so when she's at her last breath she can lower her little flag and John can tell the doctors, 'O.K., boys, rip away, get that babe'?"

"Joe!"

"Christ," I said, "it gives me the horrors."

"What should they do, pretend?"

No, not pretend. Pretending was what a lot of people did, and changed nothing. Only undoing would serve. I thought I would trade my possible ten more years of life to be God for ten minutes, to undream their nightmare for them and unravel all their careful preparations.

What is more, I didn't understand all their preparations. Some, like the heartbreaking little gifts she brought us, things that were like the gifts a serious and affectionate little girl might leave her friends when she went home from a summer at the shore or in the mountains, were plain enough, however painful. But why would she let John suspend his work for a quarter? It would have been more her style to make him go down to that lab every morning until the very day she had to be taken to the hospital. His career was at least as important to her as to him, and she would want life served, not death. And now this rejection of Debby, right when I would have expected her to be hungrily protective and possessive to the last frayed end of her strength. What about her wish to be generous and loving? Was she already so far gone that she was letting go the strongest claim on her life?

For as soon as Ruth put me to watching, I saw that she was right. Marian was systematically rejecting her daughter. And something more: John abetted her, it was some agreement between them.

In place of the two pony tails we had got used to in the station wagon, bouncing out across the bridge to piano lesson or school, now it was crewcut and small pony tail. In place of the thin bright figure that used to lean on the corral watching Debby ride, it was now

John. In the early morning when sounds rose clearly from the bottom land I heard child and father talking as they dipped rolled barley out of the bin or shook out a slab or two from a bale of hay. Marian's voice was not there any more; she was inside, in bed, in the kitchen, down in the grove reading. And on weekends and afternoons when Debby would ordinarily have been around the place, with or without playmates, John frequently took her with him into the hills while he salvaged firewood out of down trees. He didn't need all that wood, he had two or three cords of it already. But he went, and he took Debby with him.

When the child skinned her knee or walked into a blackberry vine or had her foot stepped on by the horse, it was John who answered her crying and took her into the bathroom for ceremonial Mercurochrome and a Band-Aid. If she tried to climb into Marian's lap, Marian held her away until John could take her, not always without an argument, onto his own knee. We heard her call, sometimes, yelling for her mother to come and see some skink or ring-necked snake or brick-colored salamander in the frog pond, and though Marian had spent hours and days teaching her to take an interest in country creatures and had built that frog pond herself, we observed that now she paid no attention. If John was not there to take over, the summons went unanswered.

Indications multiplied. We stopped once to pick up Marian for shopping, and here came Debby running, squawling to go too. Marian shut the car door in her face. "Lucky you," she said. "You get to stay home with Daddy." She gave me a sign, and we drove off. In the mirror I saw Debby in a brief shower of tears at the roadside, and out the door John coming, alert to provide his substitute comfort.

Or they were up at our place one Sunday afternoon for a drink. The fog had rolled over the skyline, and the wind was chilly, so that we sat on the patio side, in the lee. Debby had stripped to the hide to wade in the pool and push around a plastic boat that John—not Marian—produced for her. She gabbled to herself as she played, an innocent obbligato to our talk, which was unstrained and quiet, briefly oblivious of the madman on the intersecting road. The sheltered sun was warm, the mockingbird was singing again from the terrace, where he had sung for us the first day they ever visited us.

This was what we had come here for, this peace. We had cultivated it as strenuously as Marian cultivated aliveness. Whenever it settled upon us in its purity I was likely to think that if this was what Peck and the boys got on a sugar cube I might be tempted to join them. It lay on us that afternoon like a fine dust of gold, and especially on the child, slim and tender, a peeled willow stick, bending in the pool. She was absorbed, entirely unself-conscious. Her body was brown except for the white pants of skin that had been protected from the sun by swimming trunks. Turning, bending, shoving the plastic boat, she was the most graceful of creatures, perfect and smooth, smoothly cleft, round-limbed.

Then I took my eyes off her and found Marian watching her with so hungry an expression that it obviously embarrassed her to be caught in it. "Ah!" she exclaimed, and stretched out her legs luxuriously. "This is nice!" She reached down and picked up limp Catarrh, arching past her chair. A little flush stained the satiny skin across her cheekbone. She knew what her face had given away, and it was neither weariness nor rejection, it was devouring love.

"Hey!" Debby said suddenly, with her face bent nearsightedly close to the water. "There are *fish* in here! Little tiny fish! Mummy, come look!"

"Mosquito fish," I said. "I had the county mosquito abatement bring some the other day: we were getting a lot of wigglers."

Stroking Catarrh with so firm a hand that it slanted his blinking eyes, Marian looked toward me as if begging some conversation. The pink in her cheekbone deepened. She said nothing. John stood up.

"Mummy!" Debby cried. "There are *millions* of them!"

Her father squatted beside her with one hand on her narrow back. Touching her—I had noticed how much he touched her lately, his hand was always on her head, his arm around her—he said heartily, "Those little fish are as fierce as sharks. Here, let's catch a fly, I'll show you."

It was smoothly done. He waited, squatting, until one of our summer flies alighted on his knee. A swoop of the hand and he had it. He pinched and rolled his fingers, opened them, and dropped the injured fly on the water. From where I sat I could see the water swirl with miniature savagery as they tore it apart.

"Wow!" Debby said. She stepped out to stand, September Morn, reaching an uncertain toe back toward the water.

"You'd *better* get out," John said. "Those things would gnaw you off at the knees." His hand patted her white bottom, but she was already gone, pulling at Marian's arm. Catarrh hopped down and slid away. "Mummy, come and look. They just *gobble.*"

Sitting straighter, Marian brushed away the drops of drink that Debby had spilled on her. "Now you've slopped me."

"Come *look!*"

"I've seen them, hon."

"No you haven't."

"Others like them."

"Why *won't* you come?" Debby said angrily. *"I want you to come and see!"*

Marian withdrew herself. "If we're losing our manners we'll have to be taken home."

"But just come see!"

"You're acting very badly," Marian said. "Mummy may not want to come and see. Mummy may be tired. You go watch them all you want."

Ruth and I sat and listened as to the demonstration of a problem we had not heard stated. Now John came into it again. He picked up the naked child and held her, smiling down into her angry face. "Come on, kid," he said. "I've got a better idea. You get your pants on so we don't shock the neighbors and you and I will go over in the field and see if John Rabbit is around."

He held her between his knees and slid on her panties. Then he hoisted her onto his shoulders. "Excuse us," he said. "I've been promising to show her where a jack-rabbit friend of ours lives."

Marian was exposed to two looks, her daughter's reproachful glare and her husband's still, questioning glance. She closed her eyes, and they went away. When they were fifty steps out on the drive, and turning up toward the stile in the pasture fence, she moved her head back and forth slightly against the chair. "I'm sorry," she said, still with her eyes shut.

"Is she too much for you, Marian?" Ruth said. "Why doesn't she stay with us? We'd love having her. She'd see you every day, but you wouldn't have the care of her, or John either."

With her thumb on her cheekbone, her fingertips braced against her forehead, Marian sat looking down. Through her fingers she lifted a brief, wry smile. "It's sweet of you, but that wouldn't do it."

"Do what?"

"Oh, it's the hardest thing of all!" Marian said. Her fingertips rubbed at the crease between her eyes. "We don't want her unhappy, she shouldn't feel repudiated, but she *has* to be detached from me. She's always been too dependent. John's been away so much, and I've spoiled her."

"So you're now doing what?" I said, more sharply than I intended. "Breaking down her affection?"

"Not her affection, Joe. Her dependence. I don't want her to feel lost and shattered without a mother. I'd like her to miss me, but I know it's better she shouldn't, too much. So we're trying to phase me out and John in. But oh, it's hard! I have to turn myself into a stone!"

I said to Ruth, "Well, there's your explanation." I felt like clutching my head. How often that girl outraged me, trying to live by a theory instead of by her own sound feelings or by common sense. Or die by one. I couldn't help saying, "Does John think she should be deprived of the memory of a loving mother?"

"He agrees with me. He hates it, but he agrees."

"I hate it too," I said, "and I don't think I do agree. Good God, Marian, it's impossible for Debby, and miserable for you! Let her miss you. She'll be richer all her life for that sorrow."

She gave me her clear blue thoughtful glance, looking sidelong through the fingers still pressed against her forehead. Evidently she saw the redness of her palm, for with a grimace she laid it flat on her thigh. "Both my parents were killed when I was just about her age," she said. "I don't want her lost like that."

"*You* survived it," I said. "Not too badly."

"Joe, I had nightmares for years. I was always dreaming I was lost in some forest, or in a great bleak place like a tundra."

"And survived the nightmares too," I said. "This isn't the way you usually talk. You're always saying face up to it, experience it. Anyway, what about what Debby wants? Doesn't that matter?"

"She wants love," Marian said. "She's learning to go to John for it. He's the gentlest man in the world, she's got to discover that. Before long she'll be calling on him, not me. Then it'll be easier for both of them when I go."

Preparations, plans as if for a sabbatical year. They set my teeth on edge. Her explanation left me shaky and undone, as always when I caught her trying to assert her will against inevitability. Sometimes I almost resented her assumption that she could control the circumstances of her death; I wondered if she could be called selfish for presuming to steer the lives of those who would survive her. And inconsistent: if all experience, including pain, was good for her, it ought to be good for Debby too. And finally presumptuous. Good God, presumptuous was too mild a word.

Bothered by her presumption, I vaguely resented John's submission to it. Perhaps he resented me, too, for I could not keep still. Sometime in September I begged him to make her abort the wretched fetus that was shortening her life.

The answer that he gave me was probably the only possible answer, and he gave it to me with the emotional control, the rocklike composure, that had put me off when I met him at the airport. This active, strong, clean, easy-smiling, well-educated young American, this man whose face you could have used on posters, this *mens sana in corpore sano*, no beater of the breast or dabbler in his own insides, but a doer, a hunter of new knowledge and a believer in the future—this man you could trust to look after a child or chair a committee or conduct an impartial investigation, who could conceive an important problem and devise the system of research that might solve it, this scientist whose science was life, and who was as tender and intense about life as anybody I knew except his wife—this man so fortunate in every way but the most important looked at me somberly and said, "She's entitled to do it her way. It's her death."

So it was, so it was. And closer every morning.

5

Waiting is one of the forms of boredom, as it can be one of the shapes of fear. The thing you wait for compels you time after time toward the same images, the same feelings, which become only further repetitive elements in the sameness of the days. Here, even the weather enforces monotony. The mornings curve over, one like another, for a week, two weeks, three weeks, unchanging in temperature, light, color, humidity, or if changing, changing by predictable small gradations that amount to no changes at all. Never a tempest, thunderstorm, high wind; never a cumulus cloud, not at this season. Hardly a symptom to tell you summer is passing into autumn, unless it is the dense green of the tarweed that late in summer, against all the dry probabilities, appears in patches on the baked hills. Its odor and its unseasonable green become manifest together, until the smell covers a whole district, lifts on the slightest wind, fills the head, perfumes shoes and trousers and cats that have passed through it, and closets where shoes and trousers have been stored, and hands that have stroked the cat's fur.

In recollection, those weeks of waiting telescope for me as all dull time does. They were interminable while passing, but looked back upon they seem only an accelerating hour, scented with tarweed. When August had blurred into September, and school had begun, and John had begun taxiing Debby mornings and afternoons as Marian had used to do, the smell of tarweed was in every breath we drew.

Most of the time we were as isolated with the Catlins' trouble as if we had been adrift with them on a raft. Other neighbors, other concerns, passed largely unhailed, outside the latitude of our obsession. Tom Weld rattled in and out in his pickup, and walked the hill with surveyors. White stakes sprouted, and we saw by the paper that a subdivision plan was before the planning commission. Ordinarily it would have desolated us; in our preoccupation with Marian we noticed it only as one more betrayal of what we had come for, and hardly felt anger. Mrs. Weld blossomed into September in a yellow Impala, evidently a down payment on prosperity. Lou LoPresti, encountered on a walk, wore a pucker in his forehead and a shamed air as if he had been forbidden to speak to us. Maybe he had. Fran we practically never saw, nor Julie; when we did see Julie, she was not on her horse but in Dave Weld's Mercury, and generally headed for the skyline. Once I met Peck on the county road, buzzing along on his Honda, a messenger from nirvana with the wind like a fire hose in his beard. He did not greet me.

Wraiths, shadows of dissolving cloud, meaningless apparitions. They meant no more to us than the latest Tokyo student riot or yesterday's military coup in Syria.

Holding ourselves available for the Catlins' need, we accepted no invitations and issued none. And because they had no immediate family to call on, and had been so briefly in California that their acquaintance was small, they let us help. I like to believe that their resolution was not as rocklike as it seemed, and that they felt a little less desperate because of us. Pity was part of it, too: we took Marian's condition so hard that they both felt sorry for us.

Ruth cooked and cleaned and laundered, I played driver and yardman; occasionally we were able to take Debby off their hands. Regularly, when John was at the lab in the mornings, we stopped in to do what we could. By taking over little household jobs, Ruth released Marian to other, more troubling tasks. She put Debby's clothes completely in order. She went through her desk and storage cupboards and bundled together photographs, sorted letters, burned some, sent others back to their writers. She wrote to people she had valued and left behind in her thirty years. Slowly, saving herself and thinking about what she was doing, and resting frequently, she cleaned up the small debris of her life. From day to day we saw little change in her. Yet whenever our telephone rang we hurried to answer it with adrenalin pumping into our blood, for fear this, now, here, was the moment.

One evening in mid-September it rang while we were eating supper in the patio. I hurried in and got it in the middle of the third ring. "Hello?" I said.

Fran's voice, not glutinous but tense and tight, full of hatred and venom. Oh, she could have poisoned me through the porches of my ear. "I just wanted you to know what your beatniks have been up to."

"Fran," I said, "they're not *my* beatniks, I'm as unhappy about them as you are, and I did run them . . ."

"No you're not," she said. "You couldn't possibly be. Dirty, filthy, hairy animals! Do you know what they've done to that miserable child of mine?"

I was afraid I did, but I said I didn't.

"They've got her *pregnant*!" Fran said. Her voice swelled so that I held the receiver away from my ear; it went on shouting at me. "Pregnant! Not sixteen yet, and pregnant! And not ashamed of it one bit, my God! Throws it in my face! Runs away to live with them in that . . . coop . . . pigpen. . . ."

"Fran, Fran," I said. "I *am* sorry, believe me. When did you find this out?"

"Yesterday. Last night. Today she's gone, but I know

exactly where. I had Lou trail that Weld boy one day. He's as bad as she is, poisoned, simply poisoned by those . . ."

"Did she say who was responsible?"

Her hard, unpleasant laugh made me move the receiver out again. "Why, don't you know about modern youth?" she said. "They don't have fathers any more, there's nothing so old-fashioned as an affair. You know what she told me? My God, you know what she said? She said it might have been any of a half dozen. To my face."

"Oh Lord."

"Yes, oh Lord. I wanted you to know, I thought you'd be interested."

"Fran, honestly . . ."

"Well," she said, "there won't be any more of this, I can promise you that. I know right where that little bitch is, in their old summer cottage up there on the ridge, and I'm going up there with the police and I'm going to clean that nest out. You hear me?" I heard her all right, and I heard the strangled sound of crying underneath her furious words. "I wanted you to know," she said. "That gang should never have been allowed to form."

"I regret my part in it," I said. "I regret it very much. But Fran, if you'll forgive my speaking up, are you sure you want to go up there with the police? Wouldn't it be easier on you and on Julie if you and Lou just went by yourselves?"

"I'm going up there," said her hoarsening voice, "and I'm going to see that they're all thrown in jail! I'll have them up for using drugs, tampering with a minor, rape. I'll throw the book at the filthy things."

"But from what Julie told you, it wasn't rape."

"With a minor it's always rape," Fran said, and then her voice got away from her and she was shouting a foot from my ear. "God, who knows what it was? The dirty, lying little beast!" In the harsh pause I heard her breathing. "I just wanted you to know what you started," she said, and hung up, bang.

If I started it, Fran finished it, and she didn't wait. Before noon the next day a police car pulled up our hill and its driver, a uniformed cop from the next county, got out his notepad and took down my answers to a lot of questions about Jim Peck. How long had he lived down below? What were the arrangements, did he pay rent, or what? Had I known him before I let him camp down there? Ever notice anything queer about him or any of his friends? Act high ever? Wild parties maybe? Women coming in and out? Did I know what marijuana looked like, growing? That sort of thing.

I gathered that Peck had been raided, but the policeman wasn't telling me anything. Obviously he regarded me as a possible accessory, possibly a queen. He was alert for any dirt that blew, and his visit annoyed and bothered me so much that I did not go down for the mail, for fear I would have to talk with Marian about it. But I couldn't wait indefinitely. At three, when the afternoon paper would be there, I walked down, and of course there she was in the grove, and John with her, and they had the paper in their hands. I joined them, though I would rather have had an errand somewhere else.

It was front page, text and pictures: RAID UNCOVERS YOUTH DRUG-SEX RING. IRATE PARENT FLOORS HIPPIE. Here was Peck, beard and coveralls, holding his eye, his elbows held by stern deputies. Here was a ramshackle shingled cottage dwarfed by redwoods. Here was a disapproving district attorney with a tableful of evidence before him: a tobacco can said to contain grass, several bottles of barbiturates, a giant economy-size bottle of contraceptive pills. Here was the sex goddess Margo continued on page four, hair wild, hand raised in adjuration, while she talked sexual liberty and legalized abortion to a reporter. No other pictures of the people taken into custody, presumably because half of them were juveniles.

But luscious details, piquant beside the enthusiastically aired theories of Margo and the accusations from Peck about police harassment and invasion of privacy. Such details as were provided by some of the juveniles, frightened by what they had got into. Several said that pot was commonly smoked among the group, and that they themselves had obtained it through Peck. One admitted that he had been taken up into the treehouse in the place formerly used by the gang and there taken on an LSD "trip" under Peck's supervision. He thought that almost all of them had taken at least one trip, some many. He also said that sex was "pretty loose" in the camp, and that girls, including juveniles, were sometimes traded around among sleeping bags.

The furious father of one of the juveniles had crowded in when the gang was being booked and knocked Peck down.

I raised my eyes from the paper and found Marian sitting nervously straight, watching me. John was moodily smoking a cigarette. "I can't imagine Lucio hitting anybody," I said. "*Was* it Lucio?"

"Tom Weld," John said.

"Oh, great," I said. "The whole neighborhood gets in the act. Was that cop down here asking questions?"

Marian nodded. "Fran too. We've had a session."

"I'm sorry," I said. "I'm sorry they bothered you with it. What did she want?"

"Wanted Marian to persuade Julie to have an abortion," John said.

"What? Why you?"

She smiled a wincing smile. "Apparently I have influence over her. She'll listen to me."

It was superb. Fran charging up to Marian, pregnant and dying and unalterably addicted to life, and proposing that she advise for another the abortion she would die rather than have performed on herself. In one flickering glance I assured myself that John and I were in complete accord on that one. My sympathy for Fran, which had been considerable, and considerably mixed with guilt, instantly diminished.

"What's the matter with an old-fashioned shotgun marriage?" I said.

John laughed. "Find the man. Julie won't say. Even if she would, can you imagine Fran welcoming any of Peck's boys for a son-in-law?"

"What about Dave?" I said, and as soon as I said it acknowledged the stupidity of the remark. Through her cocker bitch, tied however snugly to the clothesline, Fran had already had experience with the Weld genius for creating consequences. She would want Dave Weld no more than she would have wanted Peck himself.

"Well," I said, "I'm sorry, I'm sorry, I'm sorry. Which does a lot of good. Are you going to advise Julie to get it aborted? You could get Margo to help persuade her."

Marian stared at me so long, with such a blank, concentrated expression, that I thought she must be watching something behind me. I thought I saw her shake her head very slightly. John stepped on his cigarette and said, "No, she's not going to advise her one way or the other. She's not going to get involved. She's not going to waste her strength feeling sorry or worrying about that kid, because the kid will do exactly what she pleases in any case. She won't tell who the father is, assuming she knows. She won't agree to an abortion. Why would she? She says they gave her pills and she threw them away. She wanted to get pregnant to spite Fran, and now she has, and that's it."

"She says?" I said. "Have you talked to her?"

"Oh, sure. Fran brought her over."

"Good God!" I said. "Hasn't she got any better sense than to . . ."

"I don't know," Marian said. "If there was something I could conscientiously do, I'd be so glad to do it! Poor sullen Julie. Poor Fran, too, she's being torn apart. And the Welds, my goodness, they had no idea what was happening, they just got called down to the station. It was like having something fall on you out of a window. You knew it was Dave who got scared and talked to the police?"

"Gunslinger? He always seemed the strong silent one."

"Julie's vicious about him. She calls him the squealer."

"Forget it," John said. "Put it all out of your mind."

She mused, relaxing back against the lounge and examining her pink palm. "I'm a naïve," she said. "I thought, because they all seemed so sort of natural and good-natured and liked the outdoors and only seemed to dislike artificial things like shaving, that we could set them some sort of example—you know, show them that all their kicks were artificial too, and unnecessary. Your own five senses ought to be more than enough. Hmmm?"

"Nothing."

"But I guess they probably thought I was pretty square. I'm sure they liked me, and I liked them, they were so full of vitality and a sort of spirit of adventure. But beliefs, that's something else. They must have thought what I believe was something suitable for Girl Scouts."

"Forget them," I said. "Forget the whole business. They aren't worth ten minutes of your time, isn't that right, John?"

"That's right," John said. "They couldn't get an abortion in California anyway. It never was your problem, Marian. You couldn't help even if they'd let you."

He did not say it, but we all understood as precisely as if he had: You've got your own problem to handle. Fran LoPresti is not the only one who has a crisis in her life.

6

Crisis turned out to be like the smell of tarweed. By the time you realized you were smelling it, you had been smelling it a long time.

That realization came to us only a few days after the Peck blowup, when we stopped in and found Marian not outside, not reading, not tidying up the details of her life, but flat in her bed, and nauseated.

It was shocking to see her down: I had the instant

conviction that I would never see her up again. The thinness that had always roused protective feelings in us had taken a sudden change and become emaciation. The face that tried to smile and reassure us through spasms of nausea was for the first time weary and pathetic. None of it was new. We had simply not noted the stages of her deterioration, despite our watchfulness. It dawned on us that for days, a week, maybe two weeks, Ruth had had trouble making anything that would tempt her appetite. She found her invalid delicacies untouched on the tray or in the refrigerator. Appetite, attentiveness, the performance of little duties, had all been growing more forced. Now suddenly she was a woman sick to death.

John was not at home—he had taken Debby to school and gone on to a meeting at the university. The place was ours, dismay and all. Ruth sent me out while she got Marian comfortable and tidied the bedroom. Outside, I stacked a lot of the wood that John and Debby had been so assiduously making, and I raked up the front yard and burned a pile of leaves.

Later I went inside, out of the nostalgic sad autumnal smell of leaf smoke, and talked a few minutes to the girl propped in bed with her hair in pigtails. Despite the nausea, her eyes were extraordinarily bright. I thought she looked at me with the soft intensity, the tenderness, that I had seen in the eyes of too many people dying of cancer—the look that says how lovely are the shapes and colors of life and how dear the faces of friends, how desirable it all is, how soon to be lost.

Because she had watched her downward progress more knowingly than we had, she knew what the nausea meant. She had discussed it all with her doctor in advance, and as usual had made preparations. Though she insisted she would not take drugs if pain came upon her, she had no objection to intravenous feeding, for that would keep her stronger for the baby. John, she said, would take her to the clinic that afternoon, and they would see if they couldn't find a practical nurse, someone who could give her the feeding at home. She would not go to the hospital, not so long before the baby was due. It would, she implied but did not say, be a fatal omen. When you went to the hospital in cases like hers, you were already dead, you lost your identity as a person, you became a case, a sickness, an obligation or an anxiety only. She knew very well she would not survive three or four weeks of the hospital. To go there this early would be to go defeated.

Nevertheless, they took her there that evening. John joined with the doctor to overrule her. But at the end of three days they brought her back again, shakily triumphant, and looking better for the three days of care. A nurse was with her, a large white-nylon person with upper arms as big around as Marian's waist. I heard her name a hundred times while she was there; I can't remember it now to save my life.

But coming home did not restore Marian to what she had been before. There was now no pretense that she was simply resting and would soon be up and around. The needle taped into her thin captive arm, the bulky figure in white nylon, were temporary, yes, but not in that way. What is more, the nurse's coming shut us out of most of the comforting chores we had formerly done, and gave us in exchange only sickroom visits, stiff and awkward and tainted with false cheerfulness.

Ours, not Marian's. She had no need of false cheerfulness. She simply opposed her will to the sickness and deflected it. Now that she had made it home, she had not a doubt that she would live to bear the child. Strengthened by the drip of maltose into her blood stream, she might even manage a normal birth. With laughter in her throat and tears in her eyes she told about meeting, on a visit to the clinic a couple of weeks before, the wife of one of John's colleagues who, seeing her obviously pregnant, had wanted to give her a baby shower. "She was kind," Marian said. "She meant only the friendliest. But it made me laugh, it was so sort of . . . orthodox."

Never with the lamp turned down, never with her mind or her resolution clouded. Whatever darkness she looked into when she was alone, or alone with John, never left the slightest shadow on her face. Yet we became gradually aware of some change of expression, a change that we might have thought the flicker of response to some thought until one afternoon, sitting with her while the nurse took a walk, I realized that Marian had stopped what she was saying. Her legs stirred under the spread. The grimace, the sickroom tic, the shadow of a thought, whatever it was, passed plainly across her face.

Across the bed, stiff and sudden, Ruth leaned forward in her chair. "Pain?"

Marian's half-closed eyes cleared, the grimace became a smile. She nodded.

"Which?"

"Which?"

"Labor, or . . . the other?"

"Ah," said Marian disgustedly, "I wish it *was* labor!"

"How long?"

"The last few days. It's not too bad, just twinges."

"Marian, you've got to let them give you something for it!"

But she shook her head, stubborn and intractable. She set her will against the pain as she had set it against time and malignancy. She did her best to ignore it. She held on. She held out.

But it must have made her desperate, as it made us grim, for it told her how little time she had. Death and life grew in her at an equal pace, the race would be down to the wire. And of all the things she might have feared, she feared pain worst, because it might obliterate in animal agony the last great experience.

John and her doctor both told her—and John told us —that they would not let her endure too much pain, they would give her drugs whether she agreed or not. She hadn't much choice: either pain or drugs would blur the climax she had set her whole strength toward. So she willed her pain small, she denied its capacity to hurt her. And who of us could tell whether she managed to make it small, or whether she only forced herself to bear more than she could?

A bleating nuisance, unable to bear her bearing of her pain, I called her doctor and asked if she could not have a Caesarean immediately. Why shouldn't she have the satisfaction of bringing forth that hard-won baby, seeing it, handling it, assuring herself that it was normal and warm? Then she could let go.

He told me she couldn't possibly stand an operation. She wouldn't live to know whether she had borne the child or not. No doctor, certainly not himself, would perform any such operation except as a last-ditch measure to save the child. The baby, he told me, was safe as long as Marian was.

"Which is not long," I said.

"No," said his dry controlled voice (Why does one so hate those who must keep their heads in human and feeling situations?), "no, it's a great pity."

A pity.

That was the afternoon when Tom Weld drove his caterpillar across the tottering bridge and began tearing great wounds in the hill. We saw him as we walked slowly home from our afternoon visit, and full of the bitterness of being able to do not one thing for Marian, we took refuge in fury at that barebacked Neanderthal and his brutish machine. I associated his mutilation of the hill with the mutilations that Marian had suffered and was still to suffer, and I hated Weld so passionately that I shook. He was a born ugliness-maker, and he was irresistible and inescapable. We couldn't move our hill or turn our house the other way; and we could no more resist the laws of property, the permit of the planning commission, and the Weldian notion that mutilation was progress, than we could stop the malignant cells from metastasizing through Marian's blood stream.

For a long time that evening we sat on the terrace, while the swallows and later the bats sewed the darkening air together over the oaks, and the crude gouge that would become a road faded into dusk, then dark. The white surveyors' stakes swam and were lost in granular obscurity. The night air was strong with the scent of tarweed, mixed now with the half-sour smell of broken adobe.

"I don't know," I said. "I guess I don't mind getting

old. I wish it would hurry up. The other day I read something in Crèvecoeur's *Letters from an American Farmer* that said it all: 'Sometimes my heart grows tired with beating, it wants rest like my eyelids.' "

"Marian would read you a lecture if you said that to her," Ruth said. "Though you couldn't blame her if she felt that way herself, poor child. I suppose we ought to wish it would come soon."

"What I wish is that she'd give up that baby and start taking some sort of treatment and give herself a chance."

"It's much too late. You mustn't kid yourself."

"I guess not," I said. "*She* never has."

We sat on in silence, and as we sat a soft darkness moved against the sky's darkness, and soundlessly an owl had settled in the oak almost level with our eyes. I could just see his outline, a Halloween cutout, on the branch. For several minutes he sat there, utterly noiseless, and then he was gone.

"What was that, a bloody omen?" I said.

"Oh, Joe, stop it! You're only making it worse."

"It couldn't be worse."

She stood up with a rustle of impatience. Then after a few seconds her hand came under my arm, and I put my own arm around her. "We'll have to do our outside living in the patio now," she said. "I don't think I could bear to watch what he'll be doing over there."

"We'll take up new positions, in other words."

"What?"

"That's the way the military reports defeats. 'Our troops have taken up new positions.' Life is one new position after another."

"There's more to it than that."

"Like what? Intelligence doesn't help, foresight doesn't help, determination doesn't help, courage doesn't help, grace doesn't help. If any of them did, Marian wouldn't be where she is."

It was too dark for me to see Ruth's face, but I could tell from the outline of her head that she was looking at me directly and hard. "But she hasn't given up," she said.

Ruth has her own variety of toughness. She is rawhide where Marian was some kind of light, strong metal. "All right," I said at last. "Tomorrow we'll take up our new positions."

We went around to the patio side and stood. It was so still that I heard the hollow rush and murmur of traffic from the choked highways of the valley. Over that way the sky was reddened, but in the other direction the hills were dark and whole. A star looked up at us from the bottomless black pool.

"It isn't as if he could ruin everything," Ruth said. "This side is getting lovely as the planting grows up. Lots of people don't have a tenth as much."

"No."

"And we won't get any dust over here."

"No."

I breathed in deeply, wanting as much as she did to take pleasure in the calm night and the peaceful patio and the oil-black pool with the splintered star in it. But aromatic tarweed flooded my nose, mouth, head, and heart, and away off in the hills, miles away it seemed, but clear as a bugle, we heard the frenzied, cracking voices of hunting hounds.

7

Our visit to Marian next day was brief, no more than ten minutes. The nurse did not want us there at all. Every move she made as she checked the jar on its stand, or the taped arm, or as she stood, a thick white disapproval, in the doorway, told us that. Marian tried. She asked about Catarrh, who had got clawed up in a fight with a wild tom. But her attempt at a smile would hold no more firmly than her attempt at interest; her eyes full of affectionate tenderness would cloud, her body would stir with insistent pain, her whole presence would retreat across an uncrossable gap. It seemed that she had shrunk in the bed, all but her mounded abdomen. Her skin was yellow, and when we kissed her she was clammy to our lips.

Our cheerful noises died in our mouths. Twice we watched her attention twist inward in spite of her attempt to hold it on us. But at the end, when we took her hands and kissed them and tiptoed to the door with a furtive sickroom guiltiness, she summoned her full smile. It blazed at us, burning through pain and everything else. "Bless you," she said. "Bless you both. I like to think you're my father and mother sent back to me." The nurse closed the door.

In the living room John had just hung up the telephone. Weakly we said, "Isn't it time? Shouldn't she be taken in? If the doctor was here, wouldn't he insist on a hypo?"

"We're waiting for Debby to get home," John said. "She won't go while Debby's away."

"Couldn't I go and get her out early?"

The look he gave me was almost ugly. A man so robust as John has really no way of showing anxiety. Where another man might sag or stumble, grow haggard under the eyes, appear with mussed hair or wrinkled clothes, he simply couldn't help his coordination and his muscular health. His tan was intact, his virile crewcut bristled. But still his look had an ugly, fleering quality, and he said, "That would make it special. It mustn't be special. It's got to be as casual as Tuesday afternoon."

It was I who stumbled and stammered, overcome by the fear that neither he nor anyone else had made any preparations. "But she *is* going in today? What about a room—is there a chance she couldn't get one? Shouldn't we . . . ?"

"The doctor's holding a room," John said. "The nurse has orders to give her a hypo if it gets too bad. We're only waiting for Debby."

"John," I said, "we don't want to be in the road, God knows. But you know how we feel about her. Can we do anything? Drive you in?"

With his arms around us both he moved us to the door. "Of course," he said. "Yes, that would be a help. I'll call you."

A smile, a pressure on the shoulders, and we were outside, simultaneously accepted for service and shut away from the intimate trouble that had room only for the family and the nurse.

As we went up the hill, we saw through the fringe

of trees that Tom Weld had put his son to work on the bulldozer. The noise of the engine, big and rough and then easing back and then big again, was like the hoarse breathing of a man heaving his weight against great stones or tree trunks. A fume of dust hung over the ravine, and there were howls and scrapings as the blade gouged rock.

The noise and dust drove us over onto the patio side, where we sat through lunch time, not really expecting the telephone to ring until after three-thirty, but listening anyway until the strain put a hum like quinine in my ears.

About two it rang, and I sprang for it. And who was it? Jim Peck, inquiring in his soft love-everything voice if he could come and get the stuff he had left behind. Because I was relieved that his call was not the one I feared, I was probably heartier than I otherwise might have been. I said certainly, sure, come ahead. Thank you, he said. There was a pause, but no click. "How's it going?" I said. "Going?" "Your case. I read that the Grand Jury is getting it." There was another pause, then the soft polite voice said, "You should know." "No," I said, with the old angry constriction in the solar plexus. "No, I don't know." "Oh," said Peck, "I thought you would." Click.

All right, you son of a bitch, think what you please, I said to the dead instrument, and went back to the patio. To Ruth's questioning eyebrows I said, "Peck. Wants to come after his stuff. At least this is the last of him."

In a little while we both went in and lay down for a nap. If waiting is a shape of boredom, habit is the best way I know to deal with it. We each went into a darkened room, and I am ashamed to say I dozed. And woke at three, and still no call. Ruth read a magazine. I repaired a sagging shelf in her closet. If we met each other's eyes, we looked away, embarrassed and gloomy.

Three-thirty, and still no call. Should we go down? But we might only be in the way. Telephone? We would only bother them. We waited.

The ring was explosive, something toward which fire had come on a long fuse. I was into the kitchen before the second burr of the bell. "Yes? Yes?"

John's voice, flat and steady. "I guess it's time. Could you come down?"

VII

AT THE DOOR we ran into a blazing afternoon. Inside our insulated and curtained house, we had not realized how hot it was, nearly as hot as a midsummer heat wave. The bulldozer growled and rumbled across the gully, and turning the buttonhook, we could see Dave Weld's walnut back and reddish head, still unshorn, as he suspended roar and motion briefly, peering ahead of the blade, and then jammed at the gears and dug in again. The hill peeled away from the steel, clods rolled, the sluggish dust lifted, and then we lost it as I whirled the car down to the left behind the screen of trees.

"Not so fast," Ruth said. Her feet were pushing hard against the floor boards, there was a pinched, hard look around her mouth.

Ahead, on the steepest part of the hill, I saw a tarantula coming. Ordinarily subterranean and nocturnal, they come out on fall afternoons and walk in bald daylight, high on their hairy legs. Maybe young Weld had rooted this one out of his hole and sent him wandering. Under most circumstances, I would have run over him, or tried to—they can jump like crickets—and squashed him into an evil smear. Now, for some reason I jerked the wheel and straddled him, and glancing back in the mirror I saw him intact, an impervious, ominous ink-blot crawling uphill bent upon carrying to us the message we had already received.

Ruth's lips were drawn back from her teeth. I knew exactly how she felt: as if the thing had crawled on her exposed heart.

I had barely cut the motor beside the Catlins' station wagon when John was in the doorway, pulling the door carefully shut behind him. A stranger would have thought him a pleasant-faced young man stepping outside to greet guests. There was no impairment of his color or his air of health, and he had himself so completely under control that he did not even seem stiff. Perhaps he was feeling a sort of relief. But there was a moment when I thought him too hatefully calm. My own breathing was constricted, and I could feel my heart.

Ruth put out her hands in an impulsive, pitying gesture, rare in her. He took them, and looking up at her from under his brows, he kissed the ends of the fingers. He wore a short-sleeved white shirt, and his arms were brown and heavily muscled.

"Bad?" Ruth said.

"Bad enough."

"You said the nurse had orders for a hypo. . . ."

"She gave her one an hour ago," John said. "Wouldn't you know, it doesn't work on her. I suppose she's unconsciously resisting it."

"Ah, but if she can *do* that! Isn't that a good sign? I mean, maybe it isn't . . ."

Into his square face came a moment's darkness, a flicker almost savage. "Isn't really bad yet?" he said. "Isn't *time*? *She* says it is."

Ruth was silent, rebuked. Accept, accept, these Catlins kept insisting. When it is unmistakable, then no blinders, no fictions. Marian was getting exactly what she had hoped to avoid: pain and dope, either of which meant the overwhelming of feeling and intelligence and will. She would not be given the chance to face it to an open-eyed ending; she would end as a guttering-out of numbed flesh. Nevertheless, no fictions, not for her, not for him.

Between ourselves, we had speculated on how John would react when the crisis came, whether he would be up to it and to her. But we would have done better to be anxious about our own responses, for now we burst out together, "What can we . . . ?" and both stopped. After waiting three months for the inevitable, we were totally unprepared. We had no plan for how we might help them. Instead of taking charge, we had to ask, we had to improvise as if in the face of an accident.

Which meant that we had never believed it was inevitable. In spite of Marian's preparations and all she had said to us singly or together, in spite of the visible symptoms of her fading life, we had not accepted as she accepted. I was ashamed for us, and relieved when Ruth said, watching him with puckered eyes, "The nurse will go with you, won't she? You'll need help with Debby."

"Could you?" John said. "It probably wouldn't be for long. I can get Marian settled and be back before dinner, if . . ."

"There's no need at all. I haven't got a thing else to do. I'll get her dinner. Where is she now?"

"With Marian."

"Don't you worry about her," Ruth said. "Stay with Marian. I can bring Debby down to see her tonight, or tomorrow, or whenever she'd like."

John was frowning at her as if he didn't quite recognize her face or hadn't quite heard what she said. His cheeks looked oddly crumpled, brown and suddenly withered. He linked the fingers of his hands and bent them backward, looking over Ruth's head. "I guess I wasn't very clear," he said. "She's saying goodbye in there now. *Goodbye,* you understand?"

"Oh, why?" Ruth burst out. "John, why? She's not that far-gone!"

"No frightening memories," John said, looking over her head. "No painful scenes. No recollections of her doped or in pain. Just—one day she said goodbye as if she were going downtown, and went away."

From the side, I saw the shine of tears in his eyes, but I did not see any fall. By some impossible act of control he sucked them back, dried them up, looked over Ruth's head until they were absorbed. Up on the hill, the bulldozer stopped. The abrupt ending of the noise left us standing sick and uneasy in the shade. On both sides of us the big oaks writhed up past the eaves, the yard sloping down toward the grove was brown and splashed with sun. Just at the juncture of sun and shade, a cloud of flies danced and jiggled, in incessant movement but held together, a galaxy of tiny sparks of life. From a crack in the weathered boarding behind John, wasps crawled out and flew, meeting a traffic of other wasps that landed and crawled in, hot with industry. I watched one alight on a post holding up the overhang and curl his yellow and black abdomen down as if anchoring himself with his stinger, and I distinctly heard the sound of his tiny mandibles gnawing on the wood.

I thought it could have been the wasp to which Marian had given back his life when he fell in her pot of jam.

From outside the circle of commitment and responsibility, neither husband nor father nor woman capable of presiding over birth or death or the living needs of a house, only a man growing old who intruded where he had no usefulness, insisting on his presence because he loved Marian Catlin and could not bear her loss—and can't yet—I said, "Does Debby know? Have you told her . . . anything?"

John's attention seemed fixed on the infinitesimal dry rasping of the wasp's mandibles. He peered at me with eyes in which the wetness of unshed tears still glittered. His frown deepened, his lips pursed, he shook his head with sharp impatience. I realized that he was listening for sounds inside the house. But he did not open the door.

Inside there, bent upon protecting her daughter as she would never have wanted herself protected, what was she doing? Reading a story? Playing a game? Planning some excursion or trip that would never be taken? I doubted that she would be that dishonest. She would sin only by omission, not outright. But could she hold herself back from tears and paroxysms of love, smothering the child to her for the last time? Yes, I thought she could. The object was to say goodbye without Debby's ever knowing it was forever. No tears, no sobbing, above all no outward sign that she was in pain. The final act of the phasing out.

It seemed to me we had been standing in the gnawed

silence for half an hour. I turned my wrist to see my watch. Ten past four. Barely five minutes since our telephone had rung.

With an opaque look at us, John opened the door. "Marian?"

"Yes," said her clear voice, lifted to carry from the back of the house. "I'm ready."

And that was no pain-shrunk or dope-numbed voice. It was as natural as laughter, it was marked only by the tuned-up fluty tone that came into it when she was excited. It told nothing of how she was feeling, it said only that she was in command. She could have sung a song through without a quaver, I believe. The sound of her voice broke me down, I was ready to cry or laugh, but above everything I was proud of her and for her. She would go like a queen, directing her life to the end, and if she was a queen bound for the scaffold, you would not know it from her bearing or her voice.

John pushed the door wide. The nurse came hurriedly in from the hall and whispered to him. "Ruth," John said, "could you come with me?" They went together into the dark room, dark at least as I looked into if from the glare of outdoors. "I'll get the car ready," I said. From the suddenly mysterious interior I heard Debby crying, "Where are you going, Mummy? Mummy, where? I want to go."

The nurse came out of the hall again with a weekend bag, ready packed as if for a honeymoon or a birth. I grabbed it from her hand and took it out to the car.

Briefly I debated between our two-door and the station wagon, and chose the station wagon because it was the easier to get in and out of. But the back end was half-full of wood, with a Swedish saw, an ax, and a splitting hammer on top of it. I am afraid it gratified me, and made me at once more critical of him and more friendly toward him, that John had not prepared better.

Climbing in, I began to throw the wood out onto the edge of the drive. The inside was like a sauna. Hurrying, afraid they would come before I was ready, I scraped out bark and litter with the back of the saw, raised up the back seat from its nest in the floor, wiped it off with my handkerchief, stowed tools and suitcase behind it, and ran down all the windows to let out the stifling heat. As I backed out, blotting my face in the damp shoulder of my shirt, I heard hoofs, and looked up to see Julie LoPresti riding through the trail gate from the bottoms.

Sentimental return to the abandoned pad of her guru? Whiff of freedom the first time her mother had untied her from the clothesline? Or perhaps a call on Marian, to dump her garbage of filial vengefulness at this roadside? She rode at a slow walk, eying the house, and I straightened up ready to warn her off. Of all the things Marian did not need at that moment, Julie ranked pretty high on the list. But if she had been planning to stop, the intention died as soon as she saw me. She touched me coldly with her hating eyes and rode on past.

I looked toward the door. From out in the blazing sun it looked as black as the opening of a cave. There was a narrow stripe of shade beginning to reach into the drive, and I backed the station wagon into it and sat waiting.

The bulldozer roared into life again, much closer than before, and bending, I could see it coming around the shoulder of the hill on a long descending angle evidently aimed at a junction with our lane about at the mailboxes. Clods broke from the wave of earth thrown downhill by the blade. Two or three made it all the way to the lane, jumped the bank, and burst like bombs.

For a minute my head was full of the thought of those Indians who had made noble speeches to Congress and commissioners, speeches in which they spoke of such reverence for the Earth Mother that they would not plow her breast. I thought of the druids who worshiped trees, and of the Great Goddess who was ancient, and anciently worshiped, centuries before she came into history on the tablets of Sumer. I swear I thought of them all, because with that destroyer tearing up the hill Marian loved, and just at the moment when she was ready to make her last trip from the country house she loved, I had to think in her terms. The earth was literally alive for her; she would suffer to see it mutilated.

It didn't help that the young fool driving the bulldozer, and his ambitious fathead of a father, would go home to a hearty supper and the satisfaction of a good day's work accomplished, while any minute now Marian Catlin, who loved the earth and its creatures in ways the Welds could not even imagine, would come out that black door and start down the lane toward the hospital where they would tape another needle in her bruised arm and jab her in the hip with a massive shot of morphine, and if a flicker of life still showed itself present, they would numb it with another needle until it gave up, and keep it numbed until it died. And then they would cut her open, warm, barely still, to get the bloody lump upon which she had concentrated her last vitality.

You ugly son of a bitch, I said to the reddish head through the dust, why can't you tip over and roll down?

And turned, and she was in the doorway.

2

She was in a wrapper of quilted white satin, but above that wedding-gown whiteness, between John's dark tan and Ruth's ruddiness, her face was death's face. In days she had shrunk on her bones. Her feet moved weakly, one, then the other, from below the hem of the robe as they helped her down the one step to the walk. Safely there, she looked up and saw me waiting by the open car door.

Even then, her whole spirit braced against the agony of parting and the agony of her riddled flesh, she could smile. Her generosity could shine across thirty feet of hot shade and give me something, reminder, acknowledgment of how much we had managed to cram into the few months of our knowing one another, and how firm the bond of affection was. Either my feelings or the effort she had to exert for that smile gave it a brilliance greater than ordinary. Doom was in it, love, gratitude, God knew what—everything that had made me wish, the moment I met her, that I had had such a daughter. It was not an expression she wore, it was an illumination. She stood between John and Ruth like a spark leaping a gap. If you had painted her at that moment, you would have had to paint her with a halo.

One instant, and then she was death again, tottering between her careful helpers. The nurse fussed behind them with her own suitcase in her hand, and behind them all came Debby carrying a flat cardboard box. I saw the picture of a barnyard with animals: a jigsaw puzzle. Later, if Debby's memory turned out to be better than Marian hoped it would be, she could put her mother's death together out of just such irregular pieces.

They stopped at the edge of the shade, and at a jerk of Ruth's head I hurried to take her place at Marian's side. Ruth stepped back and grabbed up Debby's hand. "All right, hon," Marian said in the clear, strained voice. "You and Ruth have a good time." She did not look around when she spoke. She looked at the open door of the car.

"I want to go!" Debby said. "Where are you going?"

"I told you. Just to see the doctor."

"In your *bathrobe*?"

"He's seen me in my bathrobe before."

"You'll look funny in his office."

"I guess," Marian said. She was withdrawing, her voice was indifferent. But I felt her frail weight on my arm, and looking out of the corner of my eye, I saw that her eyes were closed and that tiny blisters of sweat had come out on her upper lip. Still with her eyes closed, her back indifferently turned, she said to Debby, "You be a good girl for Ruth."

"I wanted you to help me with my puzzle."

"I'll help you with it tonight," John said through his teeth. He stooped and lifted Marian by her shoulders and knees; her bony, eloquent, beautiful feet hung down. In the haze of impressions, I saw Ruth, her eyes glazed and her teeth in her lip, pull Debby against her side, and on the other side of the car the moon-faced nurse came crawling in, creaking her slick nylon, to help John settle Marian in the seat. I slammed the door behind him, I slammed the front one after myself. As I backed around and shifted, I threw a look in the mirror. Marian was lying back against John's arm, blind to Debby's uncertain wave. The nurse was reaching to wipe her face with a Kleenex.

"Did she guess?" Marian whispered.

"No," John said. "Hold my hand."

Taking the bump as easily as possible, I eased the car into the lane. My mind was a night sky full of crisscrossing beams. I was acutely conscious of the breathing in the seat behind, but whose I didn't know. I saw the image of the brown hand and the thin one, locked together, with the precision of an etching, and I registered a blink of relief that the bulldozer had worked farther down the hill: maybe she could at least be spared that. I was already laying out in my head the route I would take to avoid the afternoon traffic and the stops and starts that would aggravate Marian's pain.

And then I was leaning forward, rising above the wheel, stiff with disbelief and fury. Ahead of us, between the mailboxes and the wobbly bridge that had gone unrepaired for fifteen months since Weld had said he would fix it, Julie was sitting straight on her horse and talking to someone driving the familiar Volkswagen bus. By the bus's rear wheel, half obscured but unmistakable, was the all-too-familiar Honda, and on it the figure in the white helmet, the cut-off jeans, the Castro beard. Thirty feet or so above them, at the end of the long rough gouge he had made, Dave Weld sat on the idling bulldozer. Unthought, Irresponsibility, Rebellion, and Foolishness held a conference or a quarrel, and blocked the road.

Julie must have known somehow that Peck was coming for his stuff, and somehow got away on her horse to meet the bus. And it was not likely that either Julie or anyone in the bus could have passed the nervous Judas on the bulldozer without pausing for some release of scorn or hatred. I have no inclination to believe that some Presence, somewhere Up, plugged a cord into a socket and sat back and smiled. But no matter how they came there, by accident or design, predestination or blind chance, those people could not have been in a worse place at a worse time if they had rehearsed for months. Coincidence I suppose it was. Yet they reacted with all the moves of guilty collusion.

The rumble of the idling bulldozer would have drowned out the sound of the car coasting down toward them, but even without it they would probably not have heard us. They were all looking up at Dave Weld now. I saw the vehement motions of Julie's head as she shouted something. Cursing under my breath, I put my foot on the brake and gave them two light blips with the horn.

If I had three wishes to last me the rest of my life, the first would be to take back those momentary touches of my wrist on the horn ring.

Guilty collusion, I said. Perhaps only astonishment that others, outsiders, intruded upon their dense enclosed groupy world. Maybe they all thought of everything outside their circle as a great faceless enemy, and it surprised them to see it bearing down on them in the shape of a station wagon and four people.

Their heads snapped around, their faces stared, startled, even as they started scattering. The driver of the bus, with hardly a break in the motion that started with his turning head, was twisting to look for backing room. Julie was lifting at the gelding's rein, swinging him left. Peck's foot stamped down and the Honda spurted smoke. Dave Weld up above snapped forward to his gears. It was like a collective start at the sound of an explosion.

Perhaps the abrupt starting of two motors, Honda and Volkswagen, frightened the horse; perhaps Dave Weld's lurch to the gears sent clods rolling to burst around the gelding's feet. Perhaps, indeed, my two touches on the horn did it all.

I had almost stopped rolling when I hit the horn. Now we were at a dead stop, twenty or thirty feet from the bus. In the narrow space between bus and motorcycle the gelding was suddenly wild. It spun and reared, the motorcycle went over and Peck dove rolling from under the hoofs. The air was dense with shouting, in my ear the nurse was crying, "Oh oh oh oh oh!" Like a broken-backed dog, the Honda circled, kicking up a great dust, and above it the horse was upright for one terrific instant, with Julie flat along its neck and its chin pulled back against its throat and her seat, that admirable heart-shaped seat, glued to the nearly vertical back.

Glass crashed, the Volkswagen rumbled like a beaten tub, the rearing horse vanished in the dust and reappeared, pawing and fighting for its head, walking on its hind feet. It must have stepped into the frantic Honda, for from mid-air, it seemed, it sprang upward and outward, away from the frenzy that had it cornered. I heard hoofs on hollow plank, Julie screamed, a long, terrible cry, and they were down, invisible behind the Volkswagen and the dust.

It couldn't have taken more than five seconds. I found myself in the road beside the driver of the bus, the rather pleasant boy named Miles. He was full of adrenalin, as who was not; he pounced rather than moved; he looked thirty-six directions at once. Darting crabwise, his eye on the bridge from which came Julie's bursts of screaming, as mindless as a steam whistle, Peck scuttled in and grabbed the broken Honda and shut it off and dragged it aside. I pushed past the stuttering Miles and ducked around the bus.

Julie was squatting just where bridge met road, holding the reins in both hands. The struggles of the horse yanked and toppled her. I saw that the gelding was through the gaps in the bridge with all four legs. Floundering with stretched neck, it gained a purchase on nothing. Its hoofs knocked muffled sounds from underneath, a haze of dust rose above it. On the right shoulder was a long slick raw wound, the skin wrinkled up like a scuff on a shoe to expose the red muscle.

Julie, her arms extended by the yanking on the reins, looked pleadingly over her shoulder, and I in turn looked over mine. John had not got out of the station wagon. He sat inside holding Marian's head down against his chest. Over her childish pigtails his eyes glared at me, warrior's eyes, hot with danger, fear, battle. The nurse's face was a moon of terror.

Desperate, I looked around again. The horse lay briefly quiet, stretched awkwardly, its hind legs spaced between two gaps, its front legs down through a single one. It seemed suspended in a grotesque rack or singlefoot. Its head thumped down on the planks.

I shouted at Julie, some advice or encouragement, foolish or otherwise. Hang on, keep him quiet, something. And I started forward with the intention of sitting on the gelding's head so that it couldn't flounder and hurt itself worse. Miles, the bus driver, had also moved, but only over to stand beside Peck. Later, thinking about it, I blamed them for not moving faster to do something, but really they couldn't be blamed. If the horse had fallen from the sky to crash through the bridge in a pulp of bones and meat and blood, it could hardly have been there with more dazing suddenness.

I moved too fast or too slow. I had taken only a step or two when the horse convulsed itself in a renewed effort to get to its feet. One stretched hind leg kinked up out of the gap, and for a split second the gelding stood impossibly on one corner, its chest jammed down on the planks and its other hind leg imprisoned. With horrible breaking noises the corner gave way and the horse fell partly on its side. Easily, at an angle that sickened me, the imprisoned hind leg came partly free. The head lay flat again on the bridge tread, the breath rattled in the stretched throat, the eyes rolled whitely.

Cautiously I edged past Julie, still hanging to the reins, and as I did so the horse made another effort to free itself. Somehow it got a front foot free and planted on solid plank. Broken, the hoof flopped aside, but still the horse pried and lifted, and then the other front foot came free.

This one was not merely broken, it was broken off. Squatting, hoarsely gasping, with its hind legs still crookedly jammed in the cracks, the gelding braced itself like a sitting dog on one flopping hoof and one peg of bloody white bone.

Julie looked, a long look, and then her whole body shuddered down until her face was on her thighs. A high whimper came out of her, unbroken, without breathing; then a hiccup; then the whimper again. It was a lovely *tableau vivant,* the propped and terrible horse, the bridge spattered with blood, the bowed girl, the two kooks and I standing stupidly aghast, the station wagon with its suffering eyes looking down on it all. "Oh, kill him!" I heard Julie saying between her knees. "Kill him, kill him!"

I am not good in emergencies. My mind was racing among alternatives like a man in a fire who grabs up things, and drops them to grab up others. What made me incoherent and frantic was not so much the horse, though that in other circumstances would have given me nightmares for months. But there was Marian up there in the station wagon, desperately needing the obliteration that the hospital's needle might give her, and no way out. The only other way out of our dead end was through the pasture where I had come on the Fourth of July. That would be rough, slow, hard on Marian, and it would bring us out not into the foothill road but into El Camino, in the worst of the afternoon traffic. We *had* to clear the bridge, kill the horse, something. The bulldozer? But how to kill it. My house. The shotgun.

I ran around the bus and saw that inside the station wagon Marian was craned around, looking back. The cords were harsh in her neck, and she fought off the nurse's hands. John had one leg out of the car, and he was waving, pushing against the air. Over the rise between us and the cottage I saw Ruth's white head and knew that she would have Debby by the hand. The bumper of the bus was behind me. I jumped on it and wigwagged, shouting, "Back! Back! Don't bring her down here!"

She saw, she heard, she stopped. I cupped hands around mouth and shouted again, "It's the horse. It's O.K., it's just the horse! Keep her back there!" With relief I saw the white head retreat and disappear. When I took my eyes off Ruth I saw John backing out of the station wagon with the splitting hammer in his hand.

Just for a moment he hung at the window. He put out his left hand and laid it over Marian's eyes. "Don't look, sweet," he said. A tic was jerking at the corner of his eye. To me he said, "Get Julie out of the way."

I ran and grabbed her by the arm, but she was limp, moaning, and heavy, and to move her at all I had to get her under both arms. She clung to the reins: I kicked them out of her hands and dragged her a dozen backward steps, and dropped her and stood up, dripping sweat, in time to see John straddle the horse's neck. The head lifted, distended nostrils and bulging eyes swayed on the stem of the neck, the peg of bone scratched and scrabbled at the planks. Then it sagged back, the head thumped down, and John stepped across it again and swung the splitting hammer, half sledge, half ax, between the rolling white eyes.

Raging, blood on his hands and arms, blood on his shirt, he threw the hammer aside. "Come here!" He grabbed up a stub of two-by-four and began to pry a hind leg out of the crack. We were slow getting to him, and without stopping his furious prying he roared at us, "Come here, help me get this damned thing off the bridge!"

Now here came Dave Weld on the bulldozer. Frozen

spectator up to now, he knew what power he commanded and saw the job clearly. But John stood up a second, estimating the pulpy bridge, and waved him back, and ultimately it was up to him and me, with Peck and Miles belatedly and inadequately helping. We struggled, slipping in thick blood, dragging at legs, mane, tail, prying at broken legs with broken pieces of plank. We got the legs free, rolled it over, pried the loose heavy shoulders and haunches nearer the edge, got its legs over, pried it closer. Resistant, sagging, sliding inside its skin, it moved reluctantly. Beside me, rank as a goat in the heat, Jim Peck grunted and shoved. His left eye was black and purple from the blow Tom Weld had dealt him at the booking. Miles was green in the face, and snorted and moaned as he worked. We pried, tugged, lifted. With a slow fleshy caving, with a tremendous loose dead weight, it toppled, gave, crashed down into the creek-bed brush.

Pouring sweat, smeared with blood, John threw the two-by-four after the splitting hammer. He said to Peck, "Get Julie home. Ask her father to have somebody with a winch get the carcass out of the creek." Dragging an arm across his face, he started for the car.

Peck turned on me a face that seemed to have shrunk inside his beard. He looked like a boy in false whiskers, which is probably more or less what he had always been. "What is it?" he said. "What's happening?"

I might have felt sympathetic to him, seeing him as scared boy. And I had been working at his side in an emergency, the only time in all our acquaintance when we had had anything in common. Though I blamed him for all this blood and anguish—why in God's name did he have to stop in the middle of the road?—I saw by his face that he hadn't the slightest idea why John was so raging mad to get the dead horse off the bridge, why a tragedy to Julie must be turned into an emergency as furious as a pit stop in an auto race.

I started to answer. The bus and the station wagon whited out, Peck's face faded, I was glaring blindly into a sheet of oatmeal paper. Then it came back, the hill steadied and deepened to its usual gold, the blood was dark on the pulpy planks, the body of the horse was shining black, laced with bright blood, among the crushed brush below me. I said to Peck, "We're taking Mrs. Catlin to the hospital to die."

It was a cruel thing to say, and if I had it to do again I would not say it. For I saw at once that he hadn't the slightest notion of Marian's condition. He thought she was pregnant. And in that moment I had a kind of rush, a revelation, an understanding of how it is with the Pecks. They think it is simpler and less serious than it is. They don't know. They fool around. They haven't discovered how terrible is the thing that thuds in their chests and pulses in their arteries, they never see ahead to the intersection where the crazy drunk will meet them.

I turned from him, ran to the station wagon, slid in, and from the glimpse I had of Marian's white face I knew she had watched it all. John took her in his arms again, where she had been when all our complicated relationships erupted into one of their consequences. In the mirror I saw her bowed, pigtailed head, his bloody shirt. Then I was easing the station wagon over the bridge while Peck and Miles stood back—staring, staring, shocked, without a word to their tongues. I felt the tires go sticky and then dry again. At the stop sign fronting the county road I stopped. Another look in the mirror.

Marian had lifted her face from John's shoulder and laid her head back against the seat. It rolled there with a strained, floundering motion like the threshing of the broken horse. Blood from John's arm or shirt had smeared her cheek. The cords were tense in her neck, her teeth were clenched, her body squirmed, her face was wet. If any of us had spoken to her she would not have heard.

Epilogue

YESTERDAY WAS FEBRUARY first. After lunch, when I went out into the yard, I found the almond trees, as dependable as the swallows of Capistrano, announcing another spring. It was a day as fresh as spring itself, the air washed, the hills green, acacias yellow down the valley, mustard yellow in the fields. And all it said to me was that a few more like it would dry the ground so that Tom Weld could put his bulldozer back to work tearing the heart out of his hill, and that on just such a day as this Marian and John had first made their way up our road, and that the last blossoms I had seen in our orchard had been those put out by the cherry tree with death at its roots.

Peace was not in anything I saw or smelled or felt. The bell jar that had protected our retirement was smashed, the dark hole that had guaranteed quiet was dug up. And no exhilaration in any of it, none of the pleasure in pain that Marian professed. Only somber thoughts and a sense of exposure and grievance. Despite her urgings, I do not accept the universe.

Knowing no other way to deal with unpeace than the way that used to work for both me and Lou LoPresti, I busied my hands. I got hoe and rake and began to basin trees and shrubs on the bank where, not quite a year before, Marian had preached me her sermon on the indomitable mushroom.

No mushrooms yesterday. The mold and matted leaves under the bushes stuck to the tarry adobe on tools and shoes. One after another I basined the flowering peaches, still in tight bud, and raked the rubbish into a pile. I would not put that on the compost heap, because the trees had peach-leaf curl that I could not seem to get rid of. Burn their litter and leaves, therefore; cauterize, imperfectly and hopelessly, another pest.

Along the fence the acacias, now ten or twelve feet high, hummed with bees. Under them too the winter had left trash. I had to reach far in to get it, and in the soft sun, in a temperature climbing into the sixties, I shed my jacket.

The wind was fresh and soft among the feathery leaves and the yellow balls of blossom. It was the sort of day that Marian would have buried herself in, powdering herself with all the pollens of life. I liked it myself, I liked the smells in my nostrils and the sounds in my ears and the feel of the sun on my bent back. But I did not forget that the peach trees behind me would shortly come out into bloom as rampant as these acacias, only to show with their very first leaves the swellings, the warpings, the obscene elephantiasis of their chronic disease. Burrowing among sunny flowers, I never lost the sense of the presence of evil.

Off in the pure blue above the hills I caught sight of the redtail soaring, a neighbor well known, but as ambiguous and unconfronted as any. He floated until he was barely a speck, and then he turned and came back toward me over the school land. Sweetly, purely, a serenity with talons, he rode the air, and his shadow dipped and raced across violet deciduous oaks and the dark mounds of live oaks and buckeyes tipped with green candles and down green slopes moiréed by the wind. Little animals, feeling that shadow, would shrink into their holes, or flatten themselves fearfully in the sweet grass.

Walk openly, Marian used to say. Love even the threat and the pain, feel yourself fully alive, cast a bold shadow, accept, accept. What we call evil is only a groping toward good, part of the trial and error by which we move toward the perfected consciousness.

Allah kareem, an Arab leper said to me once—noseless, almost lipless, loathsome, scaled like a fish—*Allah kareem,* God is kind. I dropped coins and fled from his appalling visage and his appalling faith. My impulse is to do the same when I think of Marian.

God is kind? Life is good? Nature never did betray the heart that loved her? Then why the parting that she had? Why the reward she received for living intensely and generously and trying to die with dignity? Why that horror at the bridge for her last clear sight of earth? Why the drugs that she repudiated but couldn't refuse, that killed her intelligence and will without killing her pain? Why that crucifixion death, with John hanging to one of her hands and a nurse to another and the room full of her mindless screaming?

I do not accept, I am not reconciled. But one thing she did. She taught me the stupidity of the attempt to withdraw and be free of trouble and harm. That was as foolish as Peck's version of ahimsa and the states of instant nirvana he thought he reached by sugar cube or noise or the exercise of the anal sphincters. One is not made pure by blowing water through the nose or by retiring from the treadmill. These are the ways we deceive ourselves. I disliked Peck because of his addiction to the irrational, and I still do; but what made him hard for me to bear was my own foolishness made manifest in him.

There is no way to step off the treadmill. It is all treadmill.

I was leaning on my rake thinking thoughts like this, not by any means for the first time, but with a kind of renewed bitter passion because of the brightness and purity of the afternoon, when I saw Lucio, Fran, and Julie LoPresti, followed by the mongrel dog, walking in the pasture. Once or twice they looked my way, but if they saw me behind the acacias they made no sign. I believe they didn't see me, for they seemed much preoccupied with one another, strolling slowly, watching the ground, lifting their faces to look at one another as they said something.

I had not seen any of them in a long time, and it was a shock to see Julie big-bellied, careful on her feet, leaning backward against the weight of her six-or-seven-month pregnancy. But something else struck me more. The three people walking in the spring field talking of something serious—plans to take Julie somewhere? what to do about the baby when it came? what to do about Julie's further schooling?—were a family, an intimate threesome. They were talking together in a way I had never seen them doing. And when they turned at Weld's orchard fence and started back I saw that Julie's once lank and stringy hair was in a single braid such as her mother used to wear.

So maybe Julie had got something she obscurely

wanted. I did not think that the child would be put out for adoption, as Fran in her first rage had said it would be. I expected to see mother and grandmother sharing its care. But behind the acacias, spying on their family colloquy, I could not forgive any of them for the fact that Julie's spite child would be born and that Marian's love child had been a blob of blue flesh that moved a little, and bleated weakly, and died.

Desolately I went back to raking litter out from under the yellow hedge. New growth caught in the teeth, and when I bent to look I saw that it was poison oak. Though I had sprayed every resurgent clump and bush for two years and more, and had cleaned the hill, now some bird or wind had dropped a berry and started me a new crop where it would be the devil itself to spray without killing what I wanted to preserve.

You wondered what was in whale's milk. Now you know. Think of the force down there, just telling things to get born, just to be!

I had had no answer for her then. Now I might have one. Yes, think of it, I might say. And think of how random and indiscriminate it is, think how helplessly we must submit, think how impossible it is to control or direct it. Think how often beauty and delicacy and grace are choked out by weeds. Think how endless and dubious is the progress from weed to flower.

Even alive, she never convinced me with her advocacy of biological perfectionism. She never persuaded me to ignore, or to look upon as merely hard pleasures, the evil that I felt in every blight and smut and pest in my garden—that I felt, for that matter, squatting like a toad on my own heart. Think of the force of life, yes, but think of the component of darkness in it. One of the things that's in whale's milk is the promise of pain and death.

And so? Admitting what is so obvious, what then? Would I wipe Marian Catlin out of my unperfected consciousness if I could? Would I forgo the pleasure of her company to escape the bleakness of her loss? Would I go back to my own formula, which was twilight sleep, to evade the pain she brought with her?

Not for a moment. And so even in the gnashing of my teeth I acknowledge my conversion. It turns out to be for me as I once told her it would be for her daughter. I shall be richer all my life for this sorrow.

AVAILABLE FROM PENGUIN CLASSICS

American Places	ISBN 978-0-14-303974-7
Angle of Repose	ISBN 978-0-14-118547-7
Collected Stories	ISBN 978-0-14-303979-2
The Spectator Bird	ISBN 978-0-14-310579-4
Wolf Willow	ISBN 978-0-14-118501-9

PENGUIN CLASSICS

PO #: 4500300988